NORTH FROM CALCUTTA

pecos
moon

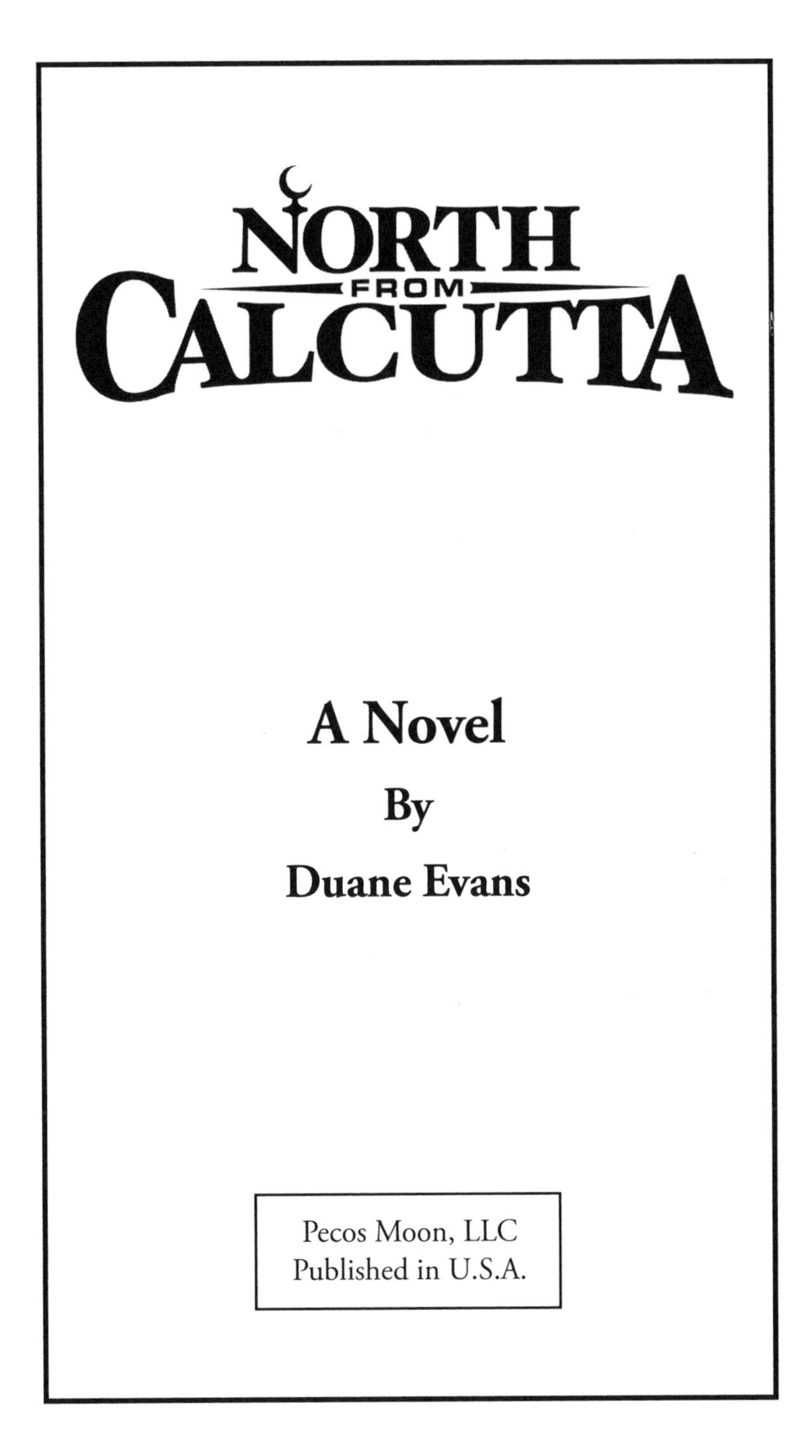

NORTH FROM CALCUTTA

A Novel

By

Duane Evans

Pecos Moon, LLC
Published in U.S.A.

This book is a work of fiction. The characters, dialogue, activities, and events described are the product of the author's imagination and are not to be construed as real. Any resemblance to actual persons, living or dead, is purely coincidental.

First Edition: May 2009

Published in the United States by Pecos Moon, LLC
www.pecosmoon.com

Cover Design by Gregory C. Gillam
Layout Design by Christopher B. Hughes

ISBN 13: 978-0-9819454-0-8
ISBN 10: 0-9819454-0-6

Printed in the United States of America

This book is dedicated to my family.

Acknowledgements

It has been famously said that it takes a village to raise a child, and no less can be said about what is required to write and produce a book. It is a community project that involves writers, editors, graphic design artists, book designers, and many others who support the effort by providing constructive comments and encouragement. I am fortunate that in the case of *North From Calcutta*, I can count all of the people who served in those diverse roles as personal friends and that has added immensely to the satisfaction I have in seeing the publication of this book.

I am particularly grateful to the following people whose advice, efforts, and work, have been instrumental in the writing and publication of *North From Calcutta*. To Victor J. Banis who was the first from the literary world to take an interest in the story and who devoted much of his time in reviewing the manuscript, I owe a great debt of thanks. Similarly, I am indebted to Gregory C. Gillam, who not only designed the jacket cover, but also maintained a dialogue with me throughout the writing of the book providing spot-on insight and constant encouragement. And a special thanks to my editor, Deborah Rhoney, whose technical skills and patience were needed in equal amounts.

I would be remiss if I did not also express my appreciation to the members of the "Kingdom" Book Club who took the time to read the manuscript and discuss with me their comments and recommendations for improvements. Finally, I am grateful to friends and family who read the manuscript and provided constructive criticism, encouragement, and support.

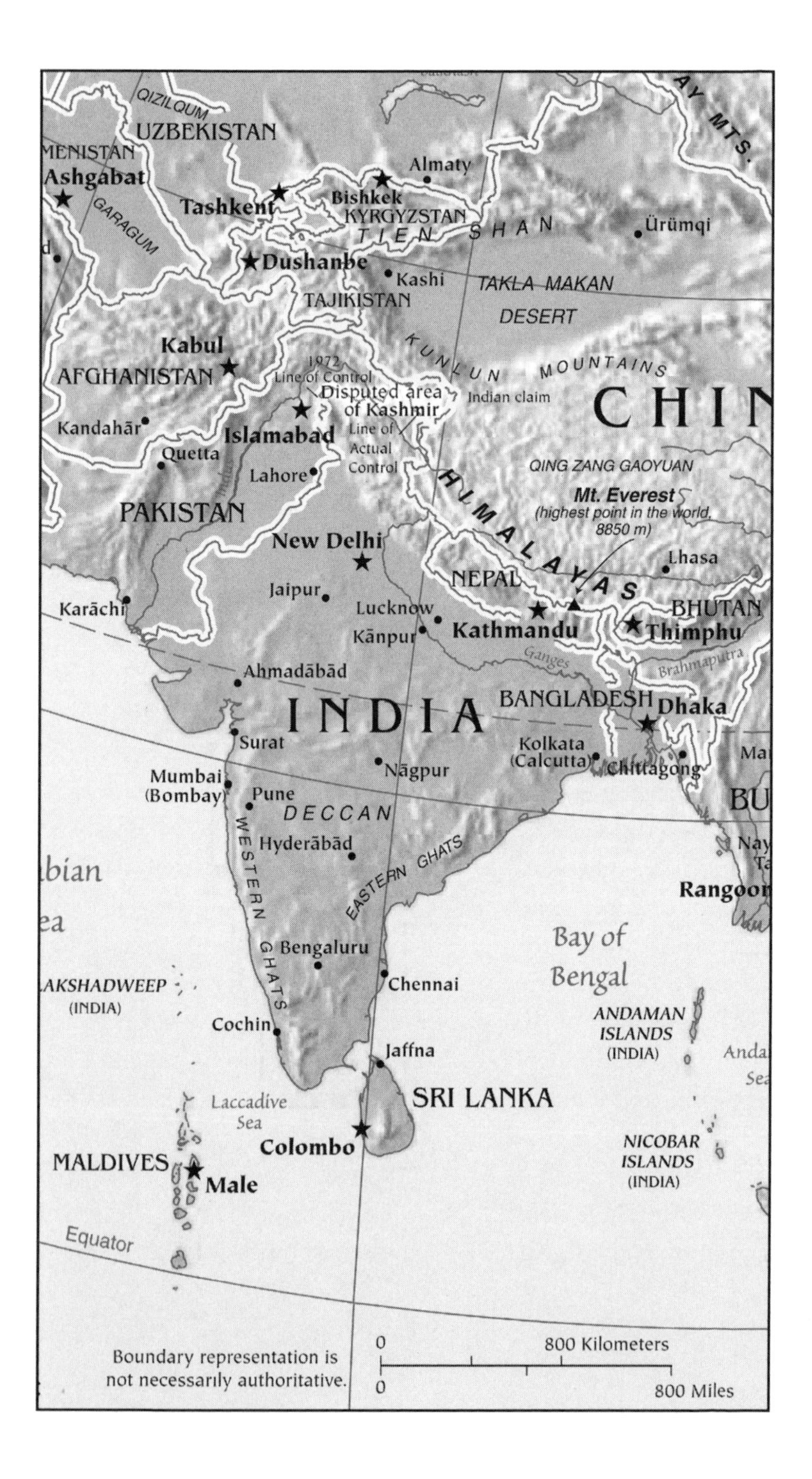
QIZILQUM
UZBEKISTAN
MENISTAN
Ashgabat
GARAGUM
Tashkent
Bishkek
KYRGYZSTAN
Almaty
TIEN SHAN
Ürümqi
Dushanbe
Kashi
TAKLA MAKAN DESERT
TAJIKISTAN
KUNLUN MOUNTAINS
Kabul
AFGHANISTAN
1972 Line of Control
Disputed area of Kashmir
Line of Actual Control
Indian claim
CHIN
Kandahār
Islamabad
Quetta
Lahore
QING ZANG GAOYUAN
HIMALAYAS
Mt. Everest
(highest point in the world, 8850 m)
PAKISTAN
New Delhi
Lhasa
NEPAL
Jaipur
Karāchi
Lucknow
Kānpur
Kathmandu
BHUTAN
Thimphu
Ganges
Brahmaputra
Ahmadābād
INDIA
BANGLADESH
Dhaka
Surat
Kolkata (Calcutta)
Chittagong
Nāgpur
Mumbai (Bombay)
Pune
DECCAN
WESTERN GHATS
EASTERN GHATS
Hyderābād
Rangoon
Bengaluru
Bay of Bengal
Chennai
LAKSHADWEEP (INDIA)
ANDAMAN ISLANDS (INDIA)
Cochin
Jaffna
SRI LANKA
Laccadive Sea
Colombo
MALDIVES
Male
NICOBAR ISLANDS (INDIA)
Equator
Boundary representation is not necessarily authoritative.
0
800 Kilometers
0
800 Miles

Author's Note

The conflict over Kashmir, which serves as the backdrop to *North From Calcutta*, has its roots in the British departure from the Indian subcontinent in 1947 when the region was partitioned into the independent nations of Pakistan and India. The goal was to provide one country for Muslims and another for Hindus and Sikhs.

At the time of the partition, Kashmir was considered an independent "princely state" and was ruled by Maharaja Hari Singh, a Hindu. The population of Kashmir, however, was predominantly Muslim. Due to circumstance and events in the aftermath of the partition, Singh agreed to India's accession of Kashmir. Fighting ensued, resulting in the first full blown war between India and Pakistan. It ended in a stalemate with India occupying over two-thirds of Kashmir and the rest of the territory being controlled by Pakistan. Two other wars were to follow in 1965 and 1971.

To this day, Kashmir remains divided between the two antagonistic neighbors. The situation has become even more dangerous with global implications since both India and Pakistan are now armed with nuclear weapons. Additionally, the emergence of Islamic fundamentalism, or transnational Islam as some prefer to say, has further complicated the issue as groups representing this dynamic have become increasingly involved in trying to drive India from Kashmir.

Both parties in this dispute make persuasive arguments supporting their claim to Kashmir, and no side is taken in this book about the rightfulness of either claim.

NORTH FROM CALCUTTA

Prologue

In a remote valley deep in Pakistan's Northwest Frontier Province, Abu Shafik sits on the dirt floor of a Lashkar-e-Taiba safe house, his back resting against the cool mud wall. To his left, a laptop computer is perched on a low table. On his right, an AK-47 lies beside him.

Taking a deep drag from his third cigarette of the morning, he listens to the unseasonable winter rain falling outside and wishes he could get a few more hours of rest. He glances down at the black face of his watch and sees it is almost time to meet his subordinate commanders. They are anxious to know what's going on, and he is anxious to tell them.

Re-energized by the nicotine, Abu Shafik gets to his feet and picks up his AK. Stepping outside the house, raindrops bead up on his parka as he walks across the muddy compound to the building where the commanders wait.

Six bearded men jump to their feet as he enters.

"Sit down," he orders.

Over the next half hour, he lays out for them what transpired at his meeting in Islamabad with the Pakistani government officials, who said their goal was the same as the LT's— to expel India from Kashmir once and for all.

"We've heard this before," one of his commanders says after Abu Shafik finishes. "Why should we believe them now?"

Abu Shafik is not surprised by the comment. "These men are not from ISI. They are very serious in what they say. I personally inspected the weapons and equipment they have for us." He pulls out a handful of photos from a plastic bag and passes them around, knowing the pictures of the weapons and equipment will give the commanders more confidence than his words alone.

Sheik Osman, whom Abu Shafik regards as his best commander, asks, "How do our new-found friends expect to overcome the Indian forces? They have almost twice as many troops in the region as the Pakistani Army."

Abu Shafik smiles at the question. It was the same question he had asked the officials.

"This has been taken into account and actions are planned that will remedy the situation. However, I gave my oath that I would not divulge the details of how this is to be accomplished until it is absolutely necessary." He deliberately fails to mention that Sheik Osman himself will play the key role in carrying out the plan to resolve the imbalance of forces problem.

"Commander, if you are satisfied that this has been properly addressed, then I am satisfied as well. I need not know the details," Sheik Osman says.

The other commanders grunt in agreement.

Abu Shafik concludes the meeting, telling his commanders that they must be patient for the next couple of months until everything is ready. But when the order comes, they must act quickly to infiltrate their forces into Kashmir.

As a final caution, he adds, "There should be no discussion of this plan with the men until our units are in place in Kashmir. Once that is accomplished and the opening attack is imminent, the men can be informed of what is to occur and the role they are to play."

Abu Shafik bids his commanders a personal farewell as each files out the door, returning to their temporary safe houses scattered throughout the area.

The last commander to leave is Sheik Osman, who pauses at the door.

"Inshallah, all of Kashmir will soon be under the flag of Islam," he says.

The two men embrace. "Go with God, my brother," Abu Shafik responds.

Sheik Osman steps through the narrow doorway, Abu Shafik watching him as he crosses the rain-drenched compound toward the main gate.

Just as Sheik Osman disappears from view, the low, gray clouds part and a burst of sunlight illuminates the courtyard.

Abu Shafik has never believed in omens, good or bad, but he knows if he did, the sun's dramatic appearance would surely be a good one.

— 1 —

Habits born of war are hard to break and Tarek Durrani woke before dawn. His breath was faintly visible in the cold air that permeated the small guest room, and it instantly reminded him that he wasn't in Cairo any longer. His return to Pakistan was not something he had wanted; he was an ISI field officer after all.

Slipping on a heavy robe, he stepped outside into the quiet garden. Only a hint of the approaching dawn could be seen and the dark sky was still punctuated by dozens of shimmering stars. Tarek knew that these final minutes before the sun's light appeared were the coldest of the day, no matter the season. He shivered, but it wasn't the cold that provoked the chill that ran through him. Hard experience had taught him that the pre-dawn darkness was also a time for cunning, a time to take one's foes by surprise—a time to kill or be killed.

Even now, standing in his sister's garden in Rawalpindi, staring into the black night and feeling its penetrating cold, if he let himself, he could be there again—watching, waiting, listening. Muscles tense, eyes straining, smelling the dew-covered earth, canvas, and leather. And for a moment, he was there again with the Mujaheddin in that bitter place... Afghanistan.

Tarek had once hoped that his memories of the Afghan war would fade with the passage of time. They had not. The memories were too strong and he knew he would carry them with him for the rest of his life.

Deciding to return to the guest room to prepare for the day, Tarek opened his eyes from his contemplation just as the very first ray of sunlight hit the eastern horizon. Its piercing brilliance seemed directed straight at him, causing his body to flinch.

Some people are afraid of the dark, but I'm afraid of the light Tarek thought, as the spreading morning light quickly filled the eastern sky. He did not bother to remind himself that he had a right to fear a flash of light from out of the darkness, especially a brilliant stabbing light like that which can come from the muzzle of a Russian sniper's SVD rifle. While the sun's light might cause temporary blindness, the SVD could make everything go dark permanently. Tarek's encounter with an SVD that cold morning in Afghanistan many years before had certainly caused his lights to flicker as the 7.62 round creased the side of his head, burrowing a deep swatch through his scalp, cauterizing the wound as it cut its hot path.

It had been Tarek's first mission for Pakistan's Inter-Services Intelligence Directorate, and the shot he took proved to be the opening round of a pre-dawn raid by an assault element of a company of Russian Spetnatz on a base camp of Mujaheddin fighters that he was traveling with. During the night, the crack Russian unit had patiently maneuvered into assault position without being detected. They were very good at what they did.

Tarek struggled to shake off the stunning shock from the round's impact, which had spun him around and knocked him flat. He heard the machine guns from the Spetnatz fire-support element open up on the camp. By knocking him down, the sniper probably saved his life; most of the Mujaheddin near him were killed or wounded by the machine guns that raked the camp seconds after he was shot.

Lying on his back on the rock-strewn ground, Tarek slowly came to his senses. He had never been wounded before and was surprised at how much it hurt. Despite the pain, he probed along the wound with his fingers and quickly determined it was not life-threatening. He knew, however, the same was not true of the tactical situation he and his Mujaheddin companions now found themselves in.

The Spetnatz commander had done his planning well, achieving complete surprise. Tarek and his comrades were pinned down by the fire pouring from two RPK light machine guns located on a small rise some 400 meters to the east of their encampment. The Mujaheddin had left three men on the elevated spot the night before to guard against the possibility of an enemy force occupying this key piece of terrain; these men now certainly lay dead, throats slashed ear to ear. Tarek knew that within a few seconds they could expect a barrage of small-arms fire from the assault force he suspected lay hidden among a thin line of boulders at the base of the rise. The assault force would likely begin its advance on the camp in teams of two with one man providing covering fire while his partner rushed forward a few yards before seeking cover.

Surveying their defensive situation as best he could, Tarek assessed that fifty or so men who had survived the initial machine gun burst had taken cover among the rocks. They were not returning fire. Tarek knew it was critical that once the Russian raiders began their advance, they be met by a storm of return fire. Lacking that, the camp would be quickly overrun. He and the Mujaheddin would be finished.

Tarek unfortunately had just run out of time to come up with a tactical solution. A burst of fire erupted from the boulders, the rounds tearing the air around him. Looking left, Tarek could make out the silhouette of Faruk, the Mujaheddin commander, crouched behind a boulder.

Tarek crawled toward him through the crackling gunfire "Faruk! Get your men to start firing. They will be coming from the boulders by the hill."

Faruk nodded, reached over and grabbed the shoulder of a teen-aged boy lying next to him. Gesturing and shouting, he ordered him to move around the perimeter to tell the men to direct their fire toward the boulders. The boy didn't move.

Seeing that he was dead, a bullet hole through his temple, Faruk grabbed the next closest fighter, this one alive, and repeated the order.

He turned back to Tarek, "We must take out those guns on the hill or we'll be dead before the sun rises."

Tarek nodded. "Where are your RPGs?"

Faruk pointed to two men kneeling behind a boulder about 20 meters away. "Alim and Omar have the new ones," he said. "I don't know where the others are."

"Keep the men firing," Tarek said. "We'll take out the RPKs."

Faruk shouted at the two men, signaling them to go with Tarek. Nodding to Tarek, he pointed his AK-47 toward the Russian soldiers and began spraying them in long bursts of automatic fire. The return fire from the Mujaheddin began to pick up, keeping the Russians from advancing, at least for the moment.

Tarek signaled for Alim and Omar to follow him, working their way around the right flank of the assault force. Somewhere ahead in the dark there had to be a Spetnatz security element posted to guard against just such a flanking movement, but Tarek hoped his small force would be able to slip by undetected.

As the men skirted past the right end of the line of boulders, Tarek saw a slight movement in the shadows a few meters directly in front of him. He raised his AK to his shoulders and fired a three-round burst into the shadow, instinctively compensating for the tendency to shoot high in a night-firing situation. He heard the distinctive thuds of rounds impacting a solid meaty object.

The sound of Tarek's gunshots were lost in the overall din of the pitched gun battle. He and his companions quickly moved around the right flank of the assault force that was still stuck in the boulders, pinned down by increasingly effective Mujaheddin fire.

Reaching the bottom of the hill's southern slope, Tarek stopped, knelt down, and signaled for Omar to pass him an RPG.

Alim and Omar dropped to their bellies while Tarek prepared the rocket launcher for firing. Checking that the grenade was fully seated in the muzzle of the launcher, Tarek insured the percussion hammer was properly aligned. He removed the protective grenade nose cap and extracted the safety pin. The RPG was ready.

He turned to the two Mujaheddin, their faces shining with sweat despite the cold morning air. "Wait here. When you hear me fire, move up the hill and attack the machine gun closest to us. I'll take out the far gun."

Both men nodded and continued to point their rifles toward the RPK's located somewhere in the dark, further up the rise.

Crouching low, Tarek headed across the hillside. As he moved between the RPK's and the assault force, he used the slope of the rise and a few scattered boulders to provide concealment from the chattering RPK's that continued to rain death on the Mujaheddin.

As he maneuvered across the rock-strewn hillside, the sound of battle raging around him, Tarek glanced up at the early morning sky and realized the sun would be up soon. If the Mujaheddin were still pinned down when the sun rose, the Spetnatz would almost certainly call in a HIND-D helicopter gunship. There was likely one already orbiting on the other side of the mountains, waiting. It might have been called in already had the Spetnatz force not been so close to the Mujaheddin. In the darkness, with only a small miscalculation, the HIND's awesome firepower could just as easily wipe out the Russian force as the Mujaheddin camp.

Lower down the hillside, Tarek could make out some of the soldiers as they fired at the Mujaheddin. Although tempted to open fire on them, Tarek knew his priority was to take out the RPK machine guns. Then he could worry about the assault element.

Finally Tarek arrived at a spot where he could see the left-most RPK. It suddenly ceased firing. *Out of ammunition*? he wondered. He saw the reason for the pause: the gunner, aided by another soldier, was changing the barrel, the first one apparently so heated that the gun had begun to misfire.

Tarek did not have a clear view of either man, just an occasional glimpse of heads and shoulders bobbing up and down over the rocks, a pair of gloved hands twisting the new barrel into place. But he could see a small rock overhang directly above their position.

Placing the grenade launcher on his shoulder, Tarek quickly located the overhang through the image intensifier, but his movement caught the gunner's attention. Having just finished refitting the RPK with a fresh barrel, the gunner simultaneously chambered a cartridge and swung the gun around, steadying his aim on Tarek.

Tarek squeezed the trigger of the RPG.

With a roar, the grenade blasted from the launcher and raced to its target, striking the low rock overhang, detonating immediately above the two-man position. Shards of jagged steel ripped through the heads and upper bodies of the Russian gunners.

The noise of the explosion drew the attention of the other machine gun position. Its gun swung toward Tarek but was immediately taken out by fire from Omar and Alim.

Tarek sprinted up the rise and dove into the destroyed gun position. It took only a glance to determine the two soldiers were dead. Pushing the bloodied bodies aside, he quickly checked over the RPK and determined that, other than a cracked rear stock, the gun appeared functional. His heart pounding, Tarek took a prone position behind the gun and looked down on the scene below.

The dawn's first light had finally come over the peaks of the Hindu Kush revealing the Spetnatz force arrayed below him like toy soldiers on a sand table. Circumstances could not have taken a more favorable turn. The RPK now had a fresh barrel and a full 75-round drum magazine with the first round already chambered, courtesy of the now-dead Russian gunner. The tide of the battle was about to change.

Tarek quickly scanned the line of Spetnatz, looking for the leader. He soon spotted him talking on a radio hand set. *Probably calling in a HIND*, Tarek thought to himself.

Tarek drew down on the commander and opened up with a seven round burst, killing him and the radio operator kneeling beside him. He proceeded to systematically search out individual soldiers hiding among the rocks, eliminating them with short bursts from the RPK.

After killing 20, possibly more, he ran out of ammunition. Tarek replaced the empty drum magazine with a full one and resumed his bloody work.

The Spetnatz troops realized they were being hit badly from the rear. They readjusted their positions as best they could and returned fire in Tarek's direction.

The Mujaheddin force saw what was happening. Wild with excitement, some of the less experienced fighters began to charge toward the Russians. In seconds they were cut down by Spetnatz rifle fire, causing the remaining Mujaheddin to be more cautious in their advance.

Being caught between Tarek's deadly enfilade machine gun fire and the close-range fire of the Muj, the effect on the Russians was devastating. Within minutes they ceased to exist as an organized fighting force. The remnants of the unit began an unorganized retreat, trying futilely to get away from the area.

In a few more minutes it was over. The Spetnatz force had been wiped out, its dead and dying littered among the blood stained rocks. The only gunfire to be heard was the sound of the occasional shot as a wounded Russian took his life to avoid capture by the Mujaheddin. Better a sudden death than what he knew waited for him at the hands of his enemy.

The battle had been Tarek's first blooding. It had changed him forever. It had made him a hero and was the foundation on which his legend in the ISI would be built in the ensuing years. As Tarek returned to the guest house to prepare for the day, he did not feel like a hero, but he did feel, as he had many times in the past, the eyes of the Russian dead upon him.

— 2 —

Tarek sat in the waiting room at ISI Headquarters, staring at a portrait of Mohammad Ali Jinnah, the founder of Pakistan, and considered his plight. He had avoided a headquarters assignment for the last 15 years but his good fortune had now come to an end, and his Cairo days were over. He hoped his impending meeting with Major General Mohammad Seyed Ali would reveal why he had been suddenly recalled to Islamabad and exactly what his new assignment would be.

Despite not wanting to be in Islamabad, Tarek was looking forward to seeing General Ali again. He had known the general for many years and had high regard for the man as both a soldier and intelligence officer. They had first met during the war against the Soviets, when Ali was in charge of ISI's Afghan operations and Tarek, as a young lieutenant, had been detailed from his commando regiment to the ISI. The eventual retreat of the Soviet forces from Afghanistan testified to the effectiveness of ISI's work during those uncertain and difficult times. Ali's key role in the effort proved to be an important stepping stone to his later selection as Director of Operations, overseeing all intelligence activities carried out by the ISI, Pakistan's most powerful intelligence organization. Recalling his own experiences in Afghanistan, Tarek knew his reward was in coming back alive.

"Major Durrani, the General will see you now," announced an office aide. "Please come this way."

Tarek followed the aide into a spacious office, where he found the General working at his desk. Military awards and framed photographs of men in uniform adorned the walls—

mementos of a long and successful career. Seeing Tarek, Ali removed his reading glasses, rose from his chair, and moved around the desk quickly, greeting Tarek with a strong embrace.

"Welcome back, Tarek! If I recall correctly," Ali said, "the last time we met you had just returned from your Qandahar trip. By the way, the Brits are still thanking us for that one."

"I'm always ready to be of help to her Majesty, Sir, especially when her service doesn't know how to get in touch with one of its own agents," replied Tarek. Ali chuckled. It was always a good laugh when done at MI6's expense.

Ali walked over to a seating area in the corner of the room. He motioned Tarek to a sofa and sat down in a chair across from him. A young corporal in starched khakis, white gloves, and spit-shined boots entered the office carrying a tray of tea and biscuits. After gently placing the tray on a low table between the two men, the corporal carefully poured two cups of steaming tea. Dismissed by a nod from Ali, the corporal left the room, closing the door behind him.

As Tarek picked up the tea cup and took a slow sip, Ali studied him for a moment, remembering the uncommon courage and soldierly skill this man had demonstrated while on missions for the ISI. These attributes, taken along with Tarek's intelligence, easy yet confident manner, and understated style, made for a remarkable and highly capable intelligence officer. Ali could not think of another ISI officer he respected or liked more.

"Have you obtained suitable quarters, Major?"

"For the moment, Sir, I am staying at my sister's home in Rawalpindi. I hope to have something more permanent arranged within the next week or two."

"I see," Ali said. "Well now, Major, tell me, how is Cairo these days?"

Tarek placed his cup on the tray and sat back in the sofa.

"Sir, the extremists continue to gain ground with their attacks and internet propaganda campaigns. I'm afraid the concept of Islamic revolution has found an audience in Egypt, and many points beyond."

Ali shook his head and chuckled. "It's classic is it not, Major? Extremists have been gaining power no matter if they are godless communists or wild-eyed Islamic fundamentalists. The principles are the same. Attack the economic structure of the country and terrorize the population, while making sure their actions are cloaked in some ideological or religious doctrine that provides a guise of legitimacy—Cuba and Iran being cases in point."

Tarek nodded. Seeing Ali's cup almost empty, he asked, "More tea, General?"

Ali shook his head.

"Major Durrani, I know you are anxious to learn of your new assignment. Unfortunately, I cannot tell you any details except that you are to be temporarily assigned on deputation to the International Relations Executive. Tomorrow you are to report directly to the IRE's Director, Ambassador Salim."

Tarek was surprised. He had assumed he would work at ISI headquarters. What could he possibly do at the IRE, Pakistan's newest government department, whose job it was to coordinate Pakistan's propaganda efforts on the Kashmir issue?

"Speaking frankly, Sir, I am not well suited or inclined toward staff work, especially outside the intelligence field. I am sure the IRE position will require experience that I simply do not have."

Ali laughed. "What operations officer worth his salt is *inclined* toward staff work, Major? And it is not clear what the nature of your work will be. Based on the criteria included in the request for one of our officers, I have a feeling, an uneasy feeling I might add, that you will be involved in some sort of initiative requiring your well-proven expertise."

General Ali shifted in his chair. "Tarek, I realize that when you are abroad you are paid to keep track of what is happening in other countries, not your own. You may know that only four months ago, Ambassador Salim was appointed as director of the International Relations Executive, an organization that did not exist until his appointment. The creation of the IRE and Salim's appointment as its chief are significant developments, in my estimation. Salim has held a number of important portfolios, most recently as ambassador to Tehran, where he is credited with reaching a modus vivendi with Iran on the thorny problems our erstwhile Taliban friends were causing at that time."

Tarek nodded. "Yes, I've heard he is an effective diplomat."

Ali continued. "And Salim's influence has been further enhanced with the appointment last month of his brother-in-law, General Kamal Huq, as the deputy defense minister. They have a close relationship and have formed a powerful informal alliance that includes a number of other important officials throughout the government—even within the ISI. Their influence in foreign and security policy has been growing daily. Prime Minister Bahir is still in charge of things, but I'm nervous about the situation. Both Salim and Huq are decidedly anti-Western in outlook and have strong empathy for some of the more extreme Islamic governments and jihad movements. Considering the current political instability in the country, not to mention our nuclear weapons, the rise of these men to prominence in the government is worrying."

Tarek had listened intently. "Sir, I understand your concern, but I am not clear on how any of this relates to my deputation to the IRE."

Ali leaned forward in his chair, his eyes had narrowed into a piercing stare. "It may have nothing to do with it, but I can tell you that Salim went to extraordinary lengths to get an experienced ISI officer assigned to him, and I initially refused his request. However, under pressure from General Huq and ISI's new civilian administrator, I was forced to comply."

"But, Sir, what do you think is behind the request?"

"Unfortunately, Tarek, I don't know." Ali relaxed a bit and sat back in his chair. The piercing stare was now gone, replaced by a wry grin. "And that is why I have recommended you for this assignment."

— 3 —

As Mohammad Abdul Salim rose from his prayers, the light of the early morning streamed through the arched windows of his airy office suite. The sunlight pierced the interior of the room in large shafts, illuminating the finely woven detail of the many Persian carpets that decorated the room. The rich tones of the carpets on the sand-colored tile floors and the gracefully arched windows had a striking effect.

Salim had a passion for Oriental rugs, and he was considered to be something of an expert. His specialty was tribal carpets, of which he owned fifty or more. Many had been presented to him as gifts during his posting as Pakistan's ambassador to Iran. In addition to the tribal collection, he also had acquired a number of exquisite Persian carpets from Tabriz, Esfahan, and Qom. The carpets from Qom were silk, masterfully colored with vegetable dyes using techniques that had been passed down for generations. The center piece decoration of his office, however, was not silk; it was a simple, although beautiful, kilim made of wool. He had bargained over half a day for it and he had it mounted on the wall like a trophy for all to see. At times Salim would simply stop what he was doing to gaze about at the loveliness of his surroundings.

Sitting down at his desk, Salim opened his leather-bound calendar and noted with satisfaction that later in the week he was scheduled to meet Major Tarek Durrani, the officer being detailed from ISI.

Salim had been waiting for weeks for Major Durrani and two officers from Pakistan's Intelligence Bureau to report to the IRE. Waiting was not something Salim did well. In his mind, the widespread unresponsiveness and ineptitude of the government bureaucracy was unacceptable. How his government had managed to produce a nuclear bomb was beyond him, although he was ecstatic it had. The bomb meant everything for Pakistan's future and some credit had to be given to the government that had created it, though Salim knew the real credit for such a wonderfully powerful tool belonged to Allah alone.

Salim reached across the desk and picked up a green folder with the words "CONTROLLED DOCUMENT" stamped across the cover. Opening the folder, Salim's eyes fell on an 8 by 10 black and white photograph of Major Durrani—a head and shoulders shot of him in full uniform, taken the previous year. Even if the Major had not been in uniform, Salim knew he would recognize him as a soldier. More than the rugged features, the eyes reflected the nature of the man. Studying those eyes, Salim knew without a doubt that this man was a warrior, yet there was something else, something more difficult to decipher. Intelligence, inquisitiveness perhaps? Salim wasn't sure, but he was intrigued and determined to find out. What was planned was far too important. The role he hoped Major Durrani might fill in that plan could not be left to an unknown quantity.

As Salim's manicured fingers lightly leafed through the Major's file, he was reminded why he had been so impressed with this operative's record the first time he read it. The Major possessed a most unique combination of talents—a mechanical engineer by education, a soldier by experience, and an intelligence officer by profession, not to mention an interesting combination of language skills thrown into the mix. And he would need all of them in his assignment. Salim knew he would be lucky to have such a man serving under him.

Putting the file aside, Salim replaced it with a gold-embossed Qur'an, and he began to read.

— 4 —

Sitting in the flowered garden of his sister's home in Rawalpindi, Tarek watched the late afternoon sun slip behind the hills to the west. The red hues along the horizon reached a purple crescendo, then faded into the early evening darkness. Tarek relished such displays of nature's beauty, viewing them as potent reminders of the cosmic forces always operating but so rarely noticed as people go about their daily lives.

He had enjoyed too few of these peaceful moments. His profession required that he live in crowded cities like Cairo, Khartoum, and Jakarta, where there was little of nature to enjoy but plenty of agents to be found. And it was in recruiting agents that Tarek excelled.

Even before joining ISI, Tarek recognized he could be a manipulative person, subtly and deliberately using his influence with people to help him accomplish what he wanted. Women, more accurately girls, had first helped him learn that. Due to his father's postings in Western countries as a military attaché, Tarek grew up abroad and had far more contact with the opposite sex than most Muslim males. As early as high school in Washington, D.C., he knew he had a natural charm with girls. Later, studying engineering in London, Tarek fully realized the power he seemed to hold over women.

While part of the attention paid to him by women no doubt came from his dark good looks, Tarek was convinced his real draw was his ability to make women feel comfortable with him. This came naturally to Tarek. He liked women, both their bodies and their minds, and he learned that if he simply paid attention to them and treated them as his equal, they were usually responsive to him. He was later to learn these same human-relations truisms could be used outside romance, in his chosen profession. He had a strong suspicion there was a direct correlation between an intelligence officer's history of sexual conquest and his success in recruiting agents to commit espionage. Tarek thought the ISI could benefit greatly by incorporating his theory into the screening and hiring practices for operations officers, but he had the good sense to keep that idea to himself.

The last light of the setting sun had faded and the night air was quickly turning cool. Tarek decided it was time to rejoin his sister, Meena, and her family inside the house.

In truth, Tarek had been delaying an interaction with his brother-in-law, Jashem Bhatti, a mid-level administrative official and a man he had little in common with. At Meena's insistence, Tarek had agreed to stay with her family for a few days while he got settled into his new posting.

He was about to go inside when Meena opened the door and stepped into the garden. "Aren't you ready to come in?" she called.

"Sorry. I was just admiring the beautiful sunset," he answered.

"I knew you would notice it. I've spent many evenings out here, and I've often thought about you. I can see you haven't changed. You're still a dreamer."

"A dreamer!" Tarek said in mock surprise. "I've been called a lot of things, but a dreamer is not one of them."

Meena walked over to him and took his hand, "That's because most people only see one side of you. I'm your little sister, remember? You can't fool me with uniforms and secret missions and all those things you hide behind."

Marveling at how much Meena had grown to look like their mother, Tarek said in a feigned whisper, "Well, don't tell anyone. Pakistani army officers are supposed to be warriors, not dreamers, and if the truth gets out about me, I'll be looking for a new line of work."

Meena let out a soft laugh and led Tarek into the house. Passing through the side foyer, Tarek stopped to look at a collection of family pictures hanging on a wall. He smiled when he saw one of his favorites—himself and Meena as children, playing in the garden while his father and mother looked on.

Then he saw another photo he had not seen in many years. His smile disappeared. The photo had been taken on his wedding day. He was in full dress uniform and Farida was beside him, beautiful and radiant.

"I just put it up the other day," Meena said. "I hope you don't mind."

"No, of course not." Tarek managed a slight smile. "We were so very young—too young really. But what choice did we have? Our parents said it was time and in those days, well, no one questioned these things."

"But they were right Tarek. Think about it. If you had not married, Farida would never have known the happiness she had as your wife."

Meena's words cut Tarek like a knife, though she had no idea they did. Only Tarek knew what their marriage had been. Happiness was not part of it. Neither was love, and only he was to blame. Farida would have been the perfect wife for most men, but Tarek had wanted something more than a wife, something Farida, with her traditional upbringing and limited exposure to the world, could never be. He had been in the West too long.

Sensing that Tarek did not intend to answer, Meena said, "Come on. Let's eat before our dinner gets cold."

In the dining room, their meal waited on a large wooden table Meena had inherited from their parents. Seeing the old table covered with steaming bowls of rice, lentils, mutton and chicken kabobs, and smelling the enticing aromas, brought Tarek sweet memories of warm evenings when his family would sit down to a dinner his mother had spent the day preparing.

As Tarek seated himself, he could see Meena was carrying on the mealtime tradition of their father, by listening closely to her ten-year-old son, Hamid, and her-eight-year old daughter, Sarah, as they told of their day's activities.

Jashem paid no attention to the children. His attention was focused on the mutton kebab and other dishes spread out before him. Finally, after consuming two plates of food, Jashem seemed to become conscious there were others present at the table, and he began to involve himself in the conversation.

Jashem and Meena knew Tarek was an ISI officer, but it rarely came up as a topic of conversation. Tarek preferred it that way. Little of what he did could be shared with outsiders— not that an outsider would really be able to understand. Jashem, like most others, had little understanding of intelligence work, and he regarded Tarek's profession as something akin to service in the Mafia. To keep peace in the family, however, he did his best to conceal his suspicions and doubts about Tarek.

"Tarek, I must say it was a surprise to learn you were coming back for an assignment in Islamabad. Is it something you wanted?" Jashem asked, mostly in an effort to break into the conversation.

"No. I was as surprised as you. I was expecting to stay in Cairo for another year and then move on to another foreign posting."

"Well, then," Jashem muttered as he reached for a bowl of dark olives, "Why did they bring you back?"

Not wishing to be drawn into a discussion of his assignment, Tarek answered, "The assignments people felt it was time I returned and did my penance. So, here I am."

"How long will you be able to stay in Islamabad?" Meena asked. "I do hope it is for a while."

"Well, these things are always subject to change, but I expect to be here for three years, which is a normal tour. I should have a better idea tomorrow after I meet my new boss." Tarek did not mention that he would not be working at ISI.

Meena beamed. "I think it is wonderful that you will be here. I couldn't be happier about it."

Tarek smiled across the table at her. "I also am glad. It will give me a chance to spend time with my favorite sister and her family and to get back in touch with Pakistan."

Tarek *had* missed Pakistan. He had missed its vivid landscapes, blue skies, and the peaceful villages found deep in its mountain valleys, nestled alongside clear flowing rivers and streams. As a boy, Tarek had spent many weeks at his father's village home in the mountains near Murree where his father took his home leave from foreign postings. Tarek had loved the Spartan lifestyle, and he longed to experience it again.

"I think you'll find your tour in Islamabad to be time well-spent," Jashem opined. "You need to get reacquainted with your government and the new direction it is taking."

"I suppose there is some value in my being here, but I'm not sure what you mean when you refer to a new direction." Tarek said.

His hunger subdued, Jashem slumped back in his chair and said, "I simply refer to our government's realization that the solutions to Pakistan's problems can be found here and among our brethren Islamic nations. The government is at last coming to the realization that the U.S. can no longer be counted on to provide the kind of help our country needs."

Tarek reflected on Jashem's words for a brief moment. "Well, you are right that our relationship with the U.S. is different than it was during our collaboration driving the Soviets out of Afghanistan and when the U.S. used us as a counterweight to the Soviet-Indian alliance. Although still, some parallels to the current relationship can be drawn."

"How so?" asked Jashem.

"I am speaking of the U.S. war on terror and its heavy reliance on Pakistan's support. Nonetheless, our relationship with the U.S. is not as close as it once was, though it has still been costly for Pakistan. After all, we lost General Masood as a direct consequence of our cooperation with the U.S." Tarek shook his head. "The assassination of a president is a high price for any country to pay."

Tarek noted the dismissive look on Jashem's face yet continued. "But if by taking a new direction you mean the government is becoming more self-reliant and is educating its youth and developing the resources of the country, then that is good news. If, however, you are referring to the anti-Western rhetoric and calls to cut ties to the West, then I believe this new direction is dangerous for Pakistan's future well-being."

Jashem slowly shook his head. "War on terror, Tarek? Let's call it what it is—war on Islam! You need not look any further than the U.S. relationship with India compared to its treatment of Pakistan. Look how over the years the U.S. badgered Pakistan about its weapons programs. Yet, the U.S. has gone so far as to support India's development of its nuclear technology. What are we to assume from this? Give me one reason why we should not turn our backs on America and all the Western countries."

Setting aside for the moment the specifics of Jashem's arguments, Tarek was surprised at his apparent new interest in international relations. Tarek could not recall having seen Jashem in such an animated state—about anything, except perhaps food.

"You make some good points, Jashem; however, it would be short-sighted and an unforgivable mistake to cut our relations with the West."

"Tarek, you are forgetting Pakistan's greatest and only true ally, Allah. Next to Allah, the West with all its technology is nothing. I predict Pakistan and our brother Islamic countries will one day again dazzle the world, perhaps not with technology, but with model societies that provide for the needs of their people." Jashem shook his head vigorously, "The Western countries are hollow on the inside. They will one day shatter from lack of spiritual sustenance."

Tarek had heard this line before, but not from Jashem. As Tarek recalled, Jashem rarely went to mosque and had never made a religious statement beyond saying 'inshallah' (God willing) when Meena told him dinner would soon be ready. Why was Jashem, of all people, now advocating Islam as Pakistan's only way to a better life? The theory was familiar; he had heard it in Cairo, Khartoum, and Algiers and had seen the blood that resulted when it was put into practice. Only now he was hearing it at home and from the husband of his sister, no less.

Tarek knew that in one sense, however, Jashem was right. Economic might had not made Western nations into model societies of contented people. The West had problems—big problems—at least a part of which he thought derived from an abandonment of religion. Aside from the American Christian ultra-conservative movement, which Tarek equated to Islam's jihadists, God seemed to be unimportant in the daily lives of most Westerners.

Meena and the children had long since left the table when Jashem rose from his chair and asked Tarek if he would like to take tea in the sitting room. No further discussion of politics or religion took place, but Tarek sensed that Jashem was proud of himself for having said the things he did. Tarek did not know what to make of Jashem, but decided to withhold judgment until he had spent some more time back in his country.

Shortly after he finished his tea, Tarek said goodnight and retired to the guest quarters for the evening.

— 5 —

Tarek arrived at the high-domed lobby of the IRE exactly 10 minutes before his 9:00 a.m. appointment. He presented his government ID to the dull-eyed guard seated behind the reception desk, who checked Tarek's name against a register.

"Please have a seat, Sir. Someone will be with you shortly."

Tarek did not sit down, preferring instead to walk about the room, admiring the architecture of the stately old building. It had been built during the British Raj era, yet was Mughal in design. Tarek was fascinated by architecture, especially buildings with the smooth curves and colorful inlaid tiles introduced by the early Islamic rulers of South Asia.

The beauty of the room reminded him of Granada's Alhambra, which Tarek had once visited during a temporary assignment in Madrid. He had spent a sunny afternoon walking through the palace's cool rooms and intimate gardens, its beauty and quiet majesty leaving a lasting impact. That the Muslims built the Alhambra during their seven-century occupation of the Iberian Peninsula had always been a source of pride for Tarek. The beauty of the building he now found himself in reflected the elegance of the Alhambra, different only in scale.

A short man dressed in a rumpled Western suit approached. "Major Durrani, I am Fakrul Rahim, Ambassador Salim's personal secretary. I will escort you to the ambassador now."

Tarek nodded, "Please, lead the way."

They ascended a circular stairwell, the sound of their steps on the hard marble floor audibly marking their climb. Reaching the third floor, Rahim directed Tarek to Salim's office.

"Please go in. The ambassador is waiting."

As Tarek stepped through the door he immediately felt as he had just entered a special place of beauty and reverence. The decor and architecture of the room were stunning.

Ambassador Salim watched Tarek's arrival and took advantage of his momentary distraction to take his first hard look at this man on whom so much would depend. As Tarek's gaze swung round to meet his own, a slight smile came to Salim's lips. Yes, he knew in an instant, Major Durrani was the man for the job.

Salim moved toward Tarek and greeted him. "Good Morning, Major Durrani. I am Mohammad Salim. I am so glad to meet you at last."

"It is a pleasure, Mr. Ambassador."

Tarek was surprised at the ambassador's height, at least six feet, 2 inches. His lean well-muscled frame gave him the appearance of an athlete and, in an odd way, reminded Tarek of himself. Salim's dark clear eyes suggested a strong intellect, but there was also a hardness about them.

At Salim's invitation, Tarek took a seat on a sofa. Salim picked up a string of emerald green prayer beads from his desk and seated himself at the opposite end.

"Bring tea," he ordered Rahim, then turned to Tarek.

"Major Durrani, I must tell you that the International Relations Executive would be privileged to have a man of your caliber and experience assigned to it," His gaze still fixed on Tarek, Salim began to slowly work the prayer beads between the thumb and index finger of his left hand. "I have read your file on more than one occasion and each time I do, I praise Allah that Pakistan has men such as yourself in its service. You have many accomplishments you can be proud of."

Tarek sensed genuine sincerity in Salim's praise, but he always suspected the motive behind praise, sincere or otherwise. Still, Tarek gave the appropriate response. "Thank you for your kind words, Ambassador."

As Rahim delivered the tray of tea the two men sat in silence. Once alone again, Salim asked Tarek about his background—his family situation, where he had lived while growing up, and his education. Salim seemed most intrigued by Tarek's experiences living abroad, particularly the time spent in the U.S. when his father was posted to the Pakistani embassy.

"I must admit, I have only been in the U.S. once and that was in New York for meetings at the U.N. I was impressed by New York, at least in some ways, but I know it is not representative of the country at large." Salim said.

Tarek nodded. "Certainly, that is true. New York is a world to itself."

Discussing Tarek's professional background, it was obvious Salim had studied the ISI file well, as he spent little time on the subject of his qualifications. He did question Tarek about his engineering degree and asked if he still tried to keep up with developments in the field.

"Yes, I try to keep up with it, mostly through a couple of professional publications I receive, but certainly I would not be candid if I said I was a technically competent engineer. My career in intelligence has been far too demanding of my time to allow that."

Salim smiled. "It is your intelligence expertise we are in most need of, Major Durrani, but your grounding in engineering is also a plus."

Long experienced in eliciting information, Tarek was able to learn a bit about Salim's background as well. One interesting nugget to emerge was that Salim's uncle was a well-known Sunni Imam who had received his religious instruction in Saudi Arabia. Salim was the uncle's favorite nephew, and he wanted Salim to follow in his footsteps by receiving advanced religious training.

In mentioning this, Salim commented, "Uncle once told me he had dreamed I would be a great servant of Allah and the Muslim people. And for a while as a young man, I felt drawn to this calling and studied the Holy Qur'an under Uncle. However, I also had a strong desire to enter civil service, and when I applied and was accepted, I decided it was the will of Allah that I should enter the government, believing that there are many ways a man can serve Allah. I can see now, having achieved this position, that my decision was a correct one."

Tarek also learned that although Salim had served as an ambassador to Iran, he was not a career Foreign Ministry officer. According to General Ali, it was in this important position that Salim had firmly established credentials as a man with vision and the drive to shape events to his liking. It was clear to Tarek that Salim had come into his own, a man of ambition and self confidence, thinly veiled by polite modesty.

Eventually, the conversation came around to why Tarek was being brought to the IRE. Tarek chose not to raise the question himself, but waited for Salim to bring up the topic.

"Major Durrani," Salim said, "the IRE is a new organization, and I had a personal hand in its establishment following my return from Tehran. The IRE has been established for the express purpose of developing an effective policy on the most serious issue confronting our country—India's illegal occupation of Kashmir. Our mission, simply put, is to change Indian policy on Kashmir by gaining and leveraging international support and applying other levers as required. To accomplish this, the IRE will work concurrently with the diplomatic, defense, security, and policy apparatus to ensure a well coordinated effort."

"Ambassador, I'm glad to hear that our government's approach on Kashmir is being coordinated. As a member of the nuclear club, it is essential that the left hand know what the right hand is doing, particularly regarding issues connected to India."

Salim smiled briefly. Tarek's reference to Pakistan's nuclear capability was an unexpected but interesting comment. Perhaps another one of Major Durrani's many talents was strategic thinking. A shame perhaps, but this talent would be wasted; Major Durrani's role with IRE was to be tactical, not strategic.

"You are correct, Major. Pakistan's nuclear capability makes the goals of the IRE even more important."

Tarek nodded. Although the on-again, off-again talks with India on Kashmir had recently been restarted after a total breakdown, the fervor of the nationalistic rhetoric, once again coming from New Delhi, was alarming. "Yes, Ambassador, the situation with India is worrisome. India will always be our pre-eminent concern."

Salim was glad to see Tarek was well-attuned to the challenge India posed for Pakistan. The recently elected nationalist government in New Delhi had made clear its strategic intentions toward Pakistan when it conducted yet another test detonation of a nuclear bomb shortly after coming to power. As had become its policy, Pakistan quickly responded to the provocation, detonating its own bomb—and two more for good measure.

Salim firmly believed that the development of the bomb and a reliable delivery system made Pakistan a military equivalent of India. This put the Indo-Pak confrontation on the same footing as the East-West standoff prior to the fall of the Soviet empire. Salim was certain the balance-of-power dynamics currently at play could be used to Pakistan's advantage regarding Kashmir, allowing Pakistan to take steps it never could have considered before, without fear of military defeat and possible annihilation.

Salim angrily shook his head, clenching the prayer beads in a tight fist. "How many years must we wait before the people of Indian-occupied Kashmir become a part of the country they have every right to belong to? They have a right to the destiny that was stolen from them by decree of imperialist powers. The

Kashmiri people have been waiting more than half a century for the UN to live up to its word to hold a referendum on their status. I believe that is far too long, don't you Major?"

Tarek well understood Ambassador Salim's frustration over Kashmir. Although the division of the region had been largely along religious lines, by a quirk of history, a Hindu Maharaja had delivered his Muslim majority territory to Indian control, splitting the area of Jammu and Kashmir between India and Pakistan, thus sowing the seeds of a dispute that continued to produce violence, bloodshed, and war.

Ambassador Salim continued. "I think we must accept that the plebiscite on Kashmir promised by the UN at the time of partition is nothing more than a child's dream, and will never take place. What we must do is change the equation so that when India does the calculus, it realizes it must make accommodations."

The tone in Salim's voice was one of determination, and Tarek simply acknowledged his remark with a nod.

"Major Durrani, our Islamic republic, with the blessing of Allah, will not be intimidated by India's Hindu extremist government. Pakistan will reassert itself in this region. We must face the Indian challenge and expose it to the world as the arrogant power it is. To do this we need smart, dynamic men who can take initiative and make things happen. I firmly believe you are this kind of man, and you will be a tremendous asset for the IRE. Consider this conversation as the IRE's formal acceptance of your assignment here."

Tarek was not surprised at the quickness of the ambassador's decision to accept him. Men like Salim seldom deliberated long on such matters, trusting their initial instincts to guide them. They were usually correct in their judgments. Sometimes, however, they were spectacularly wrong.

"You will be working exclusively on the India account for the IRE," Salim said. "No other duties or distractions—period. You should also know that everything you do at the IRE is compartmented and cannot be shared with anyone, not even your colleagues at ISI. I'm sure you are well acquainted with the 'need to know' principle. Now, if there are no other questions, I am expected at the prime minister's office in a few minutes." With that, Salim stood up, signaling the meeting was over and walked Tarek to the door.

"The India Office Director is Admiral Mohammad Nurullah, with whom you will become acquainted shortly. I suggest that before you report to work, you make sure your personal accommodations are in order, as you will have little time once you start work."

"No problem, Ambassador," Tarek responded, "My accommodations are already arranged, and there is little else in my life but my work."

"Excellent, Major, I can see you have the right attitude. Again, I must tell you how delighted I am that you are here. The IRE needs you, and more importantly, Pakistan needs you."

Salim shook Tarek's hand and, in what appeared to be an afterthought, said, "Oh, Major. You can expect to spend some time traveling. I hope that is not a problem for you."

Tarek smiled. "Not at all, Sir. Traveling has always been part and parcel of my occupation."

"Very good, then. Admiral Nurullah will fill you in on additional details at the appropriate time."

When Tarek had gone, Salim returned to his desk. A moment later Rahim joined him. "Rahim, I am quite impressed with Major Durrani," Salim said, again slowly working his prayer beads. "The ISI has certainly filled the bill by sending him to us. He is perfectly suited for the task."

"I was impressed as well," Rahim agreed.

"Still, we can't afford to take anything for granted. I want to continue our due diligence right up to the time Major Durrani deploys. He is an ISI officer after all, and it is not clear which camp he falls into---the old guard, or the new."

"With a little time, I should be able to determine on which side of the line he stands, Mr. Ambassador."

"Excellent, Rahim. Stay on top of it and please keep me informed."

— 6 —

It had been two weeks since Tarek began work at the IRE. Admiral Nurullah had assigned him to the smallest branch in the India Department. Aside from its small size, it was also distinct from the rest of the department in that it was located in a different building. Tarek was surprised to learn that most of the 15 men in his branch—there were no women—were detailed from the Army, although two were officers belonging to the ISI's domestic rival, the Intelligence Bureau.

Tarek was given a small office with just enough room for two gray metal desks, a desktop computer on one of them. The white walls were barren and dingy, speckled with the squashed remains of mosquitoes, victims of previous occupants. The office didn't matter to Tarek—he wouldn't be spending much time there.

Arriving at work, he found a package containing materials he had requested shortly after being briefed on his project. Most of the information contained in the package was unclassified—a few open-source documents, most from international news publications, along with some Foreign Ministry reports and a series of reports submitted over recent months by Pakistan's embassy in Bangladesh.

The largest document was a 54-page report produced the previous year by the Pakistani mission to the United Nations in New York. There was also a reference book on environmental studies and several maps covering the border areas of India and Bangladesh, including a 1 to 250,000 scale military version. He was primarily interested in the last item.

Tarek unfolded the map and spread it over one of the small desks. He studied it closely until he located the point where the Ganges River intersected the India-Bangladesh border. Placing his index finger on the spot, he traced the river westward into

India. At a distance of 18 kilometers from the border, Tarek saw a thick black line intersecting the Ganges. It was Farakka Barrage.

At the time of his project briefing, Tarek had known nothing about Farakka Barrage and felt embarrassed having to admit this to the briefing officer, a stuffy colonel of the Pak Army's engineering branch. The colonel, however, was not the least bit surprised at Tarek's ignorance and showed no hesitancy in saying so. He proceeded to give a standard briefing that included a description of Farakka Barrage and its significance in India's political relation with Bangladesh.

The 2,250-meter-long dam known as Farakka Barrage had been completed in 1971 with Soviet assistance at a cost of $1 billion. Although the Soviets had provided funding, the dam was still a point of pride for India, as it was designed by the internationally renowned Indian engineer Rabindranath Advani. A related project, the Jangipur feeder canal that connected the Ganges to the Hoogly River, was completed in 1975.

Farakka Barrage was built to divert water south during the dry season, keeping the river navigable and controlling the salinity of the water, particularly for Calcutta to the south. In the monsoon season, the gates of the barrage were raised to allow floodwaters to flow unimpeded eastward into Bangladesh.

In recent years, the Farakka Barrage had become a serious friction point between Bangladesh and India. The government in Dhaka blamed the barrage for the desertification of some parts of western Bangladesh, as well as the loss of vegetation and increased salinity in the Sundarbans, the world's largest mangrove swamp.

New Delhi held that the desertification was due to natural changes in weather and river patterns. Dhaka insisted otherwise and took its case to the United Nations. In its petition to the U.N., Dhaka demanded that during the dry season the barrage gates be raised, allowing water to continue to flow eastward into Bangladesh. India had refused.

Now, as Tarek stood in his office staring down at the line on the map indicating Farakka Barrage, he began to anticipate the challenges he would face carrying out his mission to collect full design specifications of the structure. According to Admiral Nurullah, flow rates of water passing through the dam could be calculated from these blueprints. From that, calculations on the amount of water blocked from entering Bangladesh and the Sundarbans during the dry season could be made. The admiral said the IRE planned to use these calculations behind-the-scenes to support Bangladesh's case against India in order to embarrass her on the world stage.

Tarek's mission was a straightforward collection operation, the kind he enjoyed most. Although his target was not military in nature, the fact that it was in India raised the difficulty level by several notches. India's intelligence and security services were highly professional, and if they were able to compromise the operation, it would add to the growing spiral of political and military tension between the two countries.

Tarek wondered if a mission to collect what could best be described as environmental intelligence was worth the risks. After all, the site had no military value, and it was located on the opposite side of the country, far from Pakistan. Other questions puzzled him too. Why wasn't the ISI given the job instead of the IRE? The ISI probably already had agents in place that could provide at least some base-line data on the dam.

He had to conclude the reason was a bureaucratic one. The IRE was a new organization, and it wanted to prove its worth and self-sufficiency, even if it was not up to the task. Asking for an ISI officer to be temporarily assigned was a compromise position, probably seen as a better option than asking the ISI to carry out the Farakka Barrage mission, and any others like it. Tarek cleared the materials off the desk, returning them to the cardboard box. Sitting down at his computer, he began to read through the daily diplomatic cables coming from Pakistan's embassies abroad. He could not read ISI operational traffic at this office; however, once every couple of days he would go to ISI headquarters and read up on developments in India. He didn't mind; it gave him a good reason to be at ISI, where he could keep in touch with General Ali.

Tarek had not for a moment taken seriously Ambassador Salim's admonition that he should not discuss his work at the IRE. General Ali was one of the very few people Tarek knew he could trust completely. Above all others, Ali, as the Director of Operations for ISI, needed to know about any intelligence operations being mounted abroad, particularly in India, a hostile nation armed with nuclear missiles, all of which were pointed at Pakistan.

Nonetheless, Tarek was being as discreet as possible in his contacts with Ali, who had cautioned him that he suspected his own movements and activities were being monitored. As a precaution, he and Tarek had agreed there would be no telephone contact between them.

Tarek decided it was time to brief Ali on how he planned to carry out the Farakka Barrage mission.

— 7 —

Sahar Advani stood at the large dining room window and gazed out at the garden, the Delhi heat penetrating through the windowpane. Stepping away, she turned and walked into the kitchen where her father sat sorting the morning's mail.

"I am certain were it any hotter even the lilies painted on my sari would wilt away," sighed Sahar. "Can the heat possibly get any worse? You must tell me we will take our retreat to the hill country soon or I will abandon you to this miserable place."

"Sahar, why do you threaten your old father? Do you think I dislike the heat any less than you? In a week's time we will leave for the tea gardens. I hope you find some comfort in this news. Were you not my only daughter, I would not be so tolerant of your complaining."

The tense expression on Sahar's face disappeared. "I guess I can persevere in that case. Besides, I still have to complete the design for the library, and I don't want to take my work with me to the hills."

"I would forbid you bringing work in any case," Advani responded sternly. "A vacation by definition means 'no work.' Modern life has turned us all into slaves. And for what? To earn more money to buy more things that we cannot enjoy because we have to work! Again I ask, for what?"

"Father, you loved your work. How many times have you talked of the pleasure your accomplishments brought you? Has retirement changed your mind?"

"Yes, it's true," Advani agreed. "My work brought me immense pleasure, but my pleasure did not come from the money I made. And I should point out that I never took my work along on any retreat. Those times are special and should be reserved for families and friends spending time together and for restoring our connection to the Divine. Ultimately nothing is more important than this. No, the time away from our normal routines must be preserved as sacred, and that means not bringing any work along."

Sahar thought for a moment, canting her head slightly and causing her thick black hair to slip from her shoulders to its full length. "You'll get no argument from me. As much as I'm enjoying the library project, I need a break from the routine—and from Delhi," she said. "If all work and no play make Jane a dull girl, then I must be the dullest girl around."

Advani paused from his mail, removed his gold frame reading glasses and looked at his daughter, his eyes reflecting a father's concern and love.

"Sahar, I am worried about you. Your job seems to have become your life. You no longer paint, you don't listen to music, and you no longer spend time with your friends. Not to mention you seem to have closed the door on the possibility of a romantic interest. You need to examine the way you are living and ask yourself if there isn't more to be taken from life. You are such a beautiful and talented woman; I hate the thought of you devoting yourself only to your job."

This was not the first time her father had voiced these concerns and it pained Sahar to know he was worried about her. She knew he was right; she needed to change the rhythm and routine her life had assumed over the last few years. But changing one's life was not easy, especially with a demanding career—and a father to look after.

As for romance, there was no shortage of interested men. But since her divorce three years earlier, her experiences with men had been mixed—and ultimately disappointing—leading to a self-imposed hiatus on romance. Her intent originally had been to withdraw socially for only a few months, but this limited timeframe had almost unnoticeably extended into years. Sahar was only now awakening to that fact, and an increasing feeling of restlessness had begun to set in.

Sahar knew that should she wish again to attempt a romantic foray, her father would not involve himself. He had played an influential role in convincing Sahar she should accept the marriage proposal of her former husband. The marriage had been a disaster, and her father had sworn never again to undertake the role of matchmaker.

Sahar walked to him and leaned down to kiss his cheek. "Don't worry. Once I have completed the designs for the library, I will be able to cut back on work and do the things I enjoy. In fact, I have already talked to my old master about resuming yoga, and he has agreed to take me back."

Her father's delight was evident. "That is wonderful Sahar! And what about your painting?"

"I'm actually thinking of bringing my things to the tea gardens to try my hand again. I know I will be very rusty, but I must begin sometime."

Her father smiled and seemed to relax. Returning to his review of the mail, his gaze fell upon a business envelope bearing a Dubai return address. He had once visited Dubai briefly, but did not know anyone from there.

His curiosity aroused, he picked up a letter opener, slit the envelope and unfolded the one-page, single-spaced letter, noting the expensive paper and the crisp professional type-face. Adjusting his glasses he began to read the English text.

Esteemed Engineer Rabindranath Advani,

It is with great honor that I open this communication with you and I pray it finds you and your family in good health. The opportunity to which I am now taking to seek contact with you is surely given to me as a blessing ordained by God in all his great mercy. I can only hope you will not find the step I have taken in sending this letter to you as an arrogant undertaking, but rather accept it as a small token of the great respect I hold for you as a master in your field, whose accomplishments have been equaled by very few men.

It is in this spirit of personal respect and professional admiration that I reach out to you to solicit your possible interest in regards to a training program I have designed on behalf of my firm, which specializes in advanced training for promising engineers. I think you may find the program interesting, as its goal is to not only improve technical skills, but to also increase creative thinking and confidence. To accomplish this, I plan to introduce these young engineers to the most accomplished engineers living today, and I hasten to add, you are foremost among this select group.

I realize you are now in a well deserved "retired" status, but I note from your recent contribution to the International Engineer Quarterly that you continue to take a strong and active interest in the engineering field, as you were quoted as saying you think you can still make a positive contribution in our chosen field. I believe, Sir, through our training program, you can indeed make a major contribution by sharing your wisdom and experiences with the engineers who will be responsible for the great design and construction achievements of the future.

If you are interested in this idea, and you could find the time to come to Dubai under my company's full sponsorship, I would look forward to discussing this project with you further. Whatever your response may be, please accept my sincere admiration for you and your work. May God bless you and your family.

Sincerely,

Tarek Durrani
Sable Enterprises
Dubai, UAE
Sable01@net.com

"Interesting," Advani said, mostly to himself.

"What is it?" Sahar asked.

"Oh, it's just another employment offer."

"You're not interested are you? You said you were enjoying retirement, with no deadlines hanging over your head, and finally having the time for your meditations and prayers."

"No. I'm not really interested. But this proposition is a bit different from the others. From what I can tell, I would not actually be working on a project."

"What would you be doing then?"

"It appears I would serve more in a professorial or mentor role, working in some capacity with young engineers," Advani said.

"That's interesting. You've always said you would not mind working in the academic field, and I know you would be a great teacher. Why don't you at least consider it?"

Advani shook his head, "No, I don't think so. They've asked that I go to Dubai for further discussions, and I really have no interest in foreign travel—at least not any time soon."

Sahar laughed, "Too bad they did not ask me to come. I could hardly turn down a trip to the shopping capital of the Middle East." Sahar sat down at the table beside her father and put her hand on his.

"Why don't you contact the company and ask that they come here to discuss the idea with you? After all, it is they who have approached you. Let Mohammad come to the mountain, if the mountain does not choose to go to Mohammad."

This idea resonated with Advani. "Sure, why not? It doesn't sound like it would take much of my time, and I do enjoy interacting with young engineers. They have so much energy and enthusiasm; it makes me feel younger when I work with them. Tomorrow I will send an e-mail to this Mr. Durrani and see what he says to my counter proposal."

Advani rose from the table, taking Sahar by the hand. "Now, let's take our morning tea."

— 8 —

Emirates flight 997 lifted off the runaway in Islamabad as Tarek gazed out the window, watching the broad city fall away below him. The day was sunny with deep blue skies, and a few high white clouds feathered by strong southwesterly winds.

Shortly into the flight, a pretty dark-eyed flight attendant, with a tight fitting skirt and jacket outlining a shapely figure, began to distribute immigration and customs forms to the passengers. Tarek had noticed her as soon as he boarded the plane and was happy to see she would be responsible for his section of the aircraft. She wore her hair pulled straight back and gathered into a simple bun the way his wife Farida had often worn hers.

As the attendant leaned over from the aisle to address Tarek, the light scent of a familiar perfume enveloped him. It was jasmine, faint but still powerful enough to send his memories reeling 20 years back in time to another young woman, equally attractive but doomed to a loveless marriage and a painful death. For a moment, Farida's face, full of sadness, flashed in his mind. "Why couldn't you love me," she seemed to ask, but just as it had been when she was still living, Tarek had no answer to give.

"Sir . . . Sir, are you a UAE citizen?"

The attendant's words brought Tarek back to the present.

"No. I'm Pakistani," Tarek responded.

She handed him the forms required for foreigners and moved on down the aisle. Whatever subtle pleasure the attendant's charms had initially evoked had disappeared with that reminder of Farida. Tarek avoided looking at the attendant for the rest of the flight, forcing himself to return his thoughts to the business at hand.

As Tarek wrote his true name on the immigration form, he wished he had been able to persuade Admiral Nurullah that when it came to intelligence work, traveling in an alias offered many advantages. Nurullah had refused the request however, as it would have required direct support by the ISI's documents section, an admission of dependence on another agency that the IRE was not willing to make. Nurullah's decision had convinced Tarek that while the admiral might have been a fine naval officer, he had no understanding of the intelligence business.

Tarek's travel to the UAE was for the sole purpose of obtaining the services of one Harun Habibi, a former asset he had personally recruited and handled while working in Algiers years before. Habibi's code name had been "Stallion Flyer/66". He had been a superb agent, but ISI's relationship with him had ended three years ago when his services were no longer needed. Tarek however, had ensured that Habibi had a contingency plan that would allow anyone with the proper bona fides to meet with him at a pre-arranged location, should the need arise.

Tarek had already activated this plan prior to his departure from Islamabad by faxing an ostensible business proposal to Habibi at his import firm in Abu Dhabi, with a key phrase inserted that signaled to Habibi the true identity of the fax's sender. The time and date of the proposed meeting could be determined by inserting the date and time of the fax into a simple false subtraction formula.

On arrival in Abu Dhabi, Tarek passed through immigration and customs without incident, the officials giving his forms only a cursory check. He continued through the terminal, following the signs to ground transportation. Though he needed a rental car, he opted not to get one at the airport in favor of getting one later somewhere in the city. The tactic did not guarantee he could not be traced to a rental car firm, but it would make it just a little harder should someone try.

Stopping at a bank kiosk, Tarek got some local currency and proceeded toward the exit doors leading outside to a taxi stand. Stepping out of the air conditioned building into the mid-day sun, the moist super-heated gulf air enveloped him as if he had walked into a furnace. He was sweating by the time he removed his jacket. A white taxi pulled up alongside of him. Tarek tossed his travel bag into the back seat and climbed in.

The driver looked back at Tarek and grinned, revealing large white teeth. "Destination, Sir?" He asked in the Queen's English.

"Take me to the Sheraton Hotel."

— 9 —

For the third night in a row, General Ali had not slept well. He got out of bed feeling all of his 60 years. At least it was Friday, he thought. He would be able to spend some time at home relaxing and catching up on his rest. As was his habit, he would attend the Friday prayer service at noon at the mosque only a few blocks from his Islamabad home. The Friday service was important to Ali; he never missed it unless he was traveling or some crisis at work kept him away. Fortunately, for the moment, tensions with India were on an even keel. Whether or not they would stay that way was anyone's guess. Ali was not optimistic. Too many things were happening. In his view, all of them were bad.

He showered and dressed, then headed downstairs to find his wife. The kitchen help was busy preparing breakfast. General Ali was almost a stranger to his own kitchen. The staff reacted as if the prime minister himself had walked in. Ali was not one for ceremony. He had no pretensions about his senior military rank. "Good morning, ladies and gentlemen," he said in a friendly tone. "Please, don't mind me. I am only looking for Madam."

"Sir, Madam is on the veranda," the senior servant said.

"Thank you, Muktar. When can I expect breakfast?"

"Breakfast is soon coming, Sir. In the meantime, I am serving tea to Sir and Madam on the veranda."

"Most excellent. Please bring the tea along as soon as it is ready."

Before the general could turn and start for the veranda, Muktar already had the kitchen boy preparing the tea. Muktar was nothing if not efficient.

As Ali approached the veranda, he could see Shahida, water pitcher in hand, moving among the potted plants. The large, leafy plants with yellow and red flowers set alongside the dark stained rattan chairs and coffee table imbued the veranda with the soothing atmosphere of a quiet woodland.

Shahida looked up as Ali arrived. "Good morning, my love," she said. "You are up early for a Friday. Do you have to go into the office today? "

Smiling, Ali said, "No my dear. I will spend my Friday with a very charming woman who floats among the plants and flowers like a whispery cloud, bringing water and sustenance to all that is green and growing".

"Anyone I know?" Shahida asked playfully.

"Why it is none other than the lovely woman who stands before me, looking more beautiful than the flowers she tends."

Smiling, Shahida took Ali's hand. "My, the compliments fall like petals from a flower. Perhaps I should see to it you always rise early on Fridays." Looking into Ali's deep-set eyes, Shahida told him, "You know a woman of my age is extremely vulnerable to such words."

"And a man, even of my age" Ali said as he pulled Shahida close, "is vulnerable to the beauty that inspires those words."

Ali's bold move and teasing words caught Shahida off guard. With a worried glance, she looked over his shoulder in the direction of the kitchen, and said in a lowered but emphatic voice, "Seyed, what has gotten into you. The servants may come at any moment. What if they should see us like this?"

Ali chuckled as he slowly released Shahida from his embrace. "Well, is it wrong to suppose that after 30 years of marriage a husband would embrace his wife in his own house?"

Shahida stepped back and straightened her clothes. "You know that your suppositions could ruin my reputation with the house servants," She said. "They love to talk about the Madam. The juicier, the better. They are such gossip mongers!"

"Well then, Madam, I shan't breathe a word. However, in the not-too-distant future, I will require payment for my silence. And it will be on my terms. But in the meantime, please summon the 'gossip mongers' and ask them about our morning tea."

Shahida's humor returned. She smiled and touched Ali's hand before disappearing through the veranda doors. Ali looked out over the tops of the high shrubbery, hoping to catch a glimpse of the green parrots that often roosted in the area. Ali loved watching all types of birds; the green parrots were always a special treat. Though he would never admit it, he still harbored a superstition he had learned as a child, that green parrots brought good luck. He searched the trees and shrubs intently, but concluded there were no parrots this day— just as had been the case in the preceding weeks.

Shahida returned, followed by Muktar carrying the tea tray. For an hour, Ali and Shahida sipped their tea while talking about the previous week and their plans for the day.

Ali did not like to mention work during these special moments with Shahida, but she had been his confidant for 30 years. There was no one he trusted more. The objective analysis and dispassionate insights she brought to difficult situations had often been of great assistance to him.

"Have you been following the press lately?" Ali inquired in a tone that indicated the conversation had changed from relaxed chatter to something of a serious nature.

"Of course."

"Well, what do you think of the reports concerning Prime Minister Bahir's difficulty with the new parliament?" he asked.

"It should be no surprise to anyone that the prime minister is having his policies challenged by this fundamentalist-leaning parliament our country somehow managed to put in office. It's obvious. They plan to take advantage of the power vacuum created by the assassination of General Masood. Let us hope the realities of politics in Islamabad will soon make pragmatists of them and that they grow weary and lose their zeal."

Ali's eyes looked down, fixed but unfocused. "Yes, but the problem is that these men are not politicians. While some might argue that is a good thing, I do not think so in this instance. Their politics are driven by Islam, or I should say, their interpretation of Islam, and Allah forbid if you do not agree with them. I've studied the dossiers on many of them, and I can tell you that the only education most of them have received has been religious training in the Salafist madrassas—the same ones that produced the Taliban movement."

"So, we should not be surprised then if the new parliamentarians do not push for an enlightened foreign and domestic policy. And about those madrassas, well the government is reaping what it sowed." Shahida said.

General Ali looked up at his wife. "You well know it was the ISI, against my objections, that was tasked with the responsibility for nurturing the madrassas and the Taliban. I never believed in the idea that an Afghanistan under a fundamentalist regime was good for Pakistan's security. Unfortunately, I was overruled."

"Overruled? Your career was nearly ruined! I have never forgiven them for the way they treated you. You were right in your prediction that once the Taliban came to power, Pakistan would lose control over them. And look at what it led to. A terrorist attack such as the world has never seen, and now a war on our border and car bombings right here in Islamabad. May Allah be praised that Prime Minister Bahir recognized that you knew what you were talking about."

Shahida was visibly angry at this point. So much for dispassionate insight, Ali thought.

"Shahida, you know I love it when you make me out to be Pakistan's most brilliant strategist, but just to keep the record straight, there were many others who held the same skeptical view of our involvement with the Taliban."

Calming down, Shahida said, "I know, I know. But within the ISI you were the most vocal in your disagreement with this policy, and for years your career suffered for it. That is what upsets me so. You have given so much to our country, risking your very life. A government should thank men like you, not punish them."

"That is all behind me now," Ali said. "And I have done very well in my career if I may be so bold to say. I never thought I would attain the rank of major general. But I was hoping to finish out my career seeing Pakistan on a stable course. And now as I near retirement, I see indications that we are beginning to go down the same path as before."

"What are you talking about? Surely, we are not going to support the Taliban again?" Shahida asked incredulously.

"We have learned our lesson with the Taliban and, as a matter of policy, we do not support them. However, they remain a potent force with strong support in the Pashtun belt on both sides of the border. And yes, there are still those that secretly support them. But what I'm referring to are developments within the government itself. There are many reorganizations being carried out under the name of improved efficiency and savings, but I am very skeptical about what is happening."

Ali paused and held out his cup for Shahida to refill and then continued. "Within the past two months, the ISI has been banned from any form of contact with the Kashmiri resistance, so we are temporarily blind as to what their plans are. This is dangerous. Their attacks against India have brought us to the brink of war on more than one occasion.

"Is this a policy you can try to get changed?" Shahida said.

"Maybe. I've managed to get a private audience with the PM on Monday. Hopefully, I can prevail upon him to let the ISI re-establish a liaison with the Kashmiri resistance. If nothing else, I will be able to reiterate my concern about what is happening in the government."

"Who else knows about this meeting?"

"I don't know. I've done everything I can to keep it close-hold, and we are meeting for lunch at the Equestrian Center, so the usual palace staff will not be around. But it is the prime minister after all, so at least a few will know. I just hope no one who opposes my views learns about the meeting and gets to him first."

Thirty years of marriage had taught Shahida a lot about her husband. She knew he would not speak to her on these topics unless he was truly concerned.

"Seyed, surely Bahir will be able to do something?"

"The PM knows about the changes, but the way they are being carried out limits his influence on things. Besides, right now he has his hands full trying to manage the new parliament. The political ground has shifted beneath him, and he is still trying to recover his balance. I just hope he is able to recover before things go too far and the confusion within the government becomes chaotic. Pakistan does not do chaos well."

"Sir, breakfast is served in the dining room," a servant announced from the doorway.

"Shall we, my dear?"

"Certainly, although I think this conversation has killed my appetite," Shahida said.

"Well, don't worry. For the time being I plan to play the role of observer and keep my cards close to the vest. Hopefully things will right themselves through the natural course of developments. However, should they continue the way they are going for much longer, then some sort of counter-offensive may be necessary."

Ali decided it best not to mention his increasing suspicion that his telephone calls were being monitored, or that just two days ago he thought a car was following him as he left the office to have lunch with an old friend. It was better to keep these suspicions to himself, he thought. After all, they could be nothing more than his imagination.

— 10 —

It was the day after Tarek's arrival in Abu Dhabi, and the recontact meeting with Habibi was on track. There had been no sign of any unusual attention paid to Tarek during his time in the UAE, where he posed as a visiting businessman interested in leasing office space. If things stayed that way, before the night was over he would be sitting face to face with Habibi, recalling old times and making new plans. As Tarek began the final leg of his surveillance check-route in a rented Toyota, he noted the sun dipping below the horizon, putting the timing of his initial encounter with Habibi at dusk. The reduced visibility would provide an additional element of security.

Having picked up no evidence of surveillance, Tarek turned right onto a major street, taking it for two blocks. He then turned off onto a narrow one-way street. A minute later he turned left into an underground parking garage.

Tarek buried the white Toyota among dozens of similar-looking cars parked on the sub-level of the crowded garage, then took the stairs up to a busy shopping mall. Walking at a casual pace, he stopped at some of the shops, as if browsing. At a sporting goods store, he paid cash for a set of binoculars coated in heavy yellow plastic to protect them from the elements. Doubling back through the mall the same way he had come, Tarek proceeded in the direction of the stairs he had used from the parking garage. Satisfied he was free of any watchers, he changed course and quickly exited at the front of the mall onto a busy city street, where he hailed a cab from the nearby taxi stand.

"To the promenade," he instructed the driver. "Drop me at the mid-point, if you can."

Tarek remained silent during the drive, gazing out the windows at the city scenes passing by. *Abu Dhabi is an impressive city*, he thought as he looked up at the modern high-rise office and apartment buildings lining the street. He noted that unlike so many other cities in the Middle East, the citizens here moved about quickly, everyone seeming to have some place to go and something to do.

Tarek knew this was a notable exception. In his travels he had discovered that too many people in the region had nowhere to go and nothing to do. In most places jobs were scarce, particularly for young people, whose access to education was limited. This was especially true for girls. Even in countries where significant numbers received university degrees, few graduates found jobs. The situation had gone on so long that people in the region had taken on a lethargic air, accepting their fate even as they watched other countries with fewer natural resources develop their economies and improve quality of life.

In cases where the state paid subsidies, as in Saudi Arabia, Kuwait and other Gulf countries, the people had the basic material goods but little else. For decades, these governments had imported foreign workers for most occupations. Tarek thought it incredible that, with few exceptions, foreigners filled virtually every occupation in these oil-rich countries, from street sweeper to chemical engineer.

"Sir, the promenade is coming up on the right," the driver said.

"Pull over just ahead please, beyond the street light." The taxi stopped, and Tarek pulled the fare from his money clip.

He exited the car, shopping bag in hand, and began walking eastward along the sidewalk for a half block, then turned right onto a narrow stone walkway. The path passed through a small grove of palm trees and connected to the wide promenade that ran parallel to the shoreline of the Gulf.

At the promenade, Tarek again turned east and continued at a relaxed pace, stopping occasionally to take in the sight of a passing ship headed out to the calm sea. He passed a mix of people as he walked—businessmen returning home from the office, several groups of young people engaged in animated conversation, walkers and joggers taking their exercise in the early evening hours.

Ten minutes into his stroll, Tarek spotted the site where he was to meet Habibi—a large fountain set back in a palm grove about 30 meters from the promenade. The center feature of the fountain was the sculpture of a dolphin breaking the surface of the inviting water, all of it illuminated by blue-tinted lights. The elevated fountain was encircled by five concentric rings of steps that served as benches for passersby who wished to enjoy the air cooled by the fine spray of the water.

Tarek walked over to the fountain, set the shopping bag down and took off his blazer. Sitting down on a middle step he reclined back against the next step and looked up to the ever-darkening sky. He took a moment to make one final check that he had not been followed. Then he reached down into the shopping bag and took out the binoculars, alternately holding them in his lap or lifting them to his eyes to look beyond the promenade and out to sea.

Your move Stallion Flyer/66, he said to himself silently.

— 11 —

Harun Habibi was a man of 'epic proportions' literally and figuratively. Though huge in girth, he wasn't particularly tall. He had a large round head covered by a tangle of tight, unruly black curls, with a beard to match. His large ebony eyes were set wide apart and had an unnerving intensity sometimes prompting strangers to think him crazy. He hardly fit the physical stereotype of a secret agent and that, in addition to his intelligence and high energy level, had been a great advantage in his clandestine work for the ISI.

Habibi was also generous to a fault. One of his long-time employees had once told him that when Habibi died, he would never be able to donate his heart to someone else. Habibi, in his booming voice and irreverent manner, asked, "Why? Because it's too fat?"

"No," was the smiling reply. "Because the body rejects gold."

Many people felt the same way about Habibi. He was simply a good man—another deviation from the stereotypic agent. On the negative side of the ledger he could be stubborn, and not always willing to listen to direction if he had a different view. As Habibi's handler, Tarek had learned to put up with it, knowing that despite Habibi's bull-headedness, his intentions were good.

Tarek had recruited Habibi only five years earlier, but the ISI had records on him going as far back as the war against the Soviets in Afghanistan. Then Habibi, who was a UAE citizen, had operated a small non-governmental organization on the outskirts of Peshawar that provided humanitarian assistance to Afghan refugees. Many years later, Tarek was introduced to

Habibi by a contact who did not know Tarek was an intelligence officer. At the time, Tarek was posted in Algiers, where he served undercover as the Pakistani defense attaché.

Habibi had come to Algiers to manage an irrigation development program for the Algerian government. Within a few minutes of meeting him, Tarek knew the access Habibi's company could provide to the Algerian countryside would be extremely useful to the ISI's efforts to obtain intelligence on the country's bloody and mindless insurgency. Pakistan's interest in the conflict stemmed from its concern that the rise of Islamic extremism in Algeria might one day reach Pakistan, a concern that time had proved to be justified.

The Algerian government had refused to cooperate with Pakistan on the issue, so there was no other option but to collect intelligence on the insurgency using independent means. Habibi proved to be an excellent operational lead toward this end, and Tarek immediately set about developing a relationship with him.

Habibi hated the violence being carried out in Algeria. Islamic insurgents were routinely going into villages throughout the countryside and butchering innocent people. Village wells were often found stuffed with bodies, even those of children whose throats had been slashed. How the perpetrators of such barbarism could claim to be followers of Islam was beyond both Habibi's and Tarek's comprehension.

Their mutual outrage at what was happening in Algeria in the name of Islam served as the basis for Habibi's recruitment. It didn't hurt that Tarek had also provided information that saved the lives of three of Habibi's employees, one being Habibi's brother, from a planned terrorist attack. The group was drilling a well in the countryside, and had been identified as an easy target. This helped to forge a personal relationship between Tarek and Habibi that was even closer than the strong relationship normally established between an agent and his handler. Now, after a hiatus of three years, Tarek's and Habibi's relationship was being renewed.

Habibi stood watching from the railing along the promenade as Tarek passed him walking toward the blue-lit fountain. Habibi knew Tarek had seen him, though he had given no sign of recognition. Habibi smiled to himself. When it came to street work, his old friend never missed a thing.

Habibi waited. When he saw the yellow binoculars, he moved toward the fountain. Dressed in traditional Arab garb, his massive bulk was covered by a white robe-like thawb that billowed about in the coastal breeze, giving the impression of a ship's sail blowing along the Promenade. Even with the formless thawb and ghoutra headdress, there was no mistaking Habibi.

"This dolphin has found the coolest spot in all of Arabia" Habibi said as he slowly lowered his heavy frame onto the fountain steps next to Tarek.

"Thankfully the dolphin does not mind sharing what he has found," Tarek responded.

Each man knew it was comic that they use this tradecraft protocol to initiate their contact, since neither had any doubt of the identity of the other, but they did it anyway, in part to see who would laugh first. Neither did.

Not wanting to prolong their public exposure, Tarek quickly told Habibi where and when to pick him up. Habibi's nod confirmed his understanding. Tarek stood up and, without another word, continued with his stroll along the promenade.

Halfway across town and exactly one hour later, a new desert-tan Toyota Land Cruiser pulled up alongside Tarek as he walked down the street. The power window on the passenger side descended.

"Get in my brother. You look like you could use a meal," Habibi said with a broad smile.

Tarek climbed into the Land Cruiser. "My mother always said not to get into cars with strangers, particularly ugly ones," he said grinning. "But she also told me to stay away from flirty girls, advice I also ignored."

"I think you confused your mother's words, my friend," Habibi said. "She told you not to get in cars with ugly girls, and yes, sadly, I fear you have probably ignored even this advice." Habibi leaned across the cabin of the car and gave Tarek a near-crushing bear hug. "I have missed you! Praise Allah we are together again," he said.

"And I have missed you as well. I have thought of you often," Tarek responded.

Habibi pulled away from the curb, the V-8 engine roaring as the vehicle quickly accelerated down the mostly empty street. "And how are your sister and her children, Tarek? I pray all is well with them."

"Yes, all are fine. And your wife and children are well?"

"Yes, yes, we have all been kept safely in the palm of Allah's hand."

"We have a lot to catch up on, Habibi. We need a place where we can relax and talk. A car meeting will not suffice. Do you have any apartments available?"

"I see you still don't like to meet in hotel rooms," Habibi said. "I thought you might like to do things the old way, so I have come prepared with keys to one of our new apartments."

"That's great. And yes, I avoid hotel room meetings, more so today even than when we worked together in the past. The security environment is much tougher now because of terrorism. There are too many ways to get wrapped up for the wrong reason."

"You will get no argument from me. And why use a hotel when I am a partner in a corporation that owns three residential buildings with at least two dozen empty apartments," Habibi said. He pointed toward a red and white ice chest in the back seat.

"I have brought a meal of lamb kabob and rice that we can carry up with us. I believe it is important that two old friends reunite over a good meal."

"You are a most thoughtful man, Mr. Habibi," Tarek said. "I saw some advertisements by your corporation when I was driving around. Things seem to be going well."

"They are. And I will tell you all about it over kabobs."

Habibi pulled up to the barricaded entrance of an underground parking garage and pointed at the five-story building standing before them. "This is our newest project. We've just begun letting out the apartments, and there are only a few tenants in the building, so we can be assured of our privacy."

Habibi pressed a button on the remote attached to his windshield visor and the barricade lifted. After parking, the two men walked to the nearby elevator lugging the ice chest between them. Habibi punched in the entry code and the elevator's stainless-steel door smoothly glided open. Inside the mirrored elevator, Habibi pressed the button for the fifth floor. The elevator ascended to its destination in a few seconds.

Habibi led the way down the semi-lit hallway to the last apartment. He pulled a set of keys from his pocket, inserted one into the lock and opened the door.

"My, my," Tarek said as he walked into the apartment. "This is nice."

"We don't call them 'luxury apartments' without cause," Habibi said.

Habibi carried the ice chest into the kitchen and began unloading its steaming contents. Tarek walked over to the high-definition wide-screen television, turning it on to provide some noise interference. It was unlikely anyone would be listening, but in his business it never paid to take things for granted.

"Name your preference," Tarek said "We've got a National Geographic special on the Himalayas, and oh, here is one of your favorites," he said as he looked toward the kitchen for Habibi's reaction.

"Baywatch!" Habibi exclaimed as he looked up from the pan of rice he was dumping onto a large plate.

"Well, what will it be? National Geographic or Baywatch? I know it's a tough choice. Both are programs about some of the world's largest natural wonders."

Habibi chuckled and Tarek could have gone on with this routine, but he refrained from any further juvenile comments. What was it about being around Habibi, he wondered, that made him want to cut up like a kid again. With Habibi, there was no pressure to be anyone but himself.

What a freedom that was. It was strange, Tarek thought, how people spend their lives not fully being themselves, 'Stringing and unstringing their instrument but never playing their song,' as Tagore once wrote. *Why do most people never play their song*? In the last few years, Tarek had begun to ask this question of himself.

"Hey, let's eat," Habibi's penetrating voice broke into Tarek's reverie.

For the next hour, he and Habibi shared the satisfying meal as they caught up on what had been happening in their lives for the past few years. The conversation tended to be one-sided, with Habibi describing what his family members were doing and what he had been doing in his business enterprises. Tarek could contribute only a few comments, aside from updating Habibi on how Meena and her family were doing. He had little to share of a personal nature. For Tarek, his work *was* his life, and work was not something he talked about.

Such was the nature of his career. He had wanted to do something challenging—and he had done that. Yet the path he chose became narrower and steeper as the years went by. He enjoyed his work and took pride in knowing he had served his nation well for more than 20 years, but he could see that the price he had paid was high. He had no wife, no children, and no hobbies, save keeping himself in shape. Tarek knew the situation was the result of his own choices, many of which he made as a young man, driven to prove himself. Now, however, he felt he had nothing to prove to anyone. Within the ISI, his accomplishments were well-known, his abilities well-proven.

Glancing at his watch, Tarek saw that it was getting late. He began to move the conversation to operational matters.

"Harun, this has been a great evening. It is not often that I can mix business with pleasure, but it is time to talk some business. I'm sure you are wondering why I have contacted you after all these years. You have been very patient not to ask."

"Tarek, as I told you at our last meeting, when was it, over three years ago? I remain your friend and faithful servant and will always be ready to help in anything you ask. I owe you that much for my brother's life. Besides, life as a businessman can become a bit boring as time goes on. I want my life to be about more than just making money. What we did in Algeria, that meant something, that was important and, well, I rather miss the excitement that you and I shared. I think about those times a lot, and I hoped that one day you would come knocking again."

Tarek had to smile at his big friend. "Well, Harun, you've gotten your wish. I'm knocking again, but I can't promise you much excitement this time around. I need a UAE work and residency permit of the same type you provided to us before. You remember the case? When we resettled the insurgent who defected? Are you still able to arrange this?"

"Of course," Habibi immediately responded. "My corporation routinely provides sponsorship for many foreign workers."

"That's great," Tarek said. "There is one complicating factor, however."

"And what is that," Habibi asked, his bushy eyebrows rising in curious anticipation.

"The document would have to be back-dated, meaning the issuance date would need to be at least five years in the past," Tarek responded, watching closely to gauge Habibi's reaction.

"Umm, that does complicate things," Habibi said. His eyebrows now descended low over his dark eyes. After a moment's pause, his face brightened.

"No problem. I will have to call in some favors, but this can be arranged. When can you give me the particulars?"

"I can give you the biographic data right now, but how do you plan to get this done?" Tarek asked.

Habibi chuckled. "My construction firm has the contract to design and build the Immigration Bureau's new headquarters building. The fact that the director general and I are classmates from our university days did not hurt in winning the contract," Habibi said with only a touch of sarcasm in his voice. "It seems the good DG was hoping his new headquarters would come complete with an indoor pool and steam room. Unfortunately, the budget does not permit this. However, with a little redesign I believe costs could be reduced sufficiently to allow the addition of these facilities."

"So exactly what are you proposing?" Tarek asked.

"I will suggest to the DG that I might be able to accommodate his desires, *if* he assists me with this one small favor concerning a residency permit."

"But Harun, this solution cannot in any way make the Director General suspicious," Tarek said emphatically.

"Trust me on this, Tarek. I know how to get this done. I'm not going to waste your time and mine by explaining every detail to you."

Tarek could see that Habibi's stubborn streak was emerging and that caution was in order. Once in the past, Habibi had ignored Tarek's instructions when he did not agree with him. In that instance it had been a relatively small issue and had not caused a security problem. Obtaining fraudulent identity documents, if not handled properly, however, could very easily affect the security of the operation at hand. Tarek had to be sure Habibi handled things properly.

"Harun, if I didn't think you knew how to do this, I wouldn't be sitting here talking to you about it. But remember, I'm responsible for making decisions on security issues. It's what my profession is all about, and I need to know how you plan to do this."

Habibi sighed. "I will cover for the request by telling the DG that by way of error, my corporation has been employing a foreign worker for several years that we failed to register with his department. I am certain at this point the DG will tell me this is a simple matter, and he will see to it the problem is addressed quietly and a permit, appropriately dated, will be issued. A small price to pay for a pool, don't you think, Tarek? As you of all people know, this is the way things sometimes get done here. Now are you satisfied?"

Tarek nodded, pleased with Habibi's imagination and resourcefulness. "It's a good plan, but keep in mind, the issuance of the permit needs to be a paper transaction. You provide the photos, date and place of birth info, and all the rest. In other words, this must be accomplished without requiring any personal appearance by the person the document is being issued to."

"Our corporation is well-known to Immigration, and our foreign employees have been exempted from any type of personal examination. We provide the required documents and Immigration issues the permit. As simple as that," Habibi said, snapping his thick fingers.

"Excellent. I need the document as soon as possible. When do you think you will have it?

"I'll see the DG tomorrow, and I expect I will have the document within a day or two. The DG will probably have his bathing trunks even before then."

"Fine. Let's plan for our next meeting based on that schedule."

Tarek never said why he needed the document. Dear friend that he was, Habibi had no need to know.

—12—

It was mid-morning. Sahar lay reading on the living-room sofa, wearing her favorite sleeping gown, her dark hair pinned up in a thick tangle of loose curls. The gown was of the finest Thai silk, a gift from a former suitor. She hadn't cared for the suitor, a prosperous merchant from Mumbai, but she loved the gown and wore it frequently on weekend mornings like this, when she could lounge around doing what she pleased. She loved the way the fine material lightly caressed her bare skin each time she moved. The gown's sky-blue color, with its gold accents, happened to match well with the studied elegance of the room. The gown, the room, and Sahar's raw beauty suggested a painting by a Renaissance master.

Realizing the morning was quickly passing, Sahar sat up and placed a bookmark in the thick novel, setting it down on the end table. She raised her arms above her, slowly stretching her back in an arching curve. Although her body was still strong and flexible, Sahar knew she was resuming her yoga class not a moment too soon. In recent months she had begun to realize that her body was not immune to the effects of time and lack of exercise.

She glanced at the gold clock sitting on a nearby table, and could not believe how much time had passed while she was reading. A sign of a good book, she thought to herself. She was actually surprised she liked the book. She had sworn off romance novels, finding them entirely too predictable. This one, though, did not fit the stereotype. She had become totally engrossed in the story and its cast of unusual but entirely believable characters. Ah, but if life were like this, she thought, full of interesting people, passion, and unexpected events.

The telephone rang, giving Sahar a start. She knew that the maid was in the laundry room and would not hear the phone so she answered it herself. The man on the phone identified himself as Mister Durrani, calling for Engineer Advani.

"Oh yes, my father was expecting your call," Sahar said. "He is out of the house at the moment but should be back shortly. . . Yes, of course. I will have him contact you as soon as he returns. Yes, please, what is the number? . . . Very well. Yes, I have it. Thank you."

Sahar walked into the kitchen and sat the cordless phone down on the table and put the note she had written next to the cane rack, where her father would see it when he returned. She headed up the stairs to shower and prepare for the day.

Ten minutes later, Advani returned from his outing. He spotted Sahar's note as soon as he entered the kitchen. Placing his brass-handled cane in the rack, he sat at the kitchen table and read the note.

"Mr. Durrani is right on schedule," Advani said aloud to himself. Reaching across the table, he picked up the phone and dialed the number Sahar had written down—a cell phone number, he surmised, based on the prefix. After two short rings, Tarek answered the phone.

"Welcome to India, Mister Durrani. I was expecting your call and I apologize for not being home earlier. . . Certainly, I am free this evening. . . Yes, the Rajastan Restaurant is excellent – but please, why don't you be my guest and come to my home for dinner instead. It really would be no trouble. . . Well, if you are sure, then I would be honored to join you this evening at the Rajastan. If there is anything I can do for you until then, please do not hesitate to call. . . Yes, I will use this number to contact you should the need arise. . . Very good, I'll see you at 8:00 p.m. this evening."

—13—

Excellent, Tarek thought as he placed the cell phone down on the nightstand. His first contact with the designer of Farakka Barrage had gone well, as had his early morning arrival in New Delhi. Tarek knew his Pakistani passport would likely draw close scrutiny by Indian immigration, but the UAE residency permit had done the trick and allayed the suspicions of the immigration officer who had quickly approved Tarek's 'Visa Upon Arrival' request.

Tarek had deliberately chosen to arrive on a weekend, anticipating correctly that the airport immigration staff would be undermanned and therefore less likely to devote extra time to conduct an in-depth interview of an expatriate Pakistani. Tarek always believed in stacking the odds however he could to reduce potential operational risks.

He had not forgotten that the operational threat level in Delhi was significantly higher than in the UAE, and he had planned accordingly. First rule: He would stay away from the Pakistani embassy and avoid contact with any Pak government personnel in India. Pakistan was enemy number one for India, and India's Intelligence Bureau no doubt blanketed the Pak embassy and all embassy officers with continuous surveillance. Should Tarek pop up on their scope, he would automatically become a target for investigation. That could lead to the mission being compromised, something Tarek had no intention of letting happen.

Second rule: Avoid using the hotel's telephone system to contact Engineer Advani. Although Tarek had no reason to believe his hotel phone would be targeted for monitoring, a common practice of security services, he also had no way of knowing for sure. Instead, he had purchased a cell phone at a kiosk during his trip from the airport to the hotel. The phone would serve as his means of communication with Advani while he was in India.

His dinner with Advani now confirmed, he stuffed some gym clothes into a small backpack and went to the hotel gym for a late-morning workout. The well-equipped gym was empty except for two Chinese businessmen whom he had seen checking into the hotel when he arrived. Dressed in white T-shirts and baggy gym shorts, the two men did not seem to know how to use the equipment. Tarek offered his assistance suggesting, a few exercises they might try. The younger of the two men pointed to a scar on Tarek's left shoulder, and asked what had happened.

"A traffic accident," Tarek said. Over the years, he had found he could most easily explain his scars by attributing them to a traffic accident he'd never had.

The truth was, each scar had a story, but they were stories never told, not even to his colleagues at the ISI. For every time he had been wounded, others had lost their lives. In Tarek's mind, to talk about such things was blasphemy. Too many people had fanciful ideas about war, ascribing noble attributes like honor, courage, and bravery to the wounds received and the men who bore them.

Tarek himself had once thought that way, but time and experience had changed his thinking. He now saw war for what he knew it really was— killing, maiming, destruction, and suffering. There was no glory in it. Yes, there was courage and sacrifice in war, but he had come to think these most high and noble of human qualities were wasted in an enterprise whose only business was death.

Tarek completed his own workout, finishing with 30 minutes on the treadmill. He rinsed off in the locker-room shower, wrapped a thick white towel around his trim waist, and stepped into the steam bath.

After a good workout, sitting alone in the hot moist air, sweat coming from every pore–that was heaven for Tarek; and it was a luxury he rarely had time for. He believed that a good workout and a steam prior to going operational was great preparation, as it both cleared the mind and relaxed the body. A colleague had once suggested to him that sex could have the same salutary effects, but Tarek took the view that finding a good gym with a steam bath was far easier and much more operationally secure than seeking out the company of a willing woman in a foreign land.

Keeping to the schedule he had planned for the day, at 12:20 in the afternoon, dressed in a set of khakis and a white polo shirt, he stepped out of the cool hotel lobby into the thick New Delhi heat, and proceeded on foot to a small Thai restaurant a few blocks away. He enjoyed a light, satisfying meal of Num Tok, served by a lovely Thai hostess who flirted shyly with him and was plainly disappointed at his lack of response.

He passed the next few hours wandering about Connaught Place, Delhi's central commercial and shopping district. Late in the afternoon, looking every bit the visiting businessman turned tourist, Tarek took an auto rickshaw back to his hotel. Most importantly, Tarek had spotted nothing during the outing to suggest he was being followed.

Satisfied with his security, he returned to his room, showered again, and rested in anticipation of his meeting later that night with Engineer Advani.

—14—

It was late on a Saturday night and General Ali sat in his office preparing the papers he would use at the meeting with the Prime Minister the following Monday. After reviewing the information he planned to present to the PM, Ali felt confident that once the PM heard him out, he would understand the dangers of restricting the ISI from maintaining a line of contact with the Kashmiri resistance groups.

His game plan for the meeting mapped out, Ali turned his attention to the most recent report from a new Lashkar-e-Taiba source, code named "Highland View/30". Even with the prohibition against official contact with Kashmiri insurgents, Ali believed the ISI was still in the business of running agents. HV/30 would be Ali's ace in the hole, providing at least one window into the activities of the LT. The reporting from HV/30 looked very good. This source had indirect access to the top leadership of the LT, and he knew about some of the LT's activities at an operational level. This penetration was particularly significant since the LT was the largest group of Kashmiri fighters and also the most effective.

HV/30's information showed that the LT was continuing to maintain a quiescent posture. There was no indication of plans for renewed attacks in India. Ali knew a serious attack could derail the reinitiated talks between Pakistan and India. Real progress seemed to have been made in the talks, and the LT had even announced it supported the negotiations, so there was reason to be hopeful. Ali, however, was skeptical that the LT was unified in supporting a peaceful compromise with India, since to achieve peace would jeopardize the LT's power and influence in Kashmir.

An important dynamic at play within the LT, which complicated assessing the group's intentions, was that the movement had changed over the years from an armed political resistance movement to an Islamic extremist movement. Its earlier purpose had been to force an Indian withdrawal from Kashmir. The goal now was to expand Islamic rule throughout the region and other areas of the world.

Ali wished he could discuss the HV/30 case with Tarek. He had received only one communication from Tarek since his departure—an e-mail sent to an ISI front company in Karachi. The text of Tarek's e-mail was transmitted from the Karachi ISI office via secure communications channels to ISI Headquarters for General Ali's eyes only. Ambassador Salim knew nothing about this communications channel. The e-mail had been sent while Tarek was in the United Arab Emirates. All appeared to be going well, with Tarek preparing for travel to his final destination, which, although not stated in the e-mail, Ali knew was India.

Considering Tarek's tasking to collect data on Farakka Barrage, Ali could understand the IRE's interest in the dam from a propaganda standpoint, given Bangladesh's complaints about the diversion of water from its territory. But to tie up the skills of an experienced ISI officer on this effort seemed to be a waste of a valuable resource.

Glancing at his watch, Ali was surprised to see how late it was. He put his work away in the corner safe and called his driver at the motor pool to take him home. Walking out of the office and down the hall lined with the portraits of past ISI directors, whose eyes seemed to stare down on him, Ali felt tired, very tired.

—15—

Tarek awoke from his nap and slowly opened his eyes. The room was quiet; the only sound was the hiss of the chilled air flowing gently into the room. Soft yellow light illuminated the edges of the window curtain, signaling the day was nearly done. He needed to prepare for his dinner engagement with Advani, but he continued to lie in the still room, where nothing moved save the slow rising and falling of his chest.

The peace and tranquility felt good. Tarek dared to let himself relax in it, putting aside all thought of doing. Such moments were rare for Tarek, and were invariably spoiled by the demons that still hounded him. Unclouded and undefended, his mind was at rest and in that moment of vulnerability, acute feelings of loneliness and sadness came forth in a forceful assault, pouring through him like soldiers through a breech.

As in previous moments like this Tarek focused quickly, and rapidly suppressed the invaders. But the feelings of doubt and questioning they provoked would remain like smoke hanging over a battlefield for some hours to come.

Tarek got out of bed and went into the bathroom to take a cold shower, hoping it would somehow break the melancholy that had come over him. He shaved for a second time that day, then put on a dark-blue gabardine suit with an expensive maroon silk tie he had purchased in Bangkok the year before. He picked up his briefcase containing information about the technical training firm he ostensibly represented. Before leaving, he examined himself in the dresser mirror. He certainly looked the part he was about to play. With the anticipation that he was about to go operational, his spirits began to rise. After a final time check, he headed out the door.

Tarek politely waved off the concierge's offer to hail a taxi as he exited the hotel lobby. He proceeded a few blocks to a small shop and purchased a local English-language newspaper before walking another two blocks in the direction of a taxi stand. Having seen no evidence that anyone was following him, Tarek approached an air-conditioned taxi with its motor running and got in the back seat.

"Oberoi Hotel," Tarek said.

The taxi zigzagged through the crowded streets, alternating between rapid acceleration and sudden stops, horn honking all the while. Tarek was reminded that some of the most frightening moments of his career had been passed in the back seat of a taxi.

In less than ten minutes, Tarek was delivered to the main entrance of the Oberoi, having once again cheated death. He entered the elegant lobby and meandered down a wide corridor of small shops. He entered a shop well stocked with piles of colorful carpets and spent 15 minutes with the shop owner, discussing the price of a Tabriz that particularly appealed to him. Tarek had no intention of consummating the deal, but the bargaining allowed him to stage the timing of the last leg of his route check.

Leaving the carpet shop, Tarek walked to the rear exit of the hotel and headed down the street in the direction of the Rajastan Restaurant. One block from the Rajastan, Tarek concluded he was clean, and he proceeded to the Restaurant.

Tarek approached the Maitre'd and identified himself. The tuxedoed man looked down at his reservation book and studied it for several seconds, his well-oiled hair glistening in the light from the gilded chandelier.

"Hmmm. I am sorry Sir, but your table is not quite ready. Perhaps you would like to wait in the bar. It should only be a few minutes more."

Looking for alternatives to the bar, Tarek spotted an interior garden area. "No thanks. I'll wait in the garden. Please let me know when Mr. Advani arrives."

Tarek followed a path through the garden's lush foliage and sat on a bench next to a fountain that gurgled with the sound of water cascading over stones. No one else was in the garden, leaving Tarek to enjoy the green ambiance alone.

Tarek thought many of the world's problems resulted from so many people being out of touch with nature, their lives spent in crowded, polluted cities, their days passed in filthy workshops or tiny cubicles. As Tarek reflected on the stresses, difficulties, and dangers of the modern world, he could think of nothing encouraging; the world seemed bent on self-destruction.

Within a few minutes, the door from the restaurant opened and a small gray-haired man stepped out. The man used a highly polished wooden cane to balance himself as he walked. Tarek stood to greet him. The newcomer's eyes met Tarek's and he smiled brightly, "Mr. Durrani, I presume?"

Tarek returned the smile. "Yes, I am. And you must be Engineer Advani." Shaking Advani's outstretched hand, Tarek continued, "It is an honor to meet you, Sir. I am very appreciative of your taking the time to see me."

"Please, Mr. Durrani, I am just a retired old man," Advani said, his clear eyes seeming to shine with a bright intelligence. "How could I refuse your kind offer for dinner? You are the one who has traveled some distance to see me, and for this I am grateful of your effort. I hope that after meeting me you will not find it to have been a waste of your time."

"I am certain that will not be the case. Please let me apologize that our table is not ready," Tarek responded.

"No need to apologize. By the way, when I inquired at the desk, the Maitre'd asked me to convey to you that the table should be ready in a few more minutes. Sometimes the efficiency of our business enterprises here in India is less than it should be, but I can assure that you will not be disappointed with the cuisine here at the Rajastan," Advani said.

"If the aromas that keep wafting through the air are any indication, I am certain it will be well worth the wait. Now, would you like to wait here in the garden or do you prefer to go inside? It is a little warm still, and perhaps you would be more comfortable in the air conditioning."

"Comfort comes in many forms, Mr. Durrani. I much prefer the garden, if you have no objection," Advani answered.

Tarek gestured at the bench. "Of course, please, let's sit down while we wait."

Seated, Advani hooked his cane over the arm of the bench and glanced around at the well-tended garden, nodding approvingly.

"This is a lovely spot, Mr. Durrani. I've dined at the Rajastan many times and noticed it, but I did not realize it was possible to come out and sit. I thought it was just for the patrons to enjoy by looking. It seems so many of things in life are that way now. Only for show, and no touching. I will definitely remember this spot in my future visits."

"I guess my discovery was just the blind luck of a tourist. I tend to be drawn toward gardens and anything green and growing. The older I get, the more I appreciate such things."

"Mr. Durrani, you are a lucky man for becoming appreciative of the wonders of nature. Many never even notice. For them, I believe, their lives are spent in a kind of ignorant distraction. A life spent without the love of nature is less than half a life. The awful loss that those who are blind to nature must feel when, in the final moments of life, the true reality opens up to these poor souls..." Advani trailed off in his speech for a moment, then finished his thought saying, "Such anguish they must endure at that moment when they realize they have missed out on life's better part."

Advani's words conveyed a deep compassion, and Tarek sensed an authority in his voice.

Despite the more serious turn the conversation had taken, Tarek managed to quickly move it back to a lighter footing. For several minutes more, he and Advani chatted on in easy conversation until they were told their table was ready.

At Tarek's insistence, Advani selected their meal, picking a delicious combination of lamb and vegetarian dishes. Enjoying the conversation as much as the food, Tarek found himself fascinated by Advani. Prior to their meeting Tarek had thoroughly researched Advani's professional accomplishments as an engineer and builder. Still, other than this information and the fact that Advani had obtained his engineering degree in London, as Tarek himself had, he had learned little else about this man.

After only half an hour of conversation, Tarek realized just how extraordinary Advani was. He was obviously a visionary, with the ability to develop complex designs to custom-fit complicated, large-scale building objectives. From their conversation and from what Tarek had gleaned in publications about his work, Advani had been thinking "out of the box" since the day he took up engineering. Just listening to Advani describe how he approached his projects was refreshing and motivating for Tarek.

To Tarek's surprise, as Advani talked on, he felt a pang of regret for not having pursued engineering as a career. It was not because he thought he might have become an engineer of Advani's stature, but because Advani took such obvious satisfaction from having worked hard and, as Advani noted, "then being able to stand back and see just what I had accomplished." This was something Tarek had rarely been able to enjoy in his profession. During his intelligence career, he had learned that his achievements often could only be seen in the abstract, if at all.

Given Advani's renown, Tarek was surprised by the man's humility and complete lack of pretense, yet he was as self-confident as any man Tarek had met. Although it took a while for Tarek to make the connection, it was in Advani's generosity and authentic nature that his confidence seemed grounded. Tarek's assessment was that Advani knew who he was, and that he needed nothing from anyone—not money, not praise, not recognition, none of the things that most men sought. Tarek thought it was a good thing he did not intend to recruit Advani as an agent, as he had little to offer that Advani would likely consider worthwhile, save perhaps his friendship, which Tarek had learned could at times be the most important commodity of all.

It was not until the meal was almost over that Tarek introduced the topic of the business proposal he had sent Advani several weeks previously. Advani asked no questions as Tarek laid out the concept, emphasizing the importance of exposing young engineers to the masters of the profession who had excelled in meeting major engineering challenges. Tarek noted that there were only a handful of engineers of Advani's expertise and experience, and added that having met Advani, he was certain Advani could be a powerful influence on young engineers, inspiring them to great accomplishments.

As an intelligence officer, Tarek was at his best in these circumstances, masterfully playing the role that the operation called for. Anyone watching and listening to Tarek would have believed the proposal he was discussing was genuine and that he was just who he pretended to be. At that moment, Tarek even believed it himself.

As Tarek got into the details of how the program would work, Advani asked a few basic questions and acknowledged that he liked the idea and was interested in the proposal. Tarek sensed a reservation, however. He doubted Advani had any concern about compensation. Deciding it best that Advani did not feel pressured, Tarek concluded his pitch by telling him to think it over for a couple of days, noting that his return flight to Dubai was not until Wednesday.

Advani nodded his head, then said, "Mr. Durrani, I feel it only right that I should give you some idea of what I am thinking at this point. As I said in my initial response to you, the idea of your program appeals to me. My main reservation stems from a personal matter involving my daughter, who, by the way is an accomplished architect. I do not wish to burden you with my personal concerns, but this matter does impact on my availability for your proposal. While my daughter has encouraged me to accept your offer, I am worried that right now she is going through some difficult times, and I am therefore reluctant to take up any activity that would take me away from her."

Tarek nodded his understanding as Advani spoke. It was obvious the issue of the daughter was a sincere one, not simply something Advani threw out as an excuse. Advani's character was such that Tarek was certain family matters took precedence above all else.

In a sympathetic tone, Tarek responded, "I understand completely. There is nothing more important than the welfare of a family member, and I in no way want you to agree to something you do not feel comfortable with."

At this point, Advani raised his hand slightly and said, "I do not want to give you the wrong impression of my daughter. She is an incredibly talented woman. It is just that she seems to be less enthusiastic about her life than in the past. Perhaps I am an over-worried father." Shaking his head, Advani continued. "I just want her to be content with her life, and right now, perhaps she needs me more than your firm does."

Tarek looked into Advani's clear eyes and saw for himself the concern this man was feeling for his daughter. At the same moment, Tarek knew that his job had just become tougher.

Tarek had been in these spots before and knew that the ops plan he had so painstakingly put together would require some on-the-fly modifications if it was to succeed.

Having nearly closed the door on Tarek's plan, Advani then opened it back up, if only a little, by saying, "All that said, I am still undecided. Frankly, I am impressed with you and your proposal. Was this not the case, I would have already declined your offer. So, I will agree to consider this further— with one provision. You must accept my invitation to have tea at my residence tomorrow afternoon. It would give us an opportunity to get to know one another better, and I can show you my project portfolio, which will better acquaint you with some of the projects I have built."

Tarek had mixed feelings about going to Advani's residence but, under the circumstances, he had no choice, and Advani's reference to his portfolio was intriguing. With some luck, it would contain information on the design of Farakka Barrage; the one project of Advani's that Tarek cared anything about.

"Of course, Engineer. I gladly accept your invitation," Tarek responded. "It will be an honor for me to visit you at your home."

"Excellent. Here is my card with my home address. I am probably no more than 20 minutes by taxi from your hotel. Please dress comfortably; there is no need for coat and tie.

Tarek and Advani spent another half-hour in conversation over spiced chai before saying their good-byes. Tarek watched Advani get into a taxi and drive away. *A remarkable man*, he thought, realizing that such experiences were what had kept him in the intel game for so many years.

The following day, Tarek stood outside the stone-columned entranceway of the Advani residence and looked through the heavy metal gate for any sign of a guard. Seeing none, he rang the bell and waited. Standing in the bright sun, he quickly began to perspire. The shaded garden on the other side of the thick wall began to look increasingly inviting. Tarek was about to ring the bell a second time when a barefooted boy about 12 years of age came trotting down the narrow walkway from the house and slowly pulled back the gate, which creaked loudly on its hinges.

"Hello Sahib," he said with a bright smile stretched across his tanned face. "Please come in. It is very hot today."

Tarek stepped through the gate.

"Sorry you had to wait, Sahib. I went for a drink and not hear you."

The sleepy look of the boy's eyes gave rise to Tarek's suspicion that the ring of the gate bell had awakened him from an afternoon slumber in a cooler spot. Noticing the small tin-roofed gatehouse baking in the sun, Tarek could hardly blame the boy for not being at his post.

"No problem," Tarek replied. "What is your name, son?"

"Amin." His smile brightening further at Tarek's interest in him.

"Well, Amin, thank you for coming so quickly to let me in. Are you the gate guard?"

"Yes, I am . . . but not night time. Then guard man comes."

I see," Tarek said. "Have you worked for the Advanis very long?"

"Not long, Sahib. My sister work here in kitchen a year, and she ask Madam if I can work too. Madam say yes, so I help gardener and guard gate."

"It sounds like you are a busy young man," Tarek said.

"Oh, very busy. And I go to school too," Amin added with obvious pride.

"Oh really?" Tarek asked, surprised that the boy's family could afford to send him to school—not often an option for children of the servant class.

Tarek followed Amin down the shaded walkway. He recalled from his research that Advani was a widower. The Madam to whom Amin had referred must be Advani's daughter. *I should put a good word in for Amin if I meet her,* Tarek thought to himself.

At the massive front door, Amin reached up and rang the door bell. "Madam say if I work, I go to school too, but my sister told her this not possible. My father he dead and my mother no has money, and that is why I want to work like sister, so I give money to mother. Madam say 'no problem,' and she put me in morning school."

"I see," Tarek said, smiling at the boy. "You are a very lucky boy. You are in school and have a job. That is very good."

"Yes. Madam and Engineer good people and they care for me and my sister. I work hard for them."

As Tarek listened to Amin, he realized how much he was enjoying talking to him. He had so few opportunities to talk with children of Amin's age, and it reminded him of his own youth, a time he remembered with great fondness.

A male house servant opened the door and Tarek said a quick goodbye to Amin, who trotted back down the walkway.

The house servant ushered Tarek into a large tiled foyer illuminated by an elegant wrought-iron chandelier.

"Please wait here, Sir, and have a seat if you please," the servant said, indicating a nearby wing chair.

Tarek remained standing. From what he could see of the house from the foyer, it was tastefully decorated with fine furnishings, some likely imported. The home did not seem to match well with the Advani that Tarek had met the day before. He had seemed such a humble man despite his great accomplishments; this house and its decorations, however, were anything but humble.

Tarek heard quiet footsteps approaching. Advani, dressed in traditional kurta pajama, entered the foyer.

"Mr. Durrani, I am so glad to see you. Welcome to my home," Advani greeted Tarek, shaking his hand and clasping Tarek's shoulder. "Please come this way. We will sit in the garden room and take our tea there."

As they walked down the hallway, Tarek was able to glimpse several rooms. All had high ceilings with ornate wood trim and tiled floors. Each was decorated with handcrafted furniture and porcelain figurines. Oil paintings adorned the walls and colorful Persian carpets were scattered here and there.

"Engineer, your home is so lovely. I can imagine you never want to leave it," Tarek said.

"I have my beloved wife to thank for the beauty of this home. She was a renowned interior designer, and every article that you see she personally selected. I learned from her that nature is not the only place where we can find extraordinary beauty," Advani said as the two men arrived at the garden room.

The room jutted out from the rear of the main house into the garden. Large windows along the three exterior walls permitted an unobstructed view of the flowers and mango trees. Well-crafted rattan furniture with floral seat cushions accented the room.

"What a wonderful room," Tarek said with an admiring glance around.

"Please sit down," Advani said. "This room is particularly special. It was designed and decorated by my daughter, and it was her first architectural project. At first I resisted having the room added on because I did not want to change the original structure of the house, which has been in my family for three generations. But Sahar can be very persuasive when she gets an idea, and now I am quite happy with the result of her work."

"If this was her first project, I can only imagine the kind of work she is doing now," Tarek said.

"You are quite right. She is a brilliant architect, and she is currently designing a new wing of the National Library. I had hoped you would get to meet her today, but she was called to a meeting by the committee overseeing the project."

"Well I'm sorry I will not be able to meet her," Tarek said, although in truth he was quite content to minimize his involvement with the Advani family. He had only one purpose in coming and that was to get a look at the design plans for Farakka Barrage.

They had no sooner seated themselves than tea and cookies were served by a young woman dressed in a green and gold sari. Tarek saw that she resembled the gate boy. He smiled at the woman as she served his tea and told her of his encounter with Amin, noting what a bright boy he seemed to be. She returned Tarek's smile shyly and thanked him for his kindness in saying this about her young brother.

When she had gone from the room, Advani told Tarek that the young woman had come to his home asking for employment after the death of her father. The head servant had told her there was no work and the woman was almost out the gate when Sahar, who had overheard the conversation, came out of the house and called her back. After talking with her briefly, Sahar gave her a job.

"I have no doubt Sahar saved her life that day," Advani said. "Had she not found work here, she would likely have become a prostitute as the only way for her family to survive. And becoming a prostitute in India is a sentence to death by AIDS."

"Allah was surely smiling on her the day she appeared at your gate," Tarek said.

"I'm sure He was," Advani said, and then after a slight pause continued, his eyes intently looking into Tarek's, "For God smiles on each of us everyday, although we seldom realize it."

Tarek was not sure what to say in reply. He had seen so much in his life that seemed to indicate otherwise that in good conscience he could not agree with Advani on this point. So many desperately poor people scattered throughout the world, barely surviving from day to day. So many tragedies, so much war, so much suffering and pain.

"I see you are considering the validity of my statement," Advani said. "This is good. Bold statements about God should not be accepted at face value, and ultimately knowledge of God can only come from direct experience."

Tarek nodded, "I'm afraid my experiences at this point in my life have not allowed me to make many conclusions about Allah although I certainly do have some ideas."

"I understand," Advani said. "So, rather than my trying to convince you of my belief, I will leave it to God to reveal himself in the way he wishes you to know him. Here in India, we have a tradition that a man spends the early part of his life becoming educated about the things of the world. When the time comes, he enters a profession, takes a wife, and raises a family. So much time is required to meet the demands of his job and family, little time is left for God. Finally the day comes when the responsibility of caring for his family is largely over, and the man retires from his profession. It is at this point, that his search for God begins in earnest."

"And is this where you are now in your life, Engineer?" Tarek asked.

Advani smiled. "No, Mr. Durrani. My search has ended."

"You believe you have found God?" Tarek asked, and although not intended, the question sounded more like a challenge.

Advani took no offense but responded in a soft voice, "To speak of one's personal experience of having direct consciousness of God should generally be avoided, as there is no experience more precious or sublime than this. Using words to describe it, even the loveliest of words, is like throwing the vilest filth on fresh fallen snow. But in answer to your question, no, I do not 'believe' I have found God as you put it. I know I have, and there is a universe of difference between believing and knowing when we speak of God."

As Tarek listened to Advani, he could feel the certainty in the old man's voice, an absolute authority that he conveyed in a powerful way. In the course of his life, Tarek had met only a couple of people who conveyed such authority when speaking of God. One had been a Sufi, the other a Christian. Now here was a Hindu speaking with the same self-evident authority. *I suppose no religion has cornered the market on God,* Tarek thought to himself.

At that moment Tarek caught sight through the window of a flock of green parrots descending into the trees of the garden. Advani also saw the parrots and said excitedly "They are back! I knew their migration had already begun, but these are the first I've seen this year!"

"They are beautiful," Tarek said.

"Yes, they are. And their appearance always comes at auspicious moments." Advani then asked, "Do you enjoy bird watching?"

Without waiting for a response, he stood up and said, "Please, excuse me. I'll be right back. I have something to show you. As a man who loves nature, you will appreciate it more than most."

While Advani was out of the room, Tarek stood and walked over to the window where he could get a better view of the parrots. As he watched the birds flitting from branch to branch Tarek began to consider his own next move. He hoped that Advani had not forgotten his offer to show him his professional portfolio. If he had, Tarek would have to remind him of it. He had not yet brought up business with Advani. As he liked the man and thought Advani liked him, he did not want to do anything that would spoil the budding relationship.

Advani returned with what appeared to be a stack of photo albums and motioned Tarek to have a seat, pushing aside the tea tray to make room on the tabletop.

"I think you will enjoy these pictures that Sahar and I took last year during a trip we made to a game park in Nepal. You will not believe the birds we found there."

Opening the book, Advani began to describe the variety of game they had seen. On the first page was a photo of an entrance sign for Royal Chitwan National Park. Standing next to the sign was a smiling woman wearing sunglasses and dressed in shorts and a light cotton shirt. It was hard to tell the woman's age but Tarek guessed she was in her mid to late thirties. What was not hard to tell was that the woman was beautiful, stunningly so.

"That is Sahar," Advani noted as Tarek continued to look at the photo. Thinking Tarek did not understand and perhaps did not remember his daughter's name, Advani said, "Sahar, my daughter."

Tarek had in fact not heard, or at least had not registered Advani's words, so taken was he by the woman in the photograph. Advani's repetition of Sahar's name did register however, and Tarek realized he was in danger of embarrassing himself.

"Yes, yes," Tarek said quickly, "a very lovely lady," and then quickly added," I have read about the Chitwan game park. It sounds like a great place to visit. Did you stay there long?"

This was all the encouragement Advani needed to resume his narration of the visit to the park while he leafed through the photos of game and colorful birds. Advani was very animated as he discussed the park and it was obvious he had thoroughly enjoyed it. Tarek however, was beginning to feel a sense of growing impatience. He began to look for a way to move the discussion to professional matters.

At last Advani reached the final page in the album and, almost as if he had read Tarek's mind, said, "Well, now. Let me show you something of more immediate interest to you." He put the photo album aside to reveal a thick leather-bound book, which he picked up and handed to Tarek.

"This is my portfolio of the major projects I have built, going back 40 years. There are eight in all, most of them dams or related structures. All the details about the projects are provided—design plans, photos, and supplemental material, along with my personal notes that describe how each project progressed. I believe this document can serve as a great source for putting together seminars for young engineers."

Tarek was impressed with the collection of projects and the way each was organized and presented in the book, which obviously had been professionally prepared and published.

Turning to the index page, Tarek noted that Farakka Barrage was listed as one of the eight projects. "This is fantastic," he said. "Very detailed. Very complete."

Advani beamed. "As an engineer yourself, I know you appreciate this work. And I want you to know that even if I do not join your project, I have no problem with you using this material in your training program. In fact, you may have this copy if you like. If I cannot influence a new generation of engineers in the flesh, at least my work can be applied toward that goal."

Leafing through the book, Tarek knew he had in his hands everything he needed on Farakka Barrage. Since Advani was willing to give him the copy of the portfolio, Tarek's mission was very near the point of completion.

"This is an excellent document, and its value as a training reference is obvious. If you are serious in suggesting that my company may use this as part of its training curriculum, I enthusiastically accept your offer." Tarek said. "Of course, I am still hopeful that we will have the creator of these projects in the flesh and before our engineers as well."

Advani smiled and said, "I have given your kind offer some serious consideration Tarek." He paused and asked, "If I may call you by your first name?"

"Of course Engineer," Tarek responded. "I would be honored to have you address me as a friend."

"Well, as I indicated at our first meeting, I have had some doubts about the wisdom of my committing to your program. I think it is a wonderful concept. However, I am dealing with some small health issues and, as I said to you before, there are issues relating to Sahar as well. Sadly, I believe I must decline this wonderful opportunity."

Advani cast his eyes downward. "I realize you have come a great distance and at some expense just to talk to me. I regret this, particularly since in my correspondence with you I perhaps gave you an overly optimistic impression about my willingness to accept your proposal. For this, I am sorry."

Advani's decision was the best news Tarek could have hoped for. It greatly simplified the operation in terms of how he would terminate contact with Advani without causing suspicion. Often this final phase of an operation could be very difficult.

"Engineer, there is no reason to apologize. This is business, and in business not everything works out as planned. I admire you for your dedication to the welfare of your daughter, and I hope your health situation is not serious. I assure you, I have enjoyed getting to know you, and I hope we can continue to be friends. Who knows, perhaps at some point in the future you will be in a better situation, and we can pick up our discussions at that time."

"Perhaps, perhaps," Advani responded. "I also have certainly enjoyed talking to you Tarek. I do like you. I believe you are a special man. You have a good heart. I can see it in you."

Tarek was caught off guard by Advani's candor. He felt a little embarrassed and was uncertain how to respond.

"I am sorry if I embarrassed you Tarek. In my old age, I have become more direct in saying what I feel. I suppose it is because I have learned that our time on this earth is very limited, and saying what we feel, particularly when it is a good feeling in regards to people we come to know, is one of the most important things we can do."

Tarek looked into Advani's penetrating eyes. "I take no offense, Engineer. Although I know I fall short of your opinion of me, it pleases me that you should think this about me."

"Good," Advani said with a quick smile. "I know you will accomplish great things in your life, Tarek. One day you will look back and realize that I was right about this. Yes, one day you will see." He paused for a moment. "Perhaps I can provide you one piece of important advice."

"Please do, Engineer. Advice from a man of your credentials is worth more than gold."

"This advice is not about professional matters, Tarek. It is about something of much greater importance, for it deals with your soul. You must learn that your true identity is not what the world says it is— not your race, nor your nationality, your profession, your religion, or even your sex. These are all superficial things that we take up when we are born into this world. Each of them has it uses, but do not make the mistake of believing they are who or what you are. They are not. What you are is buried deep within you, and you must dig yourself out if you are to become whole and truly know yourself in this life. And do not be surprised if when you uncover your true self, you also find in the same exact instant that God has been patiently waiting for you to remove that last covering from your soul. Many seek completeness in other ways—wealth, sex, drugs, professional accomplishments. Despite their best efforts, they all fail. Do not make this mistake with your life." Advani then fell silent, his eyes holding Tarek's.

For a second time that afternoon, Advani had taken Tarek by surprise. Never before had Tarek had an experience during an operation where a target had so overwhelmed him by the power and wisdom of his words. Even more overwhelming were Advani's devastating insights into Tarek himself.

Sensing Tarek's discomfort, Advani added, "Tarek, please consider my comments, and if you find them useful then perhaps in the long run they will be of greater worth to you than my portfolio."

Looking into the old man's kind face, Tarek answered, "Yes, perhaps they will be. In any case, our meeting has been a remarkable one that I shall always remember."

After a few minutes more, Tarek's afternoon tea with Advani came to an end, and the two men walked toward the front door, Tarek's thoughts having fully returned from the realm of the transcendent to the practical.

He could not believe his good fortune. In his hand was the information he had spent the previous two months planning to collect. In relation to other intelligence missions he had conducted, this one had been extremely low-cost and had been accomplished securely in a country known to have a highly efficient security service.

The situation seemed to violate one of the principles Tarek had always found to be true about intelligence work—that nothing important is accomplished easily. Tarek could only rationalize his easy success as being one of those favorable aberrations to which every operations officer is entitled at least once in a career.

The only thing remaining was to get himself and Advani's portfolio out of the country and back to Pakistan. Tarek hoped now that he would be able to get his return airline reservations for Dubai changed so that he could leave the next day, rather than in three as scheduled.

Tarek and Advani stopped at the foyer and were saying their final goodbyes when the front door opened.

"Sahar! You are back!" Advani said, surprised and pleased as his daughter walked through the doorway.

"Yes, the committee meeting was mercifully short, so I did not stay any longer than necessary." Then, immediately turning to Tarek and extending her hand, she said, "You must be Mr. Durrani."

As mesmerized as Tarek had been by Sahar's photo, it had not fully prepared him for the shock of meeting her face to face, so powerful was the effect of her physical presence on Tarek. *Surely this is what Adam felt when he first saw Eve in the garden,* Tarek thought.

Taking her hand in his and making a supreme effort to conceal his almost primal reaction to her, Tarek said, "I have heard much about you from your father. I am sure you know he is quite proud of you, and with good reason I should say. I understand you are the lead architect for a project at the National Library. That is quite a testament to your abilities."

"Oh, I am not so sure of that," Sahar laughed. "I think no one else was crazy enough to sign on to a project that is being overseen by a committee of government bureaucrats. After this meeting, I am truly convinced they are all insane."

Standing so near to her, watching her, and listening to her soft voice, Tarek was glad he had seen the photo of her prior to their meeting. It had at least prepared him in some way for the experience of a personal encounter. Her presence had energy to it and everything about her—her looks, her voice, her movements—accentuated that energy.

"I can imagine it makes your work much more difficult," he said hoping the expression on his face did not make it plain to Sahar how completely captivated he was. "As if the challenges of producing design plans weren't enough to keep you occupied, you also have to deal with a committee."

"You are so right. The design part is easy. Trying to deal with egos, all of them male, I might add, is another thing all together."

Advani placed his hand on his daughter's shoulder and said, "Don't forget Mr. Durrani has some engineering experience, and I am sure he has had similar situations in projects he has worked on."

Tarek shrugged his shoulders and said quite truthfully, "Not as much as you might think," adding, "I've spent much of my career on the personnel and training side of things." Shifting topics he asked, "When will the library project be finished?"

"We've only recently started, but it should go quickly. Another wing similar in design was renovated two years ago, so most of the problems have been encountered and worked through."

Sahar enjoyed the fact that Mr. Durrani seemed genuinely interested in her work. Her father had spoken so highly of him and, now that she had met him for herself, she judged him an attractive and educated man. She did not miss the fact that he wore no wedding band.

"Mr. Durrani, I would love to show you what we are doing in our project," she said on impulse. "If you are interested, we could go to the library tomorrow, and I could give you the grand tour."

Tarek knew his work in New Delhi was finished and that operational protocol required he leave India as soon as possible, so he was surprised when he heard himself say, "That would be lovely, Ms. Advani. I accept your invitation."

—17—

Colonel Khaja sat at his office desk in the Pak Army Corp of Engineers Headquarters building in Islamabad, thumbing through his rolodex. He prayed he had not lost the card. This was going to be a dirty job, and he did not want to have to do it himself. But if he couldn't find the card, he would have no choice—that had been made perfectly clear to him.

The second time through the rolodex he found it. It wasn't under the 'T's where he expected to find the card of the man who called himself "the Turk." The card was behind the 'B' tab. *Why did I file it there?* he asked himself, and then he remembered. It was his own little joke—the 'B' was for bomber.

Placing the card on his desk, he picked up his cell phone and punched in the number he had written on the card. He hoped the Turk was not away on a trip; there was precious little time to pull this together. After four rings, a gruff voice answered, "Speak." It was the Turk.

— 18 —

General Ali was behind schedule—of all days for this to be the case. He had less than an hour to get out to the Equestrian Center for his lunch with Prime Minister Bahir. Ali was never late for appointments, and he certainly could not be late for this one. He picked up his notes and placed them in his valet case, then he checked his pants pocket to make sure he had his car keys. He had given the office driver the day off, which gave him an excuse for taking his own car, and at the same time, avoided an entry in the motor pool log that would have shown him at the same location as the prime minister.

The telephone rang just as he was about to leave the office. It was his direct line. He picked up the phone. "General Ali here."

There was no answer. Just a click as the caller hung up.

Ali thought the call odd, but he quickly dismissed it as a wrong number.

His Kia sedan was parked in the underground parking lot reserved for senior ISI officers. Ali unlocked the car and got inside, placing the key in the ignition. He checked his valet once more to make sure he had not forgotten his notes, then cranked the engine and drove out of the garage, exiting the ISI compound through the rear gate.

Despite being pressed for time, he decided to run an abbreviated check route prior to turning onto the highway that led out of town to the Equestrian Center. He had to be sure he was not being followed.

About mid-way into his run, he spotted a car behind him that he thought he might have seen just after he had departed the ISI compound. Ali made a turn and the suspect car continued on. After a few more turns, the car did not reappear. Ali wrote it off as a "ghost," intelligence-speak for a false sighting of surveillance. Satisfied he was clean, Ali made his way to the highway and headed east.

Ali had fond memories of the Equestrian Center. Many years before, he had ridden there regularly. Once he had even owned a horse that he boarded at the center, a spirited thoroughbred gelding named "Black Dancer" that stood sixteen hands. Ali had loved that animal. He remembered sadly how the magnificent horse had to be put down after bowing a pastern. He had never felt the same about any horse after. Perhaps it was just as well, he thought, for as he had risen in rank, his time for horseback riding had disappeared.

Ali exited the highway and took the two-lane road that led to the turn off to the center. Approaching the turnoff, Ali slowed his speed and turned the Kia onto a tree-lined gravel road, bordered by broad green fields on both sides of the road. Ali lowered the windows of the car and inhaled the smell of fresh-cut hay. The sound of gravel crunched beneath the tires as he drove slowly down the road. Up ahead, parked well off the road to the right, he could see a collection of cars, bikes, and motorcycles. Ali had forgotten there was a spring-fed lake in the field where locals came to fish.

Ali looked beyond the vehicles and spotted a slow-moving Equestrian Center truck pulling an open-top, fully loaded six-horse trailer. He noted that roughly halfway between his position and the approaching truck, a small car was parked on the left, barely off the road, and directly across from the lake parking area. The car appeared to be unoccupied. It seemed odd to Ali that someone would leave their car there, when better places to park were open just across the road. *Probably it has broken down*, he thought.

The road was narrow, and the car's position would make it impossible for both Ali's car and the approaching truck to pass each other. Ali assumed the truck would swing off the road into the parking area and let him pass. But as it came nearer, it became clear the truck intended to continue straight ahead and would make no accommodation for his car to pass. Ali pulled off into the parking area, across the road from the parked car. The truck with its trailer load of Arabians slowly passed between Ali and the parked car.

Ali admired the beautiful animals standing together in the passing trailer, their ears pointed forward as they looked at him with intense, large black eyes. It was a scene that would be burned into his memory forever. An instant later he was deafened as an explosion lifted up his car and threw it onto its side.

Ali was stunned by the concussion of the blast. He could feel stabs of pain on the left side of his head, a high-pitched noise ringing in his ears. The burnt smell of cordite filled his nostrils as smoke engulfed his car.

Recovering from the shock, Ali opened his eyes. Thick gray smoke was choking him. He found himself pushed face down against the passenger's side of the car. Patches of grass stuck up through the car's open windows.

Ali slowly turned himself over. A foot above him, the front leg of a horse dangled down from the driver's side of the car. The blast had severed it whole from the animal and sent it as a projectile penetrating halfway through the side of the car. Warm red blood dripped from the leg onto Ali's face, the sticky liquid running into his eyes.

Ali began to hear shouting. He could see shadows as people moved about outside the car. He felt himself being lifted through the space where the windshield had been. Several men carried him to a shady spot and laid him down in the grass. Someone poured water over his face and washed the blood from his eyes.

"Sir . . . Sir, are you alright?" one of the men asked.

"I'm not sure," Ali managed to say.

He slowly moved his arms and legs. Other than some pain in his left shoulder, everything seemed in working order.

"Please, prop me up against the tree so I can see what happened," Ali asked the men standing over him. They carefully lifted him up and set his back against the smooth trunk of a jackfruit tree, its bark having been blown away by the blast.

Ali surveyed the still smoky scene. The carnage shocked him. A smoldering crater marked the spot where the parked car had been. The truck and horse trailer were an indistinguishable tangle of twisted metal, the proud horses Ali had only moments before admired were now ripped and shredded clumps of entrails, muscle, and tissue. Ragged pieces of horsehide were scattered about, some on fire. The stench of burning hair filled the air.

Cars with flashing red lights raced down the road from the Equestrian Center. One man, holding a cane fishing pole in his hand, knelt down beside Ali and asked, "What happened, Sahib?"

Ali looked up at the man, his eyes filled with anger. "A bomb," he said. "A bloody car bomb."

— 19 —

It was early afternoon of the day following Tarek's visit to the Advani residence. Tarek stood staring out of the front window of the hotel lobby waiting for Sahar to pick him up. Since his arrival in India, on two occasions he had gone to an internet café to check his email account for any message from Ali. The most recent check made that morning showed no message had been sent. Tarek was puzzled by Ali's silence.

As he waited for Sahar, he was angry with himself for having accepted her invitation to tour the National Library. It meant his departure from New Delhi would be delayed by a day. If there had been no flights available he could have rationalized the delay, telling himself that no harm was done, no violation of operational principle committed. But there had been a flight available that morning, had he chosen to take it. Clearly, his decision to stay another day could not be justified by operational reasons. Tarek had to confront the fact that for the first time in his career, he had let something personal unduly influence his work.

It wasn't that he was concerned his delay actually would jeopardize his mission; it was that he had violated a basic operational principle—when in a hostile operational environment, you do not expose yourself to potential discovery any longer than necessary. It was obvious that no operational benefit could come from spending the afternoon with Sahar. Tarek had gotten what he came for. That morning he had gone to a shop where he had made a copy of the Farakka Barrage material. He had mailed the original and the copy in separate packages by overnight express to two different commercial addresses in the United Arab Emirates provided for him by Habibi. So, his work was done; his only operational purpose for being in India finished.

While he silently chastised himself for his decision to stay, a baby-blue Mercedes 500 pulled up to the hotel. The driver exited the car and came around to open the rear passenger door, but the door opened before he got to it, and Sahar stepped out unaided. She was dressed in a form-fitting white and black business suit, her hair pulled straight back and tied in a neat ponytail. She looked stunning; the sight of her took Tarek's breath away.

He started toward the hotel entrance, but Sahar had already come inside. When she saw him, a bright smile spread across her face. In Tarek's mind, it lit up the entire lobby.

"Good Morning, Mr. Durrani. How are you today?" she greeted him.

When Tarek's eyes met Sahar's, he felt as if an electric current was surging through his body, a reaction that required all his discipline to conceal.

"I am very well, thank you, Ms. Advani," he answered, sounding much more composed than he felt. "And you?"

"I am feeling great, as a matter of fact. I woke up this morning very well rested and ready for a new week. I don't always feel this way on a Monday morning," Sahar laughed. "Have you had your lunch?"

"Well, I don't normally eat lunch," Tarek responded. "I'm an early riser, and I typically take a big breakfast after my morning workout."

"Oh, you make me feel guilty. I have been trying to get on a schedule of exercising in the morning but this morning, I must confess, I slept in."

Tarek smiled. "Don't feel too guilty. We all sleep in from time to time."

"I suppose you are right. I hope I will do better tomorrow," Sahar said, although from the look of his trim physique, she doubted that Tarek missed many workouts.

"Well then, shall we?"

Demonstrating her self-assuredness, it was Sahar who first asked Tarek to call her by her first name. When Tarek agreed, she immediately asked if he minded if she called him by his first name as well—a request Tarek was happy to grant.

As they came to the conclusion of their tour of the library and renovations, Sahar asked, "Would you be interested in touring an art gallery that's near here? The curator is a friend and he has offered to open up the gallery for us even though it is normally closed to the public on Mondays. I took the liberty of giving him a call last night on a hunch you would enjoy it."

Tarek smiled. "Your instinct was a good one. I'd love to see it."

The gallery featured a collection of 17th century European oil paintings, but Tarek was far more interested in a special showing of exquisitely detailed antique Persian miniature paintings. Tarek appreciated the delicate paintings not only for their beauty and the history they conveyed, but for the artists' technical expertise in rendering them, often using individual horsehairs for brushes.

While Tarek and Sahar waited for the curator to return from fetching a set of keys to the second floor, Sahar turned from one of the miniature paintings, her eyes shining with delight, and asked, "Have you ever seen such beauty?"

"No. Never," Tarek answered, his gaze fixed on Sahar.

For a moment Sahar hesitated, continuing to look at Tarek. For the first time that day, she seemed unsure of herself.

The curator broke the moment, beckoning to them from the far end of the room. Sensing her awkwardness, Tarek took the initiative. "Come, let's not keep our host waiting," he said, and taking Sahar by the arm, walked her across the broad tiled floor to the stairway where the curator waited.

To be in the company of a beautiful woman was always a treat for Tarek, but he found being with Sahar so much more than that. *This woman has me engaged at all levels,* Tarek thought to himself.

Despite the challenges Sahar posed for him, Tarek felt at ease with her. His only discomfort came from his awareness of how absolutely taken he was with her, and he feared that would all be too evident. Certainly a woman like Sahar must know the effect and power she had over men. Tarek felt sure he was only the most recent of many men who had been captivated by her. Yet for all her charms, she seemed completely genuine, which made her all the more remarkable in Tarek's eyes.

Throughout the rest of the afternoon, both Tarek and Sahar felt a subtle change had taken place in their relationship. For Sahar, Tarek was a puzzle, so different from most men, who were, in her experience, all too obvious. Tarek revealed little about himself. She knew almost nothing about him. He had told her he was originally from Pakistan, and after university study in London he had spent most of his time working for engineering firms around the Middle East.

Despite how little he had revealed of his background, Tarek seemed open and genuine, and there was an air of gentleness about him that Sahar found attractive. Tarek's reticence to talk about himself was a trait she had not found in other men, who always appeared so eager to impress her, so busy telling her the stories of their accomplishments, leaving her little opportunity to speak. With Tarek, the opposite was true.

On the drive back to his hotel Tarek asked her, "May I take you to an early dinner? It is the least I can do to repay you for the time you have spent with me."

"If you insist," Sahar teased him, "but not at your hotel. Let me suggest instead a restaurant where we will enjoy more authentic Indian cuisine."

Tarek agreed readily. He really did not care where they dined. He only wanted to prolong his time with Sahar.

The restaurant she suggested was the kind of out-of-the-way establishment only a local would know about. The food was delicious, while the intimate, comfortable ambiance only added to his pleasure in being with Sahar.

They left the restaurant after a long and enjoyable dinner, and Sahar directed her chauffeur to take them to Tarek's hotel. Upon arriving, Sahar exited the car with Tarek to say goodbye. As they stood together on the sidewalk, neither knew what to say. She asked if he had plans to return to India, but a vague, "Perhaps," was all Tarek could answer.

"Well, then," Sahar said with a confident smile, "perhaps I might visit Dubai for some shopping, and we could see each other there."

"Yes, that would be wonderful," Tarek said, without the slightest idea how he could handle a visit by her to Dubai, given his life in the UAE was entirely fictional. "You've got my e-mail address. Let me know how your shopping plans develop."

He took Sahar's hand in his. "I really have enjoyed getting to know you, Sahar. I do hope to see you again."

To his delight, Sahar smiled and placed her other hand on his, "I am glad you feel this way, Tarek. It is the same way I feel. We will be in touch." Then with a warm squeeze of his hand she said, "Until we meet again, Tarek."

Before he could respond she quickly turned from him and got back into the car, pausing to wave as the car began to move. Tarek watched as the car pulled away from the hotel. When it was out of sight, he turned and walked into the hotel, elated and more confused than he had ever felt in his life.

—20—

Dressed in loose Punjabi pants and a banded-collar shirt, Abdul Salim sat comfortably on a prayer rug atop the flat roof of his home in Islamabad. A Qur'an lay open in his lap as he read his favorite verses aloud. It was late in the afternoon on Monday, and the heat of the day had ebbed. The streets of the affluent residential area below were quiet, with only an occasional sound of a bird or distant passing car making an intrusion into Salim's solemn reverie.

Beside him sat a battery powered International Maritime Satellite Telephone. His was a compact portable model, the size of a small laptop computer, known as the "Mini-M." It had a detachable flat panel antenna that could be used remotely to gain better line of sight to the corresponding satellite. Salim had positioned the antenna a few feet from where he sat, on an azimuth of 240 degrees.

The INMARSAT was a near perfect communications system for Salim. Reliable and simple to operate, he could call any telephone number in the world without requiring the assistance of an aide or operator.

He closed the Qur'an and gently set it aside. Looking at his watch, he noted it was time to call General Huq, who was inspecting troops near the Line of Control between Pakistan and India. Salim was looking forward to talking to Huq; he had good news for him. Salim punched in the number and slowly paced around the roof as Huq's own satellite phone rang. On the fifth ring, Huq answered.

"Yes, Esfahani," Huq said, employing the alias Salim used when speaking over the Mini-M. "How is the view today?" Huq asked, knowing that Salim was probably sitting atop his roof.

"The view is wonderful, praise be to Allah, and so is the news!" Salim responded, his voice filled with enthusiasm. "We are well positioned to work with the Kashmiri firm."

"So the counter-proposal we learned about failed to change any minds?" Huq asked.

"The proposal was never delivered. The representative was delayed by an unfortunate accident," Salim said.

"How fortunate for us. So how did the second meeting with the Kashmiri firm come out?" Huq asked, knowing that the 'Kashmiri firm' mentioned by Salim referred to the representatives of the Lashkar-e-Taiba.

"Oh, very well. All is according to plan, and I believe they are beginning to trust us. And on your side? How are your sons?" Salim asked.

"They are in good spirits—fit and ready," Huq answered, referring to the troops he had spent the last week inspecting. "I am indeed proud to be their father," he added with a laugh.

"Other than the love of Allah, a man can have no greater love than for his sons," Salim said, and then quickly added in a rare attempt at humor, "And you have so many of them."

Huq again laughed. "Yes, my seeds all appear to have landed on fertile ground."

"Well, my friend, I await your return. Our enterprise is taking shape, and we and our partners have much to discuss. Call me upon your arrival. May Allah guide your steps, Khoda Hafez."

As the sun dipped behind the western horizon, the call for prayer from the local minaret blared out across the darkening sky. Salim returned to his prayer rug. Turning toward Mecca, he knelt, touched his forehead to the rug and began to pray.

—21—

Tarek learned of the attack against General Ali within half an hour of his return to Islamabad. The news shocked him and made him feel even guiltier about staying an extra day in Delhi to spend time with Sahar.

Upon learning the news, Tarek went to see Ali at his home, where he was still recovering. His most serious injury was a severely bruised shoulder. The driver of the truck pulling the horse trailer had not fared as well; he had died at the scene along with the six horses he had been transporting.

Ali quickly brought Tarek up to speed on developments since the bombing. A major investigation was underway, but few clues had been found. The car used in the bombing had been stolen the night before the attack. Based on the size of the crater it left, the car had been packed with up to 150 kilograms of dynamite, which was determined to have been stolen from a demolitions supply warehouse the year before. The explosion had been activated by command-detonation from a radio signal. It was not a particularly sophisticated device, considering the state of the art in car bombs, except for one thing: a tracking beacon had been found on Ali's car.

As far as Tarek knew, this was the first time a beacon had been used in an attack within Pakistan. Ali confirmed this was the case and elaborated further. "It was a commercial system that can be purchased by anyone for around $500 dollars, and it works anywhere cell phones work, as it communicates using the same cell-tower grid system."

"Interesting," Tarek said. "So whoever was behind this did not have to be on site to know you were in the kill zone. They only had to know where you were going and the route you were taking."

Ali nodded. "That's correct. They did not have to be at the kill zone ahead of me or to even follow me there. They could simply monitor my movements from a remote location through the beacon, which reports geocoords every 5 seconds. And when my geocoords matched those of the parked car—boom. No more General Ali to worry about."

Tarek thought for a moment. "You know, Sir, it is probably a good thing they used a beacon."

"How so?" Ali asked.

"Well, if they hadn't, you may well be dead right now."

Ali looked quizzically at Tarek.

"Sir, they did not have eyes on target. That's why they went ahead and detonated the bomb, even though there was a truck and trailer loaded with horses between you and the car. The bomber did not know they were in the way because he could not see them. Had he known about the truck and trailer, he would have either let the truck and trailer pass, or waited until your return trip."

"It is doubtful I would have been so fortunate as to have another truck get in the way the second time around," Ali said, a sober look on his face.

"Allah was looking out for you on that day, protecting you from someone intent on doing you harm. The question is who?"

"A dozen theories are being bantered about. The one with the most currency right now is that the Indians did it. No surprise there, I suppose, although you and I both know that is nonsense."

"No, I can't imagine RAW being behind this. They have done some stupid things, but this—no way. What about al-Qa'ida? They managed to kill our president. What's to stop them from going after you? After all, under your orders, ISI has been putting them under tremendous pressure and has killed more of them and their allies than anyone, even the Americans."

al-Qa'ida - assassinated president

"They certainly can't be ruled out, but I don't think their intel is that good. Whoever is behind this has to be inside the government and is probably very senior. They had to know I was going to the Equestrian Center that day to meet the prime minister. There were only a handful of people who knew that, and they all have been interviewed and have denied any involvement in the attack. "

"So, who do you think is behind it? The IRE?" Tarek said.

"Yes, almost certainly someone within the IRE. Or one of its fellow travelers. They are the only ones I can think of that would not want me to make the meeting with the PM. General Huq in particular comes to mind, or someone close to him. The trouble is, we will never be able to pin this on them. Whoever did this has covered his tracks well, and besides, there is such divisiveness in the government right now, the PM has no stomach for finding out the truth."

"So what do we do, General?"

"We do what we are good at doing. We take our time and find out who is behind this and what they are up to." Ali said.

"And then?"

"We stop them."

—22—

It was 9:00 on a Wednesday morning as Ambassador Salim sat at his desk reviewing the notes from his secret meeting the previous day. The meeting with Abu Shafik had gone extraordinarily well—Abu Shafik agreeing to all the key points of Salim's proposal. Most importantly, Abu Shafik had agreed that the LT would maintain a stand-down of its operations in Kashmir.

Keeping the LT fighters inactive was particularly important to Salim's strategy. Salim wanted the Indians to believe that the LT, under pressure from Pakistan, was being forced to abandon their armed struggle while Pakistan pursued a peaceful dialogue with India. And, especially, he also wanted Prime Minister Bahir to believe it.

According to Salim's agreement with Abu Shafik, in exchange for the continued suspension of LT operations in Kashmir, the IRE would deliver funding and material, including weapons. Salim had agreed that the LT could continue to conduct recruitment and training activities in Pakistan, and General Huq had already arranged safe havens inside Pakistan where Shafik's men could rest, refit, and hone their military skills.

The arrangement with Abu Shafik had not been authorized by the Pakistani government. Only Salim, General Huq, and a handful of officials—men who shared the same vision of the future—were aware that any agreement existed with the LT.

The arrangement exactly met Salim's needs. He could tell the prime minister that since the IRE had taken over the ISI's responsibility for maintaining communication with the LT, the group had desisted from conducting attacks, permitting Pakistan to engage in serious peace discussions with India. Once Salim was ready to put all parts of his plan into action, it would be too late for the PM to react.

Everything was shaping up nicely, Salim thought. He locked his notes in a small two-drawer safe in preparation for the briefing on Major Durrani's mission in India. Pressing the intercom button, he told his aide to send the visitors into his office.

Tarek walked in, accompanied by Admiral Nurullah and an Army engineer, Colonel Khaja, who was, like Tarek, on deputation to the IRE.

Salim greeted Tarek so warmly a casual observer would have thought they were old friends. He traded perfunctory greetings with the other two men and directed the group to a conference table where they could spread out the materials to be reviewed. The large oval table was a new addition to the office since Tarek's first meeting with Salim, one that he took as a sure sign of the IRE's growing bureaucracy.

Admiral Nurullah began the briefing. "Mister Ambassador, I am pleased to report that Major Durrani's mission has been 100 percent successful." He handed Salim a copy of the briefing materials, which Salim reviewed as Nurullah described their contents.

The first section contained the details of Farakka Barrage, including maps showing the dam's location, as well as significant population centers and facilities in the area. There was also an overhead commercial satellite photo of the dam. Another document included a history of the dam and background information on why it had become a point of contention between India and Bangladesh. Nurullah also noted that Bangladesh had recently petitioned the U.N. to again hear its complaint that Farakka Barrage was causing desertification in its western region.

Salim jotted down a note to himself on this point. "Good. Very good," he said. "I will speak to the foreign minister to see what we can do to support Bangladesh's petition. It is to our interest that Farakka Barrage becomes newsworthy."

The second section of the report was a technical analysis, prepared by Colonel Khaja, on the structure and materials of the Farakka Barrage. It was on this section that Salim seemed to focus most closely.

"So, Colonel Khaja, what does all this mean?" Salim asked. "Its complexity is beyond me."

"In a nut shell, Mister Ambassador, from an engineering standpoint Farakka Barrage is a very formidable structure," Khaja replied. "The Ganges along this stretch is particularly deep, and due to the flow rate of the water and the width of the river channel at this point, extreme forces are at work on the dam most of the year. To insure its long-term integrity, special composition concrete was poured in liberal amounts to build the dam's walls. In addition, this concrete was heavily reinforced with steel girders and other reinforcement running both vertically and horizontally. Frankly, in my view the dam is actually oversized and was over-engineered for its task."

"I am surprised India could afford to waste its resources by overbuilding a project of this scale," Salim remarked. "No doubt the waste was the result of poor engineering on India's part."

"I don't believe so, Mister Ambassador," Admiral Nurullah contradicted. "We mustn't forget that at the time Farakka Barrage was built, India was a client state of the Soviet Union. You'll note from the background material that this was, in fact, the first major joint water project between the Indians and the Soviets. The Soviets wanted to impress the Indians with what they could bring to bear on projects like this, so for purely political reasons, they perhaps went a little overboard with its construction."

"Excellent point, Admiral," Salim responded, although he would have preferred to believe it was just poor planning on the Indians' part. "Well, I think we have what we need to buttress Bangladesh's case in the UN. Let us hope that with our behind-the-scenes assistance, Bangladesh will win the U.N.

debate, and India will be forced by world pressure to close the dam for environmental reasons. Wouldn't that be a blow to Indian prestige and a great victory for the IRE?"

Turning to Tarek, Salim said, "Major, your mission to India is the critical piece in all this. Without the information we now have before us, we would not be in position to push this initiative. Now that we have the technical facts, all we need to do is present them in a convincing way to illustrate the role this structure is playing in the desertification of Bangladesh—something I'm sure we can easily accomplish. Now gentlemen, if you will excuse us, I have other matters to attend to."

Both Tarek and Admiral Nurullah were surprised at the abrupt termination of the meeting, having anticipated a much longer discussion. As the men rose to leave, Salim turned to the Admiral, "Please keep me informed of any developments concerning the debate on Farakka at the U.N. We will want to do all we can to publicize this issue leading up to and during the debate."

Uncharacteristically, Salim, who normally displayed the most gentlemanly of manners, did not walk with his office visitors to the door. "Perhaps, Colonel Khaja, you will remain for a moment," he said, and went directly to his desk. He did not even say goodbye as Tarek and the admiral departed.

Once the office door closed behind them, Salim turned his attention to the colonel, who had seated himself near Salim's desk.

"Well, Khaja, what do you think?" Salim asked eagerly.

"If we were assessing this dam for a contingency war plan, it would be classified as a target for our medium bombers, due to its size and structure, and the amount of ordnance required to destroy it. Of course, a well-placed long-range missile could also cause major damage. Unfortunately, the ability to reliably strike such a narrow linear target by missile is beyond our technical capability at this point."

Salim picked up the satellite photo of the dam and stared at it for a full 10 seconds. Placing the photo on the table, he leaned back in his chair.

"None of those weapons systems are available to us anyway, Khaja. Even if they were, Pakistan's signature would be written all over them. No, what we need is a non-attributable option. Something like a commando team."

Khaja considered Salim's words, then shook his head. "Ambassador, twenty teams of commandos could not carry enough explosives to put a dent in this dam," he said with a laugh. "No. A commando team is not appropriate for this target." He paused for a moment, and added thoughtfully, "But this assumes the ManPAD is not an option."

Salim looked quizzically at the Colonel. "Man pad? What do you mean?"

Khaja's face took on a serious expression. "Mister Ambassador, ManPAD is the acronym for Man Portable Atomic Demolition—a baby nuke, as it were."

"And a ManPAD would have enough force to destroy the dam?" Salim asked.

"With the right placement, absolutely."

"But we would still have the problem of attribution." Salim said. "If a nuclear bomb went off at Farakka Barrage, the Indians would know it wasn't the Bangladeshis who did it."

"That is not necessarily true. The Indians may not realize the explosion was nuclear in nature," Khaja replied.

"How can that be, Khaja?"

"Because the ManPAD is a very low-yield nuclear device. The entire assembly can be carried in two large rucksacks, or in the boot of a car, or in a small shipping crate. The yield is low enough that it does not emit a classic nuclear signature—no mushroom cloud, and only very low-radiation emissions. In fact, without the right equipment, it is difficult to tell that a nuke has exploded," Colonel Khaja smiled. "It is a very neat little bomb."

Salim fell silent for a few moments, pondering Khaja's words. "Do we have a stock of these devices?"

"Yes, but only a small stock. Of course, only one would be needed."

"Who controls them?" Salim asked.

"The Special Munitions Department at the Ministry of Defense."

"Where does this department fit within the MOD?"

"It falls directly under General Huq, Ambassador."

23

It was General Ali's first day back in the office since the attempt on his life. His shoulder had recovered to the point he no longer needed a sling for his arm, and the small cuts on his face had completely healed. Tarek had stopped by to welcome him back to the job, and the two men were comfortably seated. Ali took advantage of Tarek's visit to bring him up to date on what was potentially the most important new case the ISI had underway.

"Highland View/30 is the only LT source we have, so there is no immediate way to corroborate this report," General Ali said as he handed the red folder across his desk to Tarek. Tarek opened the slim folder and took the time needed to read the report thoroughly. Once finished, he closed the folder and looked up at the general.

"Well, HV/30 may be the only source we have, but thank Allah we do have at least one window into the LT. HV/30's report is interesting. On the one hand, it is positive news in that it shows no orders have been issued to begin operations; however, HV/30's interpretation of what this may portend cannot be ignored."

"I tend to agree with his instinct," Ali said. "The LT is not standing down on operations merely because of the Kashmir talks. The last time they suspended operations this long was just before they launched major attacks. And just as in that case, according to HV/30, the LT elements have been ordered into the tribal areas to await further orders. Unfortunately, trying to verify that they are there is just about impossible without mobilizing significant numbers of our forces, which I'm certain General Huq would not authorize. HV/30's next report, hopefully, will shed more light on what is happening."

"When is the next contact?" Tarek asked.

"He should signal within the next week to 10 days. Until then, we can only wait."

Tarek reached over and picked up the HV/30 file again, flipping it open and skimming a few pages. "I can't help wondering what his motivation is for reporting on the LT. Do we really know why he volunteered to us?"

General Ali nodded. "That's a good question, Major. Although it is not mentioned in the report, Captain Awal says he is motivated by his desire for peace and his belief that Pakistan can obtain peace through negotiation faster than the LT can achieve it through fighting. He also claims to be disillusioned with the LT for its extremist views, and 'lapses in moral leadership.' Unfortunately, for the present time we are left to guess what this means, as the captain did not get an opportunity to delve into this at his last meeting."

"He is saying the right things; at least the things we like to hear," Tarek said. "But I'm not sure I'm convinced. By all accounts, HV/30 is a battle-hardened fighter who, due to his age and family obligations, is now playing a support role for the LT. He doesn't sound like someone who would have a change of heart and suddenly become a pacifist."

"Indeed, Major. But men do sometimes change. An unexpected event can have a profound effect on how a man sees the world. Perhaps HV/30 has just seen too much war and its effects. However, you make a good point and we need to get a better understanding of why HV/30 appeared on our doorstep."

Tarek agreed, "Determining a source's true motivation is difficult, sometimes impossible. To quote one of my more professorial ISI instructors, 'Such are the complexities of the human psyche.' I am sure our young captain will do all he can to answer this question as he gets to know HV/30 better."

Both men fell silent, the sounds of the ceiling fans now becoming apparent.

"I do believe we are coming to some kind of crossroads on Kashmir, and things could go either way," Ali said. "The political environment today is extremely fluid. What the LT chooses to do is perhaps the greatest factor in whether or not the Kashmir talks will result in a real settlement. Should the LT initiate attacks, I think the Indians will do more than just withdraw from the talks."

Ali stood up and walked over to a small bookshelf. He picked up a book and set it down, then picked up another. Tarek could tell the General was really not interested in books. Ali turned back toward Tarek.

"Well, Major, I have told you all about the Highland View/30 case, but we have not discussed your meeting with Ambassador Salim."

"I really did little speaking," Tarek began. "Admiral Nurullah and Colonel Khaja did the talking."

Tarek described his meeting with Ambassador Salim, and in particular, Salim's intention to aid the Bangladeshi government in making its case against India at the United Nations.

General Ali simply shrugged. "Well, propaganda is his job. If he sees the Farakka Barrage as offering an opportunity to make India look bad, so be it. I just hate the fact that he had to take up the time of one of my officers to do it."

"How about the Intelligence Bureau officers who were assigned to the IRE? Do you know what have they been up to?" Tarek asked.

"I wish I knew," General Ali replied. "Unfortunately, the director general of the IB is not willing or perhaps is unable to say what his officers have been doing for the IRE. I do know that at least one IB officer traveled to Calcutta. I don't know what his mission entailed, but I suspect it was similar to your mission, a basic collection operation to provide additional ammunition that can then be used against India in some way. I'm sure Salim won't share any information about that."

"Do you have much contact with Ambassador Salim?" Tarek asked.

"Thankfully, No. I certainly don't trust the man, and I try to avoid him. And I don't think the prime minister trusts him either, although he doesn't seem to have a real understanding of Salim's politics. But he better figure it out soon. When you team Salim with General Huq and some of their fundamentalist associates, well, you have a dangerous mix"

Once again the two men fell silent. Ali's comment brought Tarek's mind to his brother-in-law's tirades against those in the government who still supported keeping good relations with the West. If Jashem's view was the predominant one held by the public, Pakistan was in deep trouble, Tarek thought.

General Ali glanced up at the clock on the wall.

"I apologize Major, but the morning staff meeting is about to start. I'll be in touch as soon we get something more from Highland View."

"Certainly, Sir. I'll wait for your call."

As they walked to the door, General Ali placed his hand on Tarek's shoulder. "These are interesting times, Major. May Allah help us to do our duty."

—24—

Since his return to Islamabad, most of Tarek's time had been spent preparing after-action reports on his mission to India. He hadn't had time to visit with Meena and her family or to do much else of a personal nature.

Sahar was ever present in Tarek's thoughts. His mind seemed split, half doing his work, half thinking about Sahar. Both halves operated in parallel but at times they inevitably merged. When they did, thoughts of Sahar assumed primacy. Never before had anything or anyone assumed more importance than his work. It was the first time in his life that Tarek had known obsession.

He made no mention of Sahar in his official report, however, rationalizing this omission by telling himself that his contact with her was irrelevant to his mission. Although it seemed a good argument to Tarek, he was not so foolish as to think it would persuade any investigating ISI security officer.

Since leaving New Delhi, he had only spoken to one person about Sahar, and that was Habibi. Tarek had met with Habibi when he traveled back through the UAE on his return from New Delhi. The meeting was at the apartment building where they had met previously, although as a security measure, they used a different apartment. There was little operational business to discuss, but Tarek wanted to talk to Habibi more for personal than professional reasons.

Habibi was his usual self, laughing and making jokes. Tarek was soon fully infected with Habibi's happy and relaxed mood. Habibi brought with him the customary amenities of lamb kabob and rice. Tarek's contributions were figs, dates, and a small selection of fruits he had purchased during the check route he conducted prior to the meeting.

It was after the meal, as the two men sat comfortably in the living room sipping tea and listening to Arabian music, that Tarek told Habibi about Sahar.

Habibi said little but simply nodded as Tarek described the day he had spent with her and the effect she had on him. Tarek had never actually mentioned that his trip had been to India, but the fact that he identified Sahar as Indian suggested this possibility to Habibi. As Tarek concluded what had become a monologue, he looked up at Habibi, and with a slight smile on his face asked, "My friend, am I a fool or what?"

Habibi returned the smile. "Perhaps you are, and your feelings for her are purely hormone-based. She sounds absolutely lovely, so it would be expected you would be strongly attracted to such a woman. But I suspect you've had your fair share of experiences with attractive women; in fact, I suspect more than your fair share, you rascal," Habibi chuckled. "But Tarek, think about it. You have hardly ever mentioned any woman to me, much less spoken at such length about one. This indicates to me this woman is truly special." Habibi made eye contact with Tarek and added, "Yes, perhaps you are a fool—or perhaps you have found the love of your life."

Habibi was the only Muslim male Tarek knew who would ever make such a statement. Culturally it was difficult, almost impossible, for a Muslim to speak openly about a man's relationship with a woman. Even in Western countries, Tarek had noted that, when speaking of relationships with women, men were superficial in their comments, and certainly never spoke of love.

Tarek shook his head. "I suppose I just never expected this. I've spent most of my life alone. My God, Habibi, I'm at a stage in life where this is not supposed to happen. After all, I'm not a 25-year-old, not even close."

Habibi studied Tarek. "What is the problem?" he asked finally. "You've fallen for a beautiful, educated woman, and it sounds as if she may have similar feelings for you."

Tarek laughed. "Think about it, Habibi. Sahar, the possible 'love of my life' as you so quaintly put it, doesn't even know who or what I am. Not to mention she is an Indian, a Hindu at that, and I a Pakistani Muslim."

Habibi raised his bushy eyebrows, "Hmm… I see what you mean," he said. "The good news is that I doubt what Sahar sees in you has anything to do with your religion, nationality, or your occupation. I suspect she sees you as a man whom she finds intelligent, attractive, and desirable. Everything else is secondary."

Tarek had to laugh. "Habibi, I can always count on you to be the optimist. I hope you are right, but it still does not change the facts. Sahar doesn't know who I am and, if I am to have any future with her, she must know the truth at some point."

Hearing Tarek speak of a future with Sahar confirmed what he had suspected: Tarek was in love.

"Tarek, my advice to you is to go home and get back to your routine, think this thing through, and let your emotions settle. Every difficult situation has a solution. You just have to find it. Remember, Allah is compassionate and he wants happiness for all his children. If it is his will, he will open the way for you."

Tarek had taken Habibi's advice to heart and returned to Islamabad, hoping to let his feelings settle. He actually hoped that he would awake one morning not thinking of Sahar. He might as well have hoped the sun would not rise.

—25—

The Farakka Barrage mission was completed and behind him, but Tarek still carried the emotional residue from the time he had spent with Sahar. An intense desire to see her again drove him to send an e-mail inviting Sahar to come to Dubai as his guest. Habibi had already promised the use of an apartment, which he could present as his own residence.

As it turned out, the ruse with the apartment was unnecessary. Sahar responded to Tarek's e-mail with a counter-invitation asking Tarek to join her in London, where she would be attending a business conference.

Tarek was ecstatic with her proposal. It made things for him much simpler, but even more thrilling was that it made clear to him that Sahar was interested in seeing him again.

Still, Tarek knew that sooner or later he would have to deal with the problem of the deception through which he had met her. He didn't want to lie any longer, but he had yet to devise a plan for telling her the truth. He feared doing so now would risk losing her forever. And who would blame her if she turned her back on him?

As he saw it, his only hope was to spend more time with Sahar, time for their relationship to deepen and so reach the point where she would fully trust him and want to be with him no matter what secrets he revealed to her. The planned rendezvous in London provided that possibility.

Before that could happen, however, it was necessary for him to secure approval to take leave that included travel to the U.K. To that end, he was scheduled to see Admiral Nurullah in just a few minutes, and he was still deliberating what reason he could give for wanting to take the trip.

As he walked from his car to the office building for his meeting, he carefully avoided stepping in the puddles of rainwater that had gathered from the previous evening's downpour. It had been the first rain Islamabad had seen for some time, and it had cleansed the air, leaving the morning sky exceptionally clear.

The fresh, cool air sparked his imagination. He pretended, if only for a moment, that he was breathing the mountain air of Nepal, and Sahar was by his side, trekking through the lower elevations of the Himalayas, the snowcapped peaks of the Annapurna towering above them. What a wonderful image, Tarek though. Perhaps one day he would make his dream a reality.

Thoughts of Sahar and the Annapurna faded as Tarek arrived at the admiral's office. Greeting Tarek with a smile and a warm handshake, the admiral called to his office assistant, "Tea and biscuits, please." Returning to Tarek, he said, "Please Major Durrani, come in, come in."

As the two men sat down on adjacent chairs, the Admiral inquired, "And how was your weekend, Major? Pleasant, I hope?"

"Indeed it was, Sir. I spent both Saturday and Sunday with my sister and her family, which was a pleasure for me. It was the first time I had been able to visit them since my return from India."

Speaking in such favorable terms about his visit with Meena, Tarek ignored the fact that Jashem had used every opportunity he could to talk about Islam and the necessity that the government of Pakistan become purely Islamic in character and action. In Tarek's view, Jashem's behavior showed all the characteristics of a new convert—insistent, domineering, and uncompromising in his position. The kind of person Tarek thought of as truly dangerous. He had to wonder just how many others like Jashem there were in the Pakistani government.

Nurullah nodded, "Time with family is time well-spent. It seems these days none of us get to spend as much time with our families and friends as we would like," he said, going on to describe the weekend he had just spent with his wife, their children, and grandchildren. Listening to the Admiral, Tarek realized he was seeing a side of the man he had not seen before, and he liked him better for it.

After tea was served, Admiral Nurullah told Tarek how pleased he was with the results of Tarek's mission to India, saying, "We could not have done it without you, and for that Ambassador Salim and I are most grateful."

He offered a second sugar biscuit, which Tarek declined.

"Of course we do not expect this to result in the closure of the dam," the Admiral went on in a more serious tone, "and frankly we do not care about that. What this campaign will do is portray India for what it is—an arrogant country that has no respect for its neighbors or international law. Through this portrayal, we will link India's hegemonic practices to its unlawful occupation of Kashmir."

So this is what propaganda is, Tarek thought as Admiral Nurullah laid out the campaign strategy: Nothing more than an adult version of a rumor campaign carried out between playground rivals. Tarek was glad his part in it was finished.

Admiral Nurullah continued, "Major, your efforts on the IRE's behalf are particularly noteworthy as the IRE is not your professional home. I know it was a sacrifice for you to be recalled from your posting abroad, although frankly, that decision was not ours but the ISI's. Let me assure you, however, that we are glad you were the officer selected. You have been remarkably efficient in accomplishing your assignment."

"This is what I do for a living, Sir."

The Admiral smiled. "And we are so fortunate to have men such as yourself that we can call on from time to time. Ambassador Salim and I understand, however, that the ISI has its own important work to do and, with the completion of your mission, it would be wrong for us to delay your return to your organization. So Major, I suspect you will be pleased to learn that as of today, your deputation to the IRE is formally ended. Late last evening, Ambassador Salim signed the order releasing you from the IRE back to ISI."

It was all Tarek could do to keep from smiling. He had hoped that he would be released from IRE service, but he had not suspected it would occur so quickly. Best of all, there was now no reason to discuss his leave plans with the admiral, although he would still need to raise that issue with General Ali.

Tarek thanked the admiral for the news and, their business concluded, both men rose from their seats and shook hands. The admiral said, "Ambassador Salim was most impressed with you, Major. He has written a memo to this effect and is sending it to your superiors."

"Please thank the ambassador for his kind gesture," Tarek responded.

As Tarek made his exit, Admiral Nurullah laid his hand on his shoulder and said, "Please stop by and see us from time to time, Major. You are always welcome here."

"Thank you, Sir. I will do so," Tarek answered out of courtesy. Both men knew he would not be back.

Tarek picked up the few things he had in his office and left the IRE building, for the last time, he hoped. Small thermals of steam rose off the black pavement as he crossed the parking lot. The rising temperatures of the morning made it hard for Tarek to again imagine himself and Sahar walking through the cool mountain air of Nepal, so he dismissed Nepal from his mind and thought only of Sahar.

—26—

General Ali did not know if he should be happy or disappointed by Ambassador Salim's decision to release Tarek from further duties. Tarek was Ali's only reliable source of information on the IRE. Not knowing what was happening inside that organization made him feel very uneasy.

On the other hand, Tarek's return to the ISI was something of a Godsend. Two days before, the ISI captain who had recruited HV/30 had been seriously injured in a car accident. He was out of action for the foreseeable future.

Ali was not about to have the Highland View/30 case picked up by just anyone; it was simply too important. With his return to the ISI, Tarek was the ideal choice to run the case. As he expected, Tarek readily accepted the assignment, but to Ali's surprise, he requested permission to first take a week's leave so he could travel to London. Tarek had said he wanted to visit an elderly uncle, his father's last living brother.

As the next scheduled meeting with HV/30 was three weeks away, General Ali approved Tarek's request. And why not, he thought. The man had not taken a day of leave in over two years and who knew how much time was left for him to see his uncle?

In fact, Tarek did have an uncle in London, whom he had for some time wanted to visit, but his assignment to the IRE and his trip to India had prevented him from doing so. The delay now worked to his favor, providing him a perfect cover story, with no need to mention Sahar.

With his leave permission secured, Tarek quickly made his travel arrangements. Two days later he was on a British Air flight bound for London.

— 27 —

The man who climbed down from the top of the dust-covered bus was indistinguishable from the dozens of others around him. Dressed in simple garb with sandals on his feet and a brown skullcap on his head, he easily could have been one of the local villagers returning home from a week spent working in one of the larger towns in the region. No one would have suspected him to be Sheik Osman, the most able combat commander of the LT.

Glancing around as the bus pulled away, he quickly spotted what he was looking for. Just down the narrow street, a faded red rooster carved from wood stood out from the corrugated tin roofs of the small shops and tea houses. Sheik Osman had been riding on top of the bus for more than six hours. He was exhausted. The thought of a hot cup of tea and a good night's rest brought a smile to his lips. Hefting a leather satchel over his shoulder, he walked down the street and entered the Red Rooster tea house. He dropped his satchel on the floor as he sat down at a corner table, his back to the wall.

"Sir, what may I bring you?" asked the young waiter.

"Chai," he responded. "And fresh naan as well."

When the waiter returned with his order, Sheik Osman lifted the cup to his lips and slowly sipped the steaming tea, savoring its flavor and invigorating warmth. Only after the cup was empty did he reach into the breadbasket, take out a piece of naan and down it voraciously.

Sheik Osman's bus had broken down twice on the trip from the North-West Frontier Province. Now he was behind schedule and worried that his contact might have given up on him. When the waiter came to pour him a second cup of tea, Osman said, "I am seeking the Little Grey One. Has he been to the shop today?"

The waiter nodded. "Yes, Sir. Mr. Mahmoud was here earlier. He left but said he would return before dark."

Relieved, Sheik Osman began to slowly sip his second cup of tea, settling himself more comfortably into the cushioned seat of the cane chair.

The effects of his tiring journey took over and Osman began to nod off to sleep. Only seconds after his eyes closed the battered door of the shop silently opened, and a short man with white hair and white beard stepped inside. He spotted Sheik Osman sitting in the corner, and walked over to him.

"Brother!" he exclaimed.

Startled, Osman sprang from his seat and grabbed the little man, throwing him to the concrete floor, his head striking it with a dull thud.

"Brother it is me—Mahmoud," the man cried out.

Realizing his mistake, Sheik Osman helped Mahmoud to his feet. A large blue welt had already formed above his left eye.

Staring coldly into Mahmoud's eyes, Osman said in an icy voice, "Never surprise me again, you jackass."

Mahmoud quickly apologized. "I am sorry. I thought you saw me come in. I did not mean to surprise you."

His better humor returning, Osman smiled. "I am like a horse; I can sleep even when I am standing," he said. "And as you have learned, I can kick as well. Now, let us go. I have been here too long."

"At once, Brother. My car is outside."

Mahmoud reached down to pick up Sheik Osman's satchel, but Osman pushed his arm away. "I've got it," he said slinging it over his shoulder. "Now let's go."

He followed Mahmoud out of the teahouse and down the street a short distance.

"That's it," Mahmoud said pointing to a white Toyota. "You can put your bag in the back if you like."

"It's fine here," Osman said as he settled into the front seat and placed the satchel on the floorboard squarely between his legs.

"How far to your place?"

"It's close, not more than an hour from here."

Sheik Osman looked out through the cracked windshield and saw the afternoon light quickly turning to twilight as the sun sank behind the mountain that overlooked the village.

"Good," Sheik Osman said. "It will be dark when we arrive. That is always better. Less chance of a nosy neighbor getting a look at the arrival of guests next door."

Mahmoud nudged the Toyota into the steady stream of motor scooters, bicycles, and automobiles moving down the narrow street. "This is true, brother, but this house has the added benefit of being secluded away from any other house. So you do not have to concern yourself that we will have unwanted visitors. It is much better than the place I had when you last stayed with us."

"I'm glad to hear this," Sheik Osman said. "I wasn't comfortable there. Too many people always walking by. Not good for security, Mahmoud."

"Yes, yes, brother, I know. That is why I moved."

"And how is your family? Are they with you at your new place?"

Mahmoud unconsciously flinched at the question.

"All are with me but Soriya, my oldest," he responded.

"Where has she gone?" Sheik Osman asked, turning his head toward Mahmoud.

Mahmoud tensed, looked out the corner of his eye at Osman, and said as evenly as possible, "She is working for a family in another village." Then he quickly asked, "And your family, I pray they are well?"

"Yes, the news from them is good, praise Allah. I hope to arrange to see them in a few weeks. But only Allah knows if this will come to pass. They are still being watched by security, so I have to be very careful in meeting with them."

"Yes, of course," Mahmoud responded.

At last they were clear of the village, the car picking up speed as it moved down the gravel road and through the darkening river valley. Sheik Osman's eyes grew heavy as the motor droned steadily on.

"Wake me when we arrive," Osman commanded. He shut his eyes and settled down into the seat.

"Of course my brother. Rest easy. We will be there soon."

Tarek stood near the doorway where the international passengers exited the customs area at Heathrow's terminal four, his dark eyes searching for any sign of Sahar. As he waited, his mind began to fill with doubts. *Maybe she is not what I remember at all*, he thought despondently. *Maybe I have lost my mind and should never have agreed to see her.*

The area filled with more and more people exiting customs as waiting relatives and friends searched for familiar faces. Tarek found himself pushed about by the milling crowd.

He knew what he was doing was wrong. At least he knew that ISI would see it that way. But he knew as well that if he reported his contact with Sahar, he would be ordered to terminate the relationship, and that was something he simply could not do.

There was a time in his career when he would never have even considered flouting ISI's regulations. That was no longer true, and he felt no remorse for ignoring the rules. He did feel badly about having misled General Ali, a man he respected, and about misleading Meena as well. As he saw it, he really had no choice. He would be with Sahar again, no matter the consequence.

Finally, he saw Sahar walk out from the customs area into the main terminal. In an instant, all doubts about what he was doing vanished and in the same instant, he knew he was somehow changed forever. The intensity of his feelings actually made him afraid. The truth hit him that, despite the improbability of a life with Sahar ever becoming a reality, it somehow had to be. Sahar *had* to become a part of his future.

"Tarek, Tarek," Sahar shouted as she waved and moved toward him through the crowd. When they met she gave Tarek a hug and it thrilled him.

"Oh Tarek, it is so good to see you. I was afraid that maybe you would decide not to come," she said.

Tarek smiled. "How could I not come?" he said and silently added, *I have thought of nothing but you since I left New Delhi.*

Tarek pushed the luggage cart as he listened to Sahar excitedly tell him about her trip from Delhi and the funny things that had happened along the way. Her laughter and the sweet sound of her voice were music to his ears.

Traffic from the airport to the hotel was light, and the taxi arrived at her hotel in less than half an hour. During the ride, Sahar told Tarek about the International Architect's Conference she had come to attend. "I will be making one presentation myself," she said, somewhat hesitantly. "If you would like to come..."

Tarek wanted to spend every minute of his time in Sahar's company, but he only replied, "We shall see. I do need to spend some time with my uncle."

"I understand," she said, but he could see she was disappointed.

Arriving at the hotel, Sahar checked in at the desk, and then walked across the lobby to where Tarek had taken a seat. Sitting down beside him, Sahar smiled. For a few moments, neither of them spoke.

It was Tarek who broke the awkward silence. "Sahar, I am so glad we are here together," he said. "The day we spent in New Delhi passed so quickly, and although we were essentially strangers to each other, I felt so comfortable and it was . . . well, it was just a special day for me. I didn't know if it would be possible, but I wanted somehow to see you again, and I was so happy when you suggested we meet here. I know you are in London on business, and I do not want to interfere with that, but I hope we can spend time getting to know each other better."

Listening to Tarek, Sahar realized how much courage it had taken for him to say this to her. She became aware of an openness in Tarek that she had not often seen in men. Still, there was this mystery about him, something she could not quite put her finger on. He appeared to be genuine, with no pretension despite his obvious charms, yet there was a quality of seriousness and distance that seemed to lie behind it all. Tarek, Sahar decided, was a complex man.

She put her hand lightly on Tarek's. "Thank you for putting into words the very same thoughts I have had. We will have time together, Tarek. I promise you that." After a moment's pause she continued, "Oh, I wanted to tell you, my father sends his regards, and he also invites you to return to India."

"I do hope I have the opportunity to see him again. Sahar, your father is a very special man whom I greatly enjoyed getting to know." Tarek did not add that the possibility of his ever returning to Delhi was remote, since the operation that had taken him there was now concluded.

"He thinks very highly of you Tarek, and he is a tough judge of character. He said he would be honored if you could come to a special event that is being held to commemorate the 35th anniversary of the opening of Farakka Barrage. It will be held late next month. Father thought you might like to see the project first hand."

Not wanting to make a commitment, Tarek replied, "Well, I would love to come, but it may be difficult for me. I have a busy schedule around that time."

"Oh, I hope you can make it Tarek. It would mean a lot to Father and, as an engineer, I think you would be impressed with Farakka Barrage. It is going to be a big event, with some senior government officials in attendance, as well as foreign dignitaries. The whole thing has already created some international controversy."

"Really?" Tarek responded. "What is at issue?"

"Bangladesh has resumed its claim that the dam is causing parts of the country to dry up and is demanding that its gates be permanently opened. They are highlighting the ceremony in the international press, saying it proves India's arrogance, since it is taking place at nearly the same time that the issue will be debated at the U.N.," Sahar said. "But whatever the case, please try to come. You can stay with us, and then we can all go to Farakka together. It is in a remote area some distance north from Calcutta."

"We shall see." Tarek said. He stood up and clasped Sahar's hand. "I know you must be exhausted from your trip. You need some rest so you don't fall asleep on the opening morning of your conference!"

They walked to the elevators together. When the doors opened, Sahar squeezed Tarek's hand and stepped into the elevator.

"I'll call you tomorrow once I know my schedule," she said.

Tarek said goodnight, stepped back from the elevator and watched the bank of lights until Sahar's safe arrival on the 10th floor.

He decided to walk to his hotel instead of catching a taxi. He needed time to think, and he did his best thinking when he was out in the open air and moving. As he strode down the quiet street, it became more apparent than ever to him that his relationship with Sahar would take him into uncharted territory. How it all would end was completely beyond his knowing.

—29—

The time spent in London with Sahar passed as if in a dream— a very good dream. On the first day of her conference, Sahar had attended every session while Tarek spent time with his Uncle Omar. Later, they met for dinner. Tarek selected a French restaurant where he had once dined during a liaison visit to London when he was hosted by MI6. His British intelligence counterparts had chosen the restaurant in part due to its well-regarded cuisine and in part due to its intimate atmosphere, which had allowed for maximum privacy.

In making the dinner reservation, Tarek was reminded once again how the requirements of intelligence work and romance often mirrored each other. The conditions the Brits had sought in choosing a restaurant for a meeting on sensitive matters were the same conditions Tarek wanted for his first evening with Sahar: No interruptions, no distractions, no one to eavesdrop on their conversation. Only he and Sahar—enjoying good food, the warm atmosphere, and each other's company.

The evening proved to be as lovely as he had hoped, lovelier than any evening Tarek could remember. Each time he looked at Sahar, no matter how often, he was taken anew by her striking beauty. When they looked at each other, he had to limit his eye contact lest his intense feelings for her became all too obvious.

This was a new experience for Tarek. As an intelligence officer, he had always sought to be the one who controlled any relationship he had—with man or woman. Tarek knew this would be impossible with Sahar. She had taken control the first moment they met, and he would never be able to reverse the tables. He felt completely vulnerable to her, and as disconcerting to him as that was, it did not matter. If that was the price he had to pay to be with her, he would gladly pay it and more, if necessary.

The five-course dinner was perfectly prepared and served, complete with excellent French wines. Sahar knew Tarek was Muslim, but the fact that he drank wine somehow did not surprise her. Still, she was curious how he rationalized this breech in Islamic conduct.

"Tarek, you obviously know your wines. This is delicious," Sahar said as she lifted a glass to her lips. After taking a sip and setting the glass down on the white linen tablecloth, she asked, "How is it that a Muslim is so knowledgeable about wine? Not that I'm complaining, mind you."

Tarek chuckled and said, "I've enjoyed wine for years. I don't drink in the presence of other Muslims, as it may offend them. However, when this is not an issue, I sometimes will have wine with dinner. Is this a violation of Islamic teaching? Yes, it is. Do I regret that I do not follow this edict against alcohol? If I am honest with myself, I must answer, no, I don't."

"And why is that?" Sahar asked as she again took a sip of the dark Burgundy.

"I suppose it is because I do not believe that Allah concerns himself with such things. I know many religious people, and not just Muslims, disagree with this, but this is what I believe. I think on matters of food and drink, I have to agree with the prophet Jesus when he said it is not what goes into a man's mouth that defiles him, but that which proceeds from it."

"Are you also a student of the teachings of Jesus?" Sahar asked, once again surprised by Tarek's eclectic knowledge.

Tarek reached for the bottle on the table and slowly refilled Sahar's glass. "I have studied the teachings of many of the world's great masters, including Jesus. He is a highly revered prophet in the Islamic faith and is quoted many times in the Qur'an. In fact, he is considered to be the very spirit of God. I have also studied his teachings in the New Testament."

"I see." Sahar said. "And what else have you concluded from your studies?" Sahar was becoming increasingly interested in Tarek's comments on religion, especially given her Hindu upbringing.

Tarek again softly laughed. "I am no spiritual master, so my conclusions may disappoint you. And besides, I think your father can speak much more authoritatively on this subject than I can."

"No, really. What do you believe? I would like to know," Sahar persisted.

"What I have concluded is certainly not original," he said after a moment's reflection. "I simply believe there is an underlying truth or reality to existence, and that truth or reality is what we refer to when we speak of Allah or God. I believe that most of us can only understand Allah in a very limited sense, although a few special people sometimes are able to connect in a more direct way, and they are profoundly transformed by it. Your father, I believe, is one of those special people."

"Are you against orthodox religion? Sahar asked.

Tarek lifted his glass and looked for a moment at the rich red liquid before taking a drink and setting the glass carefully back down on the table. He thought it a bit ironic that they were talking about religion, a subject he hadn't expected to come up, at least not over a romantic dinner.

"No. I am not against religion. I just believe that true experience of Allah cannot come through organized religion because the nature of Allah is so vastly different from the nature of what we call religion. Religion teaches important values that can help us along our journey to Allah. But ultimately, as your father once told me, a person can truly only know Allah by direct encounter."

"And you, Tarek, have you found God?"

Tarek remembered he had asked the same question of Engineer Advani. He shook his head, saying, "No, I have not found Allah, but I think I've found the place to look for him."

"Where?" Sahar asked intently.

Tarek leaned across the small table and placed his hand lightly over Sahar's heart. "Right here. As Rumi wrote, He can be found nowhere else."

Sahar could not help but smile. "Tarek, I think you may just be a 'spiritual master'."

He shrugged. "Well, you wanted to know what I believed, so now you know. Now, it is your turn. What do you believe, Sahar? "

Sahar laughed. "It is too late in the evening to begin that discussion. You will have to accept a rain check. As much as I hate to end this lovely evening, I do have my presentation to give first thing in the morning."

Tarek smiled. "I will accept your rain check, but only on condition that we resume this conversation soon."

Sahar returned his smile. "Oh I agree to that. You have not only my rain check, but my word."

Tarek paid the bill in cash. As they exited the restaurant, he took Sahar's delicate hand in his and walked to a nearby taxi, which quickly whisked them back to Sahar's hotel. The street was empty as they stood outside the hotel's entrance. Sahar regretted the night had to end.

"Tarek, would it be possible for us to meet tomorrow afternoon?" she surprised herself by asking.

"Of course it would," Tarek responded, surprised as well. "But won't the conference be in session?" he asked.

Sahar moved closer to Tarek and softly responded, "Yes, but I would rather spend the time with you."

As Sahar spoke, her eyes met Tarek's, and he could no longer resist the attraction he felt for her. Pulling her toward him he kissed her briefly on the lips and then, as she embraced him eagerly, he kissed her again, this time more deeply, his passion quickly rising.

At last Tarek pulled back and holding both of Sahar's hands in his, softly said, "I must let you go. You have a big day tomorrow, and I want you to do well."

Sahar nodded and stepped back without taking her eyes off Tarek's face. Then, abruptly, she turned and walked toward the hotel entrance. Just before she stepped inside, she called back over her shoulder, "Until tomorrow."

—30—

The next morning, Sahar gave her presentation on her work on the National Art Gallery renovation in New Delhi. To her surprise, Tarek attended her briefing. Seeing her in her professional milieu, Tarek was again impressed with Sahar's subject knowledge and self confidence. Her talent was as obvious as her beauty.

Sahar's presentation was her last appearance at the conference. For the rest of the week, she spent almost every moment with Tarek. They toured what seemed to be every site of architectural interest in London. Both relished being able to share the experience with someone who also loved architecture. Tarek took time each day to visit with his Uncle Omar, but as much as he loved the old man, each minute away from Sahar was torture. He kept his visits short.

On Wednesday night, following a satisfying meal at an Italian restaurant, Tarek invited Sahar for dessert at his hotel's restaurant, which was famous for its cakes made on the premises. Arriving at the hotel, they found the restaurant filled to capacity with a waiting list of a dozen names. Up to this point, the evening had been perfect, and neither Tarek nor Sahar wanted it to end.

"We can always do room service," Tarek suggested, not quite knowing how Sahar would respond.

Sahar's eyes met Tarek's and then she smiled. "What a wonderful idea!"

The two walked hand in hand to the elevator and took it to the 15th floor. Once inside Tarek's room, Sahar tossed her wrap onto the bed, its covers already turned back, and walked over to the window. Pushing the sheer curtain aside she took in the view of the city for a few seconds, then let the curtain fall and turned to face Tarek.

They stood several feet apart. For a few moments, neither spoke. They did not need to. Their eyes said everything. Tarek crossed the floor in two strides and Sahar was in his arms, warm and willing.

Tarek had once read that some perceived sex as a spiritual experience, an idea Tarek gave no credence. For him, sex was definitely physical, not spiritual—although he could not deny that when he lay with Sahar, her perfect body soft and warm, it was heaven on earth.

—31—

For the remainder of the week they were together every moment, waking and sleeping. But inevitably, their time together came to an end. Bidding Sahar farewell was the most difficult goodbye Tarek had ever said. He felt as if his heart would burst. The tears that welled up in Sahar's amber eyes and rolled down her cheeks told him it was as difficult for her as well, though they both tried with little success to put on a brave front.

As they stood at the airport just outside the security gate, Sahar again reminded Tarek of her father's invitation.

"You know I will come if I can arrange it," Tarek told her. "But if I can't, we will find a way to see each other soon. This I promise."

"Oh Tarek, we must," Sahar said, tears again filling her eyes. "I'm going to miss you so. I don't know how I will survive when I return to Delhi. I know my life will not be same as it was before I came to London. It's crazy, I know. But it is how I feel."

Tarek knew the feeling well. He had felt it to one degree or the other from the first moment he had laid eyes on Sahar.

"Sahar," he said looking intently into her eyes, "I am crazy about you. We will be together soon. Let me just take care of some details at work."

The pre-boarding announcement for Sahar's flight boomed over the loudspeakers.

"All right, my love," Sahar said. "Just stay in touch."

They kissed once more, and Sahar walked to the nearly deserted security checkpoint, passing through it quickly.

Many thoughts went through Tarek's mind as he watched her walk down the concourse and disappear into the crowd of people moving toward the departure gates. As she vanished from his sight, a crushing sadness swept through him.

Are you alright? Meena asked, lightly touching Tarek's shoulder. "Is something wrong?"

Tarek looked up. "No, nothing is wrong. This is just the first chance I've had to sit still since my trip, and I've got a few things running through my mind. I'm sorry if I'm not being a good guest this afternoon."

They were sitting in the sun-lit living room of Meena and Jashem's home in Rawalpindi, the day after Tarek's return from London. Jashem was in the bedroom taking his daily nap, and the children were occupied in other parts of the house.

In an effort to get Tarek to engage in conversation, Meena playfully asked, "Well, tell me Tarek, what are you thinking about? Is it work, or is it a woman?"

Tarek laughed. "Meena, in the first case, I could not tell you on grounds of national security. In the second case, I would not tell you because you would hound me with questions for the rest of the afternoon."

"If you are thinking about work, well frankly, I don't want to hear about it anyway. But if you are thinking about romance, now that is something worth talking about," Meena said "And who but me would you discuss such things with?"

Meena had a point. With the single exception of Habibi, there was no one else, and Habibi was a long way away. Although Tarek would have liked to tell Meena about Sahar, his relationship with her was too complicated to try to explain.

"Well, I hate to disappoint you, but I was not thinking about a woman," Tarek lied. "And I was not thinking about work. I was thinking about the great dinner you promised me. Never forget Meena, food is almost always on a man's mind."

This time Meena laughed. "Tarek, do you forget that I am married to Jashem? Believe me, I know about men and food, although I think Jashem is an extreme example."

Of that there is no doubt, and in more ways than one, Tarek thought to himself. In his last couple of contacts with Jashem, his brother-in-law seemed even more radicalized in his politics and religion. Tarek could not even hold a conversation with Jashem if it touched on politics, international or domestic, as Jashem would become agitated and almost belligerent in tone. The last time they had talked, Jashem had all but called Tarek a Western lackey and anti-Islamic.

Tarek had decided that in the future he would not allow himself to be drawn into any political or religious discussions with Jashem. It was obvious Jashem's mind was closed on both subjects. Tarek found it sad and disappointing that his brother-in-law had become such an ignorant, biased man, and he could not understand how this had occurred. Tarek thought something dangerous was happening to the Muslim psyche. It bothered Tarek that Meena had to live with Jashem, and that their children were subject to his influence.

Despite his misgivings about Jashem, Tarek still managed to enjoy the afternoon leading up to the evening meal. He kicked the football with Hamid and Sarah, then went for a walk with them and Meena through the tree-lined streets, taking in the early evening air. Tarek felt less stressed when they got back, setting the stage for a relaxing dinner. Even Jashem did not seem so bad this particular evening.

The visit to Meena's house proved therapeutic for Tarek. For the first time since his return from London, he was able to think of something besides Sahar. As he drove back to his apartment that night, Tarek's mind had cleared, and he was able to focus. The next day he had to be at his best– he had an agent to meet.

It was late afternoon when Tarek turned his car onto the road to Wah. Intense sunlight penetrated the windshield as he headed westward out of Islamabad toward the silhouetted hills a few kilometers in the distance.

Tarek reached into the car console and retrieved a set of dark sunglasses and put them on. The air conditioner was on its highest setting, but the air in the car was still warm and sweat ran down the middle of Tarek's back as he concentrated on determining if anyone was following him.

The four lane highway leading out of Islamabad was crowded. Canvas-covered transport trucks vied for supremacy with colorful but poorly maintained buses packed with passengers. Sprinkled among these vehicles were private cars as well as a few hired cars, many held together by little more than wire and tape.

The vehicles sped along, their drivers seemingly unaware of the hazards posed by the chaotic mix of rolling metal. The occasional donkey-drawn cart ambled down the road as well, the donkeys appearing more alert to the dangers of the road than their human masters. For Tarek, these driving conditions were unexceptional, no worse than in Khartoum, Cairo, or Jakarta.

The traffic was at its heaviest in Rawalpindi, but lightened noticeably after Tarek passed through the towns of Golra and Taxila. He was certain enough now that there was no surveillance behind him. Relaxing a bit, he took in the familiar scenery where he had spent so much of his youth.

A moment of melancholy came upon him as he drove past the sign indicating the turn to Murree. It was the same sign he would anxiously watch for as a child when his father had driven the family to their summer cottage high in the cool mountains.

The memories of those times were so precious to him that recalling them brought tears to his eyes. Tarek wiped his eyes with the back of his hand and wondered how it was that memories of events so long ago could provoke such powerful emotions. He remembered how, in anticipation of his wedding, he had imagined that he and Farida would have children and he would give them the same happy childhood experiences he had enjoyed, spending idle days in cool mountain forests. *How did that dream slip away?* he thought.

He knew the answer . . . love for Farida had never taken root in his heart. Farida had known that too, and she died because of it. Of that, Tarek was certain. Her disease was only the instrument of her death. His unkindness toward her was it's cause. And that was the beginning of the end, not only to that dream, but to all of Tarek's dreams. His work became his life. And all these many years later, he was still working.

Had he more time, he would have taken that turn off to Murree, to try and find the old cottage, if it even still existed. *But to what end?* he thought. Would that not be just a futile attempt to somehow recapture a lost past, as much behind him as the landscape passing in his rearview mirror?

There was no use in trying to reclaim a pleasant past when it just brought on a present pain. Tarek knew he should look to the future, but thoughts of the future did not necessarily come without pain either, particularly when he thought of Sahar and how uncertain he was they would ever be together. Tarek knew Sahar was now the dream, but he recognized only too well that dreams did not always come true.

The right front wheel of the Land Cruiser dropped into a deep pothole. The sudden jolt brought Tarek back into full mental focus, forcing the thoughts of his past and future into the far recesses of his mind. Glancing at his watch, he estimated he had less than an hour left in his trip and would arrive in Wah just after sunset, his preferred M.O.

—34—

Exactly one hour later, night had fallen and Tarek was in Wah. The light traffic and poorly lit streets created the ideal operational environment for a clandestine meeting with an agent, and Tarek felt completely at home in it. This was what his profession was all about. It was one of the things that had kept him in the business. There was nothing like working in secret, robbing opponents of the information they wanted to keep hidden. And while it was true that the desire to serve his country had led Tarek to an intelligence career, at some point along the way, it was the work itself that had become the sustaining motivation. The clandestine nature of his profession was to Tarek like nicotine to a heavy smoker and he had to have his fix.

As he neared the pick-up point, Tarek adjusted his 9mm H&K to insure its ready access from his ankle holster. Some ISI officers preferred to slip their pistols under a thigh in a car-meeting situation, a technique that had been taught in training, but one Tarek had argued against and thought ludicrous. In the course of his career, he was aware of at least two accidental discharges that had resulted in some very nasty injuries.

The fact of the matter was that, in case of an ambush, the best chance of survival was to use the car to get out of the kill zone, using it as a weapon if necessary, and to do so as quickly as possible.

Many of his colleagues, most of whom had never been involved in a gunfight, disagreed with Tarek's approach to dealing with an ambush, arguing that driving away would be cowardly.

"Better to use the car as cover and shoot it out," they said. According to their argument, at least this would show the attackers that Pakistani intelligence officers had courage and were not afraid to engage with firearms, and this defiance would dissuade future attacks.

Tarek thought these officers were imagining the excitement a gunfight would afford them, as well as the opportunity to show their courage. Tarek knew something of gun battles, and he knew something of courage. He thought the first was overrated and the second misunderstood. In any case, meetings that were supposed to be discreet but turned into shootouts did not go over well at headquarters.

Having firmly established that he had not been followed, Tarek entered the final approach to the pick-up point. He turned left onto a two-way street, then right onto a one-way street. Ahead, he spotted a short man holding a large white plastic bag in his left hand, the signal Tarek was looking for.

Tarek pulled the car up alongside the man, the passenger side window already rolled down. The man stepped forward and leaned over to look into the vehicle. He was obviously surprised to see Tarek and not the young ISI captain he normally met with.

"Could you direct me to Malik Street?" Tarek inquired, invoking the parole that had been given to HV/30 by the ISI captain.

"Yes." HV/30 responded. "It is the next street past Gol. If you would like, I can show you."

The word "Gol", told Tarek he had the right man.

"Get in," Tarek said.

HV/30 opened the passenger door and got in the car. The interior of the car remained dark as he did so, Tarek having removed the bulb from the ceiling light shortly after renting the car. By the time HV/30 shut the door, the car was half-way down the block and gaining speed.

"Where is Mr. Chowdhury?" HV/30 asked, using Captain Awal's operational alias.

"Mr. Chowdhury sends his regards," Tarek said. "But unfortunately, due to a family crisis, he cannot meet you, and he asked that I come instead. My name is Rashid. I am a colleague of Chowdhury's."

"Please tell Mr. Chowdhury I will pray for his family. He is a good young man, and I am sorry to hear this bad news."

"I will tell him. He says you too are a good man. Someone we can trust. Is that true, Mahmoud? Can I trust you?" Tarek inquired, to see how HV/30 reacted to such a direct question.

"My friend, I just got in the car of a complete stranger, and you just picked one up," HV/30 said. "Whether either of us likes it or not, we have already taken a chance on each other. Now you tell me, what other choice do we have but to continue to trust one another if each of us is to get what we want."

Tarek turned right on onto a quiet street. "You know what we want—information on the LT," he said "But what is it you want?"

"I want these bastard jihadis to quit squandering the help that Pakistan has given them," HV/30 said, his voice reflecting irritation at being aggressively questioned by a man he had just met. "We have all heard about the break in relations between the LT and ISI, and I thought your people would like to know that all the support you have given to throw India out of Kashmir is being used to finance a rich lifestyle for many in the LT leadership. Also, you should know that once the Indians withdraw from Kashmir, these jihadis will take control and try to establish an Islamic state independent of Pakistan. The last thing I want is for Kashmir to become another Afghanistan, ruled by corrupt men who want total control."

HV/30 paused for a moment. "I told Mr. Chowdhury this," he added, still irritated. "I am surprised that you do not already know it, Mr. Rashid. Don't you know anything about me?"

"Yes," Tarek replied in a gentler tone. "I know everything that you have told Chowdhury. I just like to hear things for myself. Please forgive my directness, but the nature of this business sometimes requires one to act in a way he would not normally act."

Tarek's conciliatory words had a calming effect on HV/30. He turned so he could see Tarek's face and said, in a less hostile voice, "Yes, I suppose it is a tough business you are in, with no room for sentimentality."

Tarek checked the rearview mirror for perhaps the twentieth time and reassured himself that it was only HV/30 that he had picked up. He pulled over at a quiet spot along the street and stopped, putting the car in neutral and leaving the motor running. He set the emergency brake and took his foot off the brake pedal, eliminating the red glow of the brake lights.

"Any problems getting to Wah? Tarek asked.

"No, none."

"Does your family know you came here?"

HV/30 nodded. "I come here every couple of weeks to pick up supplies I can't get in the village, so my trip here is a routine occurrence."

Tarek already knew this from the file, but he wanted to see if HV/30 told him the same story he had told the Captain.

"Have you seen anyone you know since you arrived in town?"

HV/30 shook his head. "No, no one."

"Good," Tarek said. "Is anyone expecting to see you tonight?"

"No," HV/30 again responded.

"So we can have a couple of hours together? That is not a problem?"

"I assure you Mr. Rashid, I am completely free of obligations this evening."

Satisfied with HV/30's answer, Tarek was ready to move from security questions to the more substantive issues on Abu Shafik's plans and activities. He hoped that in the process he would gain a firmer understanding of HV/30's motivation as well.

Releasing the emergency brake, Tarek put the car in gear and drove away from the curb, turning on his lights only after he had gone down the street half a block. He turned left onto a wide road that led north and out of town. As he made the turn, light from the corner street lamp dimly lit HV/30's face and gave Tarek his first opportunity to get a good look at the man.

"Did you have an accident?" Tarek asked. HV/30 automatically reached up and touched the bump on his head.

"Yes, I fell and smacked my head on the door when I was bringing wood into the house. It hurt like hell," HV/30 said.

"It looks pretty bad. When did it happen?"

"Two or three days ago. It doesn't hurt anymore. Not even a headache."

Tarek had no reason to doubt HV/30's story and did not pursue it any further. He drove out of town for 5 kilometers, slowed down, and pulled off the road into a large graded parking area at the point where the road narrowed to two lanes. There were at least twenty cars, several heavy transport trucks, and a bus parked in the area in no particular pattern. The drivers and passengers were taking a last break, getting drinks and snacks at several small food stalls prior to continuing the grueling and dangerous journey on the twisting two-lane mountain highway that led to the badlands of the Northwest Frontier Province.

Tarek did not intend to proceed any further north. To do so risked running into Pak Army road checks manned by trigger-happy conscripts, or worse, being ambushed by bandits. But the parking area provided good cover for being stopped on the road and afforded Tarek the opportunity to have a more extended conversation with HV/30. He found an isolated spot to park in, then turned off the lights and killed the engine.

"Would you like a Coke?" Tarek asked as he reached into the rear seat and opened a small plastic ice chest.

"Sure. Thanks," HV/30 replied.

Tarek took out two ice-cold bottles of Coke, handing one to HV/30 and opening his own. He took a long drink. HV/30 opened his bottle and followed Tarek's example. For a moment both men sat silently.

Tarek half switched on the ignition key and lowered the windows. The air had cooled dramatically from its daytime temperatures, and it gently wafted through the car. Save for a few muffled indistinguishable voices in the distance, the night was quiet.

Tarek reached into the Land Cruiser's center console and took out a small metal aviator's clipboard with a notebook already attached. Setting the clipboard in his lap, he switched on a battery powered light at the top of the clipboard that faintly illuminated the paper pad.

"Let's begin," Tarek said, breaking their silence. "Have you any information concerning Abu Shafik for us?"

"Yes . . . yes, I do, Mr. Rashid. There was a meeting, an important one. Abu Shafik was there, as were his subordinate commanders."

Tarek took out his pen and began to make notes. "When was the meeting, and where did it take place?"

"It happened a few weeks ago near Chitral. I don't know where exactly."

"So you were not at the meeting?" Tarek asked.

"No, I wasn't there but my friend Yasin, who I told Mr. Chowdhury about, he reported it to me."

"Was Yasin there at the meeting?"

HV/30 shook his head. "No. He found out about it from Sheik Osman. Osman is one of Abu Shafik's commanders. I only learned about it from Yasin yesterday when he stopped by."

Tarek knew who Sheik Osman was, but he gave no indication of it to HV/30. Tarek still wanted to nail down the source of the information, but he decided to move on with the intelligence debriefing and come back to the sourcing later.

"What was discussed at the meeting?"

"Well, Yasin only picked up a few odds and ends. But the main thing he learned was that Abu Shafik is in contact with some Pakistani officials who have promised equipment and weapons for his fighters."

"Who were the Pakistanis? Were they military officers?" Tarek asked, careful not to reveal his excitement at learning this bit of information.

HV/30 shook his head. "Yasin does not know who they were. Sheik Osman did not say."

"What kind of weapons and equipment did the officials say they would give, and when did they plan to do it?"

"Yasin said Sheik Osman mentioned getting new clothing and gear, like backpacks and grenade carriers. The officials said they would also provide 2,000 new AK's and 500 RPG launchers, as well as a lot of ammunition. I don't know when they will give this equipment to Abu Shafik. Yasmin did not find this out."

"Did Sheik Osman tell him why the officials were doing this? They must want something in return."

"Sheik Osman did not say. I would be surprised if he told that type of information to Yasin."

After another 10 minutes of questioning, Tarek concluded HV/30 had nothing further of intelligence interest to report. It was always hard to get details when the source obtained the information from an unwitting sub-source.

Tarek returned to the question of sourcing.

"So why do you think Sheik Osman told your friend Yasin about this? I thought Yasin was just the safehouse keeper for Sheik Osman?"

"Yes, he is, but Sheik Osman is a big mouth who likes to smoke hashish and screw whores. Then he brags to Yasin about how important he is. Yasin hates this man."

Tarek was surprised at HV/30's answer. Sheik Osman was known to employ stringent security practices, and Tarek found it hard to believe that Abu Shafik would have a senior commander that was hooked on hashish. Whether or not he used the services of prostitutes, who knew? ISI had limited information on LT commanders. Perhaps this was some new intelligence.

"Do you think Yasin would be willing to meet directly with me to talk about Sheik Osman?"

For an instant, HV/30's eyes grew wide. "No! That would not be possible."

"Why not?" Tarek probed.

"Because Yasin is sick and cannot travel far."

"What's wrong with him?" Tarek pursued.

"I am not his doctor, Mr. Rashid. I don't know what is wrong with him. Cancer maybe. He does not talk about it. It distresses him."

Tarek thought for a moment. "Well, perhaps we could help him with medicine or something. We could even send a doctor under a pretext to his village, who could then diagnose and treat him. In this way we help him, and then he could help us by supplying more information on Sheik Osman and Abu Shafik."

HV/30 shook his head. "I'm sorry, Mr. Rashid, but I don't think there is any way he would meet with ISI. He hates you guys because he thinks the government has not done enough for the LT, and he knows that ISI has broken relations with the LT."

Having seemingly run into a brick wall on a meeting with Yasin, Tarek closed the discussion, started the car, and drove back to Wah. During the drive back, Tarek went over the arrangements for the next meeting and had HV/30 brief them back to him.

"Remember," Tarek told him, "I will see you in two weeks. But if something comes up before then that is important, you must signal us immediately, using the number I gave you, and we will meet the day after your call at the same place and time."

HV/30 nodded. "I understand."

A few minutes later, Tarek dropped HV/30 off on a deserted street a few blocks from the bus station. Aside from bus fare, HV/30 refused to accept any money for his information.

Tarek pulled back onto the street and started on the drive back to Islamabad. He decided the info he had obtained, even though somewhat dated, was too important for him to delay his return by staying overnight in a local hotel. Pakistani officials promising military supplies to the LT was news General Ali would want immediately.

As the adrenaline rush of the ops meeting began to wear off, Tarek shifted into fifth gear, accelerating the Land Cruiser down the highway into the black night. He rubbed his tired eyes and, if only for a moment, thought he might be getting a little too old for this business.

—35—

Ambassador Salim sat at the head of the oval conference table in his office, his expression serious. Also at the table were his personal assistant, Fakrul Rahim, as well as Brigadier General Kasurie, who was General Huq's Chief of Staff and close confidant, and two other trusted functionaries on the IRE staff.

Looking up from the material he had been reviewing, Salim addressed the waiting men. "Gentleman, it is critical that we coordinate closely with the Ministry of Foreign Affairs on how we proceed on this. Our instructions to our U.N. office must be crystal clear and given in a timely manner. Thanks to our hard work, Farakka Barrage is formally back on the agenda at the special session of the UN, and India is already beginning to feel the political heat." Salim's expression changed to a look of satisfaction. "This is exactly what we have been working toward. Allah has rewarded us for our efforts."

In a voice bordering on exuberant, Rahim said, "According to the Ministry, the Bangladeshis are absolutely ecstatic about this development."

General Kasurie added, "Perhaps for once, the Foreign Ministry has made a useful contribution to something that is actually of importance for Pakistan."

"Indeed." Salim commented. "The Ministry can be an effective organization if properly guided and influenced. And I want it to continue to be seen as having primacy on pushing the Farakka Barrage issue. The IRE cannot be identified as being involved in this. Not publicly and not even within our government. I trust you all will do the needful to keep our hand hidden."

After a few more minutes of discussion on specific actions to take, the meeting broke up, although Ambassador Salim asked General Kasurie to stay for a few more minutes. Once everyone had cleared Salim's office, Salim motioned to the seating area where he and Kasurie sat down.

"I'm sorry that General Huq could not attend the meeting, but given the circumstances I understand his absence," Salim said. "I realize that the forces under General Huq's command have no role at this juncture, but I asked you to come to this meeting because it is critically important that you and General Huq stay in touch with me as the U.N. debate gets underway. For yours and General Huq's information only, the IRE is now well-positioned to affect just how that debate goes. We have close allies in this, and more than one agent of influence awaits our direction. In short, we will be in control from the opening round and can make it play out anyway we want." Salim paused for a moment, then looked squarely at General Kasurie. "I estimate your forces will probably be needed within days of the of the UN resolution on Farakka Barrage."

Nonplused, Kasurie asked, "And when will that be Ambassador?"

"Unfortunately, it is a bit too early to tell," Salim responded. "What I can promise you is that the debate will be over before the rains come. Once the resolution is reached, your forces must be prepared to move very quickly."

"Very well, Sir. We will be ready."

"Perfect," Salim replied. "And how will you explain the movement of your troops? What will Army headquarters think is happening?"

General Kasurie smiled. "As is required by headquarters, we had to put out the corps training and unit rotation schedule for the next six months. General Huq realized this would not do, and we would need some flexibility in terms of timing, so he requested and obtained Army's concurrence to carry out a surprise exercise, to be executed sometime prior to the rotation of combat units along the line of control."

"Excellent. This exercise will give you the cover you need to execute the operation?"

"Precisely. And because it is a surprise exercise, we can determine the timing." General Kasurie frowned slightly. "However, it will probably only buy us a couple of days at most. Hopefully, by then, if all goes according to plan, the world will see all of Kashmir under the control of Pakistani troops. The big question is, will the rest of the army join us?"

A look of anger flashed across Salim's face. "General, why do you ask such a question? Of course it will join you, as will all of Pakistan. This has been a festering sore for us far too long. Once they realize your troops have already seized control, there will be no reason to hesitate."

"Even if Prime Minister Bahir orders the army to stand down? You believe the army leadership will disobey him?" Kasurie asked.

His facial features softening, Ambassador Salim chuckled. "Civilian rule of Pakistan is a fragile thing, General. Look at the facts: Prime Minister Bahir has only been in power for a year, and his ascension was solely the result of General Masood's assassination. Each day, the PM's position becomes weaker in the eyes of the people. Such nonsense, to think we can negotiate with India. History has made it plain that India will not budge on Kashmir. So, we must make her budge."

"Very well, Ambassador. I will relay all this to General Huq."

Salim nodded, "Thank you, General. When do you expect him back?"

"He is scheduled to meet with our friends tomorrow night. He will travel back the following day, depending on road conditions. He did not want to fly, as it would be too easy for his travel to be noted."

"Yes, of course. It is good that the General is taking such precautions. We all must follow his example from here on out," Salim said. "I am looking forward to learning the results of the meeting."

General Kasurie stood up and shook the Ambassador's hand, bidding him good-day.

After the General had left the office, Salim slowly walked to the wide center window, hands clasped behind him, and looked out over the city of Islamabad. From his office window he watched as General Kasurie exited the building directly below him, entered his waiting sedan and drove away.

Seeing the General from this lofty perspective, Salim was reminded of his disdain for military men. Soldiers are nothing more than men who are still boys, he thought cynically. All their sacrifices and suffering, driven by their needs to glorify themselves instead of glorifying Allah. Such fools!

Shifting his view, he could see the minaret of the city's largest mosque outlined against the blue sky. The sight brought a smile to his lips.

All is well, he told himself as he turned from the window and moved toward his desk. *All is well indeed.*

Since her return from London, Sahar's emotions had swung from a feeling of happy contentment to a deep sadness that bordered on full-blown depression. The ache in her heart for Tarek and the uncertainty of the future of their relationship kept her emotionally off-balance and unable to focus.

Advani had noticed a change in Sahar soon after her return. He suspected something had happened between Tarek and his daughter, so he was not particularly surprised when she told him of her relationship with Tarek.

Advani was quite pleased that his daughter had at last found someone she felt strongly about, particularly a man he very much liked himself. Even so, he was disturbed by the obvious emotional pain she was experiencing. He tried to encourage her and give her hope that it would all work out in the end.

One evening after dinner, he and Sahar took a stroll in Lodi Park near their house. Over the years, the expansive park had been of priceless benefit for them, serving as a refuge from the stresses of life in New Delhi.

They were both silent as they slowly walked arm in arm along the hard-packed dirt pathways. Seeing a bench up ahead and sensing that her father needed a rest, she suggested they sit for a while to enjoy the quiet and the last of the fading sunlight.

"So, my dear," he said when they were comfortably seated, "what is the latest from Tarek? Any plans to visit soon?"

Sahar shook her head, "No, not soon if you mean in the next couple of weeks. In his e-mail last night he mentioned that he still hopes to attend the commemoration ceremony, but even that is not certain, given the unpredictability of his work schedule."

"I see," Advani said gently. "Well, the ceremony is still some weeks away. In the meantime, if he can't come, why don't you go pay him a visit? You said you wanted to go to Dubai for some shopping."

"Yes, I know. But he is traveling and even if this were not the case, I could not go right now. The library renovation is getting into the critical phase, and I must be here to make sure it proceeds according to plan."

Advani smiled. When it came to her work, his daughter was just like he had been, totally dedicated to making sure the job was done right. Even her love for Tarek would not make her compromise on that.

"Well, let's be patient," he said. "Tarek will come as soon as is possible for him. I know it is hard for you, Sahar. It was the same for your mother and me. Just after we were engaged, my company sent me to Africa on a major project there. It was agony. Remember, in those days, phone service was nothing like it is today, and e-mail did not even exist. Imagine having no means of reliable communications. Oh, how my heart ached for your mother."

Sahar squeezed her father's hand. He had loved her mother so much that her passing a few years ago had almost taken him with her. Sahar knew that the only reason her father had not followed was because of his devotion to his daughter.

"Just remember, Father, I am not engaged to Tarek. I am only, how should I say. . . involved with him."

"Involved or engaged, it makes no difference. The point is the two of you are in love. This much I know. And because of your love, you will be together again. It may be in two weeks or in two years, but you will be together. Truly, love finds a way to overcome all obstacles."

Advani paused for a few moments, seized by a profound truth, a truth not founded on science but on personal experience. "Even death itself is defeated by love," he murmured softly.

As he looked at Sahar, his eyes shone brightly with his love for her. He realized again how lucky the man would be who could claim her for his own.

Reaching his arm around her shoulders he pulled her a little closer, and the two relaxed in the hushed quiet of the park as the night completed its descent.

—37—

Three weeks had passed since that first meeting between Tarek and Highland View/30. A second meeting was to have occurred two weeks later, but just a few hours before Tarek was to depart for Wah, HV/30 had signaled via a coded phone call that he would not be able to make the meeting. Tarek was in a holding pattern, waiting for another call from HV/30 to signal he was ready to meet.

Tarek was not overly concerned about HV/30's last-minute cancellation. This was the nature of operations with agents in remote areas, particularly agents closely involved with militant or terrorist groups. Unavoidably, things came up that made it hard for an agent to keep to the meeting plan without creating unwanted suspicion. An agent under suspicion in HV/30's circumstances is only one step away from being a dead agent. Knowing this, a good ops officer always told his agents, as Tarek had advised HV/30, to play it safe. Better to get the information a week later, then to never get it at all.

Still, he was anxious to see HV/30. Tarek believed the information HV/30 had provided him at the first meeting was accurate, but he had doubts about the sub-source, Yasin. If it turned out HV/30 was dissembling about the source, it could call into question all the information he had provided.

General Ali had been alarmed at HV/30's information, but given the implication of the report and the fact that the sourcing was still not clear, he was unwilling to share the information with anyone, much less forward it through normal distribution channels. Ali knew the report was dynamite. If true, and the wrong people got their hands on it, it could blow apart the government of Pakistan, factionalized as it was between secular moderates seeking compromise with India and Islamic fundamentalists determined to see a military solution to Kashmir.

Ali's gut feeling was that the report was accurate and he suspected the IRE, and General Huq in particular, were involved. There had been an unusual number of personnel changes of Army officers, officers who would play critical roles in any Pakistani military operation concerning Kashmir. Young officers were being placed in combat command positions all along the Line of Control, and these assignments were taking place out of the normal rotation cycle. Most of these officers were known to have fundamentalist leanings. One unit in particular, a newly established element of the Special Security Group, which often operated in sensitive areas along the LOC, had essentially become the Islamic fundamentalist equivalent of Hitler's Waffen SS. Just as the Waffen SS, this SSG unit functioned outside the normal military chain of command.

Seeing all the changes occurring in the Army, Ali was surprised he had managed to stay in his position as the Chief of Operations for ISI for as long as he had. Ali was anything but a fool, however, and he had concluded that his days in the job were numbered, making it all the more important that he learn what Abu Shafik and the unidentified Pakistani government interlocutors were planning. Once known, he would have to devise a strategy to neutralize the effort. The problem would be in finding reliable allies.

General Ali had become so concerned about the direction and speed of events that he was taking special precautions to protect HV/30. First, he told Tarek to say in his report that after confronting HV/30 with his suspicions, the agent had admitted that everything he had previously reported was a fabrication, through which he hoped to ultimately trick the ISI into paying him a large sum of money.

Ali also had Tarek conclude his report by saying he had terminated HV/30 on the spot with no plans for future contact.

Falsification of reports was an extreme measure, but General Ali believed—and Tarek agreed—it was necessary to protect HV/30. From the initiation of the case, only a handful of officers had known about HV/30. Now the number of people who knew that HV/30 was still reporting information on the LT was reduced from that initial handful to two, Tarek and Ali.

Ali's second precaution was that he and Tarek no longer discussed anything related to Highland View/30 in his office and certainly not on the office phone—not even using the secure line. Instead, they met at General Ali's home and then only spoke about the case while outside in the garden.

Sitting in his garden listening to a CD of his favorite evening raga, General Ali considered the situation. For perhaps the first time, he felt that maybe the cards were stacked too much against him, and ultimately, he and others like him, would not be able to stop the momentum that was building.

The house boy appeared to announce that Major Durrani had arrived. Ali told the boy to have the Major join him. A minute later, Tarek, dressed in black slacks and a tight fitting cotton shirt, entered the garden. Ali waved him over to the sitting area. After their greeting and brief handshake, the two sat down.

"Major, you are looking fit these days. Are you still jogging?" Ali asked.

Tarek smiled and shook his head. "Not as much as I used to, Sir. I try to get out three to four times a week for about 10 kilometers. But that is about it."

"Good Lord, man!" Ali responded. "The heart only has so many beats in it. Why push your luck?"

Tarek chuckled. "Running is supposed to be good for the heart, so I'm hoping it has added to the number of beats, not lessened them."

"You can try to add beats to your heart if you like, Major, but the number of our days is written on our foreheads by the Almighty himself, and there is nothing we do can do to change that number," Ali said matter-of-factly.

"You may be right General, but I'll keep running just the same. I find it therapeutic, and that alone makes it worth the effort."

"Well there is nothing wrong with that I suppose," Ali said, then asked, "Can I get you something to drink? Water? Or a soda perhaps?"

"Thank you, Sir, but I'm fine."

Ali raised his eyebrows. "How about a brandy, Major? It's been a while since we shared one of those. Oh, and don't worry about Madam chastising us, she is with her family in Lahore for the week. "

Tarek pondered the offer for a moment. Although he did not often drink hard liquor, there was something about the thick night air and the soulful raga playing in the background that made the thought of a good brandy sound very appealing.

"Thank you, General. I accept your offer," Tarek responded.

"Good. I was hoping you would. It gives me an excuse to indulge myself in the interest of being a good host. Certainly Madam would understand that."

Ali walked over to a rattan cabinet under a sheltered area of the tiled patio, took out a bottle and two brandy snifters, and returned to his chair.

Pouring a double shot into each glass, Ali offered a toast. "To Pakistan."

Tarek raised his glass and touched it to Ali's. "To Pakistan," he echoed.

Each man took a brief drink. Tarek found just one sip had an immediate relaxing effect. He could not help but notice that the General seemed melancholy. As the evening progressed, and they consumed more brandy, it became clear that Ali was in a pensive mood.

An hour later, Ali sat comfortably back in his chair, his empty brandy snifter dangling from his left hand, a smoldering half-smoked cigar in his right. He took a draw off his cigar and asked, "Still no word from our friend, I assume?"

"None, Sir. But I should hear something soon."

"The sooner the better, Tarek. Maybe I'm paranoid, but the complete stand-down of the LT is ominous, as contradictory as that may sound, and with HV/30's report on the meeting between Abu Shafik and these mystery persons from our government, the situation only looks worse. My belief remains that Abu Shafik is stopping operations in order to refit, with the intention of resuming operations at a critical moment."

Tarek took a sip of his brandy, savoring the smooth taste as it slipped down his throat.

He set his glass down and said, "If HV/30 has some news at the next meeting, we may get answers that will clarify things."

"I'm counting on it, Tarek," Ali responded. After a moment's thought, he asked, "Do you think you can get to the bottom of this sub-source of his at the next meeting? We've got to know where this information is coming from."

"I'm going to do everything I can, General. The last meeting was a car meeting, but this fellow did not open up to me much. I wanted to get a little further with him before taking him to a safehouse, but I don't think I have a choice at this point if I'm going to create an environment where he feels safe enough to really talk. In fact, I've already procured the house"

"It makes sense to me," Ali said, nodding his approval. "I think we have to push the envelope on this one."

Tarek could see General Ali's eyelids were becoming heavy and that he was starting to fade. Looking at his watch, Tarek was surprised to see how late it was. "Sir, I believe I've kept you up well past your bedtime and mine as well. It is time for me to leave before I wear out my welcome at the Ali home."

The two men stood up. "Tarek, you know that will never happen," Ali said, and then to Tarek's astonishment, he added, "You are like a son to me."

Tarek knew whatever he said in response would be insufficient for the moment, and all he could think to say was "Thank you, General. That means a lot to me. You have always had my deepest respect and admiration."

Ali put his arm around Tarek's shoulder and walked him down the pathway to a side gate that led out of the garden to the street.

Tarek stepped through the gate and started to walk away but Ali stopped him.

"If you hear anything from HV/30, call me immediately. And, just so you know, I will be out of my office tomorrow afternoon. The ISI director has invited me to lunch. You can always call my highline, however, and leave a message. And let's hope our friend signals soon."

"Exactly right, Sir," Tarek said. "And let us hope this luncheon is less disastrous than your last."

—38—

The heat from the late morning sun was intense. Despite having all the office windows open and the ceiling fans at maximum speed, there was nothing Anil Deshmukh could do to cool himself. There simply was no escaping from the heat of late spring in Calcutta. The smell of rotting refuse and the cacophony of cars, horns, motorcycles, and shouts of vendors rising from the street poured into the fourth floor suite of the West Bengal Protocol Office. Anil did not know what annoyed him most—the heat, the smell, or the noise.

These were not the conditions he had imagined he would be working under when he accepted the provincial governor's offer of a job as the protocol officer for the province. Governor Ghule had made the offer almost two years ago while he and Anil sat ever-so-comfortably in the governor's tranquil air conditioned office, sipping ice-cold Coca-Cola served to them by the governor's office assistant, truly one of the most beautiful women Anil had ever seen. Looking back to that meeting, he had to admit that Governor Ghule had not exactly promised him an air conditioned office, or that he would be "assisted" by a beautiful woman. But still, the implication was there. At least in Anil's mind it was.

Since then, Anil had somehow grown to accept the reality of his current station within the West Bengal government. After all, he was very fortunate to have landed a government job of some responsibility, given his young age. He had a steady, if low, salary, and employment with the government meant that he received some health benefits. Should he endure until retirement, he would have a pension in his old age.

The job had other benefits, as well. As the protocol officer, he had met a number of celebrities who had visited the city, most having come to make highly publicized donations to organizations that helped Calcutta's poor.

He had also organized open-air concerts for Western rock bands, primarily from the U.K. who came to Calcutta while on tour. This had happened with much more frequency prior to Mother Teresa's death, but still, every now and then, a band of tattooed long-haired rockers would arrive. Some were actually unaware Mother Teresa had died years before and would no longer be available to see them when they visited her orphanage, their mouths dropping open in shock when told of her passing.

No, his job was tolerable, as long as he kept reminding himself that his current post was only temporary. Anil was convinced the job in Calcutta would be his stepping stone to a position in India's Ministry of Culture, with all of its possibilities—service abroad, perhaps, maybe even New York on assignment at the United Nations. This had been his dream for as long as he could remember, and he was confident he would one day fulfill that dream and the world would be his oyster.

But for the present time he had no oyster, only cold left-over lentils and hard naan to sustain him. Pushing the unappetizing food aside, he picked up the large manila envelope, which had only that morning arrived from New Delhi, and for the third time pored over its contents.

His office assistant, Mathir, walked into the room carrying a stack of old newspapers. "What is it?" Mathir asked. He was a short pudgy man of about 45 years, a far cry from the office assistant Anil had imagined when he accepted the job.

"A lot of work." Anil answered.

"That's not good." Mathir said as he unceremoniously dumped the papers he carried out the open window. They crashed down onto a large garbage heap, conveniently located on the street only 30 feet below the office window.

Anil turned and glared at Mathir. "How many times have I told you not to throw things out the window? We are not slum dwellers."

Mathir, tired of hearing this particular refrain, retorted, "How can you say this? We *are* slum dwellers. Look around. There is garbage everywhere. Bad odors are everywhere. There are poor people everywhere. Where do you think we are Anil? In the south of France?"

"But we are not slum dwellers!" Anil fairly shouted, shaking his head emphatically. "This is not our home!"

Angry with himself for getting mad, Anil made a conscious effort to calm down. After a couple of long breaths, he once again reminded Mathir that a move to a new office was budgeted for the following year, and it would be in a much better part of Calcutta.

Mathir had a simple formula for responding to almost every statement Anil made. He would either respond, "That's good," or "That's not good." He had learned that these two responses had the least chance of provoking the volatile Anil.

In this case, after listening to Anil wistfully speak about the new office, Mathir chose to respond, "That's good." This seemed to satisfy Anil, who once again was pondering the contents of the manila envelope.

Mathir walked over to Anil's desk and picked up the envelope, which bore the seal of the Ministry of Waterways. "So what is this one about?" he inquired.

"The same thing as the last one," Anil replied absent-mindedly, "the Farakka Barrage ceremony."

"You're joking? I thought everything was worked out on that," Mathir said.

"Apparently not. Based on this new list of VIPs, Delhi wants to make it a bigger deal than what was originally envisioned. I think the only one from the government who won't be coming is the prime minister."

Mathir picked up the list Anil had been studying. Although Anil had exaggerated a bit, there were many important officials who were now invited—about 25 senior Indian government personnel, it appeared at a glance, ranging in rank from assistant deputy minister to full minister. India's deputy representative to the U.N. was on the list as well.

There were foreign dignitaries too, most notably the Russian ambassador to India, and the resident chief of the American Agency for International Development.

Also on the list was Engineer Advani, who had designed Farakka Barrage and oversaw its construction. Advani's daughter would accompany him as well. According to a footnote at the bottom of the page, as a courtesy, the Ministry of Waterworks was also allowing the Advani's to bring up to five guests with them, who would be identified prior to arrival. A second footnote indicated that a group of foreign investors might also attend—if they could be identified quickly enough.

As Mathir read the list, Anil commented, "The Russian ambassador is no doubt invited in acknowledgment of his country's support in building the dam during the days of the Soviet empire."

"And the American embassy official? And the foreign investors? Why are they coming?" Mathir asked.

"Think about it, Mathir. India has been trying to encourage foreign investment to develop the economic infrastructure in West Bengal for the last few years. I'm sure the government sees this as an opportunity to get some exposure for West Bengal in this regard."

"But Farakka Barrage is in the middle of nowhere. Isn't this going a bit overboard?" Mathir asked. "After all, it is just an old dam. You might as well just dump your money in the Ganges."

Looking up at Mathir, Anil responded in a serious tone, "It is more than an old dam. It is a symbol of India's technological prowess and its sovereignty. Here, read this." Anvil handed Mathir a second page. Mathir read it.

"Hmm, I see. The picture is becoming clearer now. Farakka is to be debated at the UN again. I wonder if the debate will take place before or after the commemoration ceremony," Mathir asked.

"The next UN session begins in only a week, and it will last for about a month, so any discussion of Farakka should take place very near the time of the ceremony." Anil, who kept track of anything having to do with the U.N., said. "It's actually a clever strategy, whether India wins or loses in the debate. A high-profile ceremony highlighting the dam will emphasize the point that India bows to no one on internal issues. Obviously, that is why our deputy U.N. rep will be here."

Mathir put down the paper, "That's good."

"Yes, it is good. But now we must think about what it is we have to do to properly organize for the ceremony and related activities, particularly in light of these additions to the list of invited guests. Obviously, we will need a larger *shamiana* for the VIPs in case of rain. We also will need to recalculate our catering order for the dinner. And that is just the start of it."

"Indeed," Mathir responded. "We will need to line up more buses to transport the invitees to the various locations here in Calcutta and get them from Malda to Farakka. That, I think, is all easily accomplished. However, arranging for more aircraft to transport the invitees from Calcutta to Malda will be a challenge, putting us way over budget. We also cannot forget that we will need to coordinate with the police regarding the need for more security."

Despite his frequent frustration with Mathir, Anil had to admit that when it came to planning events, he was a master.

"All good points, Mathir. Let's sit down this afternoon and make a list of everything we can think of that needs doing. This must come off well,"

Mathir shook his head dejectedly, "Oh, God, I'm dreading this. Governor Ghule is going to be even more demanding now that there will be more VIPs coming. He is such an ass."

"Mathir!" Anil said sharply. "You will not say such things about Governor Ghule. He is not an ass. He is just under a lot of pressure. He has personal issues to deal with plus the demands of this job. Do you know his wife has left him?"

"That's not good." Mathir responded.

"No, it's not. The man is beside himself. So let's not be so callous about his situation. It could happen to you too, you know."

Mathir started to reply that he did not think so, since he was not involved with a beautiful office assistant that his wife could find out about, but he thought better about making such a provocative comment to Anil. Tired of the conversation, he simply said, "Well, it's not good. Let's discuss what we will need to do after lunch."

The two men locked up their office and walked down the four flights of stairs to the street level, stopping at the front door to tell the *chokidar* they were leaving and not to let anyone go up to their office.

Mathir hailed a motor-rickshaw, and the two men shared the ride to the middle-class area of town where they both lived. There they parted company, each making his way on foot to his own apartment.

With the day's heat at its peak, the first thing Anil did upon arriving at his apartment was to turn his window-mounted air conditioner on high. The small unit only cooled the living room, which was closed off from the rest of the house by a glass wall and door. The chilled air felt so good that Anil lay down on the cool tile floor directly under the air conditioner.

As he lay there drinking in the coolness, he imagined what it would be like when he finally could live in an place where creature comforts weren't such a rarity and his work would always be interesting. To his mind, the United Nations in New York was the perfect place for him.

Just before drifting off to sleep, the thought occurred to him, and not for the first time, that his role in organizing the Farakka Barrage ceremony could be his ticket to New York.

39

Well into his ten kilometers, Tarek had entered the zone. His mind was clear and still, his pace steady and strong. With each stride, the surface of the dirt trail rose up to meet his feet in an effortless rhythm. The heat of the day and the exertion of his body felt good. Tarek savored every moment. This was his meditation. This was what renewed him time and again.

It was only one week since his last meeting with General Ali, but much had happened since that evening. The day following the meeting had been a fateful one for Ali. At his luncheon with the ISI director general, Ali was informed that he was being assigned as the ISI representative to Washington, effective immediately. The DG had tried to put the best face on it, telling Ali it was safer for him to go abroad, as the "miscreants" who had tried to kill him were still at large. The DG also noted that the position in Washington was highly coveted.

Ali thought the desirability of the Washington job was debatable and under different circumstances he might have been happy to take the assignment. But given what seemed to be afoot in Pakistan, Ali knew that now was not the time to be exiled half way around the world. Realizing General Ali did not seem particularly excited about the news, the DG went on to say, "It is fortunate that General Baluch has announced his intention to retire and return from Washington. Had this not happened, I do not know where we could have placed you."

Ali understood the DG was saying that if he did not accept the Washington job, retirement would be his only other option. He knew that, as difficult as it would be to try to influence events from his post in Washington, if he retired he would be completely out of the game, with no influence at all.

The DG had apologized for the short notice, offering the excuse that given the importance of Pakistan's relationship with the U.S., he needed to get a replacement for General Baluch out to Washington as soon as possible, and he did not want to work through the normal personnel process, which could take weeks. General Ali was to be in Washington by the following week, and Shahida could join him later.

As Tarek slowed from a run into a cool-down walk, he started to think about the implications of General Ali no longer being accessible to him to discuss developments concerning HV/30.

Written communications through official ISI channels would not be possible, as officially the case was dead. Any mention of it would attract unwanted attention. Official secure voice communications would be risky as well, since ISI routinely monitored most if not all official conversations. Calling General Ali over commercial telephone systems would be fairly secure in terms of the ISI finding out about them, but other unwanted listeners could tune in. E-mail might be a good alternative but that had security risks like those of the telephone. Clearly, communication was going to be a problem.

Tarek had hoped HV/30 would signal for a meeting before Ali departed for Washington, but it was now too late for that to happen. General Ali was getting on the plane that night.

The situation was unlike any Tarek dealt with before. He knew how to deal with external threats, but he did not know how to deal with threats from within his own government. Without General Ali available, he would have to make decisions, possibly critical ones, on his own.

Anticipating the problems Tarek would encounter after his departure to Washington, Ali had assigned him to a position as special programs officer, from which he reported only to Ali and could travel as needed with no approval necessary. Equally important, Ali also authorized an off-the-books budget for Tarek's use. With this arrangement, Tarek could continue his handling of the HV/30 case without his ISI colleagues becoming aware of it. Still, this arrangement was good only until Ali's replacement was on the job. Once the new chief of ops arrived, things would undoubtedly change. Tarek guessed he had only three or four weeks at most.

Ali's unexpected assignment to Washington added yet another element of uncertainty and confusion to Tarek's life. It had been weeks now since he had last seen Sahar, and he longed for her. They wrote to each other by e-mail almost daily and spoke on the phone several times a week. All the while, she believed he was in the UAE. While their frequent communication helped sustain the relationship, for Tarek they were no replacement for being with Sahar. Not even close.

Needing to plan something definite, during their last phone call Tarek had committed to coming to India for the anniversary ceremony at Farakka Barrage. Sahar had almost squealed in delight on hearing his decision. Tarek thought his attendance at the ceremony would be an important milestone in their relationship and a good way to put his relationship with Advani on a different footing, one he hoped would lead to Advani accepting him as a deserving suitor for his daughter.

Tarek's great concern was that he might have to cancel the trip if something related to HV/30's information developed. He prayed he could go to India before anything happened. Earlier in the week, he had gotten General Ali's approval for the necessary leave, telling him only that he planned to see an old friend in Abu Dhabi. Of course, the only friend Tarek planned to see in the UAE, before proceeding to New Delhi, was his old agent, Habibi. It bothered Tarek that he continued to deceive Ali about this one area of his life. But what could he do? His desire to be with Sahar outweighed all other considerations.

Returning home, Tarek showered and dressed before heading to Islamabad International Airport where he met with a dozen other ISI officers and members of General Ali's family to bid farewell to the general. Given the crowd of people, Tarek had only a limited opportunity to say a personal goodbye. Ali's final words to Tarek were simply, "Stay safe."

After the General boarded the Gulf Air 777, the group stayed to watch it taxi down the runway and lift off into the night sky. As the lights of the plane disappeared from sight, Tarek said goodbye to the others in the group and headed toward the main exit.

Just as he stepped outside, he felt his cell phone vibrate. He pulled the phone out of his inside jacket pocket and flipped open the cover to read the text message.

To anyone else, the message would have seemed innocent enough, just another unsolicited advertisement for car insurance. To Tarek, however, it was much more important than that.

It meant he would be meeting HV/30 the following night.

Tarek departed Islamabad late-afternoon and arrived in Wah shortly after nightfall. He parked several blocks away from the contact point, then approached on foot through the nearly deserted streets passing by shuttered shops and tea stalls.

Rounding the last corner he saw HV/30 arriving at the designated spot, white plastic bag in his left hand. After closing the distance between them, Tarek gave a slight cough. HV/30 looked his way and recognized Tarek immediately.

The two men started up the street together. As they walked, Tarek provided him with directions to the safehouse, telling him to be there in an hour. Tarek had HV/30 repeat the directions, then parted company with him.

Tarek returned to his car and drove to the safe house, a residence in a middle-class neighborhood. While renting the safehouse, he had arranged for an illiterate old man to live at the residence in the servant's quarters, adjacent to the main house, to serve as the caretaker and *chokidar*. The man's wife lived with him, and both believed the house had been leased by a wealthy man from Islamabad who periodically did business in Wah. They were happy with the arrangement and had no inclination to question it.

At the entryway, Tarek beeped his horn. Wearing rubber flip-flops and a threadbare plaid jacket, the bearded old man peeked through the pedestrian doorway. Seeing Tarek, he swung open the heavy metal gate. Tarek pulled inside. After an initial greeting, Tarek told the man to wash his car and to be alert for the arrival of a villager who was interested in selling his property to Tarek.

HV/30 arrived as instructed. Tarek had brought a generous meal to share with the agent: ample servings of chicken kabob, rice, and freshly baked naan, with a juicy ripe pomegranate for dessert. HV/30, who had not eaten since early morning, ate voraciously. Tarek did not spoil the atmosphere by talking about business. Instead, he used the time to talk about his own background—his family, his likes and dislikes, all in an effort to establish a rapport with HV/30. Ninety percent of what Tarek said was true. The rest were lies necessary to protect his identity from HV/30.

HV/30 responded to Tarek's apparent candor by opening up about his own background. Over the next two hours, Tarek learned more about HV/30 than a headquarters file could ever provide. During the conversation, he at last learned the truth about what had motivated HV/30 to betray an organization he had once risked his life for.

HV/30 recounted how at the age of 30 he had married a young woman from his village. The couple had been together for 20 years, deeply devoted to each other and their five children. Their first child was a girl named Soriya. HV/30 spoke of how disappointed he had been when informed that his first-born was female. At first, he did not even want to go to see the child, but wanted to shelter his wife from his disappointment. So he went to his sister's home, where the child had been born, determined to conceal his unhappiness.

HV/30 smiled as he told Tarek that this had been easier than he had imagined. The moment he first saw the tiny girl, with her dark curly hair and a soft round face, he knew she was "a gift from Allah," given to him to care for and protect. HV/30 said he loved all his children, but with none of them, not even his sons, did he feel such a profound sense of love and responsibility.

"I suppose it was because she was the first," he told Tarek, "or maybe it was because she was just special. Whatever the reason, I have always been devoted to her more than any of the others."

Tarek was surprised when HV/30 mentioned that, for reasons of economy, Soriya no longer lived with the family, but stayed with his sister's family. This struck Tarek as strange. Customarily, a young girl left home only after marriage, but Soriya was still unwed. It would have been acceptable to send a son away if necessary, but to send a daughter away was unusual. Tarek began a subtle elicitation campaign to get to the truth of the matter.

"Mahmoud, I had no idea you had sent one of your children away. This is not right; a young girl should be at home with her family," Tarek said, partly because he believed it and partly to affect empathy with HV/30's situation. "If you have need of money, there is no reason to have your daughter stay with your sister. I can give you a stipend every month that will more then pay any expenses she may cause you."

"No Rashid, your money is really no solution to the problem, although perhaps there is something else you can do for me."

"Of course, Mahmoud. I will do whatever I can to help you."

"I thank you for that," HV/30 responded. "But first it is important that I explain myself. You see, since its founding, I have given my all to the Lashkar-e-Taiba, and I did not refuse when I was asked to give occasional refuge to one of its commanders, even though this put not only me but also my family at great risk. At first, they would not even tell me who this commander was, and not until I took him under my roof did I learn that it was none other than Sheik Osman."

HV/30 stopped and took a deep breath, letting it out slowly. "I told you at our first meeting that my friend Yasin was assisting Sheik Osman, but that was a lie. While I do have a friend named Yasin, he knows nothing of Sheik Osman. I was not ready to tell you of my connection to Osman, but since our last meeting, I have thought this over. Now I want to set the record straight. I am the one who hides him."

Tarek showed no umbrage at HV/30's deception and was careful not to interrupt HV/30's story.

"Of course, I had heard of him, but never had I laid eyes on him. So although I was frightened, I was honored that Abu Shafik had entrusted me with his best commander's safety. This man was a hero to our cause. Totally fearless in battle, he has personally killed more Indian soldiers than any other LT fighter. This, and the fact that he is very smart, makes him an exceptional warrior."

HV/30 paused for a moment, his eyes filling with hatred, and said, "But after I brought him into my home and gave him shelter and food, I learned that he is also arrogant and impulsive, and he does what he wants. And why shouldn't he? Who can challenge him? He is untouchable, or at least he thinks he is."

HV/30 did not look at Tarek. He gazed downward, his eyes glowing with intensity.

"So, is Sheik Osman staying at your home now?" Tarek asked.

"No, he was with me until early yesterday. That is why I couldn't come to the meeting before now. I had to wait until he left." HV/30 gave a slight smile. "But I think the inconvenience for you will have been worth the trouble."

"Why do you think so?" Tarek asked.

"Because he hosted a meeting at my house in which some plans were made— plans that I think you will be interested in."

Tarek was very interested, but he knew he had to understand what was between HV/30 and Sheik Osman if he was ever going to learn why HV/30's was betraying the LT.

"I do want to hear what happened at that meeting, Mahmoud, but first, tell me, why do you hate Sheik Osman?"

"Is it that obvious?" Mahmoud asked.

"It's pretty obvious." Tarek said.

HV/30 slowly lifted his head and looked at Tarek as tears replaced the hatred in his eyes. Softly he said, "Because he raped Soriya. The bastard raped my little girl."

HV/30 began to sob so intensely he was unable to speak. Tarek was the first person he had ever told about the rape of his daughter, and months of pent-up emotion came to the surface all at once.

HV/30's pain was difficult for Tarek to witness. Reaching over, he placed his hand on HV/30's shoulder. "Brother, I am so sorry. May Allah give you strength."

Tarek could see the great difficulty this situation presented for HV/30. In a rural village, it was rare to hear an accusation of rape, which usually resulted in severe punishment, not for the accused, but for the accuser. Often, victims who made these accusations were beaten, even killed. The lucky ones were simply exiled from the village, sometimes after being permanently disfigured to mark them for life as a whore. In Soriya's case, the fact that the attacker was a fabled LT commander would only work against her.

Regaining his composure, HV/30 confirmed Tarek's assessment of the situation and explained what had happened. The attack had occurred the first time Sheik Osman stayed with HV/30. The day it happened, HV/30 and his wife had walked into the village to get bread. When they left, Sheik Osman had been sleeping, and Soriya was in the courtyard hanging up the laundry to dry. HV/30 and his wife were gone for less then an hour, and Soriya was no longer in the courtyard when they returned. They did not suspect anything, assuming she had gone down to the river to wash another basket of clothes. After an hour, Soriya still hadn't returned, so HV/30 walked to the river to check on her.

He found her near the river, sitting in the tall grass and crying. When she told him what had happened, he nearly collapsed in shock. For a moment he thought he was dying. He held Soriya in his arms and cried for a long time. As he cried, his pain turned to anger, and he resolved to kill Sheik Osman. He would have done so that very day had Soriya not stopped him, ultimately convincing him that people would still blame her for what had happened. Then both he and Soriya would be punished. Soriya demanded HV/30 promise that nothing be said to anyone.

Despite his burning hatred for Sheik Osman, HV/30 agreed that for the good of the family there was no other choice but to remain silent. He told no one, not even his wife, about what had happened. The most difficult part was not allowing Sheik Osman to see that he knew of the rape.

To get his revenge, HV/30 had even considered approaching Indian intelligence to set up Sheik Osman for capture. No doubt the Indians would love to get their hands on him. But he himself was on the Indian's wanted list. It was more likely the Indians would imprison him for many years, impoverishing his family.

With the Indian option closed, HV/30 decided the ISI would want to know what the LT was up to, particularly information about leaders like Abu Shafik and Sheik Osman. And if he could convince the ISI that Sheik Osman had stolen the money the ISI had provided to the LT, then there would be hell to pay.

Tarek listened to HV/30's story in silence, nodding his head at key points in HV/30's litany of wrongs, real and perceived, done by Sheik Osman, and by association, Abu Shafik and the LT. At last, HV/30 seemed to have run out of words to say.

"Mahmoud, you have been carrying a great burden. I want you to know that I am outraged about what has happened to Soriya. This is a terrible crime, one that makes me ashamed to be called a man. But Soriya was right. Had you taken action yourself, only more harm would have come from this despicable act. You and your family would have suffered gravely."

HV/30 nodded. "I know you are right Rashid, but somehow, this must be avenged. And this is why I need your help. I need you to help me avenge Soriya in a way that protects her and the rest of my family."

Tarek understood HV/30's feelings, but for the moment, Sheik Osman was the means by which HV/30 was obtaining information on Abu Shafik and his involvement with the still unidentified Pakistani officials. To take any kind of action against Sheik Osman now would mean shutting off that information stream, something Tarek knew he could not do.

"Look, Mahmoud. I will have to study this situation. We have to be very careful and patient if we hope to make Sheik Osman pay for his crime. At this moment, I cannot tell you what I can do to help. I can only promise you that if there is a way I can help, I will do it. But you must be patient."

"Rashid, I have been patient. But I do not know how much longer I can endure."

"I know, Mahmoud. Still, you must be patient a while longer. There is a saying that applies here, perhaps you have heard or read it."

"Rashid, you know I am not a well-educated man. Please, tell me this saying."

Tarek smiled and again placed his hand on HV/30's shoulder. "The saying goes like this. 'Revenge is a dish best served cold.'"

Mahmoud lifted his gaze up for a moment, as if looking away at a distant sight. "Hmm," he said. "I think I like this saying."

—41—

After HV/30 departed the safehouse for his village, Tarek headed back toward Islamabad. As he drove, Tarek mentally reviewed the information he had gleaned from the meeting. HV/30's deep-seated need for revenge for the rape of Soriya was the key to understanding his motivation for cooperating with the ISI, which meant that Tarek was now in a better position to manage HV/30 and, if necessary, manipulate him to accomplish the operation's goals.

Tarek had not forgotten to debrief HV/30 on the details of the meeting Sheik Osman had hosted. It was clear that something big was underway. Three days ago, a group of seven LT fighters had arrived at HV/30's doorstep. HV/30 knew only one of the seven, a neighboring villager and old LT stalwart named Latif. The rest were strangers.

HV/30 was able to learn bits and pieces of what transpired during the meeting as he moved about serving food and tea. It became clear from the conversation that the fighters had been hand-picked for a special but unspecified mission to take place in India. Sheik Osman would lead the mission after some training that would occur soon.

Curiously, all of the men were fluent in Bangla, which HV/30 himself spoke, having lived much of his early life in East Pakistan, before it became Bangladesh. Based on the team's language abilities, Tarek had to assume the mission would be carried out somewhere in eastern India, most likely in Calcutta, the largest city in Bangla-speaking West Bengal. Tarek remembered Ali telling him that one of the Intelligence Bureau officers assigned to the IRE had traveled to Calcutta. Tarek thought it possible the officer's travel there might be related to what the LT team was up to.

HV/30 had not learned the timing of the team's mission, only that the men would receive training shortly. The mission would quickly follow the training, Tarek thought. HV/30 had also not learned anything concrete on the involvement of Pakistani officials with Abu Shafik, but he did hear Sheik Osman tell the men that the "equipment package" would come from the "uniforms."

Tarek shook off his sleepiness as he drove through the night. He would have to get word to General Ali to keep him informed of developments. With the general now in Washington, doing so securely wouldn't be easy.

An even more difficult problem was how to obtain additional details about the LT operation. Once Sheik Osman and his team departed for India, HV/30 would be left behind and Tarek would have no means of keeping tabs on the group's activities. This was the most serious operational problem Tarek faced. An attack by the LT in India would undoubtedly lead to a cancellation of the negotiations going on between India and Pakistan. If Pakistan were directly implicated in supporting the mission, the consequences would be far, far worse. It could mean war.

After what seemed like an eternity of driving, Tarek could see the dim glow of the lights of Islamabad in the distance. Approaching the city, he had an idea on how to deal with HV/30's impending loss of access to the team. Though the plan was relatively simple, he would have to call in some favors to pull it off. Tarek knew he had no alternative. When the LT team left for its mission, HV/30 would have to go with them.

—42—

At a remote airstrip in southeastern Pakistan, a steel aircraft hanger sat baking in the sun. Long streaks of rust ran down its sides and the once-black tarmac had long since faded to gray, its surface broken and cracked, covered in places by patches of weeds. Inside, the hanger was empty save for a coffin-sized wooden shipping crate.

Two soldiers wearing the distinctive camouflage fatigues of the Special Security Group were positioned just inside the open hanger door, taking advantage of the protective shade it afforded. Around the airstrip, hidden in the dense vegetation, a full SSG platoon provided perimeter security and in the distance, the whop-whop sound of a helicopter grew louder by the second.

As the helicopter came into view, the two soldiers stepped out from the hanger into the sun. One soldier carried two white flags on wooden handles, one in each hand. He walked away from the hanger, facing the helicopter fast approaching from the north, and raised his arms, crossing them in an 'X' pattern. The other soldier knelt down in a position off to the side, watching as the green transport chopper slowed its forward speed and began its descent to the steaming tarmac.

Touching down, the helicopter rolled forward on its wheeled triad, stopping 50 meters from where the soldier with the flags stood leaning forward into the rotor blast. In well-practiced movements, the helicopter crew chief opened the door behind the pilot compartment and, one by one, ten men, each carrying backpacks, exited the aircraft, heads bent low as the aircraft's powerful rotors cut through the air above them.

Two of the passengers wore Pak Army uniforms. The rest wore civilian clothing, but uniforms nonetheless—black tennis shoes, dark polyester slacks, and white cotton shirts. Most of appeared to be in their 30s, except one who looked a decade older. All were dark-skinned and bearded.

As soon as the men were clear of the rotors, the aircraft engines revved and the bird was once again airborne, rising slowly and turning back toward the north. None in the group bothered to look back at the helicopter as it disappeared into the cloudless sky.

The senior Pak soldier with the group wore the rank of full colonel, but that was all his uniform said about him. He wore no unit patch, no branch of service insignia, and no name tag. The second uniformed member of the group was a young well-muscled captain. Aside from his rank, his uniform bore no other identifiers.

The colonel led the group into the open bay of the hanger, telling them to wait as he walked over to the soldiers who had been guarding the hangar, now once again inside its bay. He conferred with the senior of the two. The soldier, a tough-looking sergeant, reported to the colonel that there had been no visitors since the colonel had been there the day before. Satisfied, the colonel returned to the waiting group, then led them to the back of the hanger where the crate sat on the cool concrete floor.

"This is it. It is all here. I inspected it myself when we prepared it for transport," the colonel said.

The captain tapped two of the men on the shoulder and handed them a sack of tools he pulled from his rucksack. "Your first test is to see if you can get this thing opened," he told them.

The men glanced at each other and approached the crate warily.

"Why are you afraid? It isn't going to bite you," the captain scolded.

The men set to work opening the crate, first using cable cutters to remove the six thin steel bands, three running horizontally and three running vertically, around the crate. Using crowbars, they pried the top off, surprised to find yet another smaller but similarly bound crate inside. The man with the cable cutters stepped forward to cut its steel bands, but the colonel stopped him. He reached into a side pocket on his backpack and took out a small electronic meter with a single probe hanging from it. Setting the meter on top of the inner crate, he pulled a multi-tool knife from his belt and opened out a short Phillips-head screwdriver, which he used to remove a screw located in top center of the crate.

The colonel closed the knife, put it back on his belt, and turned his attention to the electronic meter. He flipped its power switch, then took the metal-tipped end of the probe, pushing it deep into the hole where the screw had been. A small light on the face of the meter begin to glow green. The indicator needle of the meter moved to the positive position while a digital display registered the number 50.

"Excellent," the colonel said. "The electronic seal has not been disturbed." He nodded for the man with the cable cutters to proceed.

The team soon pried loose the top of the inner crate. A plastic-coated wire was attached to the underside of the crate's top, at the point where the colonel had inserted the lead wire, and this was hampering the effort to completely remove the top.

"Cut the wire," the captain ordered. Once that was done, the top easily lifted off.

Looking down into the crate, the men could see the top of a steel object, but the view was impeded by dense black-colored rubber packing material that encased the object on all sides.

Although it would have been easier to remove the object by breaking up the crates, the colonel wanted to preserve them intact.

"You are going to have to lift it out," the colonel said. "It's heavy. I suggest four of you position yourselves on each side of the crate and lift it out of the box in a team effort."

The men did as the colonel suggested and were able to lift the object out of the box, setting it gently on the hanger floor. The captain stepped forward and pulled off the rubber packing material to reveal a black steel canister a little less than a meter in height and 60 centimeters in radius. Its appearance resembled an old-fashioned milk can.

Upon close inspection, they could see that the device was divided into two parts, an upper and lower casing. The fit between the two halves was so precise, it could have been mistaken for a solid object but for four internal locking ports that were evenly spaced around the equator of the device on slightly raised areas.

Intrigued, one of the civilians squatted down next to the canister and ran his hands along the smooth surface.

"It's beautiful isn't it?" the colonel asked.

"Yes," replied the man. "You can tell the steel is of extremely high quality and much time went into making this."

The colonel chuckled. "Believe me, brother, you have no idea."

Another one of the civilians took a closer look. "I don't see any kind of controls. How does it work?"

"A good observation," the colonel said. "Here, you two help me lay it on its side."

Two men stepped forward to assist the colonel. Oblong in shape, the canister was stabilized on its side by the raised internal locking ports, two of which at any point prevented it from rolling.

The colonel knelt down beside the canister, pointing to the end that served as the base of the device when it was standing upright.

"If you look here, you will see there is a recessed area. This is where the control panel is plugged in and the device can be programmed. You have a choice of setting it for use with a timer, remote control, or manually; the latter option is reserved for emergency situations only."

"So that is all there is to it?" asked one of the men. "Just plug in the control panel, set it, and it is prepared?"

"Not quite," the captain answered. "The sequence is like this. First the control panel is inserted and a security code is punched in. This code opens the four locking ports. Second, the two halves are separated and a special barrier in the center of the device is removed. Then the two halves are reattached and locked using the control panel. Finally, the device is programmed for operation. When these steps occur will be dictated by the operational situation at the time."

"Will all of us be trained on this?" asked another member of the team.

"Of course," answered the captain. "Before you leave here, every one of you will know this process so well you will be able to do it in the dark, which, I suspect, will be the exact conditions you will operating under when you put this into action."

At that point, the older-looking civilian spoke for the first time since the group's arrival at the airstrip.

"Brothers, conditions on the ground can never be fully predicted. All of you must know how to activate the device. We will only have one chance. We must get it right. Your job over the next two days is to learn how to operate this device properly. And then you must remember what you learned when you return home from here and we wait for our transportation arrangements to be finalized. Do you understand?"

The men responded in unison, their voices rising. "Yes, Sheik Osman! Allah Akbar!"

The colonel was startled by the loud response, but quickly recovered. "Alright then," he said. "We don't have much time. Let us begin."

It was almost eight o'clock in the evening in Abu Dhabi and Habibi was ready to go home. His day had started early, and he had not even had time to take lunch. Now here it was an hour past the time he had told his wife he would be home. She would be angry, but she would forgive him—he hoped.

Just as he stood up from his desk, the office phone rang. Picking up the receiver, he noticed the call was on his personal line. He braced himself, anticipating an angry blast from his wife. To his surprise, he recognized the voice asking for Mr. Harun Habibi. It was Tarek.

Habibi had not forgotten the rules of telephonic contacts and responded using Tarek's operational alias. "Yes, Mr. Rashid, this is Habibi. It is so good to hear from you".

"I wanted to touch base with you about our next transaction."

"Of course, Mr. Rashid. As I told you previously, my company stands ready to assist you at any time. What can I help you with this time?" Habibi asked.

"I would like for you to duplicate my last order as I have a similar requirement as before. Can you support this?"

"Certainly. What is the anticipated delivery date?"

"In about three weeks time, but I will provide a more precise date in the next few days."

"That should not be a problem. I will personally oversee the necessary preparations."

"Excellent. By the way, there is another thing too. I may need your assistance in assessing a project I am considering. Would you be available for travel in the next few weeks?" Tarek asked.

"Mr. Rashid, I am an international businessman. Of course I can travel if the deal is right."

Tarek chuckled, "That's what I assumed. I will be discussing this with you in future correspondence, as soon as I have a few more details in hand."

"I look forward to hearing from you."

"Very well. I'll be in touch. Good night, Mr. Habibi." Tarek hung up the phone.

Habibi was delighted to have heard from Tarek. It was a rare event when Tarek used the phone to make contact, but Habibi knew he would not have done so if it had not been necessary, and he would have taken all the necessary precautions beforehand.

Habibi guessed Tarek was headed back to see Sahar, for it was obvious on Tarek's last trip through Abu Dhabi that he was in love with her. As to Tarek's remark about Habibi possibly making a trip, he had no clue what that was about. Even so, he was ready to go anywhere Tarek needed him.

—44—

As Tarek walked away from the International Telephone Exchange office in a poor section of Rawalpindi, he imagined the thoughts that must be running through Habibi's mind. Undoubtedly his call had raised Habibi's curiosity.

Things were moving quickly. Tarek was already making plans for his trip to see Sahar to attend the ceremony at Farakka Barrage. It now appeared likely that he would be in India at the same time as the LT team.

The situation presented an opportunity to monitor the team's activities, but Tarek needed help to do it. Habibi had helped Tarek before with such matters, particularly in Algeria. Tarek would have to rely on him once again, this time to help uncover and, if possible, stop the LT plot in India.

In Sahar's last e-mail, she had asked if Tarek knew any businessmen in the UAE who would consider investing in infrastructure projects in West Bengal. She had suggested he could invite them to the ceremony, which was to include a tour of the area, organized by the West Bengal government, to promote trade and investment in the region.

The invitation to foreign businessmen provided an ideal cover for Habibi to go to India. Tarek knew he would feel more confident about his chances of success if Habibi were there to help. There was a down side, however. If Habibi traveled to India, he would be directly involved. If something went wrong, it meant Habibi would be in harm's way, both from the Indian security services and from the LT.

Tarek saw no alternative. Were he operating under the authority of the ISI, he could call on his colleagues to help him, but that wasn't an option. For all intents and purposes, he was running a rogue operation, completely without official sanction.

Even with Habibi's help, lacking information from HV/30 on the LT team's movements, Tarek would have no chance of learning anything of its plans, much less be able to do anything to stop an attack. He was about to implement a plan, however, to address that problem.

—45—

The weather in Washington had been pleasant and mild since General Ali's arrival, although he had hardly noticed, busy as he was trying to settle into his new job as the senior ISI representative in the U.S. He was charged with overseeing the ISI's liaison relationship with the U.S. intelligence community. While in theory, this included liaison with all U.S. intelligence agencies, the reality was he dealt almost exclusively with the Central Intelligence Agency and, in particular, the National Clandestine Service, previously known as the Directorate of Operations.

Dealing with the CIA had always been a complicated affair, charged with political sensitivities for both sides. Now changes brought about by the reorganization of the U.S. intelligence community following the 9/11 attacks had only made the situation more complex. Within the already sprawling U.S. intel community, new levels of bureaucracy had been established, along with new agencies that had overlapping and unclear areas of responsibilities.

Ali's view of the CIA had been shaped primarily by its role in the war against the Soviets in Afghanistan. The CIA had impressed him with its ability to make things happen quickly, and this same high standard of performance was apparent in the early aftermath of the 9/11 attacks.

More recent experience, however, had made it harder for Ali to maintain a positive view of the agency. The once-aggressive organization appeared to have become hamstrung by internal confusion, bureaucratic bloat, and politically driven oversight. Ali's predecessor had warned him that morale at the NCS while on the upswing from its nadir in the months and years following the 9/11 attacks, still was not close to where it had once been and over the last few years, the agency had seen a large exodus of experienced officers frustrated by the situation that had befallen the organization.

Ali had reached the sobering conclusion that the CIA and ISI were both victims of Islamic extremism. The irony was the two organizations were not working as well together as they should against a common enemy. Ali didn't know how they would be able to once again establish strong momentum against the terrorists, but he had every intention of doing his part to stop the extremist movement that had taken the life of Pakistan's former leader and now was promoting events that could plunge his nation into war with India.

The letter Tarek had recently sent the General, using Shahida as a courier, had not improved Ali's outlook. It contained the disturbing news that an LT team was being prepared for a mission into India.

The LT had previously attacked the Indian Parliament, provoking a massive military build-up on the border with Pakistan, whom India held responsible. Other major attacks against civilian targets had taken place in New Delhi and Mumbai. One more large-scale attack would almost certainly cross a red line for the recently installed Indian Nationalist government.

Looking at his day planner, Ali noted his scheduled meeting with his primary interlocutor at the CIA, Dan Barlow, the chief of the South Asia department of the NCS. Barlow was an imposing and distinctive figure, dark skinned, six-feet tall, and solidly built. He kept his head cleanly shaven and was always well-dressed, with a penchant for wearing pastel-colored shirts and matching ties. At their first meeting, Barlow had reminded Ali of a fortyish male model that might appear in ad for menswear at Macy's.

The thought of Barlow as a fashion model made General Ali laugh to himself. Barlow had the deserved reputation of having a no-nonsense, call-it-as-you-see-it approach to things—characteristics that Ali liked in a liaison partner. Ali felt he could work with Barlow and was hopeful they would have a productive relationship, the internal problems of the CIA notwithstanding.

The single item on that day's meeting agenda was the proposed multi-intelligence service conference on the growing opium trade in Afghanistan. Neither Barlow nor Ali was excited by the topic, both believing that the burning issue was the resurgent Taliban, not narcotics. As was often the case, though, it seemed U.S. political considerations were behind the push for the conference which had been urged by the British, who were the ungrateful recipients of the increasing opium production.

Ali spent the morning attending embassy meetings, then after lunch called for his chauffeur to drive him across the river to Langley for his meeting with Barlow. Ali had begun to look forward to his trips to CIA headquarters. The drive down Canal Road and across Chain Bridge was picturesque but, more importantly, it provided him an escape from the dull grind of embassy existence and the demands of an overbearing and irrational ambassador.

In addition to Dan Barlow and Ali, two representatives from the Counternarcotics Center participated in the one-hour meeting to discuss plans for the opium conference. Ali thought it a waste of time, as nothing new was discussed and no decisions made.

"My friend, such meetings are the life blood of bureaucracies," Barlow noted sarcastically as he escorted Ali to the building entrance.

Walking past the memorial wall in the main lobby, Ali stopped to look at the dozens of stars carved in the white marble, each symbolizing a life lost by a CIA officer in the line of duty.

"You know," he said, "I was recently given a tour of FBI Headquarters, and they also have a memorial to their fallen special agents. I am surprised to see that the CIA actually has suffered more casualties than the FBI."

Barlow nodded. "Many people are surprised to learn that the Agency has lost about twice the number of personnel as the FBI, despite the fact that the FBI is a much larger and older institution. People understand that an FBI agent's work can be very dangerous. What they don't grasp is that intelligence work can be more so. Of course, our losses earn us no sympathy; we have no political or popular constituency," Barlow added. "The media and our own politicians have convinced the American people that the CIA is an incompetent, perhaps evil institution. Certainly no president or congressman is going to be re-elected on the basis of his or her support for the CIA."

Thinking of the ISI's own losses, Ali gave an emphatic nod. "It is much the same with the ISI. Intelligence agencies always provide political leadership an easy scapegoat." Ali shook his head. "But what can we do?"

Still looking at the starred wall, Barlow responded, "Our jobs, General. We can do what we signed on to do."

—46—

Tarek was at his apartment when the call finally came at midnight.

"Good evening, Captain Ahmed. You have news?" Tarek asked.

"Indeed, Sir. You were right. The man is in our custody now. He claims not to know anything about the contraband—says he is innocent, of course. But we have it. At least 10 kilos of good-grade opium."

"So, a very good catch, I would say. Any trouble with the apprehension?"

"None at all, Sir. We picked him up as he drove through the checkpoint. I think he was surprised that we would actually search his truck. You would not believe the look on his face when we started pulling the bags out. He said he had no idea how it got there, which is hilarious. I pulled a bag right out from under his seat."

"He will have a hard time explaining that," Tarek said.

"Well, he can tell it to the magistrate. We are almost done with him. He is a simple trucker from the village and no doubt was duped into this."

"I suspect you are right," Tarek said. "How much time do you think he will get."

"It is hard to say. At least five years, possibly more. But you know, he was stupid to get himself involved in this. He has no one to blame but himself."

Tarek was silent for a few moments. "Yes, he will have to live with the consequences of his actions, just as the rest of us do."

He told the captain goodnight and set the phone down on the table beside his chair, continuing to stare blankly at the barren wall across the room for several minutes. What he had done had been necessary, he thought. Still, he took no satisfaction from it.

It was another warm day in Islamabad, and General Huq had worked up a sweat in his walk from Army Headquarters to the IRE building. Ordinarily, he had his driver transport him the six blocks in air-conditioned comfort, but his waist line was in an expanding mode of late, and he had begun taking every opportunity to get in a little exercise. General Huq was a short man who did not carry extra weight well. As a uniformed officer, he knew there was nothing more unsightly than a soldier with a belly hanging over his belt.

The general was not looking forward to his meeting with Ambassador Salim. The team had suffered its first setback, and Huq was not sure how Salim would take the news. He knew Salim's temper—like an angry cobra, some had described it. So far, the general had managed to avoid being on the receiving end of it. Today, however, he suspected that he would not be spared Salim's venom.

After the initial greetings and Salim's offer of tea, Huq got straight to the point. The ambassador said nothing for a few moments, but listened in silence to Huq's explanation of the "problem." When he did speak, it was obvious Salim was doing all he could to control his rage.

"Huq, explain to me, how could a man like this have been selected to be part of this team?" Salim demanded, his face livid. "My God! A drug smuggler! Everything depends on this mission, and we are trusting drug smugglers to carry it out? I thought Shafik handpicked these men."

"It is a shock" Huq said. "Particularly coming so close to the team's deployment. But I want to assure you we have a plan to deal with this."

Salim said nothing but again listened in silence.

"I considered intervening with the police to get the man released, but he had already appeared before a magistrate, and any intervention at this point could result in unwanted attention."

"I agree," Salim said. "We must do nothing to bring any attention to ourselves. There are still those in this government who oppose us. We must not give them any ammunition that they can use to undermine us."

General Huq nodded, relieved that the firestorm of Salim's temper seemed to be past him. "Fortunately, Abu Shafik has a replacement that is particularly well-qualified to fill in. He is the same man who has been sheltering Sheik Osman when he comes out of Kashmir. Additionally, he is a fluent Bangla speaker and has excellent area familiarization."

"Does he trust him?" Salim asked.

"Yes, he does. He would not trust the security of his best commander to the man otherwise."

"I suppose that makes sense. But what about the technical training?"

Huq shook his head. "It is too late for that. The device has already been prepared for shipment and will be loaded on the boat in Karachi within the next three days. Within a week it will be in Chittagong."

"So he doesn't need the training?" Salim asked.

"Ideally, it would be a good thing for him to be trained, but as a backup only, in case something happens to the others. But his primary job will be in a support role—driving a truck, getting supplies, that sort of thing. With his language ability and his knowledge of the area, he will be a true asset for the team even without the training."

"I see," Salim responded. "It sounds workable. But what about our drug smuggler? He has been through the training. He knows the mission is being supported by someone in the Pakistani government. He will be expecting someone to come bail him out. If no one does, he may start talking."

"Yes, that is unfortunately true. We cannot afford to run this risk. I have already discussed it with Abu Shafik, and he will take care of it."

"How?" Salim asked.

"It is necessary that you know the details. Rest assured, Mohammad; the problem will be handled appropriately. "

"Damn it, Huq!" Salim shouted, his eyes intense and his fists clenched. "I will decide what is necessary for me to know. Not you, and certainly not Abu Shafik."

His head bowed, Huq responded, "I apologize. There are a number of Abu Shafik's men currently in custody at the same facility as our drug smuggler. Abu Shafik has provided instructions that the drug smuggler be eliminated as soon as possible."

"Fine," Salim responded, his voice starting to return to normal. "Let me know as soon as this man is dead. I do not want anything left undone in this matter."

"I will. You can count on that," Huq replied.

Apparently satisfied that the matter of the arrest could be laid to rest without any compromise, Salim turned his attention to other details of the mission.

"Now, Huq, let us review. How will we get the device to where we want it?"

"Initially, it will travel by ship. Once the ship makes Chittagong, the package will be transferred to a train. It is marked as manufacturing equipment for a garment factory in Dhaka, and it will have all the necessary paperwork to get it as far as the receiving office at the Dhaka freight office. There, an employee who is a trusted LT sympathizer will take control of it and hold it until our team makes contact. Once the team arrives, they will be put it on a truck that will transport the device and the team to the objective area. At that point, the team will procure a boat for the final approach to the target."

Salim interrupted, "Will it be in assembled form during shipment?"

"No. Again for security, it is better that the device not be assembled, so that should it be examined, it will not appear to be a weapon. Also, the team will need it disassembled in order to carry it in their packs. Except for a systems check, it will not be assembled until the team is in the objective area."

"But how do they plan to get across the border from Bangladesh into India?"

"Where they plan to cross is an open border. Neither government wants to interfere with the flow of goods and people, as it feeds the economy on both sides of the border."

Salim thought for a moment. "So what happens once they are across?"

"The team needs to approach the objective from the up-river side in order to be able to manage the current and get the right placement. To do this, they will proceed to Crowe's Bazar, the closest town of any consequence, and there they will obtain a boat for use in their final approach."

Salim shifted in his seat. "I am not a military man, Huq, but all these transportation arrangements make me nervous. Do you think the team can actually get there without being discovered?"

Huq smiled. "I know they can Ambassador, because we have already done it. A full dress rehearsal was successfully completed last week, using another team of men who had no clue as to the true nature of the mission. I suspected at some point you would raise this question, and I wanted to be able to give you a proof-of-concept. And we have it."

General Huq reached inside his jacket pocket, removed a three-by-five photograph and handed it to Ambassador Salim. In the photo, five dark-eyed men dressed in Bengali *lungis* sat in a boat, all with wide grins on their faces. Behind them in the distance was the faint silhouette of a linear structure rising above the dark water.

Salim looked from the photo to Huq.
"Farakka Barrage?" Salim asked.
"Farakka Barrage," Huq responded.
Salim looked again at the photo and began to smile.

HV/30 did not wait long to signal Tarek for an emergency meeting. He had big news and needed to talk with Tarek immediately.

Tarek arrived at the pick-up point, confident he knew why HV/30 wanted to meet. HV/30 was no sooner inside the car when he literally reached over and grabbed Tarek by the arm. "Rashid, praise Allah you made it. Sheik Osman wants me to go with him on the mission. He ..."

"Settle down, Mahmoud," Tarek told him as he drove away from the pick-up point. "Tell me, calmly, what has happened."

HV/30 released Tarek's arm and sat back in his seat. "O.K., O.K. Here is what happened. One of the team members was arrested."

"By whom? The Indians?" Tarek said, feigning ignorance.

"No! By the provincial police. He was carrying opium in his truck!"

"How do you know this?"

"Because the man arrested is the man in the group that I knew. Remember? He is the one I told you about. Latif. Remember? The trucker that lived in the next village."

"Oh yes, I remember. You didn't say he was a drug smuggler."

"That's because I didn't know!" HV/30 exclaimed. "I am surprised. We all thought he was a religious man. But because he was arrested, Sheik Osman sent word that he wants me to take Latif's place."

"What answer did you give him?"

HV/30 nodded. "I told the messenger that I would go."

"What instructions did he give you?"

"He told me to be in Karachi next Tuesday and to stay at the Royal Guest House. He made me memorize the address, but I wrote it down for you."

HV/30 handed Tarek a slip of paper. Tarek glanced at the note and stuffed it into his shirt pocket.

"Did he give you any other instructions?"

"Yes, he said to bring a couple of changes of clothing. He also said not to tell my family or friends that I am going to Karachi, but to make up a story about where I am going."

"Did he say how long you will be gone?"

"He said not longer than two weeks."

"Did he give you a telephone number or name of who you were to contact in Karachi?"

"No. He said I would be contacted at the guest house by a brother."

At this point, Tarek spotted a place to pull over, stopping the car on the side of the road near a shuttered teahouse.

"Alright, Mahmoud. This is great news. Do you feel up to the task?"

"Definitely. I was afraid that once Sheik Osman left, I would never see him again. I believe now that I will have my vengeance."

"You'll get your revenge, Mahmoud, but you need to do exactly as I tell you. Do you understand?"

"Yes, of course. But how will we be able to stay in touch once I leave Karachi?" HV/30 asked.

"This will be the tricky part; communications always is. I will need to meet with you just prior to your departure from Karachi. By then you should know more than you do now. At that point, I'll provide instructions and a telephone number where you can reach me at any time. Once you have met your contact and have learned as much as you think they are going to tell you about the mission, you will need to call me at the number you already have to set up a meeting using the same procedure I have already taught you. The only difference is that the location of the meeting will have to be in Karachi. Make sure you do not call me from the guesthouse. Go to a public phone exchange and call from there. And Mahmoud— make sure you aren't followed."

"I will make sure, Rashid. But where can we meet? I don't know Karachi at all."

"It will have to be at a location away from the guest house, somewhere that is easy for you to find and gives you a chance to make sure you are not being followed."

"Do you know a place?" HV/30 asked.

Tarek thought for a moment. "I think I do. There is a Navy memorial a few blocks away from the main entrance to the Mohammad Bin Qasim port. It sits back from the street, but it is easy to spot, as it has a tall white ship mast that serves as a centerpiece to the memorial. On the back side of the memorial, opposite the street entrance, is a small courtyard with a fountain. There are steps leading down from the fountain to a larger courtyard where there are some benches. I'll meet you there at the time you signal for. The place is outside and open to the public, so we can meet at anytime that you think is safe."

HV/30 nodded. "Alright, then. I think I have it."

Just to make sure, Tarek took out the aviator notebook and drew a sketch of the site and showed it to HV/30.

"So, think you can find it?" Tarek asked.

"No problem."

Tarek checked the side view mirror, pulled the car back onto the street, and continued driving as he went over some additional points to help prepare HV/30 for what might lay ahead. Once he had finished, he drove back to the general area where he had picked up HV/30 and looked for a place to drop him off.

"You know, Rashid, we do reap what we sow. That is Allah's justice, and through it all things are made right."

"What do you mean?" Tarek asked.

"Latif dealt in drugs and was arrested, and now he is dead and his family will be destitute. This was his punishment. But because of it, I am taking his place, and I will have an opportunity to take vengeance against Sheik Osman for attacking Soriya. This is my reward for my faithfulness and patience. This is true justice."

Tarek had heard nothing beyond the news that Latif was dead. "Latif is dead? How?"

"The day after he was arrested, he was found stabbed to death in the prison yard. Everyone suspects that the gangsters Latif was working for arranged his killing so he would not talk. You know talk in that kind of business is dangerous."

After a few moments, Tarek said, "Yes, talk is dangerous. I guess Latif could have compromised the whole enterprise if he had started talking."

"Yes, he could have. But he isn't talking now."

Tarek suddenly had no interest in continuing with the meeting. He slowed the car and pulled to the side of the street.

"O.K. Mahmoud, this is where you get out. I'll see you in Karachi as we discussed. Until then, be safe. *Khoda Hafez.*"

"You as well, my brother." HV/30 got out of the car and disappeared into the night.

Tarek quickly pulled back onto the street and made his way to the highway headed toward Islamabad. The news of Latif's death, a man he had never seen, was so unexpected and disturbing that Tarek could think of nothing else. As he left the outskirts of Wah and drove down the black empty road, a cold rain began to fall.

Tarek tried to console himself that Latif's death was an unintended consequence of a necessary action and that the man was involved in a plot that could lead to Pakistan's destruction. Still, Tarek could not avoid the great darkness that engulfed him.

— 49 —

It was late when the phone rang. Sahar, who had just dozed off to sleep, was instantly wide awake, her heart racing, hoping it would be Tarek. She hadn't heard from him in more than a week and was desperately worried something had happened. She picked up the phone to hear the voice she longed for.

"Sahar? I hope I have not awakened you. I know it's late, but I could not make myself wait until tomorrow to call you." Tarek said.

"Tarek, I am so glad it is you. I was so worried that something was wrong. Are you alright?"

"I'm fine. I'm sorry I have not been in touch, but I have been so busy with travel that I have hardly had a moment to sit still. I feel terrible that I made you worry."

"You are forgiven," Sahar said, "but only if you tell me you will be in New Delhi next week as you promised. I think I will die if you say you cannot come."

"Nothing could stop me from being with you next week, Sahar. I miss you so badly. I ache for you, body and soul," Tarek said.

"And I for you, Tarek."

The sweet sound of Sahar's voice was both a soothing balm and an inflammatory agent for Tarek's increasingly strained emotions. If he had ever forgotten how badly he needed this woman, he was again acutely aware of it.

"When will you be here?" Sahar asked. "I want us to spend some time together before we travel to the ceremony. Once we leave for that, we won't have much time alone."

"I was thinking the same thing. I have reservations to arrive a week from today."

"That's wonderful! That will give us three days here in Delhi before we go to Calcutta. From there we will travel by air to Malda, then take a bus to Farakka Barrage for the ceremony. It is going to be great, Tarek! We have to make up for lost time."

Tarek smiled to himself as he imagined once again being with Sahar. "I will do my part," he said.

Sahar laughed. "Of that I have no doubt. Are you bringing any business contacts to tour the area for investment possibilities?"

"There is a prominent UAE businessman and friend who is very much interested in making the trip," said Tarek. "I'll send you his name by email tomorrow."

"Oh, that's great!" Sahar said. "I will pass his name along with yours to the protocol office."

They talked for another half hour, and it was all either of them could do to say goodbye. After he hung up the phone, Tarek gave some thought to what Sahar had just said. The fact that they would first go to Calcutta before traveling to Farakka Barrage was news to him. He wondered how it would play into his efforts against the LT team.

On the surface, it seemed it could work to his benefit. Calcutta was at the top of Tarek's list as the likely target for the team. But there were so many uncertainties it was impossible to say what if any advantage would come from his being in Calcutta. Only time would tell.

— 50 —

A hot wind was blowing off the Arabian Gulf as Habibi waited for Tarek at the arched entryway of a shopping mall a few kilometers east of Abu Dhabi. The mall's location on the coast gave it a commanding view of the Gulf, and Habibi passed the minutes watching giant cargo ships slip slowly by.

Stoic as he could be about physical discomforts, the heat was beginning to get the best of him. He was about to take temporary refuge in one of the air conditioned shops when he spotted Tarek in the back seat of a taxi pulling up to the curb.

Habibi waited a few more moments until Tarek left the car and, after establishing eye contact, turned and walked through the entryway into the outdoor mall. Tarek followed and for the next five minutes shadowed Habibi as he window-shopped, admiring the glittering gold jewelry and fine Swiss watches that were prominently displayed.

At last Habibi turned into a narrow alley that led to a covered parking lot. Tarek followed a short distance behind him. Habibi walked to his Land Cruiser, unlocked the doors by remote and got in the vehicle. Tarek walked to the opposite side, opened the front passenger door and climbed inside. The two men turned toward each other.

"Salam Aleikum, my friend," Habibi said. He leaned across and bear-hugged Tarek.

"Aleikum Salam," Tarek replied with some difficulty, as Habibi nearly squeezed the life out of him.

Habibi released Tarek and slapped him on his knee.

"You know, you have brought me out of my air conditioned office on the hottest day of the year. You will owe me for this my Pakistani friend. I hope you are here to discuss a trip to Oslo, or perhaps Zurich, where I might cool off a bit. If this is the case, your debt will be smaller."

Tarek laughed as Habibi cranked up the Land Cruiser, put the AC on high and began to work his way out of the parking lot. Glancing at Tarek, he raised an eyebrow and said, "All right, just exactly where is it you would like me to go?"

"India."

Habibi chuckled as he pulled onto the coastal highway headed toward Abu Dhabi. "Well, I have to say, I had assumed this would be the case. But I did have hopes that perhaps we would be going where it was a bit cooler."

"It will not be cool but I promise you, it will be interesting," Tarek said.

"All things with you are interesting my friend. I think that is the only reason I put up with you. Well, then, if you need me to go to India, so be it. I will go. Although I find Indian men can sometimes test my patience, this is more than made up for by the beauty of the women and the fantastic cuisine."

"I'm glad you are not blind to the benefits of my travel plan," Tarek responded. "I'll fill you in on the details when we get to the apartment and can relax. In the meantime, tell me about what you have been up to. And the family? I pray they are all well?"

For the remainder of the drive, the two men talked of family and Habibi discussed some of his most recent business activities. Tarek relished every moment of the light discussion. It had been so long since he had an opportunity to just relax and talk in the company of someone he counted as a friend.

Habibi took Tarek to the same apartment building where they had met the previous times. The number of cars parked in the underground garage indicated the occupancy rate of the building had gone up considerably.

"Habibi, are you sure you have an empty apartment for us?" Tarek asked.

"Not only do I have an apartment, I have the best apartment. I think you will be impressed."

Habibi parked the car, then the two men left the vehicle and walked to an elevator. Stepping in, Habibi swiped a card in front of an electronic sensor and pushed the button for the top floor. After the non-stop ascent, they exited and walked down the hall to a double-wide doorway. As he punched in a combination to an electronic lock, Habibi turned to Tarek with a grin. "I wish all doors could be this wide."

Tarek was indeed impressed. It was a penthouse apartment decorated in a modern motif, with clean lines and a minimalist style.

"This is beautiful. Why isn't it leased? You could get a fortune for it."

Habibi motioned for Tarek to have a seat in the living room, where wide windows provided a spectacular view of the coast. In the city below, the evening lights were starting to shine as dusk turned to night.

Sitting down in a red leather chair, Habibi looked at Tarek and said, "I've been keeping this apartment off the market for a while, thinking that a certain friend from Pakistan might like to entertain his lady in style. But alas, he has yet to make good on his claim that he would return with her."

"You are kidding, aren't you?" Tarek asked, dumbfounded that Habibi was not renting it out so he and Sahar could perhaps one day stay there.

"No, I am not kidding. But don't worry about it." Habibi said. "I have let a few of my out-of-town business contacts stay here. It makes for good business." Habibi paused and said in an emphatic manner, "I really do want you and Sahar to use it. I know how much you care for her, and I want the both of you to stay here and enjoy yourselves."

"But Habibi, by not renting this place you are forfeiting a lot of money. I do not want you doing this on my account."

"That's your problem Tarek." Habibi responded, an edge in his voice. "You never permit anyone to do anything for you. Why do you think you are so different? Everyone needs a favor or a good break every now and then, even ISI officers. You know Tarek, you are human. I've known you for many years now, and you always are thinking and planning ahead. You are always working hard, devoting every moment of your life to your work. It is as if everything is a crisis, and only you can prevent disaster. Have you ever thought for a moment that the world might just be able to get along even if you are not out there trying to save it?"

Tarek was a little taken aback by Habibi's tone, but he knew the words were well-intentioned. He also knew Habibi was right. He *had* spent his entire career immersed in working one crisis after the other, always heading toward the sound of the guns.

But what was wrong with that, he thought. He was a professional intelligence officer, after all. It was his job to do the tough tasks.

Even so, Tarek had seen problems develop in officers who always followed that same philosophy: a certain distancing of themselves from anything routine and a general inability to keep their attention on any one thing for very long—almost a compulsive restlessness. Tarek knew he fit that profile.

"Habibi, I know what you are saying, and I don't disagree with you. The rush of adrenaline is probably part of why I'm the way I am, but that may not completely explain it."

Habibi nodded. "I've watched you for a long time Tarek, and I think I can put my finger on it. You use your professional life to escape from real life. Some people use drugs, or video games, or whatever—but you use your work. The question you need to ask yourself is, 'Why?' You have become a martyr to your profession. The only difference between you and one of those fanatical suicide bombers is that you are not killing innocent people. But you are sacrificing a life nonetheless—your own life. And you know what? You don't have to. You are not the only one doing your job. My God, at this point you have more than met your professional obligations. It is time for you to back off a bit and put some balance in your life, while you still have some good years ahead of you. Think about it Tarek; you could retire if you wanted to and do something completely different. Start a new life. Even go into business with me."

Habibi stopped and smiled for an instant. "And I would be your boss, which I think would be a very nice turn of the tables. And now that you have met Sahar, what a great time to make a change."

As he listened, Tarek thought that it sometimes seemed as if Habibi were his conscience, reminding him of truths about himself he already knew but refused to deal with.

He did want to make a new start. He already was imagining himself and Sahar sharing all the good things that life had to offer. Maybe even raising children, or traveling the world. It suddenly became clear to Tarek: If he was to ever have a chance at such a future, the time to take that chance was now.

For an instant he felt as if a great weight had been lifted from him. This was the time for him to make a change, and it suddenly seemed urgent that he do so. There was just one more thing he had to do.

"Habibi you are a persuasive man, and a true friend. I have heard your words, and I plan to heed them," Tarek said.

Habibi smiled widely. "I think you actually mean it."

"Oh, I mean it."

"But?" Habibi said with a touch of suspicion in his voice.

Tarek looked Habibi in the eye. "I have one last thing to do, and that is why I need you to come with me to India."

"Did you hear anything I just said, Tarek? Does it have to be you that does this? Surely the ISI has someone else who can go on this mission. Sure, you should go to India, but not for work. Go there to lay claim to Sahar."

Tarek shook his head. "There is no one else who can do this, Harun. In other work I've done, others could have filled in. But not now. Not this time. I'm a one-man show, and that's why I need your help. I still plan to 'lay claim to Sahar' as you so quaintly say, but I, or rather we, have to stop something from happening. If we don't, it could mean millions will die."

Habibi studied Tarek's face and sighed, "Oh that's not fair, Tarek," he said. "Millions may die! Did they teach you this stuff at ISI's spy school?" Shaking his big head in resignation, Habibi said, "Okay, my brother. So we're still going to India. Now tell me, what on earth are we going to do there."

Tarek had to smile at his large friend. "Habibi, you are as loyal as they come. Make yourself comfortable. We have a lot to talk about."

For the rest of the evening, as the lights of ships anchored far off the coast twinkled through the window, Tarek discussed the situation with Habibi, providing him with as many details as he thought prudent. Tarek explained about HV/30, calling him by his true first name, and his information on the LT team. He also briefed him on likely support to the LT mission by sympathetic Pakistani military elements that were in touch with Abu Shafik. Tarek explained that his mission was not authorized by ISI headquarters, and the only person knowledgeable about it was his former boss, General Ali, now assigned in Washington.

When Tarek was finished, Habibi asked, "Why don't you just go to the Indians? Let them stop it."

"I wish it were that simple," Tarek responded. "If we told the Indians, we would be taking a huge risk. Just the fact alone that members of my government are behind the plot might be enough for the Indians to go to war with us."

"Do you really think so? Going to war is a big step," Habibi said.

"Harun, you have to keep in mind that the new government in Delhi is nationalistic to the extreme. Part of their campaign in winning office was a pledge to go to war with Pakistan should it be involved in supporting terrorism against India. Telling them information about this plot might give them just what they need to justify an attack. No, Harun, I have to do everything I can to stop this first. Only if I get to the point where I know there is no possibility of succeeding can I take a chance and go to the Indians."

"Well, I'm not sure I agree, but you're the boss. What can I do to help?" Habibi asked.

"I met with Mahmoud less than 48 hours ago in Karachi. He told me that the following day, now yesterday, he was to board a ship bound for Chittagong," Tarek said. "Unfortunately, he did not know the name of the ship or when it would arrive in Chittagong."

"And you want me to try to identify the ship they sailed on?" Habibi asked.

"That's right. According to Mahmoud, one of the LT members told him the ship's last port prior to arriving Karachi was Dubai. I thought your contacts at the port might be able to provide some helpful information."

"Of course there are a number of ships that leave Dubai for Karachi on any given day, but some of the details that Mahmoud gave you should help narrow it down."

Tarek nodded. "But how about in Chittagong? Do you have anyone who could help you find out about the ship there?"

"Maybe. I don't know any Bangladeshi port officials, but I do have a shipping agent there whom I keep on retainer. We don't do a lot of business out of Bangladesh, but occasionally we handle a few containers coming from there."

"That could be useful. Where is his office?" Tarek asked.

"He has offices in both Chittagong and Dhaka. He primarily deals in garment shipments, and most of the factories are in Dhaka."

Tarek turned the discussion to another area of critical importance—communications. "Habibi, because this operation is off the books, I have no access to communications gear and without communication we are dead in the water. The problem is that the cell coverage in some of the areas we will be in is spotty at best, so we need a dependable back-up to our cell phones. I know you use satellite phones for some of your company's construction projects in remote areas. Do you have any we can take with us to India?

"Only a room full," Habibi said with a chuckle. "How many do we need?"

Tarek breathed a sigh of relief. "Four. We each will need one plus a back-up, plus chargers and spare batteries."

"No problem."

"Well, there still may be a problem," Tarek said.

"What is that?"

"We need to get them into India without drawing any suspicion to ourselves, so I'd rather we didn't bring them with us on the plane."

Habibi laughed. "Tarek, you are so paranoid. I take the damned things with me all the time. No one gives them a second glance."

Tarek smiled. "It's my job to be paranoid, Habibi. We can carry cell phones in. That is no problem. Everybody has a cell phone, but few have satellite phones."

"That's true, but I still think we could just bring our sat phones with us."

Tarek shook his head. "No way."

"So what do you suggest?"

"As I recall, you have a company rep in Delhi. Could you send the phones there via DHL and ask the rep to hold them for you?"

"Consider it done," Habibi responded. "But Tarek, how will Mahmoud be able to contact us? He doesn't have a phone, and he doesn't know any of the phone numbers of the phones we will ship out to India?"

"Well, he will have to call us from telephone exchanges whenever he can do so safely, and he already has two telephone numbers." Tarek replied.

"What numbers are those?" Habibi asked, puzzled.

"He has my cell phone number, and I took the liberty to give him your personal satellite phone number that you have on your business card, so you will need to make sure that your phone is one of those you ship to your New Delhi affiliate, and then let me use it."

"Thanks for handing out my number to a stranger," Habibi said, affecting irritation, which Tarek ignored.

"Now another question: How are you funding your travel and expenses, since this operation is not officially sanctioned?" Habibi asked.

"Ah yes, the funding," Tarek replied. "Thanks to General Ali, I do have some funds that he approved for my use while he was still Chief of Operations, which means that from the money side I am covered, although if I ever do my accounting, I may have to get a little creative."

"Ah, don't worry about it. You'll be headed toward retirement soon."

Tarek chuckled, "Or jail, depending on how this all works out."

By the end of the evening, Tarek felt like they had a workable plan. Now if only HV/30 could do his part, there was even a slim chance of the plan succeeding.

—51—

For the next three days, Tarek and Habibi continued to plan for their travel to New Delhi. Habibi had quickly shipped the satellite phones to his affiliate office and had already received confirmation of the package's safe arrival.

Tarek had been so busy making final preparations that he had little time to think of Sahar. As he and Habibi finally relaxed in the apartment a few hours before their departure from the UAE, Tarek turned his mind from the mission to think about being reunited with Sahar. Once again, doubts began to enter his mind. Although their long-distance relationship felt strong, he worried that once they saw each other again, Sahar might decide she no longer felt the same way about him. Tarek knew he would be devastated if that happened.

Habibi sensed Tarek's thoughts. "Brother, this is all going to work out. And when it does, you will be on your way to a new life with the woman of your dreams. You are such a lucky man. A new beginning and a beautiful woman to be there with you. Praise Allah."

Tarek had to laugh. Habibi could be so optimistic, so positive. It seemed life was just one big joyous party for him, and he could make the people around him feel that way too.

"You're right, brother. It will be fine. And speaking of women, why don't you go spend some time with your wife, and I'll see you at the airport in three hours. Give my regards to her, and tell her I will keep care of you."

"My wife likes you, Tarek, but she does not like you taking me away from her. She is so possessive, you know. I think all women are like that."

"Yes, it's true," Tarek agreed. "Meena is the same way. She hates it when her husband goes away, though I have no idea why, since I don't think she really even likes the man."

Habibi looked at Tarek and said, "You know, I doubt that Sahar will be any different."

Tarek thought for a moment. "That's fine with me," he replied. "I don't ever plan to leave her."

* * * * *

Three hours later Tarek cleared airport security and walked to the British Airways gate. He spotted Habibi, but did not approach him and he took a seat in the waiting area. Shortly afterward, the flight began to board. As Tarek passed the ticket agent, Habibi entered the jet way a short distance ahead of him, a huge grin on his face as he imagined the adventure he and Tarek were embarking on.

It was just like old times.

—52—

Five hours after taking off from Abu Dhabi, Tarek's fantasy became a reality – he was with Sahar again after so many weeks of separation. Any doubts he had about how she would feel about him were vanquished with their first embrace. At their introduction, Tarek could tell Sahar and Habibi would get along well. Engineer Advani had not come to the airport but warmly greeted them when they finally arrived at his residence.

A light meal had been prepared for the travelers. Later, tea was served and the four of them sat comfortably in the living room engaged in easy conversation. The occasion provided an opportunity for Habibi to talk about his business interests, which Advani was very interested in discussing. Both having worked on projects in North Africa, Advani and Habibi had many similar experiences. The conversation ultimately led to Advani explaining the plan for the trip to Farakka Barrage and the associated tour of West Bengal Province.

"Well, gentlemen," Advani began. "So far there are about 100 individuals signed up to take the tour, all potential international investors and representatives of companies specializing in rural development. Our Trade and Industry Ministry is extremely pleased with the level of interest, as is the governor of West Bengal, who happens to be the son of an old friend of mine going all the way back to my childhood days."

"I don't know if you knew this, Tarek," Sahar interjected, "but Father spent his youth in Calcutta."

Tarek nodded, "Yes, I know. We talked about this quite a bit when I first visited here." Turning to look at Advani, Tarek added, "I recall that you told me the house that you grew up in was very near Tagore's childhood home. In my humble opinion, his poetry is the best ever written."

"Your opinion agrees with that of many others," Advani responded. "I believe within a few more decades he will be as widely regarded as Rumi or Hafez. Do you agree, Tarek?"

Tarek nodded, "I place him in their ranks now. One has only to read *Gitanjali* to know he is equal to them both. Do you think I might have the opportunity to visit his home while we are in Calcutta? I understand it is possible to visit there."

"Yes, of course. I will arrange a special tour. After all, I am connected to the governor," Advani said with a wink.

"I hate to be the one to bring an end to this most enjoyable time, but I believe if I do not get to my hotel soon, I may embarrass myself by falling asleep right where I sit," Habibi said,

"Please, won't you change your mind and stay here with us? There is a spare room in the guest house right around the corner from where Tarek will stay," Sahar pleaded.

Habibi smiled and thanked Sahar for the offer but for a second time he declined, saying he had already arranged a meeting at his hotel the following morning with a representative from his company's New Delhi office.

Habibi's representative would be bringing the satellite phones Habibi had sent by DHL. Tarek would feel much better once they had the phones in hand. Next to maintaining security, establishing reliable communications was the most critical operational requirement.

"Alright then, Sir, if you must go, my driver will take you."

At Advani's words, the group rose and made their way to the residence entrance, bidding goodnight to Habibi. Then, Advani said goodnight to Tarek and Sahar and slowly climbed the stairs to the upstairs bedrooms.

Tarek and Sahar walked to the side door leading out to the garden. A softly lit walkway led to the small guesthouse where Tarek would stay.

A slight breeze was stirring as they stepped outside. The leaves of the trees and shrubs rustled lightly, and the sweet scent of tube roses filled the air. Being with Sahar, alone in the garden after so many weeks without her, was almost too much for Tarek, who wanted nothing more than to have her right there. As they embraced and kissed, his desire became even stronger.

Sahar's own passion rising, she pulled away, softly saying, "No, wait. Not now."

Tarek knew she was right. He would have to be patient until the right time came along. Perhaps at some point during the trip to Farakka they could find some time to be alone together.

As Sahar stepped back from him, she squeezed his hand and softly said, "Come this way."

To Tarek immense surprise, Sahar led him down the garden path and into his room, then closed the door. A small table lamp burned in the corner, casting a dim yellow glow. Sahar kissed Tarek and pulled a pin from her hair, letting it fall to her shoulders. She kissed Tarek again, this time much more slowly than the first, and walked to the bed. Looking back over her shoulder at Tarek, she unpinned her silk Sari. It slipped off her smooth skin to the floor.

Sahar stood looking at Tarek, her body perfect and inviting. She was the most delicious sight Tarek had ever seen and he did not, could not, delay in taking her—or perhaps, he thought later, it was she who took him.

Now that he was in New Delhi, there was little Tarek could do but wait for HV/30 to call. He expected the next communication with HV/30 would likely be critical and might even provide him with the LT team's target. Once that was known, he and Habibi would have a much better idea of what they could do to stop the team before it struck.

Tarek continued to believe the target would be in Calcutta. The team members all spoke Bangla and were going to Chittagong. From there, it would be a relatively quick trip to reach Calcutta by traveling across the southern part of Bangladesh via Kulna and Jessore. Crossing the Bangladesh-India border would pose no problem for the team members, as they all could easily pass as locals.

Late on the third day, Habibi came through with a nugget of information. His shipping agent's office in Chittagong had determined that only one ship from Karachi had made port in Chittagong in the last several days: a Moroccan-flagged vessel named the Desert Star had arrived just the previous day. According to its itinerary, the last port of call prior to Karachi was Dubai.

The itinerary matched perfectly with the information about the ship that HV/30 had provided Tarek at their meeting in Karachi. If it was the that HV/30 and his companions had traveled on, it meant HV/30 would be contacting him in the near future. All depended on HV/30's ability to get away from his fellow travelers long enough to find an international telephone exchange.

Tarek did not have to wait long for the call. Mid-morning on his final day in Delhi, Tarek was packing his clothes when his cell phone rang. It was the most welcome sound he had heard in a long time. Taking the phone from the battery charger, he answered, "Yes."

"Brother!" Tarek recognized HV/30's voice instantly.

"Mahmoud, it is good to hear your voice. How are things?"

"Things are good, and I have some news but only a little time to tell you, so please listen carefully. We arrived in Chittagong two days ago and we leave by bus for Dhaka tonight or maybe tomorrow."

Tarek was surprised. If Calcutta was the team's destination, traveling by way of Dhaka was taking the long way.

"What is your final destination?" Tarek asked.

"I don't know," HV/30 said. "I've been instructed to rent a truck or van once we get to Dhaka and to get some food and other provisions. We will pick something up there, a crate with some equipment in it that Osman said we will need for the job. And no, I don't know what the equipment is or what it will be used for," HV/30 said, anticipating what Tarek's next question would be.

"What about the team? Is it intact or have some members split off?"

"No, we are all here."

"And Sheik Osman?"

"He is here as well."

"Has anyone contacted the team since your arrival in Chittagong?" Tarek inquired.

"No. Not that I'm aware of."

"How were you able to get away to call?"

"It was easy. I am responsible for obtaining the supplies for the team. Sheik Osman wants the team to keep a low profile, so they are staying in a guesthouse while I go out to get whatever is needed. Oh, that reminds me. When we get to Dhaka, I am supposed to buy cell phones for each of team members."

"Interesting," Tarek said more to himself than to HV/30. "Once you make the purchase, make sure you copy the numbers off each phone and give them to me when you are able to call."

Even as he said this, Tarek realized there would be nothing he could do to exploit the phones since he was on his own and had no access to any technical monitoring systems. Still, as an intelligence officer, the force of habit was too strong. He wanted those phone numbers.

"Alright Rashid, I'll do it, but I need to go now. I don't want to stay away too long. I will try to call you from Dhaka if the opportunity comes along."

"Excellent. Good work my friend. Be careful. Khoda Hafez," Tarek said.

"Khoda Hafez," HV/30 said and hung up the phone.

Tarek felt a sense of relief that contact with HV/30 was now reestablished. That feeling, however, was quickly replaced by a sense of foreboding as Tarek realized that the team was now closer to India and things were coalescing toward some as-yet-undetermined conclusion.

Tarek considered calling General Ali in Washington to give him a cryptic update. Although he knew there was nothing Ali could do about the events that were transpiring, Tarek wanted someone else to know what was going on. He decided to wait, however, until after the next contact with HV/30. Hopefully, he would then have more details to share with Ali.

He finished packing his suitcase for the trip to Calcutta. As he started down the walkway to the Advani residence, he spotted Habibi coming from the other direction.

"Salam Aleikum," Habibi said, his voice booming.

"Aleikum Salam. You are later than I expected. That is not like you. I was beginning to worry."

"Oh, I just was moving slowly this morning," Habibi replied.

"Did you speak with Sahar?" Tarek asked.

"No, the house girl said they were upstairs preparing for the journey. She offered me tea, but I said I would come see you first."

"Well I'm glad you are here," Tarek said. He motioned to some patio chairs. "Come let's sit for a few minutes. I have news."

Habibi eyes grew wide. "Our friend called?"

Tarek nodded.

"Where was he? In Bangladesh?"

Tarek nodded again. "In Chittagong with the LT team."

"And?"

"Well, there is a surprise. The team is moving to Dhaka either today or tomorrow. Mahmoud believes that is only a temporary destination, however, as once they arrive, he has been tasked to get a truck and supplies, including cell phones for the team. He also said they will be picking something up in Dhaka, but he does not know what it is."

"Hmm. Why Dhaka if they are going to Calcutta?"

"They must need whatever is in Dhaka, so to Dhaka they must go." Tarek hesitated for a moment.

"But?" Habibi said, his eyebrows arching over his wide-set eyes.

"It is always possible my theory is wrong. They may be headed to another part of India and not Calcutta. For all I know, they could even be headed here to New Delhi. The last LT attack here was a couple of years ago."

"Yes, I know. They blew a shopping market to bits, killing dozens. I doubt the LT would try again in Delhi though, and certainly not Mumbai. Not after all the carnage they caused there. They have heated both cities up too much and, as we have seen, the Indians have a lot of police on the streets. And besides that, why would everyone on the team speak Bangla if they are coming to Delhi?" Habibi asked.

"Well, it could be they need the Bangla to do whatever it is they are going to do in Dhaka."

"I don't buy that," Habibi said shaking his big head like a bulldog with a bone locked in its jaws. "These guys need the Bangla language for their mission in India, and Calcutta is the center of the universe as far as Bangla is concerned."

Tarek chuckled at Habibi's decisive assessment. "I'm thinking the same thing, brother. I just needed to hear that you agree."

"Did Mahmoud say how long they would be in Dhaka?" Habibi asked.

"No. He didn't know. My guess is it won't be long—a couple of days probably. Why?" Tarek could tell Habibi had an idea.

"Well, I could fly to Dhaka from Calcutta. That way I would be in position if Mahmoud comes through and provides us with some actionable information. Of course, I would have to bow out of the tour and the commemoration ceremony, but I could tell our hosts that a business emergency has come up and I need to get over to Dhaka to sort it out. I'm sure they would understand."

Tarek considered for a moment. "As much as I hate to admit it, particularly since I did not think of it myself, it is not a bad idea. Having you in proximity of the team could make all the difference, particularly if Mahmoud can give us some details to work with."

"That's right," Habibi said. "It's been a while since I've been there, but I'm sure I could check some things out if I had some basic leads to go on."

"And you do have your shipping agent there; he could be helpful." Tarek said.

After considering the suggestion for a couple of seconds, he made his decision. "Alright Habibi, let's plan on your going to Calcutta as scheduled, but if we have not heard anything further from Mahmoud by the time of our arrival there, you will need to get to Dhaka."

"That should not be a problem," Habibi said, glad for the prospect of action. "I'm sure there are at least a couple of flights a day between the two cities. The worst part is I may have to fly on Bangladesh Airlines."

"Oh, don't worry brother, flight time between Calcutta and Dhaka can't be very long. Once you leave Calcutta, you'll be back on the ground before you know it."

"Yes, that's what I'm afraid of," Habibi chuckled.

Tarek relaxed a bit and sat back in the patio chair. "I feel better now. We have a plan and are taking the initiative. I hate waiting around, being dependent on somebody else making a move."

"I feel the same way. We are taking a little bit of a risk, since the team may not be in Dhaka long enough for me to find out anything, and they still could show up in Calcutta. In that case, you would be on your own until I could make my way back. But by staying here, you will continue to keep your cover should anyone be looking at you."

"At this point, screw the cover," Tarek responded. "I have to do everything I can to find out where these guys are going and somehow get them to abort their mission. Cover or no cover."

"Aren't you worried about Indian security? The Farakka Barrage ceremony and the tour are government sponsored events, you know. They have got to be paying attention to the foreigners on the guest list, where, may I remind you, both you and I are prominently listed." Habibi flashed a smile. "I, however, am not Pakistani, but a well-established Arab businessman. You, Sir, are neither of these things. Although your ex-pat UAE residency papers may buy you some consideration, the fact of your Pakistani origins will not be lost on them."

"Thanks for the encouragement, my Arab friend," Tarek said.

The two men looked at each other for a moment, not really wanting to think too much about all the things that could go wrong.

Finally Tarek said, "Let's go say good morning to our hosts and see if we can beg some tea."

—54—

The thick haze over Calcutta was an ugly brown, the air still and stifling hot. Standing on the outdoor observation platform at Calcutta International Airport, Anil was oblivious to it all. His eyes searched the sky for the plane carrying the visitors. Seeing nothing, he turned to Mathir and asked for the tenth time, "Are you sure all preparations have been made and that you've left nothing undone?"

"Please Anil, give me credit here," Mathir replied patiently. "I have worked for the Protocol Office since the time you were a boy playing with sticks in the mud. Everything is prepared. The police are in place ready to block off the major intersections, and the hotel is prepared to receive our VIPs."

Anil nodded. "It sounds good, Mathir. You have done your planning well. Let's hope we have not forgotten anything. I want . . ." Anil stopped in mid-sentence, a panicked look on his face. "Oh, did you remember to talk to that police Captain? He seemed somewhat agitated when I talked to him."

Mathir nodded, "Yes, I talked to him and an Intelligence Bureau Inspector as well."

"An Intelligence Bureau Inspector?" Anil's eyes went wide. "What did he want?"

"He just asked me to bring him our visitors' passports before I turn them over to the hotel for registration."

"Why? If he wants to see the documents why doesn't he just get the hotel to give them to him?"

Mathir laughed. "He could, but the Intelligence Bureau doesn't work like that. They don't trust anybody, particularly not some hotel clerk. They prefer to work with people they know well and can trust. People like me."

Anil was becoming annoyed. "I am the senior protocol officer in West Bengal. If Intelligence Bureau needs my office's assistance, they need to come to me, not you."

"Yes, yes, of course. I'll be sure to tell them," Mathir answered. The IB had already informed him they wanted as little to do with Anil as possible.

Mathir looked back toward the main runway. "Well, it looks like our guests have arrived."

"What?" Anil spun around to see. "Oh, my God! The plane is already on the ground. Let's go! Let's go! We must be at the gate when they disembark!"

Mathir shook his head and chuckled as he watched Anil scurry into the terminal.

A short while later, Anil and Mathir were greeting Engineer Advani and his small entourage. "Your baggage claim tickets, please," Mathir told the group. "I will arrange for the bags to be transported to the hotel and," he added, addressing Tarek and Habibi directly, "if I may have your passports, they will be needed for hotel registration, which I will handle personally for you."

As Mathir departed, passports and baggage claim tickets in hand, Anil invited the group to follow him through the airport terminal and out a special exit, where a black Mercedes sedan waited. Anil opened the right-rear passenger door and motioned grandly for Sahar to enter the car. Tarek and Advani joined Sahar in the back—without invitation—and Habibi sat in the front.

"I hope the ride to the hotel is comfortable," Anil said through Sahar's open window. "It should take about 30 minutes to get there. I'll be in a separate vehicle right behind you."

With that, he waved for the driver to go. As the Mercedes drove away, Anil took out his cell phone and called Mathir.

"What?" Mathir answered as he struggled with six pieces of baggage.

Mathir's impolite response sent a bolt of anger through Anil.

"Don't say 'what'," Anil scolded.

"Why?" Mathir replied, which only exasperated Anil further.

"For God's sake, man! You are a protocol officer! Now act like one."

"I would," Mathir responded, "but right now I am acting like a bellboy pulling two carts full of luggage, and I am dripping with sweat. You know, I just had this suit cleaned!"

"Why didn't you get someone to help you? The office can afford a few rupees for these kinds of expenses," Anil asked, without the slightest sympathy in his tone of voice.

"Because the rules have changed! Airport security does not allow baggage bearers to come inside the airport. They have to wait outside. I told you this last week."

"You did no such thing," Anil said.

By this time Mathir was furious, and quickly tiring of this pointless discussion. With all the self-control he could muster, he responded in a conciliatory tone. "It doesn't matter now. I have reached the car and will be on my way to the hotel."

"Wonderful!" Anil said. "I'll see you there. Remember, we are taking them to the VIP room for tea and biscuits upon arrival at the hotel. That should give you enough time to get their bags to the rooms. Oh, how about the passports? When will you get them to the Intelligence Bureau?"

"It has already been done. My IB contacts met me a few minutes ago and looked at the passports in their office here at the airport."

"Fine, then. Our foreign guests should not be troubled by the IB during their visit here."

"Not unless the Intelligence Bureau determines they are terrorists," Mathir said.

"Really, Mathir! Somehow I doubt that Engineer Advani would invite terrorists to the commemoration of one of his crowning achievements."

"Well, Anil, as you are fond of saying, there is no accounting for taste, and they were interested enough to make a copy of Mr. Durrani's passport."

"Please, Mathir. You are wearing my nerves thin, and this is only the first group to arrive. Thank God the others don't come until tomorrow evening. I must be in tiptop shape. Our rep from the UN will be in one of those groups, and I do not want to disappoint."

"Right," Mathir responded with feigned interest. "Listen, the bags are in the car, and I'm going. So goodbye."

Anil stood for a moment looking at his silent cell phone, then snapped it shut and started off toward his car, cursing Mathir as he went.

Thirty minutes later, all was well and Anil's anger with Mathir was forgotten. The Advani entourage was checked into the Taligange Hotel and had gathered in the VIP lounge awaiting the arrival of Governor Ghule.

Tarek and Sahar were seated together on the couch. Advani stood admiring a painting by a local artist when Habibi entered the room, a disturbed look on his face.

"What is it?" Tarek asked. "Is something wrong?"

"I'm afraid so," Habibi responded. "It seems a cousin of mine who runs a clothing import business is having problems with his supplier in Dhaka. The supplier has not delivered on his agreement to ship a large consignment of garments that my cousin needs to meet his contract obligation with an American buyer."

By now Advani had picked up on the conversation and walked over to where Tarek and Habibi were talking. "Is there something we can do to assist?" Advani asked. "I have many contacts in Dhaka who might be able to help in this matter."

Habibi smiled at Advani. "Thank you for your kind offer Engineer," he said, "however, my cousin wishes to handle this as quietly as possible, as he is concerned that the U.S. buyer might somehow get wind of the delay and possibly cancel the deal. The problem is, the supplier is in Bangkok on business and my cousin has been unable to reach him. Fortunately, my corporation also retains a shipping agent in Dhaka who is well-connected to the company in question. He should be able to help out but, to make sure it gets done quickly, I'm afraid they will require my presence."

"Then you must go?" Sahar asked, disappointed at the prospect.

"I am afraid so, Sahar."

"Mr. Habibi, you should not feel badly." Advani said. "You must do what you can to protect your cousin's interest. This is only right. In any case, the ceremony isn't for another three days. You will have time enough to go to Dhaka and still join us for the ceremony. After all, it is only a short flight from Calcutta to Dhaka."

"I assure you, Sir, I will do all I can to be back in time."

Habibi then excused himself in order to pursue travel arrangements for the late night flight to Dhaka.

No sooner had Habibi departed the room than Governor Ghule, accompanied by his security detail, arrived at the front of the hotel. Anil and Mathir were waiting in the hotel lobby for his arrival. When Anil saw the governor's car, he immediately started for the lobby door, but Mathir reached out and grabbed him by his shoulder to hold him back.

"Anil! Don't you remember the last time you rushed out to meet the governor? His guards almost shot you. Do you want to tempt fate again?"

Anil flashed an angry look at Mathir and was about to scream at him when he realized that Mathir was right. He did not want to again be looking down the barrel of a pistol held by some brute whose greatest wish was to fulfill his duty by shooting someone.

"You are right, Mathir. Let's wait for the Governor to come into the lobby before we greet him."

As Mathir took his hand off of Anil's shoulder, a plain-clothes member of the governor's protective detail entered the lobby, immediately followed by Governor Ghule himself, dressed in a well-tailored double-breasted suit. Anil noted that the governor had a new hair style as well, wearing it well-oiled and slicked straight back. Certainly not movie star quality, Anil thought, but the governor did cut a dashing figure, nonetheless. Anil stepped forward to greet him and escort him to the VIP lounge.

When they met a moment later in the lounge, the governor greeted Advani warmly. Advani turned to Sahar and Tarek to introduce them.

"Governor Ghule, this is my daughter, Sahar," Advani said. "I am sorry that I have never had the opportunity to introduce her to you before."

For a moment, Ghule could not speak and could only stare. "No, Engineer," he said finally, "It is I who am sorry not to have met your beautiful daughter before today. It is my greatest pleasure, Ms. Advani."

Sahar smiled. "It is an honor, Governor Ghule." She nodded toward Tarek. "This is Mr. Tarek Durrani," she said, "A friend of mine, and as it would happen, an engineer as well."

"An honor to meet you, Mr. Durrani. Are you resident in New Delhi?" The governor greeted him with a handshake.

Tarek smiled and shook his head, "No, I am from Dubai, where my business is located."

"Wonderful," Governor Ghule said. "I love Dubai. It is one of my favorite places to visit."

"Mr. Durrani is most interested in visiting Tagore's childhood home." Advani said. "Could that be arranged?"

"Why yes, of course. I'll have my staff work in a private visit tomorrow during our tour of the city."

"That would be wonderful," Advani replied.

The group engaged in several minutes of conversation about the schedule of events planned for the following day. Tarek excused himself in order to check on Habibi's preparations for his trip to Dhaka. He found Habibi in his room.

"How do you think it went?" Habibi asked. "Was I convincing?"

"What? Your cousin doesn't have a business problem in Dhaka?" Tarek asked with a smile. "No, it was perfectly natural. You are good at this business, my friend. That is why I like working with you."

Tarek sat down in a wing chair and motioned for Habibi to sit in the other one. "Let's take a few minutes to go over the plan."

"Ah, yes, the plan," Habibi said.

"First, where will you stay?" Tarek asked. "Do you know yet?"

"Oh yes, I have reservations at the Sonargaon. It is a great hotel near the downtown area." Habibi handed a folded piece of paper to Tarek. "If you are ever unable to reach me on my cell or satellite phone, here is the number for the hotel. I've also included my shipping agent's name and number."

Tarek unfolded the paper, looking at it for a moment, then refolded it and put it in his pocket.

"Since I will essentially be in a hold pattern until you call with more information, all I can really do is check in with my shipping agent," Habibi said. "I have already notified him that I am paying a visit to Dhaka and stopping by his office sometime tomorrow."

Tarek nodded. "As soon as I hear something from Mahmoud, I'll let you know. Hopefully, he will be in Dhaka when he calls. It is possible of course, that he might not get the opportunity to call, but that is a chance we will have to take."

Tarek paused for a moment and looked steadily at his old friend. Habibi returned the look, then broke into a soft laugh. "We are flying by the seat of our pants on this one, aren't we, my commander," Habibi said.

Tarek's nod was almost imperceptible. He stood up and walked over to the window. "I can't say what you will be able to do, if anything. It really will depend on what Mahmoud tells me. In a general sense, what I am thinking is that if we can somehow create a situation that attracts the attention of the local authorities to the team, they might abort, even if their actual mission has not been compromised. The LT is a careful lot, and if they suspect someone may be on to them, they will likely stand down from their plan."

"But don't you want these guys permanently put out of action, either by arrest or otherwise?" Habibi asked.

"Right now, all I care about is stopping their attack. Whether they are arrested or killed is secondary," Tarek responded. "Let's be honest, Harun. Our ranks are thin. It's just you and me. Under these circumstances, our methods will by necessity be less sophisticated than we otherwise might want."

"Well, put that way, I guess you are right. If we can derail them from their plan, through whatever means, we will have succeeded."

Habibi looked at his watch. "It's time for me to go. I don't want to miss this flight as it is the last one for the evening."

"Alright, let me help you with your bags. Sahar and Advani said they would be in the lobby to say goodbye. They really like you, you know."

"And why shouldn't they? I am a most likeable fellow. Both handsome and charming, and all this nicely fitted into one rather large package."

"Oh, you left out modest too," Tarek said.

"Because that's so obvious."

The two men left the room with Habibi's bags in tow. Sahar and Advani were waiting in the lobby to say their goodbyes to Habibi, making him promise he would try to return in time for the ceremony.

Habibi handed Sahar a sealed business-sized envelope. "I saw that tomorrow the program calls for a visit to the orphanage founded by Mother Teresa. Would you be so kind as to deliver this small donation to the administrators there?"

"Certainly. This is so nice of you." Sahar took the envelope and placed it in her purse. She had no idea that inside the envelope were ten countersigned traveler's checks each in the amount of $500, made out to the orphanage.

A few moments later, Anil entered the lobby and approached Habibi.

"Sir, I am so sorry to learn of the need for your departure. There is a car outside, courtesy of the Office of Protocol, which will take you back to airport."

Habibi thanked Anil and said his final farewells, waving goodbye to the assembled group as he exited the hotel.

Tarek watched for a few more moments as Habibi got into the waiting car, which quickly drove off into the night.

Go with Allah my friend, Tarek said silently, go with Allah.

—55—

The smoky yellow-hued streets smelled of burning dung, which only exacerbated HV/30's depressed mood as he and the LT team made their way via bicycle rickshaws from Dhaka's central bus depot to the White Swan guest house in the Banani district of the city. HV/30 missed his wife and children, and doubts about what he was doing had been seeping into his thoughts since the day he boarded the ship in Karachi. As much as he had tried to ingratiate himself with his companions, he knew the team viewed him as just a last-minute stand-in, selected for the job because bad fortune had befallen their comrade.

During the cramped bus ride from Chittagong to Dhaka, HV/30 had seriously considered abandoning the group. He might have acted on the idea had it not been for Sheik Osman's secret instruction to him. Osman, who sat squeezed next to HV/30, had leaned close at one point and said in a low voice, "Mahmoud, when we arrive in Dhaka, I want you to find me a woman for the night."

Osman had even instructed that HV/30 not share a room with the other members of the group, but instead find a room at another guest house. This was ostensibly for the sake of security, but HV/30 saw now that it was to facilitate his pimping for Osman—he was to bring a prostitute not to Osman's room but his own, and wait there with her for Osman's arrival.

It was the last part of Osman's instructions, however, that gave HV/30 new-found determination and strength to complete what he had set out to do. "And Mahmoud, don't bring me some old hag," Osman had informed him. "She should be no more than 16 or 17. Those are the ones I like."

With those words, HV/30's great hope was renewed that soon he would see Osman dead.

56

As HV/30 and the LT team were making their way from the bus depot to the White Swan, Habibi stood at the baggage carousel at Dhaka International Airport. After what seemed like an eternity, he at last spotted his two bags rounding the corner on the slow-moving conveyer. Thinking he was through the worst of it, he picked up the bags only to find himself standing in line for a second eternity, waiting to clear immigration and customs.

At last through the formalities—and the Bangladeshis were nothing if not formal in these matters—Habibi proceeded out of the customs area into the main terminal, mobbed with hundreds of people, all of whom seemed desperate to help Habibi with his two bags.

In circumstances like these, Habibi's massive girth worked to his favor. He waded into the crowd, the people parting like tall grass in response to a rhino as it moves across the savannah. Many of the Bangladeshis were stunned at Habibi's size, and those closest looked at him with absolute terror in their eyes, afraid he would crush them if he should step on them.

As he plowed toward the exit sign, Habibi spotted a man in coat and tie holding a placard above his head that read "Sonorgaon Hotel." Habibi approached the man and identified himself.

"Oh yes, Sir, you are on my list," the greeter said. "The other two guests are already in the van. Please let me take your bags."

Outside the terminal, yet another crowd of hundreds of people stood watching as the travelers walked through the door. Moving beyond them, Habibi squeezed himself inside the minivan with two other male passengers, both of whom were British. As Habibi's bags were loaded in the back, one of the Brits commented, "I've never seen any airport quite like this. What in the name of God are all these people doing?"

Habibi smiled. "They are here for the show," he said.

"The show? What on earth do you mean?" the man asked.

"I mean they come to watch you and any other foreigner who walks out that airport door. This is the most exciting thing these people ever see. You are their entertainment, as it were. They are here every night and every day, whenever the flights come."

The Brit stared out the window as the van pulled away, looking at the multitude and trying to imagine how different his existence was from that of the people who stared vacantly back at him.

After arriving at the Sonargaon and registering at the hotel reception desk, Habibi proceeded to his room. He had only been in Dhaka a handful of times, but he had always stayed at the Sonargaon, a cool, modern oasis amid the crowded and sultry city. He looked forward to his stay, even if it would likely be brief.

Habibi unpacked his bags, then called his shipping agent to confirm their appointment the next day. After showering, he ordered up a late-night meal of biriyani and chicken kabob, which he ate while watching a BBC news program.

Soon his eyes grew heavy. He turned off the T.V., stretched out on the king size bed, and quickly fell asleep.

—57—

HV/30 did not comply with Sheik Osman's order. When Osman showed up later that night at his room, HV/30 claimed that the only prostitutes he could find were old and ugly. Much to his surprise, Osman accepted his excuse without argument. *Probably owing to his exhaustion from the trip,* HV/30 thought. Osman returned to the White Swan to rest for the night.

Only after Osman departed did HV/30 realize that by not being with the team at the White Swan he would have much more freedom of movement in Dhaka. He decided to complete all the tasks Sheik Osman had assigned him before calling Rashid. In that way, he would have much more to report, he thought.

His first task was to find a suitable truck to rent. Then he would purchase the supplies and cell phones Osman wanted, being sure to copy the numbers as Rashid had instructed. As he saw it, the best time to contact Rashid would be immediately after picking up the supplies and cell phones. After that, he was to return to the guesthouse and pick up the team. From there they would proceed to the freight office in the Dhanmondi section of town. Once he was with the team, it was unlikely he would have a chance to slip away again before they left Dhaka.

As he prepared himself for bed, HV/30 felt strangely calm and at ease. He knew he was playing a role in events that were taking a course that could not be changed, events with momentous consequences.

The following morning, HV/30 rose early and walked down the street to the White Swan. He found Sheik Osman sitting in the small dining area of the guest house, sipping his morning tea. HV/30 walked over and sat down at his table.

"Good Morning, Mahmoud," Osman said, his voice friendlier than HV/30 expected.

"Salam Aleikum, brother," HV/30 replied.

"Tell me your plan for the day." Osman said. HV/30 quickly laid out his schedule.

"That sounds good," Osman said with an approving nod of his head. "I want to leave tonight, and I want everything in order. Make sure you get everything on the list."

"No problem," HV/30 answered. "I better get started."

"Oh, Mahmoud, one more thing. Pick up two five-gallon Jerry cans and a funnel. We'll need a boat later, and I have it on good authority that most of the river boats around here have diesel engines. We'll want to take some extra fuel along just in case. We can get the petrol for the truck and fill up the jerry cans with diesel just before we leave Dhaka. And I want a full tank of gas before we get on the road. We want to be able to get as far as Rajshahi before getting more petrol. Then we will push on to Crowe's Bazar. Since you are the driver, you need to make sure you know the way."

HV/30 was intrigued by this new information, but he knew better than to pursue the topic. Crowe's Bazar was a former English trading post in India, not far across the border from Bangladesh. He could not fathom why the team would be headed there. Again he was tempted to ask questions but he restrained himself, knowing he must do nothing to raise suspicion.

"I know the way," he said instead. "It is fairly straightforward to get there, although the road is in poor condition and can be very crowded."

Osman nodded. "That is one of the reasons why I want to travel at night. There should be less traffic, and we can make better time."

"Alright then. If there is nothing else, I will be on my way."

With a flick of his wrist, Osman waved him away. "Khoda Hafez, Mahmoud."

"Khoda Hafez," HV/30 said, then walked out of the guest-house and into the street that bustled with morning traffic.

—58—

While HV/30 talked with Sheik Osman in the White Swan guesthouse, Habibi was making his way in a hotel taxi to the office of his shipping agent. Joseph Bilal had been in the shipping business for over 40 years, and he knew as much as any man about the nuances of import/export in Bangladesh. Habibi had not done a lot of business using Bilal's services, but he was always impressed with the man's ability to get things done in a country racked by poverty, corruption, and political paralysis.

Bilal was dressed nattily in a green sport jacket and tie when Habibi arrived. He appeared happy to see Habibi, thanking him for taking the time to come see him.

"I must apologize for the short notice," Habibi said. "There were unexpected business developments in Calcutta that required my presence, and since I was so close, I thought it made sense for me to come by and see how things are going here."

"No matter," Bilal said, "You are always welcome, anytime."

They spent 20 minutes discussing a few business matters, none of great consequence, then Bilal invited Habibi to dinner. Habibi was reluctant to commit, but after a moment's consideration, he accepted the invitation. As he saw it, if developments arose, he could call Bilal to cancel the engagement.

Their meeting concluded, Habibi returned to the Sonargaon and retired to his room to nap for a full hour.

While Habibi slept, HV/30 was completing his shopping. He had leased a closed-body Hyundai truck that was in serviceable condition and had purchased all the supplies on his list. His last purchase was the cell phones for the team. After copying the phone numbers, HV/30 went to the main telephone exchange in downtown Dhaka and called Tarek.

Tarek sat waiting in the hotel lobby for Sahar and Advani when HV/30's call came. Tarek's heart jumped as the phone started to ring. He knew it had to be HV/30.

"Hello," he answered.

"Brother, I have big news," HV/30 said in a rush. He then quickly relayed all that he had learned since their last conversation, including that the team's destination was Crowe's Bazar. Tarek listened without once interrupting and hastily wrote down the cell phone numbers and the information on the truck HV/30 had rented. He repeated it all back to HV/30 for accuracy.

"What about the package? Did you learn any more about that?" he asked.

"No, Rashid. I thought it safest to call you before we picked it up as it might not be possible to call you afterward."

"Good thinking, Mahmoud. You have done well. But once you find out what is in the package you must try to call me. Try my cell first, but by tomorrow, I may not be in range of a cell tower, and you probably will have to call my satellite phone to reach me. Rajshahi will have a telephone exchange, so that may be the best place to call me from if you are able to get away from the others."

"Okay, Rashid, I will do my best," HV/30 said, and asked in a worried voice, "But, Rashid, how far do I go with the team?"

Tarek knew what he said next was important. "Mahmoud, you have to go all the way. Wherever they go, you need to go with them."

"Alright, I will do as you say. You know what my goal is here. I am counting on you to help me make it happen."

"Your goal and my goal are compatible my friend. You can count on me to do my part." With that, Tarek said goodbye and the phone went dead.

As he slipped his cell phone into his shirt pocket, Tarek's mind was reeling. The team was not coming to Calcutta at all. It was headed to Crowe's Bazar! He did not need a map to know where Crowe's Bazar was; he'd seen it on a map all too recently. The implication hit him like a fist in the face.

The team's target was Farakka Barrage.

—60—

Habibi was napping soundly when the ring of his cell phone awakened him. The bed creaked loudly as he rolled onto his side and grabbed the phone.

"Hello," he said, still not fully awake.

"Wake up, brother. I've got news," Tarek said. "I spoke with Mahmoud not more than 10 minutes ago. He and his friends are not coming to Calcutta."

"Where are they going?" Habibi asked, not sure if he really wanted to know the answer.

"The same place we will all be tomorrow night."

Habibi thought for a moment before responding to this news. As what Tarek had just told him sank in, he slowly said, "Oh...my...God."

"It can't be coincidence that they are headed to the area of Farakka Barrage at the same time the commemoration ceremony is planned." There was silence on the line for a few seconds, as Habibi considered Tarek's words.

"But how would they know about the ceremony, and why would they care?" Habibi asked.

"It's no secret. It has been talked about in the press in the lead-up to the UN vote. And the protocol officer here just advised us that last night the UN voted on the side of India, meaning no sanction was issued. The Bangladesh delegation walked out in protest. An attack during the ceremony, even if a small one, would be very symbolic. It also could be catastrophic, if the sponsorship of the attack is linked to Pakistan."

"So what do we do now?" Habibi asked.

"What we set out to do. We have to stop the attack."

"But how? We don't have anything to work with."

"Mahmoud passed along some details that should help. Let me lay it out for you. I know where they are staying at least for the next hour or so. I've got a description and tag number of the truck they are using, and I have the address of the freight office where they are going to pick up this package that they have been talking about. I have a rough timeline for their travel to Crowe's Bazar. I also have their cell phone numbers, although that is probably not going to help us, running solo as we are. Still, the more information we have, the better."

Habibi wrote down the information as Tarek relayed it to him. When finished, Habibi said with rising determination in his voice, "Well, they are in Dhaka right now and so am I. If we are going to stop them, Dhaka is our best bet. Let me go over and spot them out at their guest house and see what I can do to create a little disturbance, something that will bring the police on the scene. With a little luck, they will have some contraband that will get them arrested."

"It's a good concept," Tarek said. "But according to Mahmoud, they have nothing incriminating with them at this point. No guns, no explosives, not even knives. I suspect that will change when they pick up the package. It has to be weapons and probably explosives. Once they have weapons, if they are stopped and searched by the police, they will definitely be compromised. I suspect they would shoot it out before submitting to arrest."

"So, I should wait until after they get the package?"

"Yes, but they will not be returning to the guest house once they have the package. Sheik Osman's plan now is for everyone to check out of the guesthouse just before going to the freight office. This means you need to get over to the freight office and see if you can spot them picking up their cargo."

"Alright. I'll get going and figure something out once I know they have the package."

"Harun," Tarek said his tone of voice serious. "I've already figured something out for you."

"Why am I not surprised?" Habibi said.

"Listen, this is too important to fly completely by the seat of our pants. You have to have a definite means of stopping these guys in their tracks, and I mean that literally. If we depend on getting the Dhaka police involved through some diversion, we are leaning on a weak reed."

"Alright, so what do you suggest, my commander?

"First, rent a car—a big one. Then take it down to the freight office, find the truck, and confirm that they have the package. Then, at a time of your choosing, you need to take that car and drive it right into them, preferably at a 90 degree angle, right into the middle of their vehicle. Going 45 or 50 kilometers an hour should do the trick. Coming in from the side like that, the impact for you will be less severe, but it will do maximum damage to their truck. Mahmoud should be driving it. As long as you aim for the middle section of the vehicle, he should be okay."

"Crude, but effective," Habibi said.

"Oh yes, very. And what's nice is it will look like it was an accident—unlike, say, walking up to someone and putting two rounds through the head, which tends to look a bit contrived."

After a pause Habibi said, "Well, our man Mahmoud should be okay, but what about the others?"

"I have to protect Mahmoud— that is my obligation. As to the others, Allah can protect them. But I also have to protect you. Now listen Harun, you have to remember to make sure you use your seat belt, which I know you don't like to do. It will not be enough to rely on an air bag. I think in a contest between you and an air bag, you would win—which means you would lose, if you know what I mean. I don't think the police will give you a hard time over the accident if you stage it so it really does look like an accident. You are a respected foreign businessman, bringing commerce to their country. The LT team? Well, once the police find their weapons, assuming they survive, they will be arrested or killed while resisting arrest, and their mission to India will be stopped cold."

"And we win."

"That's right. We all win. India wins. Pakistan wins."

"Alright, I better get going," Habibi said. "I can rent a car right here at the hotel. I think a Land Cruiser would do nicely."

"An excellent choice," Tarek replied. "Just be sure that when the rental car agent offers you their overpriced insurance you don't decline."

Habibi chuckled. "You are just full of advice today aren't you?"

"It's my job. Call me when you have something to report. And, Harun –may Allah protect you."

—61—

It was close to midnight Washington time when General Ali concluded his phone conversation with Tarek. Ali had been almost panicked that Tarek had not called sooner, imagining all the things that might have gone wrong. Even after talking to Tarek, his anxiety level was not much improved. Tarek was still on the trail of the team, but stopping them had come down to the laws of physics when applied to a car crash.

Half-way around the world from the action, Ali felt helpless. Tarek had passed to him a great deal of information about the LT team that in another time and under different circumstances would have allowed him to employ the human and technical resources of the ISI to shut the team down.

This was not possible now. None of the ISI officers he could trust were in any position to help him. Like him, they had been marginalized and replaced by other officers with fundamentalist credentials. He dared not report the information to his headquarters for fear someone who was involved in the mission would see the report. If that happened, both he and Tarek were dead men. The only hope now was that Tarek's plan would be successful. It was simple enough, and the ISI had successfully used the car-ramming tactic on other occasions.

Ali tried to relax. Tarek had promised to call as soon as he learned anything from his man, Habibi. Ali brushed his teeth and went to bed in hopes of sleep. He had an early appointment the next morning at CIA.

Worried as he was about what was about to transpire in Dhaka, he slept fitfully. He woke up feeling vaguely ill, and not wanting to miss a call from Tarek, he called his office to tell his secretary he would not be in and to reschedule his appointment at CIA.

Replacing the phone on the hook, he lay back down and began the wait for Tarek's next call.

—62—

At half-past noon the Dhaka sun was showing its strength, as Habibi made his way in the rented Land Cruiser from the hotel to central Dhaka. The air conditioner blew cold air as Habibi sat in comfort negotiating the crowded streets.

At last he spotted the billboard sign with a black arrow indicating the entrance to the central freight office. Habibi turned into the large compound and within a few minutes had determined there were eight warehouses within the compound, divided into two rows of four buildings each. The compound was alive with the activity of dozens of moving vehicles. Most were large transport trucks but there were a few smaller trucks similar to the one the LT team was supposed to be using, but none carried the license tag he was looking for.

According to HV/30's info, the warehouse where the package was to be picked up was in Building 8. Habibi found it at the far end of the second row of buildings, and negotiated his way through the gauntlet of trucks until he found an empty parking space some 200 meters away from the building. He parked and waited. Initially thinking the truck must not have arrived yet at the freight office, his heart skipped a beat when a freight truck pulled away from the north dock of Building 8 revealing a white Hyundai truck parked there.

That's it, Habibi said to himself, his pulse quickening. He could see two men sitting in the truck cab. Deciding he needed to get a closer look, Habibi left the Land Cruiser. The heat of the day hit him like a furnace blast and within seconds beads of sweat began to form on his forehead.

Careful of the trucks moving about, Habibi crossed the road to a brick walkway that separated the two rows of warehouses, making his approach to the truck. Coming 30 feet behind the

Hyundai, he stepped off the walkway and approached, moving at a slight diagonal angle to the truck but close enough to read the license tag. Excitement raced through him as confirmed the tag number.

There were no windows in the back of the truck and Habibi had no way of knowing if the package had already been picked up or not. He decided to return to the Land Cruiser where he could continue to watch the Hyundai.

Just as he turned and started to go, the driver's door of the Hyundai suddenly swung open and a short white bearded man jumped out. Both men were startled by the other's unexpected presence. Neither man spoke, nor looked away from the other, their gazes seemingly frozen.

Although they had never met, Habibi surmised that this was Mahmoud, based on the description Tarek had given him. Although Habibi wanted to tell Mahmoud that he was a friend sent by Tarek, he knew to do so might confuse Mahmoud and inadvertently complicate the situation.

Finally, Mahmoud nodded ever so slightly to Habibi and continued around to the back of the truck. He used a key to unlock the rear door, but left it closed, then returned to the front of the truck, climbing back into the cab.

Habibi quickly headed back to the Land Cruiser, worried that their unexpected encounter might have made Mahmoud suspicious. There was nothing he could do about that now.

The interior of the vehicle was so hot that he immediately cranked the engine and turned on the AC, making himself as comfortable as he could while he continued to watch the Hyundai.

Ten minutes later, a man with a thick black beard man stepped out of Building 8's administrative office, followed by two other men pulling a cart containing a wooden crate. Whatever was in the crate was heavy, as it was clearly difficult for the men to maneuver the cart down the ramp to where the

Hyundai was parked. HV/30 and the other man in the cab of the truck got out and moved to its back. When they opened the rear doors, several other men clambered out of the truck.

Habibi watched as the crate was loaded, noticing that the body of the Hyundai sank lower on its rear axle when the crate was set inside.

Once the crate was loaded, all the men began climbing back into the truck. Almost as if he sensed Habibi's presence, HV/30 looked around before he got into the cab. Habibi felt a powerful sense of respect for the diminutive man, whose head barely rose above the steering wheel. He knew the courage it took for such a man to take such great risks.

Don't *worry, my friend. I'll make sure you come out of this okay*, he thought to himself as he turned the Land Cruiser around and drove straight to the exit of the freight compound.

Vehicles exiting the freight compound had to make a right turn onto the street. To go in the opposite direction, a driver had first to travel five blocks to a traffic circle, where he could then reverse course.

Habibi's plan was to position himself on the last side street before the traffic circle. The cars had to slow down in single file as they approached the circle, and this would make it relatively easy to run into the Hyundai. He would park and wait, then when he saw the Hyundai approach from his left side he would accelerate out from the side street and crash into the vehicle's right side. As the road out of the compound was a single lane, there was no risk of another vehicle coming between Habibi and his intended target.

Turning into the side street, Habibi drove for a block and turned the Land Cruiser around in the driveway of a small market. After driving back down the block, he parked 100 meters from the intersection with the road that the LT team would be traveling on. A stone wall paralleled the road and might have blocked Habibi's view of the vehicles approaching, but it was in a bad state of repair, some sections having collapsed to nothing but piles of broken stones. Habibi had a good view of the road through these open sections. He was confident he would have plenty of time to spot the approach of the Hyundai.

Realizing the moment of truth was fast approaching, Habibi broke into a sweat, and he could feel his heart pumping harder. He tried to calm himself by staying focused on the mission, making sure everything was properly prepared. He turned off the air conditioner so the Land Cruiser would have maximum power available, and he lowered all the windows to minimize the amount of glass that could fly about during the crash.

Habibi did not normally use a seatbelt, as his large girth made it uncomfortable, but given the current circumstances, he was willing to make an exception. He reached down beside the seat for the belt but couldn't locate it. Looking down he realized there was no seat belt to be found.

Glancing around the car's interior, he realized that the vehicle did not have air bags either. He had assumed the Land Cruiser he rented would be equipped with the same modern safety equipment as the one he drove in the UAE. *A bad assumption*, he thought, *I am in Bangladesh, after all.*

Realizing he had become distracted, Habibi quickly looked over at the vehicles approaching from his left. Instantly he spotted the white Hyundai headed his way. Seat belt or no seat belt, he intended to stop that truck. He pulled out from the curb and began to accelerate toward the line of vehicles passing in front of him. As the Land Cruiser lunged down the side street toward the Hyundai, Habibi knew he would be spot on for colliding with it. He instinctively tensed in anticipation of the coming impact.

That's when he saw her, a young woman carrying a baby in her arms, walking into the Land Cruiser's path, oblivious to the vehicle rushing toward her like an angry bull. Habibi instinctively reacted, yanking the wheel left, sending the Land Cruiser over the sidewalk, missing the woman by inches. Habibi spun the steering wheel violently back to the right but not quickly enough to avoid slamming the Land Cruiser into the wall. The impact completely collapsed the corner, sending stones and dust flying. The Land Cruiser stopped dead in its tracks.

The swirl of dust and debris that went shooting into the street next to the white Hyundai caused its occupants to flinch. "My God, what was that!" one of the men exclaimed.

There was so much dust in the air as they passed the accident scene that HV/30 could barely make out the crumpled Land Cruiser, but through its shattered windshield, he could see the driver, slumped behind the steering wheel.

"Poor man," HV/30 said. "May Allah have mercy on him."

—63—

It was mid-afternoon as Tarek and Sahar finished their tour of the Tagore residence. They were standing in the sun in the front garden. Tarek motioned toward a bench under a flowering Plumeria tree and said, "Let's sit there while we wait for your father and the governor. After all, we are neither mad dogs nor Englishmen."

It was the first time that day that Tarek and Sahar had actually been alone with each other and, despite the heat, they sat close together, their legs touching and Tarek holding Sahar's hand. For a few moments, Sahar watched the gateway where her father should soon emerge. Then turning toward Tarek said, "You don't seem to be yourself, Tarek. Is there something wrong? Are you not feeling well?"

Tarek squeezed her hand. "I'm fine," he said. "I guess I'm a little concerned about Habibi. When I spoke to him this morning, he said he should have his business finished by 1:30, and he would give me a call to confirm his return to Calcutta. It's past 3:00 and still no word."

"I'm sure he is fine. Perhaps his appointments were delayed or he got caught up in traffic. I understand Dhaka can be terribly congested."

If for some reason he was not able to carry through with the plan, he would have called by now, Tarek thought to himself. Tarek had tried to call him on his cell phone a few minutes earlier, but could only reach the message service. He knew something had gone wrong.

Still he responded to Sahar in a positive tone. "I'm sure you are right, but I haven't been able to reach him on his cell. I have the number for his shipping agent, so I think I will give him a call while we wait. Hopefully, he will be able to put me at ease."

"Well, while you are doing that, I'll fetch some mineral waters at the shop next door," Sahar said, giving Tarek's hand a squeeze.

Tarek took out the slip of paper with the telephone number for Habibi's shipping agent and carefully punched in the number. He was surprised how quickly the call went through.

Almost immediately, a voice on the other end answered, "Joseph Bilal, here."

"Yes, Mr. Bilal, this is Tarek Durrani speaking. I am a friend of Mr. Harun Habibi. I have been trying to reach him but have been unsuccessful. He gave me your number as a point of contact while he was in Dhaka. I thought perhaps I would give you a ring and ask your assistance in locating him."

"Oh, Mr. Durrani, I have very bad news," he said. "Mr. Habibi was seriously injured in a vehicle accident and is at the Dhaka General Hospital."

Bilal's response made Tarek feel like he'd been punched in the stomach.

"My God, how badly is he hurt?" Tarek asked, bracing himself for the worst.

"He was unconscious for a couple of hours, but he is awake now and seems to be in full command of his facilities, although the doctors believe he may have suffered a concussion. He also cracked his sternum and fractured three ribs. While he is in some pain, according to the physician attending him, praise Allah, he is not in a life threatening situation,"

"Thank God," Tarek said. "How did the accident occur?" Tarek prayed that Bilal's response would include mention of another vehicle matching the description of the LT truck.

"Traffic conditions are daunting here, particularly for foreigners, and Mr. Habibi was very near our freight center when the accident happened. That can be one of the busiest areas of town."

The mention of the freight office raised Tarek's hope that despite the unintended consequences, Habibi had still been successful in his attempt against the team.

"But exactly what happened?" Tarek persisted

"You must understand, Mr. Durrani, Dhaka is full of ignorant pedestrians—poor villagers who come to the city for work, and then think they can walk in the street like it is some country lane. They are killed by the dozens. Poor Mr. Habibi crashed into a wall in order to avoid running over a beggar woman who stepped into the street in front of him."

"That sounds like Habibi," Tarek said. "He cares about people."

"Yes, I can tell. Mr. Habibi has a good heart. I am so sorry that he has been injured."

"Do you know if I can call him?" Tarek asked.

"No, I'm afraid the doctors have forbidden calls for at least 24 hours. However, I have enlisted my personal physician to assist in his care. He was trained in the U.S., and he is very good. If you would like, I could relay a message to Mr. Habibi through my doctor."

Tarek thought for a moment. He was certain there were no commercial flights into Crowe's Bazar from Calcutta. In an instant he made his decision. "Yes, thank you very much Mr. Bilal. I do have a message. Tell Mr. Habibi I'm coming to Dhaka."

— 64 —

The sound of Ambassador Salim's Mont Blanc pen moving swiftly across the IRE stationary could be heard on the other side of the office where General Huq sat at the oval meeting table, which was covered with the maps of India and Bangladesh that he had brought with him.

Huq was usually a patient man, but he was growing irritated as he sat waiting for Salim to finish his scribblings and join him. Although Salim was his brother-in-law, some respect was due. He was a general officer, after all, and the deputy defense minister of Pakistan to boot. Having to wait like a tea boy for a civilian, even one of Salim's stature, was most annoying.

Finally Salim rested his pen. "There," he said, as he carefully laid the pen inside its decorative silver case. "I think this note will make clear to my executive officer that he is not to procure any office furnishings for senior IRE officers without my personal approval. I will not tolerate any furnishings of poor taste being associated with the leadership of this organization. It sends the wrong message about the kind of people we are. My God, I walked into Colonel Hassan's office this morning, and I had to cringe. The man's couch was upholstered in camouflage and his meeting table was made of metal. Does the man think he is still posted to the Siachen Glacier?"

Relieved that Salim was at last coming to the table, General Huq chuckled. "You must forgive him, Mohammad. Colonel Hassan is one of those officers who fancies himself a 'Rambo'."

"Rambo! What a stupid thing for a grown man to think himself. If he wasn't otherwise competent in his duties I would replace him in an instant."

Salim sat down, his prayer beads in hand, and turned his attention to the map-strewn table. "And what do you have for me today, Huq?"

"A new message from Sheik Osman. The team now has the package and is departing Dhaka as we speak."

"So, no problems? The package arrived in Dhaka in good working order?"

"The package appears to be in great shape. Of course they have not yet had a chance to run a systems check to make sure. They will do this once they are away from Dhaka," Huq said.

"When do you expect to hear from them again?"

"They will call me after they cross into India and have reached Crowe's Bazar."

"That is fine, but I want you to make sure we have contact with the team right up until they execute the mission. And . . ." Salim paused to emphasize the next point, "I want to be the one that gives the final okay. This will be the catalyst on which all our plans depend. There is no room for error. It must succeed. We know there is no hope of taking Kashmir by force as long as Indian forces in the region are up to full strength. They are simply too powerful. The diversionary attack on Farakka Barrage is the key to getting them to shift their forces."

"Do not worry. We will be in control right up to the very last second. Right now we are using cell phones to communicate, since there is reliable service in the major towns. However, once they leave Crowe's Bazar, the cell phone infrastructure is poor and therefore our communications plan requires that Sheik Osman revert to his satellite phone."

"Is it secure?"

"Yes. Reasonably so, anyway. We acquired a state-of-the-art commercial encryption system, and then we tweaked it a bit. Even if the Indians, or anybody else for that matter, picks up the signal, they will not be able to decipher what is being said. Besides, we won't be up on the air for very long, so it is unlikely the signal will come to anyone's attention. It will simply be a blip on a screen—an electronic anomaly—and then it will be gone."

Salim nodded. "And even if someone suspects something, at that point it will be too late. There will be no means to react to the signal."

"That is correct."

Salim continued. "Now, what about the other preparations?"

"That is why I brought the maps," Huq said as he spread out a map of northeast India. "We have coordinated with two indigenous insurgent groups. Within the next 12 hours, they will begin to step up their operations here and here." Huq pointed to areas in Nagaland and Manipur. "I might mention that this is the first time that they have cooperated operationally, and neither group is Islamic; they are ethnic minorities with long-standing grievances against India."

Salim nodded approvingly. "The principle of 'the enemy of my enemy is my friend' seems to apply well in this situation."

Huq continued, "Their activities should get the Indians' attention, so their military commanders will already be looking to the east and considering the need to shift forces in that direction."

Huq paused for a moment and hit the map with the heel of his fist on the serpentine blue line demarcating the Ganges River at the location of Farakka Barrage. "And when we take Farakka down, the Indians will immediately shift forces to the east, sending them all the way to the Bangladesh border and beyond."

Huq added a caveat to his bold statement, however, expressing a lingering doubt that he had harbored about the plan from the beginning. "That assumes, of course, that the Indians attribute the attack against the dam to the Bangladeshis."

"They will," Ambassador Salim responded confidently. "They will be forced to this conclusion, given the bellicose statements coming out of Dhaka in the wake of the UN decision not to intervene in the water sharing dispute."

Salim smiled at Huq. "You see, my friend, diplomacy, propaganda, and a little arm twisting can make a critical difference in determining the fate of nations. It is not always the Rambo's of the world who achieve great victories for their countries and their faith."

"I must concede this point to you. The IRE has truly done a masterful job in manipulating the UN in this regard. The IRE victory has given our effort a real opportunity to succeed."

Salim smiled again. "I am quite pleased to hear such an acknowledgement coming from a military man. But Huq, you know Allah will ultimately decide if we succeed or fail.

General Huq stood up and began to collect and fold his maps. "Mohammad, one final point. We have notified Army Headquarters that we are starting our surprise exercise."

"So you will now have an ostensible reason for the movement of forces that will be used in the attack." It was a statement from Salim, not a question.

General Huq nodded. "That is correct. We are moving selected units under the commanders who are allied with us to the Line of Control. We are also moving a few battalions which we are not sure we can count on out of the area. The Indians will believe we are just reorganizing for the exercise. Still, we will keep our major forces out of the immediate area of the LOC until after we see Indian troops being shifted east. My staff estimates this should happen within 24 hours of the attack on Farakka Barrage. Once they move east, we will reinforce into the LOC and then, with elements of the SSG in the lead, launch our attacks. Abu Shafik is ready to set up blocking positions for any Indian counterattacks. We will drive east, link up with the LT fighters and continue operations until we have overrun Indian-controlled Kashmir."

Salim stopped the general. "Yes, Huq, I am familiar with the plan. But you must control your commanders. They are not to go into Indian territory beyond occupied Kashmir. Pakistan has no design on India, and we will make that clear to the world upon initiation of hostilities. Any violation of territory outside of Kashmir will work against Pakistan's interest in the diplomatic arena. Our success in holding on to Kashmir will depend not only on our military capability, but also on getting the UN to pressure India to negotiate on the issue. The longer we can keep the Indians talking, the better chance we have of consolidating our defenses and keeping what is rightfully ours. We have to be smart about this."

"And what about the prime minister?"

"This is a sensitive issue I have struggled with since the beginning," Salim said. "But I have made my decision. We will place the PM under house arrest at the time the orders are given for our forces to cross the LOC. We will also declare martial law."

"And the defense minister?"

"He will be made to resign, and you will take his place."

Huq sat expressionless, contemplating Salim's statement.

"Well, General, are you up to the task?" Salim asked.

General Huq cast his gaze to the floor for an instant, then looked Salim square in the face. "Of course. I am ready."

"Good. You and I are about to make history together."

—65—

Within hours of learning that Habibi was hospitalized, Tarek arrived in Dhaka at the General Hospital. Sahar and Advani understood Tarek's decision to cancel his plans and leave Calcutta immediately to go to his injured friend. What they did not understand, and what Tarek could not tell them, was that a team of Kashmiri fighters with hostile intent was making its way to Farakka Barrage, and he had to stop them.

Tarek did not stay long at the hospital, only long enough to check on Habibi. Convinced that his friend was receiving the best medical care possible, and entrusting Joseph Bilal to make sure the care continued, Tarek set out in a rented four-wheel-drive Mitsubishi for Rajshahi, in hot pursuit of the LT team.

Tarek prayed he would get an update call from HV/30 when the team reached Rajshahi. To help insure the satellite signal came through, Tarek used a magnetic mount to attach the phone antennae to the roof of the Mitsubishi.

He felt exhausted as he drove through the early morning. So much had happened within the last 24 hours. Not only were events moving much more quickly, but the complexion of his mission now had become very personal. An attack on Farakka Barrage could not only lead to a war between India and Pakistan, but it might well take the life of the woman he loved. The fact that he himself had collected information that was being used in the terrorist mission was hard to accept. He would stop at nothing to prevent the terrorist team from carrying out its plan.

It was 4:30 in the morning, as Tarek was passing through the town of Pabna, 50 kilometers southeast of Rajshahi, when the call came through. The conversation was short. HV/30 relayed to Tarek everything he had learned since they had last spoken.

HV/30's news was not encouraging. The team had already arrived on the outskirts of Rajshahi, on the opposite side of town from Tarek, and would be leaving within the next 30 minutes. There was no way Tarek would be able to catch up to them there. He would have to find them at Crowe's Bazar.

According to HV/30's information, that might just be possible. The team planned to stop in Crowe's Bazar and switch their transport to a diesel powered boat. Finding a suitable boat and transferring the team's gear would likely take some time, possibly several hours. The mention of a boat had sent chills up Tarek's spine. He imagined a boat loaded with a fully armed team making its way down the Ganges toward Farakka Barrage as the commemoration ceremony got underway, Sahar and her father seated as guests of honor in the front row at the river's edge overlooking the dam, guests and dignitaries seated behind them, and not one aware of the approaching danger. The images were too frightening; Tarek had to force his mind into the present.

HV/30 had provided another piece of critical information: Sheik Osman had a satellite phone with him, his means of communicating with his controllers back in Pakistan, Tarek presumed. HV/30 had not been able to see the brand of phone, but he had gotten a look at what may have been the phone's number, handwritten on a piece of paper taped to the phone. Although he had seen the entire number briefly, he could remember only the last four digits. He also reported that the crate contained 30 hand grenades and AK-47's, one for each team member, except himself.

HV/30 had not been allowed to help unpack a separate smaller wooden crate contained within the larger crate. He could only speculate that the smaller crate contained explosives, as the team members seemed to be extra cautious in its handling. The unidentified items in the smaller crate had been divided up into two backpacks.

At first, Tarek had agreed with HV/30's assessment that the smaller crate must contain explosives, probably Semtex or some other plastic explosive. But as HV/30 provided additional details, the possibility of Semtex seemed less likely. According to HV/30, the small crate was heavy to the point that three men were needed to move it. Semtex packed in a crate the size of HV/30 had described would not be so heavy. Also, the contents of the crates had been placed into special backpacks with frames made of flat brushed steel. The packs themselves were made of a heavy black ballistic material. Each pack had only one large compartment with no exterior pockets. Particularly odd were the fasteners, six in number, set two inches apart, and aligned horizontally across the lower part of the pack. After the team had packed the material into the backpacks and snapped the fasteners closed, a thin steel cable was run through pre-drilled holes in all six fasteners, and then crimped on each end.

Hearing these puzzling details, Tarek was convinced there was something other than plastic explosives in the backpacks. He could not even speculate what the material might be but whatever it was, the team had gone to a lot of trouble to get it to Dhaka, and he knew it was lethal.

Tarek wasn't sure how he could stop the LT team. He considered another attempt using a vehicle, but if that was not possible, he really had few options, especially lacking a weapon. Then again, with seven armed LT members walking around, at least he knew where he could get one.

—66—

Prior to Tarek's departure for Dhaka, he had notified General Ali of the failed attempt by Habibi to interrupt the LT's plan. Now, with the latest report from HV/30, it was time once again to give the general an update. Tarek didn't bother to pull over to the side of the road but punched in Ali's home phone number as he drove through the night toward Rajshahi.

It was late afternoon in Washington, and Ali was home when the phone rang. He sat in silence as Tarek briefed him using double talk to mask the information as best he could. Ali interrupted only once to ask Tarek to repeat the partial number HV/30 had seen on Sheik Osman's sat phone.

When Tarek finished, Ali asked, "So what's your plan?"

Tarek managed to chuckle. "It is still a work in progress, but I might try to succeed where Habibi failed, using the same tool he used. If I can't make that work, then I might borrow another kind of tool from our little group."

General Ali followed his meaning easily but hoped anyone else listening, who did not know the background of the events that were unfolding, would not be able to make sense of it.

"The party in question may object, and it could get messy," Ali responded.

"Well, there is always the DFF option, but that certainly would not be any less messy," Tarek said. Diesel fuel and fertilizer were standard field-expedient materials for making a bomb.

"Agreed," Ali said. "What is the backup in case you miss your friends at Crowe's Bazar?"

"I have the governor's sat phone number, which he carries when traveling into remote areas, and he will be traveling with the delegation."

"You propose to notify him?" Ali asked.

"If I can't stop our friends, yes I do. I have to tell them to cancel the ceremony."

"I suppose," Ali said. "You realize that you will have to convince him you are serious. To do this you will have to acknowledge who you work for, and there is a likelihood that once you tell the Indians about the team, they will simply jump to the conclusion that our government is behind their plan. Even if the Indians are successful in preventing the attack, it still could lead to the very same consequences we are trying to avoid—war with India."

"I know," Tarek said. "But if I can't stop them in Crowe's Bazar, there are no other options."

Both men were silent for a few moments.

Dispensing with the double talk, Ali, said, "Tarek, there is no choice here. You cannot fail. The team must be stopped. One way or the other, it must be completely shut down."

"I assure you, General, my very life depends on it," Tarek said.

Unaware of Sahar, the general did not grasp the full significance of Tarek's words.

"Call me as soon as you have any more information," General Ali said, and added, "I wish Allah's protection for you."

Hanging up the phone, Ali walked through his kitchen and out onto his wooden deck. He leaned against the railing and looked out over the trees at the late afternoon sun. He suddenly felt a tiredness born of frustration and helplessness.

Over the course of the last year, in the wake of the assassination of General Masood, he had watched as the political landscape of his country had changed, with Islamic fundamentalists assuming key positions in the government. He and many of his ISI colleagues had become victims of a current of radicalism that was running through Pakistan. He had barely escaped a car bomb, and his influence within the ISI had been marginalized by his transfer abroad. Now, with the continuing purge of loyal ISI officers, he could not trust anyone, and he found himself unable to act to counter crucial events happening half a world away.

For the first time in his professional life, Ali was reduced from the role of a primary actor to the status of an inconsequential observer. He did not like it, not one bit.

—67—

At the same time Tarek was approaching the Indian border-control station, the first group of dignitaries bound for Farakka Barrage were gathered at the Calcutta airport, waiting to board the plane that would take them to Malda, the first stop of their journey to the Farakka Barrage. From Malda buses would carry them to the dam, some 30 kilometers away.

Sahar was still upset by the news of Habibi's accident, followed immediately by Tarek's departure to Dhaka. Both she and Advani were disappointed Tarek wouldn't be attending the anniversary commemoration, but for Sahar it was more than disappointment. She had an odd sense of foreboding. Sahar tried to convince herself the feeling was caused by the shock of Habibi's accident and the sudden change of Tarek's plans. Still, she could not rid herself of the feeling that something was wrong, and her intuitions had often proved accurate.

In an effort to lighten her mood, she approached Anil, who was checking the passenger manifest.

"Mr. Deshmukh," she greeted him, "I have not yet had a chance to thank you for all the work you have done in arranging for this ceremony. You have done a marvelous job. The hotel arrangements and our outings in Calcutta were perfect. My father and I have had a wonderful time, and I know that is due largely to your efforts."

Anil couldn't hide his excitement on hearing Sahar's remarks, particularly coming as they did from such an attractive woman. Mathir, who had done all the hard work in organizing the event, was out of earshot, leaving Anil free to take all the credit.

"Please, Ms. Advani, you owe me no special recognition," he said with unconvincing modesty. "This is my job after all, and if I may say so, I know what I am doing when it comes to these types of affairs."

Sahar smiled, "I should say so, if what I have seen is any indication of your ability."

"All you have seen is a reflection of that, Madam."

"I am curious. How long have you been in charge of the West Bengal protocol office?" Sahar asked.

"Oh, only about two years. Just long enough to get things on track." Anil paused for a moment and glanced at Mathir, who was still busy on the other side of the waiting area talking to an airline official. "When I first arrived here, I am sorry to say, the office was a disaster. And I have had to train my assistant, who was quite incompetent. Governor Ghule hand-picked me, you know." While this was technically true, Anil chose not to mention there had been no other candidates who met the basic qualifications needed for the position.

"Well, I am truly impressed," Sahar responded. "Where will you go from here? To Delhi, perhaps?"

"No, I don't think so. In fact, Ambassador Singh, who I think you know is our deputy representative to the UN, has asked me to consider an assignment in New York."

Ambassador Singh was indeed among the visiting dignitaries waiting to board the plane, but Anil's version of their conversation was a loose interpretation of what had actually transpired. However, when a man spoke of his future possibilities with a woman as beautiful as Ms. Advani, truth was often the first casualty—a phenomenon Sahar was well acquainted with, having seen it demonstrated more times than she cared to recall.

"Oh, New York, that would be wonderful indeed." Nodding to Anil she quickly retreated to rejoin her father.

Advani took out a copy of the schedule and reviewed the day's planned events. "After a quick stop in Malda for tea with the mayor, we will depart on buses at 11:30 and arrive at the Farakka Barrage Administration Building. After room assignments, we will lunch with the chief administrator and his senior staff at 12:30."

"And the afternoon schedule?" Sahar asked.

"We get an hour break from 1:30 to 2:30, when I suppose we can relax a bit. Then comes the tour of Farakka Barrage, which I see includes a short cruise up the river."

"I hope they have scheduled time to freshen up before the ceremony," Sahar said, imagining what she would look like after a mid-afternoon cruise on the wind-blown Ganges.

"There should be plenty of time. The boat returns around 5:00, and the ceremony doesn't start until 6:30 in the evening."

"Oh, that will be nice. It will be starting to cool and the sun will be setting over the river. It should be beautiful." Sahar's sense of depression started to lift as she imagined the picturesque scene.

"And after the ceremony, there is a formal banquet scheduled. So, it sounds like we have a full day ahead of us."

Speaking from the airline gate counter, Mathir announced that the plane was ready for boarding.

"Are you ready, Father? This is a big day for you," Sahar said.

Advani slowly stood up and gesturing toward the gangway with his wooden cane said, "It is indeed. It is the day I return to Farakka Barrage."

The sun had just risen above the tree-lined horizon and a thin gray mist filled the air as Tarek approached the Indian border checkpoint. A faded sign indicated transport trucks should pull into the right lane and other vehicles should proceed straight ahead. Tarek continued forward, passing a line of parked canvas-covered trucks waiting for the Indian border authorities to process them.

Two cars were in front of Tarek, and he imagined he would be through the border check and on his way to Crowe's Bazar in a matter of minutes. The Indian border inspector, with a clipboard in hand, waved through the cars ahead of Tarek without so much as a single question. Tarek expected similar treatment as he pulled up next to the inspector.

"Good Morning, Sir. May I see your passport?"

Tarek handed over his passport with his UAE residency permit attached. After taking a moment to review the documents, the inspector said, "I note there is an exit cachet from Calcutta airport stamped only yesterday afternoon. May I asked why you are returning to India so soon, and why are you doing so by a land crossing?"

Tarek had anticipated the question.

"I was in Calcutta as part of an official delegation that is traveling to Farakka Barrage this very morning," he said. "Unfortunately, yesterday morning a very good friend of mine from the UAE, who was in Dhaka on business, was involved in a serious motor accident, so I came right away to see him. He is recovering, and now I am trying to make my way to Farakka Barrage to join the delegation. I did not have time to fly back to Calcutta to make the flight from there, so my only recourse is to drive."

"I see," the inspector said. "Please pull forward into the space on the left. I will be with you in a moment."

Tarek was not particularly concerned about being put into secondary, but he was unhappy with the delay. He had one shot to catch the team in Crowe's Bazar. If he missed them there, nothing he could do would stop them.

The inspector waited for Tarek to pull forward, then walked into the administration office, taking Tarek's documentation to the commander of the station as he had been instructed to do. The commander took the documents and thumbed through Tarek's passport.

"You'll note the valid multiple-entry Indian visa issued in Abu Dhabi, and that he is a long-time resident of the UAE," the inspector pointed out.

"Yes, I see that," the commander responded. He picked up Tarek's International Driver's Permit, which showed it was issued in Abu Dhabi. He leafed through the pages and then handed the documents back to the inspector.

"There is no doubt that Mr. Durrani is the subject of the Intelligence Bureau communiqué," he said.

"Why do you think the IB is interested in him?" the inspector asked.

"In their wisdom, or should I say arrogance, the IB did not see fit to let us know that, inspector. You know they treat us like poor second cousins."

"I don't know which is worse, IB or RAW."

"Don't waste your time trying to figure it out," the commander said. "They both think they are the only government organization that has an important job to do, so they ignore the rest of us and treat us like crap." He stood up and walked over to the window that looked out on the inspection lanes. "That's him in the Pajero?"

"Yes, Sir. That's him. Should I have his car searched?"

"Not yet. Just let him sit until I get further instructions from Calcutta. But keep your eye on him. I don't want him wandering off."

"Right, Sir. I need to get his vehicle registration documents. I'll do that while you talk to Calcutta."

The inspector left the office while the commander picked up the phone and called the number included in the IB communiqué. On the third ring, the call was answered.

"Intelligence Bureau, Calcutta"

"Yes, please put me through to Inspector Thomas Singh."

The call was immediately transferred.

"Inspector Singh, here. How may I help you."

"This is Crowe's Bazar Border Station Commander Chowdhury. I'm calling regarding the communiqué on Subject of Interest Pakistani national Tarek Durrani."

"Yes, what about it."

"Your SOI is presently here at my station, and I wish to know if I should formally have him detained."

"Is he alone?"

"Yes. He is alone."

"How is he traveling? By bus?

"No. He's driving a Mitsubishi Pajero with Bangladesh tags. It's probably rented."

"What color is the Pajero?"

"Red."

"How long as he been there?"

"Only a couple of minutes, Inspector."

"Alright. What is your number? I will get back to you in a few minutes and, for the moment, do not let him enter the country."

"No problem. We have him waiting while we check his documents and vehicle registration."

"That's fine. I'll call you in a few minutes. Please stand by."

Inspector Singh hung up the phone. His supervisor was not in the office yet, but it did not matter. The instructions the Intelligence Bureau Headquarters had issued for this contingency were very clear. The IB knew from it's source that Durrani was pursuing a terrorist team intending to strike India, although Singh himself had no details about the planned attack. After Durrani's departure from Calcutta, the decision had been made to take the ISI officer into IB custody if he tried to return to India. The assumption was that if he returned, it meant he had learned more details about the terrorists' plan, and he was back to try to foil the attack. No one in the IB chain of command was willing to rely on a lone Pakistani intelligence officer to stop an attack in India. No, if the attack was to be stopped, the Indian IB would do it.

Singh picked up the official Intelligence Bureau telephone directory from his desk and thumbed through the pages until he found the listing for Crowe's Bazar. According to the document, only one IB inspector was assigned there.

Singh called the number for Inspector Reza and got through immediately. After giving him instructions, Singh called Commander Chowdhury.

The border inspector was just returning from copying Tarek's vehicle registration documents when the commander hung up the phone.

"That was Calcutta," he said. "The IB doesn't want us to detain him any longer. They say they have the situation under control."

"Should I at least search his car?"

"No. They don't want us to do anything that might raise his suspicions. I don't know what is going on here, probably some stupid game the IB is playing."

"Then my orders are to release him?"

"Those are your orders, inspector."

Tarek had been sitting in the secondary inspection zone for over 30 minutes when the border inspector returned with all of his documentation. Passing the documents to him, the inspector thanked him for his patience and wished him a pleasant trip.

Tarek pulled back out onto the road. He had made many border crossings in his career and being put into secondary was not a new experience for him, yet it did raise his suspicions. The Indian security services were as professional as they came. At this point, though, he could not let it slow him down. He had only a few short hours to find and stop the LT team.

— 69 —

The congested streets of Crowe's Bazar were full of the sounds of beeping horns and engine exhaust hung thick in the unmoving air.

HV/30 left the team at a restaurant on the edge of town under instructions to find a suitable boat that could take the team down the Ganges to Farakka Barrage. Walking, he made his way through town in search of a cut-through to the river that bordered the far side of the commercial area.

The commercial zone consisted of dozens of small shops packed into a few short blocks. He had asked for directions to the marina but the directions provided were never clear. It was only by chance that he at last broke through the last section of shops and spotted the river. Some 500 meters from where he stood, he saw a marina of sorts, with a collection of riverboats tied up to the piers. Most appeared to be fishing boats, but there were also three or four flat-bottomed boats used for carrying sand collected from the river bottom.

The sand boats were long and shallow, sitting well down in the water, presenting a low profile. Outfitted with slow but powerful diesel engines, the boats had ample capacity to handle the currents of the Ganges. One of the boats had a structure of bamboo and woven hyacinth covered by a yellow tarp that provided a sheltered area at the rear of the boat. This was a feature Sheik Osman had specified.

In short order, HV/30 struck a deal with the boat's owner, a dark-skinned old man with a wispy white beard and eyes clouded by cataracts. He looked to be 90 years old, but HV/30 suspected 65 was probably a more accurate age. Life in places like Crowe's Bazar was hard.

Despite his fragile appearance, the boat owner drove a hard bargain. HV/30 ended up settling on a price half again as much as he had intended. While he was doling out a third of the sum in order to ensure the boat would be made ready, HV/30 explained that he would return in an hour or so with his colleagues. The cover story that Osman and HV/30 had prepared between them was that they needed the boat to transport themselves to the entrance to the Jangipur Feeder Canal where they would meet a boat from Calcutta bringing goods they planned on trading in Crowe's Bazar.

The old man waved his hand as if brushing a fly away. "I don't care what you need the boat for," he said, "but whatever the purpose, one of my sons will accompany you to navigate the river."

Certain that Sheik Osman would not be happy with this stipulation, HV/30 tried instead to negotiate a security deposit. But the old man held firm.

"Nobody on the river would risk their boat to strangers," he insisted. "My son will accompany you, or no boat."

In the end, HV/30 had no choice but to accept the condition. He paid his deposit and left, but he had one last task to complete before rejoining the team.

He had already checked his cell phone and found that there was no service. He stopped at a shopping stall full of garment-factory overruns and asked directions to the nearest telephone exchange. He was certain the crowded conditions of the town would make it impossible for Tarek to find the team without some directions from him.

The owner of the shop stepped out of the stall and pointed down the street, "One block, that way," he said.

HV/30 walked for three blocks before he finally spotted the telephone exchange and went inside. He had to wait a few minutes until one of the booths came open and the exchange manager motioned to him that it was his turn. HV/30 dialed the number for Tarek's satellite phone. After three rings he heard the voice he wanted to hear.

"Rashid, this is Mahmoud."

"Mahmoud, I'm almost to Crowe's Bazar," Tarek said. "Are you there?"

"Yes, yes, but only for another hour or so. My friends are at a restaurant at the edge of town. They sent me out to rent a boat, and I have to go back to get them soon. Sheik Osman wants to get out on the river in time to reach our destination soon after sunset."

Tarek had no doubt as to what the team's destination was, but he had to confirm it.

"Has he told you where you are going?"

"Sheik Osman has said nothing to me, but I overheard some of the others say we were taking the boat to a place called Farakka Barrage."

Tarek's heart sank with the confirmation of their destination, and with the further revelation that Sheik Osman wanted to be there the very night of the ceremony.

"Do you know anything about Farakka Barrage?" HV/30 asked. "Is it an Indian army base? I did not need to come to the far side of India only to be shot by Indian soldiers."

"It's not an army base. It's a dam. That's all," Tarek said, only half listening to HV/30. He could not free his mind from thoughts of the danger Sahar would be in.

"All this trouble to go to a dam in the middle of nowhere? Sheik Osman is crazy. Why come here when there are far better targets closer to home?"

"It really doesn't matter at this point. They have to be stopped before they get on that boat."

Tarek's own words helped to refocus his attention on the challenge that lay ahead. "Where is the restaurant that the team is at?" he asked. "And also, where is the marina, in case I miss them."

He listened carefully as HV/30 gave him the directions. "Do what you can to slow them down without getting into too much trouble," Tarek said, when he was sure he had the directions clear. He paused for a moment, pondering how he should phrase his next statement.

"Mahmoud, if I cannot intercept the team before it gets on the river, then you will have to do something to stop the mission."

"How, Rashid? They are heavily armed. I don't even have a knife."

"I can't tell you how, Mahmoud. You will have to look for opportunities and figure something out."

There was silence on the line. Finally, HV/30 said, "Maybe I can do something to the boat. Or if not the boat, I can try to damage the engine."

That suggestion gave Tarek a thought. "What about the diesel fuel you bought for the boat. Do you think you could contaminate it with something?"

Now it was HV/30's time to think for a moment. "Maybe, but it will be hard to do. At least one of them is always guarding the truck, and the jerry cans are in the truck."

"I understand, but try to do it. Use dirt, sugar, rice, or whatever you can lay your hands on, and get as much of it into the cans as possible."

"Alright, but even if I can spoil the fuel, I doubt we will need to refill before we get to the dam. The extra cans are only a reserve."

"Then try to convince Osman to top off the tank before reaching the dam. If he knows anything about engines, he will know a diesel is hard to get restarted once it runs out of fuel. The last thing he will want is to run out of fuel right after carrying off an attack and not be able to restart the engine."

"Okay, I'll do what I can," HV/30 said.

Tarek knew the fuel contamination option was a long shot, but he wanted to generate as many possible contingency plans as possible. If all failed, he would immediately call Governor Ghule on his satellite phone and tell him of the threat. That would at least give sufficient time to cancel the ceremony and evacuate the attendees from the area, saving many lives, including those of Sahar and Advani.

But the bitter truth was, even if the team was captured or killed by Indian forces before carrying out an attack, it still could mean war. If he was forced to call Governor Ghule, it would be rolling the dice on the question of war on the sub-continent.

"Rashid, my call time is almost up. Is there anything else?" HV/30's voice brought Tarek back to the present moment.

"No, my brother. There is nothing else to say. All we can do is try our best."

"It is in Allah's hands. Khoda Hafez."

"Khoda Hafez," Tarek replied.

As Tarek placed the phone back in the car console, he believed there was a very good chance he'd heard HV/30's voice for the last time.

—70—

There were now only three kilometers left before Tarek reached Crowe's Bazar. Knowing he would likely be in action soon, he began to ready himself mentally. According to HV/30, the restaurant where the team was waiting was at the edge of town. This meant Tarek would be there within the next five minutes. He had no firearm, but he had purchased a Nepalese army-issue Gurkha knife at a roadside stand where he had stopped for water. The large, distinctively curved knife was a formidable weapon. Nevertheless, he hoped his effort to stop the terrorists would not come down to a bloody knife fight.

Tarek prayed that the team would still be inside the restaurant when he arrived. Since they could not openly carry their AKs, they would have left them in the truck, relying on a guard to keep their weapons and gear safe. If Mahmoud was the guard, Tarek's task would be much simpler. If not, he planned to employ the shiny Gurkha to eliminate the guard. Assuming the keys were with the truck, he could then simply drive off with all the team's weapons and explosives. *Now that would be a grand coup*, he thought.

If, however, there were two or more team members outside with the vehicle, Tarek would have to resort to using his Mitsubishi as the weapon of choice and try to accomplish what Habibi had failed to do.

Despite these plans, anything could happen. He might still end up having to face one or more of the team members in hand-to-hand combat. Although he had worked hard to keep himself strong, he knew he was not as quick or as strong as he once had been, and he would be facing much younger and equally fit opponents. His only advantage would be surprise, and his first priority would be to get hold of one of the AKs. If he could accomplish that, he could level the field— literally.

As he contemplated the likelihood of violent action, he realized that it was not only his physical condition that had changed over the years; his attitude about killing had changed, too.

As a young Army commando and through much of his ISI career, Tarek had been detached when it came to the business of killing. While he never liked it, he had accepted the notion that when killing was done to vanquish the nation's enemies, it was justified. There was no need for further discussion or reflection.

With age, however, had come doubts as well as nightmares.

Up until he had learned the target of the LT team, he had told himself his objective was to stop a war between India and Pakistan. Now, with Sahar's life in the balance, it was clear to him that his motivation was no longer driven by any noble nationalistic goal. He would kill for one reason and one reason only: to save Sahar. The lives of every man on the LT team for her life. And he had no qualms about the arrangement.

Then he saw it—the white Hyundai truck just ahead on the left side of the road in a dirt parking area next to a cinder-block building. A sign on top of the tin roof of the building simply read, "Restaurant."

Several other vehicles were parked in the lot as well. Tarek drove past without pulling in, looking the scene over carefully to make sure he fully understood the situation before committing himself to a plan of action.

There was one man seated in the cab of the Hyundai and another standing next to it. Neither was HV/30.

Tarek continued past the restaurant for about half a block and pulled into a gas station on the opposite side of the street. The location provided good line of sight with the restaurant.

He decided to go ahead and fill up the Mitsubishi, which would provide him cover while he continued to watch the truck and finalize his plan.

As he pulled up to the diesel pump, he saw in his rear-view mirror a Toyota sedan pulling into the station behind him, coming from the same direction as he had come. He had not seen the car before, but the car's two occupants struck him as odd. Both wore Western attire—open-collar shirts with light sport coats and sunglasses.

It was the sport jackets that bothered Tarek the most. No one drove around wearing a sport jacket in this heat unless they were concealing something.

The men pulled up behind Tarek and exited their car. "Damn," Tarek said under his breath. He knew at a glance they had to be cops or criminals—or both. Something about the way they kept eyeing him convinced him they would be trouble. Whatever they intended, their timing was very bad.

Pretending to pay them no attention, Tarek got out of his vehicle and started pumping diesel into the Mitsubishi. The gas station owner began cleaning Tarek's windshield of the thick scum of insects that had accumulated during his all-night drive from Dhaka.

After pumping almost 80 liters of diesel into the Mitsubishi, Tarek removed the nozzle from the tank and replaced it back at the pump. As he was replacing the gas tank cap, the two men approached him.

"Good afternoon, Sir," the oldest and tallest of the two men said.

"Good afternoon," Tarek answered.

"I am Detective Jumblat, of the Crowe's Bazar Metro Police."

Tarek nodded but said nothing.

"I see your vehicle has Bangladeshi plates. May I ask your business here?"

"I am making my way to Farakka Barrage as an invited guest for a ceremony that begins in just a few hours. I plan to catch a river launch here in Crowe's Bazar.

"May I see your passport?"

"Certainly," Tarek said, pulling out his passport and handing it to the detective. "You will note the entry cachet, which I obtained at the border crossing earlier this morning. Everything should be in order."

The detective briefly looked at the passport and handed it to his partner, then returned his gaze to Tarek. "I'm afraid there are some formalities that must be handled before you continue on your journey. You will have to accompany us to our office in town."

Tarek groaned inwardly. His position was deteriorating rapidly. A change in strategy was in order.

"Detective, I have been invited by the government of India to attend an official function, and you are interfering with that. As a municipal official, you do not, under these circumstances, have any authority to detain me. Now if you will return my passport to me, I will be on my way."

"You are quite right, Mr. Durrani," the younger of the two said. "Detective Jumblat has no authority in this case, but as an Intelligence Bureau official, I do." He held out an IB credential for Tarek to see. "I am Inspector Reza. I assure you, this will only take a few minutes of your time, and then you can be on your way."

Tarek heard an engine start in the distance. Looking past the two men, Tarek saw to his horror that the LT team had loaded into the truck and was beginning to pull out of the restaurant parking lot. For a brief instant, the thought crossed his mind that he should tell the IB inspector about the LT team, but to do so, would, at least on its surface, implicate him in the plot. If the IB were able to establish he was a Pakistani ISI officer, he would likely meet with little mercy for a long time to come.

Having run through his analysis at lightning speed, he gambled that it would take the team a while to get to the marina, load the boat, and make the final preparations before departing. With a little luck, he would be through the "formalities" quickly and be able to catch up with the team at the marina. Under the circumstances, he really had no choice—to try to neutralize two Indian officials in public sight next to a major street was simply not a good option.

Tarek watched as the Hyundai passed by in route to the marina. It was all he could do to stand still and watch. *Patience, Tarek, patience*, he told himself.

"Alright Inspector, let's get this over with. I'm expected at Farakka Barrage tonight."

—71—

Sahar sat silently gazing out the window of the bus as it rolled down the highway from Malda toward Farakka Barrage. Next to her, Advani dozed in his reclined seat. Many of the other delegation members were napping as well.

As she watched, wide expanses of jute fields flew past, featureless, except for the dark green color, the intensity of which seemed to glow in the late-morning sun. The scenery and the low drone of the bus had a mesmerizing effect on her, and her mind was quiet.

Up until they had arrived in Malda, Sahar's feeling of uneasiness had continued, but now, it was gone. She felt relaxed and peaceful. She was no longer upset that Tarek was not with her. She had accepted that it was not meant to be, and she took comfort in the thought that within a few days, maybe even less, he would come to her in New Delhi. Then she would never let him go. She felt a powerful connection to Tarek and an equally powerful confidence that Tarek felt the same way about her. They would spend the rest of their lives together. It was meant to be.

Sahar had never believed she could love a man as she loved Tarek. The feeling surprised her, since in many ways Tarek was still an enigma to her. If he were any other man, she might consider his opaqueness a warning flag, but not with Tarek. She would not hesitate to go with him anywhere he wanted to go, as long as she could be with him.

Sahar looked away from the window and reached into her travel bag to take out the schedule for the day's events. Her appetite starting to stir, she was glad to see lunch was scheduled soon after arriving at Farakka Barrage.

She thought of Tarek and wondered if he was eating properly and taking care of himself. Somehow she imagined Dhaka as the kind of place where taking care of yourself might be a difficult thing to do. But Tarek was resourceful and well-traveled.

Tarek is probably just fine, she told herself.

—72—

The drive from the gas station to the entrance to the Intelligence Bureau office was brief, encouraging Tarek to think he could be on his way soon, with enough time to catch up to team at the marina—*if* the IB inspector kept to his word.

Reza drove through the unguarded entryway of the walled compound and parked next to a small office building a couple hundred meters from a larger building. The words "Crowe's Bazar Municipal Police" were stenciled in large block letters on the building's stucco exterior. Tarek deduced that the smaller structure was a satellite IB office, a tenant facility on the municipal police compound.

Immediately, Reza and Detective Jumblat exited the sedan. Reza opened the rear door for Tarek, who stepped out of the car. Tarek's Mitsubishi pulled in behind them, driven by the attendant from the gas station they had just left.

Tarek noted that except for the Mitsubishi and the sedan they had arrived in, the small parking area was empty. He also noticed bars over the few windows in the back of the smaller building, leading him to suspect it was not an administrative office for dealing with formalities, but was a detention facility.

Reza walked over to the gas station attendant and gave him a handful of rupees for his trouble, then sent him on his way.

"This way, Mr. Durrani," Reza said, gesturing toward the building. The three men walked the short distance to the front door, which was the only door the building appeared to have. Reza took a heavy key ring with several thick brass keys from his jacket pocket. As he opened the door, a musty smell drifted out the building.

Standing a few feet outside, Tarek saw there were no lights on, and the building appeared to be empty. The sun light coming in through the windows provided sufficient illumination for Tarek to see just inside the door to a small office with a single desk and two chairs. Beyond this, a corridor ran down the middle of the building to the back wall. On each side of the corridor were jail cells, all unoccupied, their doors standing open. Tarek's muscles tightened as Inspector Reza's intention became clear to him.

Reza stepped inside the office and turned on the lights. "Step inside, Mr. Durrani, and empty your pockets of their contents and place them on the table," he said in an authoritative tone.

"Certainly," Tarek said in a calm voice, as he stepped through the doorway. Jumblat following close behind.

As Tarek walked past Reza, he focused his mind and, in a sudden move, slammed his right elbow into the side of the inspector's head, the blow instantly dropping him to the dusty concrete floor.

Jumblat, initially startled, reached for his service revolver under his jacket. Tarek dropped him with a straight-line punch to the chin before the pistol had cleared leather. It was over in less than three seconds.

Tarek quickly pulled Jumblat's limp body inside the doorway and took his revolver, tucking it into his waistband. He searched Reza and found a small 9mm semiautomatic, which he stuffed into his pants pocket. After shutting the office door, he picked up the ring of keys from the floor and quickly checked the pulses of both men, finding they were strong.

He dragged each of the men into a separate cell. Spotting a small supply cabinet in the office, he rifled through it to find masking tape and twine, which he quickly used to bind their hands and feet. Finding a moldy towel in a latrine, he ripped it in half to make gags that he secured with tape around their heads. After matching the keys on the key ring with the locks, Tarek locked both cell doors and the door between the office and the cell corridor.

Tarek looked out the window at the parking area. Seeing no one, he stepped outside the building and walked quickly to the Mitsubishi, where he found the keys still in the ignition. After climbing into the vehicle, he pulled it around to the back of the building, making sure it was out of sight. Reaching into the back seat, he grabbed a small pack that contained his phones, maps, and binoculars. He exited the Mitsubishi and walked back to the other side of the building, where he entered the Intelligence Bureau sedan, found its keys in the ignition, started it up, and drove out of the compound in search of the marina.

—73—

It was now mid afternoon. HV/30 and the other team members were loading the last items of gear onto the rented boat while Sheik Osman stood watching, his arms crossed.

Where is he? HV/30 wondered as he handed the boxes of concealed weapons and rucksacks down to the men in the boat. He feared Rashid would not get to the marina before they departed. The thought of Sheik Osman succeeding in his mission did not sit well with HV/30. The man would become an even greater hero within the LT, and he did not deserve to be a hero. He deserved to be dead.

HV/30 was glad he had taken the risk to contaminate the diesel fuel as Rashid had advised. If he could convince Sheik Osman that they should top off the tank before they reached the dam, then the engine would foul, and the mission could not proceed.

Still, HV/30 decided this in itself would not be enough. It might stop the team from carrying out its mission, but it would not achieve his own driving ambition to see the death of Sheik Osman. With this thought in mind, he had pilfered a hand grenade from the cache the team had picked up in Dhaka. When the time came, he would stand next to Sheik Osman and tell him he knew that he had raped Soriya. Then he would detonate the grenade.

All that remained to be loaded on the boat were the two jerry cans of contaminated fuel. As HV/30 prepared to pass the first can down to the others on the boat, the wizened owner of the boat stopped him

"Only my fuel," he said angrily. "There is too much bad diesel on the market. I know that my supplier can be trusted. I know nothing about yours."

"There is nothing wrong with this fuel," Mahmoud argued. "You are just trying to make us pay more for your fuel."

"It is my boat," the old man insisted. "Only my fuel can be used."

"Mahmoud, forget it," Sheik Osman interrupted. "Leave our fuel and take his. We need to get moving. I don't care whose fuel we use."

It was all HV/30 could do to set aside the contaminated fuel containers and load the ones provided by the boat owner. Now the grenade would be his only option.

The old man's son, who appeared to be in his mid-20s, had been working on the boat's motor. He called up to his father, "She's ready." The old man waved, looked at Sheik Osman, and then nodded to the boat.

"Alright, everyone on the boat," Sheik Osman ordered.

As HV/30 started past him toward the boat, Osman put his hand on his shoulder, stopping him in his tracks.

"Not you, Mahmoud," he said. "I need you to stay here and make sure nothing happens to the truck. We should be back well before midnight. Make sure it is gassed up in the meantime and ready to take us out of here."

HV/30 could not believe what he was hearing. He *had* to get on the boat. "My brother, I have come all this way," he said. "Please! I must go with you. I must do this."

Sheik Osman smiled, "Mahmoud, I am impressed by your dedication and your courage. May Allah bless you for this. But we must maintain control of the truck." Then lowering his voice he said, "This is not a martyrdom operation. We will need to return to our homeland. I assure you, Kashmir will need us in the coming days."

Were the grenade in his immediate possession, HV/30 would have gone through with his plan and killed Sheik Osman right then and there. But he had hidden the grenade in his backpack, which was already on the boat.

Thinking quickly, he said, "Alright, my brother. I will do as you command. Let me get my pack off the boat."

Sheik Osman nodded and began walking toward the boat. As he did, he called out to the men now waiting onboard, "Throw Mahmoud his pack."

The boat engine roared to life. One of the team members grabbed HV/30's pack and tossed it high in the air. The throw was long. The bag sailed over the narrow dock and landed at the river's edge. By the time HV/30 managed to get down off the dock and scramble down the short, steep incline to retrieve the pack, Sheik Osman and the boat were well into the river, at far too great a distance for HV/30's grenade to reach.

He stood in shock, watching the boat head farther and farther out into the wide river, his plan shattered beyond recovery. The only thing that lay between the team and their target was water, and even that worked in the team's favor, as it flowed swiftly in the direction of Farakka Barrage.

—74—

The late-afternoon sun sat low over the Ganges as the boat tour of Farakka Barrage and the Jangipur Feeder Canal came to an end. One by one the visitors climbed the short ladder from the river launch to the dock.

Sahar was amazed at the transformation that had occurred since their departure for the tour only two hours before. The huge dock, built to handle the largest of river-going ships, had been converted to a venue for the evening's ceremony. A massive open-sided *shamiana* tent had been erected to cover the entire seating area. Sahar estimated that as many as 200 chairs had been set up in neat rows facing the wide dam stretching across the Ganges. A smaller tent was set up nearby for the banquet that was to follow the ceremony.

Governor Ghule approached. "Well, Sahar, this looks very nice," he said. "The staff here has done a great job in getting ready for tonight's festivities."

"Yes, it looks lovely," Sahar said.

The governor looked intently at Sahar, a smile on his face. "I hasten to add, your presence here adds to that loveliness."

This was not the first time Governor Ghule had let it be known how taken he was with Sahar. From the moment they had first met in Calcutta, he had waged a low-level campaign of pursuit. When Tarek had left for Dhaka, the governor had been encouraged in his designs, using every opportunity he could find to get close to her. His tactics were like arrows hitting a stone wall. Sahar was well acquainted with his type; she saw him for the womanizer he was.

Ignoring his compliment, she asked, "Do you know where my father is? The last time I saw him on the boat he was with you."

Governor Ghule was disappointed he had not gotten a more receptive response to his comment, but the night was young, and he would be spending much of the rest of it with Sahar, having arranged for her to be seated next to him both at the commemoration ceremony and the banquet.

"Yes, I believe I saw him get off the boat," he answered. "He was walking with Ambassador Chernikov. He is probably just up ahead."

"Thank you, Governor. I should catch up to him so we can coordinate our plans for the evening."

Sahar turned and headed off toward the guest lodgings in search of her father, Governor Ghule taking in her every step and move.

—75—

Tarek made his way toward the marina on a road that ran alongside the river. Seeing the marina ahead, he pulled the sedan into the parking lot of a vegetable market and buried the Intelligence Bureau car among dozens of parked vehicles.

Before getting out of the car, he put Detective Jumblat's large six-shot service revolver into a side pocket of his pack. Taking out Reza's 9mm semiautomatic, he removed the magazine and used his thumb to flick out the rounds onto the seat, counting each one as it popped out of the magazine. There were only seven rounds plus the one still chambered. *That will have to do*, he thought. Tarek quickly reloaded the magazine and snapped it back into the pistol butt.

Tarek made his way to the marina on foot, blending in as best he could with other pedestrians walking along the river-front road. Looking ahead, he could see the top of what appeared to be a van in the marina parking lot on the opposite side of the street.

Still walking with the crowd, Tarek surveyed the scene. The truck was the Hyundai he was looking for, but there was no sign of anyone around it. More disturbing to Tarek, the dock area was quiet, with only a couple of workers moving about. The team was not there. He had missed them.

Tarek's feeling of exhilaration as he anticipated action was instantly replaced by a feeling of crushing disappointment—his life's dream vanishing as he imagined the team making its way down the Ganges toward Sahar.

Disheartened, Tarek walked across the street, dodging rickshaws and bicycles as he approached the truck. After glancing inside it, to ensure no one was there, he walked over to the river's edge and sat down on the grassy bank placing his pack between his legs. He took from his wallet a small slip of paper on which he had written Governor Ghule's satellite phone number.

He had waited as long as he could to make the call, but now there was no choice but to notify Ghule of the approaching danger. Tarek removed the sat phone from his pack, punched in the numbers and waited as he listened to the phone ring.

—76—

Governor Ghule leaned against the railing at the Farakka Barrage dock and sighed wistfully as he watched Sahar disappear from his view. Glancing at his watch, he decided he also should return to his room to rest up for the night's activities. He wanted to be in top form for his next run at Sahar. With a little luck, who knew what the night might hold?

Just then his bodyguard approached and handed him his satellite phone. "It's ringing, Sir," the bodyguard said.

Ghule took the phone and looked at the number displayed in the caller ID panel. At first he did not recognize it, but then remembered; it was Mr. Durrani's number. He had given it to him just before Durrani had left for Dhaka. Ghule started to answer the call, but then stopped.

Why should I answer this? he thought. He probably wants to speak with Sahar, and that certainly would not do, particularly at this moment. Ghule handed the phone back to the bodyguard.

"I don't want to be disturbed with phone calls for the rest of the evening. Please shut this thing off."

The bodyguard took the phone and pressed the power button. "Done, Sir. Please enjoy your evening."

—77—

After listening to the phone ring for over a minute, Tarek put the phone away, planning to wait for a minute before trying again. "Damn" he said out loud. The Governor had assured him the phone was always with his bodyguard. *Why wasn't he answering?*

As he thought through the possible reasons no one had answered his call, he heard the sound of a car engine being started. Standing up quickly, he turned around. To his shock, he saw the Hyundai start to move. He immediately recognized HV/30 behind the wheel.

Grabbing his bag, Tarek dashed toward the truck as it started toward the exit to the street. "Mahmoud," Tarek yelled. He ran toward the vehicle as it moved away from him. Just as the truck reached the exit, Tarek caught up to it and slammed the heel of his fist against its side. "Mahmoud," he yelled again.

The truck stopped abruptly, and HV/30's gray head popped out the driver's window.

"Rashid!" he exclaimed as he climbed out of the truck. The two men embraced.

"Are the others still here?" Tarek asked.

"No," HV/30 shook his head sadly. "They have left, and we have failed, my brother."

"How long ago did they leave?" Tarek asked urgently.

"Not more than half an hour ago. I'm supposed to wait for them to come back." Tears welled up in Mahmoud's eyes. "I tried to stop them, Rashid, I swear I did. But everything I planned failed."

Tarek grabbed HV/30's shoulders. "Mahmoud, I know you did everything in your power to stop them. But we are not done. Not yet anyway."

"You think we still have a chance? You think we can catch them?" HV/30 asked.

"It will be close, but if they only left half an hour ago, I think there is a way. Does the truck have gas?"

Mahmoud nodded. "I filled it up right after they left. I was just going to go pick up some food at the market and then you banged on my truck." HV/30 paused. "Rashid, what are we going to do."

Tarek smiled. "We are going after them." He walked around to the other side of the truck and got in. Pointing to the road he said, "Let's go. We will take this road east along the river. There is a cluster of fishing villages about 15 kilometers downstream. According to the map, this road is hard-surfaced the entire way, which means we should be able to make up some lost time."

"But then what?" Mahmoud asked.

"There is bound to be a boat we can get our hands on. And then we get on the river and try to intercept them. What do you think, Mahmoud? Are you ready to make another run at this?"

"Yes I am ready, Rashid. This dish of revenge I have been carrying is getting colder and colder."

Despite the gravity of the situation, Tarek had to laugh.

"Excellent, Mahmoud. So let's get going. While you drive, I must make a couple of calls."

Tarek reached into his bag and took out the remote antennae for the sat phone. Reaching out the window, he slapped its magnetic base on the roof of the truck just over his head. After attaching the antennae cable to the phone, he tried another call to Governor Ghule. This time there was not even a ring.

What the hell is going on? Tarek wondered.

He punched in the number for General Ali. Tarek knew it was early in the morning in Washington, but Ali would just have to wake up.

To his surprise, when the call was answered Ali's voice was chipper; it was obvious he had not been sleeping.

"Tarek," he said. "I wasn't sure I would ever hear your voice again. Thank Allah you are alright."

"General, I'm okay for now, but things are getting down to the wire. I won't go into the details, but the bottom line is that we have not been able to stop the team, and it is already on the river having left Crowe's Bazar about 30 minutes ago. I have linked up with Mahmoud, and we are in pursuit, paralleling the river in the truck. Our plan is to get a boat further downstream, then try to intercept them."

"Keep after them," Ali said. "There are no guarantees here, but the situation may not be as desperate as you think."

—78—

As the guests and dignitaries began to gather under the shamiana for the ceremony, a U.S.-chartered cargo jet with a crew of six men was flying at 35,000 feet, two hundred kilometers to the west of Farakka Barrage. It was bound for Seoul, having departed the Persian Gulf state of Qatar five hours earlier. The aircraft's approved flight plan called for it to follow the international air traffic lane for South Asia, and it was dead on course, skirting the massive Himalayan mountain range 100 kilometers to its north. As the civilian-registered aircraft passed over the Indian city of Patna, the pilot alerted his crew to get ready.

In the bay of the aircraft, secured by wood blocks and cargo straps, sat a long and narrow object that looked like a five-meter-long cigar with a bulging center measuring a little more than a meter across. Despite its aerodynamic design, its dimensions were much too small to accommodate even a single human passenger, nor was it intended to. It looked to be sculpted from a single block of material.

It was this unique visual characteristic and the way the aircraft modified its own shape while in flight that led to its name "Transformer"—the latest generation of U.S.-produced unmanned aerial vehicles.

The Transformer was the product of a joint-development program between the U.S. Air Force, the CIA, and the U.S. Navy, the goal of which was to develop a UAV with greater reach and capability than possessed by the in-service "Predator" UAV. Like the Predator, the primary mission of the Transformer was armed reconnaissance. But the Transformer's capabilities far exceeded that mission.

The Transformer could be air delivered to a target area using another aircraft, giving it superior range and a faster response time. With its state-of-the-art ultra-light weight, and the radar-absorbing material used in its construction, the Transformer could operate in more sophisticated air-defense environments than the Predator. It was almost impossible to detect, even as it loitered for long periods over a target area, and the loiter time was extraordinary, due to the incorporation of a very small hybrid electric-gas turbine engine.

Perhaps the most unique feature of the Transformer was its ability to change its shape to a stable air platform once deployed. Although cigar-shaped while in the bay of the aircraft, once it deployed from the rear of the aircraft, two short wings would extend from the wide center, causing the UAV to assume the proper flight attitude in relation to the earth, much as a sky diver might extend his arms and legs to stabilize his free fall.

With stability established, an additional six feet of wing on each side telescoped out from the fin, each wing equipped with four small but extremely powerful motors which, as the wings telescoped out, rotated from the bottom side of the wing, locking in place on the front side

The Transformer carried only one specially adapted Hellfire missile inside the elongated body of the airframe. When the time came to fire the missile, a launching mechanism dropped down below its center.

As impressive as it was, the Transformer onboard the aircraft that night was little more than a prototype, having never been deployed operationally— until this mission. None of the crewman, not even the pilot, knew what the actual target of the Transformer was; they only knew that their job was to deliver it to the specified location.

Ten minutes after the pilot had given the alert, Transformer was ready to be deployed, and the aircraft began to slow its forward speed almost imperceptibly. Switching from internal comms, the pilot activated the encrypted satellite communications channel dedicated specifically to operations involving Transformer.

"Base, Base, this is Alpha six," the pilot said. "How do you read, over?"

"Six, this is base," was the reply. "We got you five by."

"Base, we're ready to roll a cigar. You got a light."

"Roger, six. We're just waiting on you."

"Roger Base, stand by."

The pilot switched back to internal comms and told the loadmaster to prepare for deployment.

On his instrument panel, the pilot watched the rear ramp light come on, indicating that the ramp was opening and being lowered to a position horizontal with the floor of the aircraft. After checking with the navigator to confirm they were in the deployment zone, the pilot told the crew to release the cargo straps and remove the blocks. When he was informed this had been accomplished, the pilot gave a final command: "Stand clear."

The pilot pulled back on the yoke, elevating the nose of the aircraft. In less than three seconds, the Transformer rolled down the floor railing and sailed out the back of the aircraft into the coal-black night.

"Base, this is Alpha six. The cigar has been rolled. All she needs is a light."

"Roger Six, we already have her and she is responding well. Thanks for the help, and we'll take her from here."

—79—

Thousands of miles away, a young co-pilot sitting in an air-conditioned trailer at a secluded military base in the American southwest stared at a high-definition flat screen in front of him.

"Wow!" he said, turning to the pilot seated next to him. "The Ganges is damn near as big as the Mississippi!" His southern U.S. roots were obvious in his broad drawl. "Now which one of them little boats is the one we're looking for, do you reckon? There are at least 20 in our sector, and right now they all look a lot alike."

"Well, we're just going to have to sort that out aren't we," responded the pilot. "The target profile is already programmed into the electro-optics and IR systems, so let's start checking them out one at a time. Aside from the technical identifiers, we know we are looking for a boat that should have five to seven people in it, carrying lots of gear. Also, the analysts believe it will not be in the central river channel. Those parameters should narrow the suspects down to a manageable number."

As the Transformer flew over Farakka Barrage, the eastern limit of its search pattern, the co-pilot pointed up at the flat screen to the place where the dam cut across the Ganges. "Some kinda shindig going on down there. Lot of light . . . activity. . . people movin' round. I wonder what's up with that?"

"No clue," the pilot said, "and it's not our job to find out. Our target is supposed to be a little boat full of bad men. If we need to check out the party, I'm sure somebody will let us know."

With that the two men fell silent and began the routine of checking flight controls and making minor adjustments to the Transformer's flight path and altitude, while the Transformer's electro-optics and infrared package did its magic.

The hunt had begun.

— 80 —

The boat Tarek and HV/30 ended up renting at gunpoint was a good one. At a fishing village of thatched huts with small boats pulled onto a small white beach, they had bartered with the boat's caretaker. Frightened that when the owner returned he would be angry, the caretaker was not interested in renting, no matter the price offered. He was more frightened, however, when Tarek and HV/30 pulled their pistols, and he was happy to accept the more-than-generous payment.

Unlike the sand boat that the LT team had rented, the boat Tarek procured was much smaller, with a powerful outboard motor and no covered area to create drag. The boat moved along at a surprisingly high speed. And it was the boat's speed that gave Tarek some hope they could catch the team, but they had to do it before nightfall or the game would be lost.

It was now dusk and the light was quickly fading. Tarek navigated the river while HV/30 sat in the forward bow and used Tarek's binoculars to check out the boats that were moving east with the flow of the Ganges. The binoculars' ability to gather in light was helping to extend the time available for the search, but it would only last a few more minutes.

HV/30, his white hair and beard blown back by the fierce wind as the boat raced down the river, pointed off the starboard side and yelled for Tarek to head toward a distant boat, its shape barely visible on the horizon. Tarek sped toward the boat. Thirty seconds later, Mahmoud jabbed his index finger repeatedly at the boat and yelled, "That's it! That's it! I can see the yellow canvas!"

Tarek's heart skipped a beat. Immediately he broke off his direct approach and changed course, cutting across the boat's wake to fall in behind it, gambling that the darkness, the diesel engine noise, and the shelter that blocked the team's view to the rear would prevent the LT team from detecting their presence.

HV/30 had replaced the binoculars with the big six-shot revolver Tarek had given him. The dark silhouette of his unkempt hair, long beard, and large revolver reminded Tarek of a scene in an American cowboy movie.

Tarek signaled for HV/30 to join him at the back of the boat. "Okay, Mahmoud, I want you to take over navigating the boat. For now, just hold our position behind them. Even in the dark, we should be able to follow them as long as we stay inside their wake."

Tarek retrieved the satellite phone from his pack and called General Ali.

Ali answered. "Tarek, tell me you have good news."

"We found them, Sir. They are still traveling on the river, and we are about 300 meters directly behind them."

"Excellent. Good work, Tarek. Can you give me a GPS coordinate?"

Tarek looked at his sat phone. It displayed Tarek's own location using an embedded GPS system. Tarek provided the ten-digit coordinate to Ali, emphasizing it was his location and not that of the LT team. "Our bearing is due east with the LT team positioned about 300 meters further east than our position."

"That's great intel," Ali said. "I'll pass this along. Stand by for a call from me and be ready to move out of the area. I don't want you to become collateral damage. In the meantime, continue to monitor the team."

"Standing by," Tarek said.

—81—

Night had settled on the Ganges as the LT team made its way eastward. The sound of the diesel motor drowned out the noise of the water crashing against the bow of the boat as it cut through the dark river.

Omar, the boat-owner's son, prepared to light the lanterns that he would place fore and aft. Sheik Osman, who was sitting on some straw mats on the floor of the boat, raised his hand.

"No. No lanterns," he said.

"But Sir," Omar protested. "We must put the lanterns out or risk being run down by a river barge."

"I said there will be no lanterns."

The young man liked neither the message nor Osman's tone. "This is my father's boat and we use lanterns," Omar said sternly. Sheik Osman suddenly stood up, blocking Omar and shoving him hard, causing him to fall backwards onto the boat's floor.

The rest of the team, who had been watching the encounter unfold, suddenly became alert.

"Grab him!" Sheik Osman ordered. Instantly, three of the team jumped on Omar, pinning him to the boat's floor.

"Tie his hands and gag him, and put him in there," Osman commanded, gesturing toward the canvas-covered part of the boat.

Within seconds, the team had bound and gagged Omar, and two of them dragged him under the shelter, Sheik Osman following behind them. The space in the covered area was largely taken up by the team's gear, leaving little room to move for Osman, the two team members and Omar.

Omar was shoved to his knees. The two team members crouched down, holding him on both sides. Sheik Osman reached up under his shirt and pulled out a 9mm semi-automatic.

As he did so, he instinctively tapped the bottom of the grip, making sure the magazine was seated before drawing the slide back just far enough to check that there was a round in the chamber. Satisfied, he raised the gun to Omar's head.

One of the team members, a hardened LT veteran, cried out, "No! You cannot do this! This man is a Muslim!"

Unaccustomed to being challenged, it was only respect for the LT member's combat record that prevented Sheik Osman from striking him with his pistol butt.

"Brother, Muslims kill Muslims every day," he said. "Besides, we have no choice. We can't risk having any witnesses around. This operation is too important. This man can go to Allah knowing he is a martyr to our cause." Sheik Osman placed the end of the hard black barrel on the center of Omar's forehead, as the smell of urine filled the crowded space and Omar's body trembled uncontrollably.

"Sheik Osman! You know you cannot do this! A Muslim may take the life of another Muslim only if a *fatwa* has been issued declaring him an apostate!"

Sheik Osman knew the man was right. He lowered the pistol. "Well, what do you suggest? Look around, brother. Do you see any *mullahs* to give us a *fatwa*?"

"Let Allah decide his fate," one of the other team members said.

"Allah decides all our fates," Sheik Osman replied impatiently.

"Right. So give him to the river and let Allah decide."

Sheik Osman thought for a moment. "Alright then, take him out and throw him overboard."

"What about his hands?"

"Leave them tied and leave the gag in. I don't want him shouting. And may Allah have mercy on him. Now, do as I said; we have things to do."

Kicking and thrashing, Omar was lifted up off the floor like a heavy sack of grain and heaved overboard into the dark river, his body making a loud splash plainly heard by all in the boat.

"Alright," Sheik Osman said. "Forget him. We are about to do what we came here to do. Remember your training. We cannot make any mistakes."

As one of the team members continued to pilot the boat, the others began collecting the rucksacks of equipment into one area. One by one, and in the order taught them, they removed the component parts of the device from their rucksacks. Now, as the boat approached Farakka Barrage some 10 kilometers in the distance, it was time to put their package back together again and run a final systems check.

The two halves of the highly-machined steel device were so black it was difficult for the men to see them in the dark, even with the parts right in front of them. They took two dark rain ponchos from one of the rucksacks and snapped them together, then used the joined ponchos to cover themselves in order to use a red-filter flashlight without fear of it being seen while they assembled the device.

The assembly procedure was straightforward. The base half was stood upright and the top half was set on top. The most difficult part was to make sure the male and female parts of the four internal locks were perfectly aligned before the full weight of the top half was allowed to rest on the bottom half. Not done correctly, the locks could be damaged, and the device would not function. In a training situation, the special barrier would also be placed between the two halves to protect the locks, but this was not a training situation—this was real, and the barrier was tossed overboard.

When the two hemispheres were fitted together the device was laid on its side, and the waterproofed electronic control panel was snapped into the recessed area under the base. Once it was determined that the connection between the control panel and the base was good, the team ran a systems check to make sure all electronic components would function and the device would detonate according to the programmed instructions.

Finally, the internal locks were electronically activated, which insured a precise seal was established between the two hemispheres. Ten minutes after the team started, the device was fully assembled.

All that remained was to set the desired detonation time and to initiate the system using a six-digit code followed by the single push of a button. Detonation would then occur at the programmed time.

Sheik Osman oversaw every step of the assembly, and he was satisfied that all was ready. Looking downstream, he could see a glow of lights stretching across the river. His target was now in sight. There was only one thing left to do before putting the device into operation.

Digging through his pack, Osman found the satellite phone. Although he could see the dam, it was still several kilometers away, so he decided to wait to make the call to make sure no problems occurred during the final approach to the dam. He put the phone into the cargo pocket of his pants and turned to the team. The men watched him closely, waiting for his orders.

"Sheik Osman, what should we do now," one of them asked.

"Pray," Osman answered.

— 82 —

Rashid, did you hear that? HV/30 asked, his eyes straining as they searched the black river.

"I heard something." Tarek said. "Quick, cut the engine."

The outboard motor fell silent. The sound of the LT team's diesel motor could be heard up ahead in the darkness. But there was another sound as well. Something between the two boats was splashing around in the water. They drifted with the current for a few seconds. Tarek thought he saw movement on the surface of the water only a few meters ahead. HV/30 saw it too.

"It's one of them!" HV/30 said, pulling the revolver out from his waist band. "I'll kill him myself," he said as he edged toward the side of the boat.

"Mahmoud, if you shoot it will alert the rest of them. Put the gun down and get the motor going again. Let's see what this is all about."

"Let's just leave him," HV/30 said. "None of them deserve our help."

"We can't. He may have some useful information," Tarek said.

"Why should he tell us anything? They are his friends."

"Really? Then why haven't they tried to fish him out of the river?"

"Maybe you're right," Mahmoud said. "Can you see him?"

"No, but I can hear him. He's still thrashing about."

Suddenly Mahmoud spotted the man. "There he is, off to our right."

"Quick, bring the boat around," Tarek said. "Let's try to pick him up."

HV/30 started the motor and maneuvered the boat, bringing it up alongside the man who disappeared under the water for a few seconds, and then resurfaced. Tarek reached down and grabbed him by his arms and with HV/30'S assistance, dragged the man onboard. It appeared he might already be dead.

"Which one is he?" Tarek asked.

"May Allah have mercy!" HV/30 said. "This is the son of the boat owner."

Tarek immediately yanked the gag out of his mouth. The young man began to cough and spit up water.

"Look! They tied him up. Those miserable beasts!" Mahmoud said in disgust.

"I'll untie him, Mahmoud. You get back to driving the boat and get us closer to their boat. I want to see what this boy can tell us."

"Alright, Rashid, but you better do it fast."

Tarek instantly looked up and saw what had prompted the comment. It was Farakka Barrage, still some distance away, but approaching fast.

pace

—83—

The portable lighting set up around the shamiana did a good job of illuminating the scene for the ceremony. With Advani on one side and the ever-persistent Governor Ghule on the other, Sahar watched the other guests as they arrived and took their seats. This was the first time all the invitees had been assembled in one spot during the trip and she was impressed by how large a gathering they made.

"Father, isn't this exciting!" she said. "So many people have come and all of them here to recognize you for this wonderful achievement. Oh, I am so proud of you. If only mother were here to see it."

Advani smiled lovingly at his daughter whom he loved so dearly and squeezed her hand. Leaning close, he said, "It is you who are wonderful. And it is you that I wish your mother were here to see. She would be so proud of what her daughter has become."

Sahar reached her arm around her father and gave him a gentle hug.

Just then, the chief administrator of Farakka Barrage, Engineer Seyed Kamal, stepped onto the speaker's platform and asked for everyone to take their seats as the ceremony was about to begin. Sahar felt a tinge of sadness that Tarek was not going to witness the honoring of her father. As she thought of him, she wondered where he was and what he was doing.

Had someone told her the answers to her questions, she would not have believed them.

—84—

Sitting well forward in the bow, the occasional splash of water hitting his face as the low-riding sand boat cut through the river, Sheik Osman no longer needed his binoculars to see the details of Farakka Barrage some 800 meters in the distance.

He was surprised at how well lit the dam was, and he realized the lighting that ran along the length of the structure would make the boat visible once it came to within a 100 meters.

Previous reconnaissance with his binoculars had revealed no hint of a security force on the dam and he believed that the security personnel would be deployed at the site of the commemoration ceremony, about a thousand meters from where the device would be dropped overboard.

The lights on the dam made it easy to see the target destination, a five-meter "L" shaped, recessed area built into the dam about 300 meters from the central gate. The spot was used for docking maintenance boats when work was needed to work on the lower aprons of the dam. It was an ideal spot to drop the device as the recessed area formed a natural eddy in the flow of the river that would protect the device from the otherwise swift current.

Sheik Osman estimated that the boat would reach its target in five minutes. Making his way back to the center of the boat, he signaled for the helmsman to cut speed and hold steady in the current.

Seeing the assembled device, Sheik Osman was hit with the realization that the time had come for him to put it into action and, in so doing, play a dramatic part in the ascendance of Islam as a force to be reckoned with in the modern world.

It was time to make the call. To steady himself, he sat down on the floor of the boat and reached into his cargo-pants pocket for his satellite phone. He entered the 10-digit telephone number and waited for the call to go through.

The phone was answered almost immediately. He recognized the familiar voice of Abu Shafik who was sitting in a safe house in Islamabad. Across the table from him sat Ambassador Salim, his prayer beads in hand.

"Hello," Abu Shafik said.

"This is Samad. Is Muhammad there?" Osman asked.

"One moment." Abu Shafik looked at Ambassador Salim.

Salim's eyes met Abu Shafik's. For a moment neither man moved. Salim then slowly nodded.

Abu Shafik spoke into the phone. "Muhammad is at a birthday party. Can you call tomorrow?"

"Yes. I will call him tomorrow. Please wish him well and tell him I am well."

"I will tell him. Khoda Hafez."

Osman turned off the satellite phone and put it back into his pack. Standing up in the boat he looked at the men who crowded around him, expectant expressions on their faces.

"Allah Akbar! The mission is approved."

* * * * *

The detonation timing was critical, as it would determine how much time the team would have to get away from the area. During the training in Pakistan, Sheik Osman was told that any structures within a 1,000 meter radius of the explosion would be totally destroyed. Even beyond this distance, tons of debris would be propelled into the air out to a radius of 1,500 meters.

Sheik Osman glanced across the river to the site of the commemoration ceremony. It would be decimated, if not by the initial shock wave, then by the rain of cement that would follow. Farakka Barrage was soon to become a disaster zone.

It only took a few seconds for Osman to make his decision. He would set the device to go off in 30 minutes, allowing the team enough time to get out of harm's way but still be close enough to witness the event. Sheik Osman looked at his watch, calculating that the detonation would occur two minutes before 8:00 p.m.

A feeling of exhilaration ran through him. He had just decided the exact time that the world would be changed forever.

—85—

The infrared images of the boats plying the Ganges appeared light gray on the otherwise black river. The locations, sizes, and the speeds of those images varied, but apart from that, there was little to distinguish one boat from the other—with the exception that boats with the larger motors appeared whiter in color due to the increased heat signature they produced.

When the Transformer's sophisticated electro-optics and infrared sensors were employed against a selected boat, all was laid bare. Before that happened, there was a necessary process of elimination to be sorted through and that was taking time, too much time. Having watched the same scenes for almost an hour, both the pilot and co-pilot, remotely flying the Transformer from their grounded cockpit, were growing weary of the monotony.

But it wasn't only the two pilots who were watching the scene. Thanks to satellite communications, many other spectators scattered around the globe were watching it as well. Staff members at the U.S. Pacific Command in Honolulu, Hawaii, the U.S. Central Command in Tampa, Florida, the Ops Center at the Pentagon, and the Counterterrorist Watch Center at CIA Headquarters in Virginia, which had overall responsibility for the operation, were all seeing the same scene as the two men in their ground-based trailer in the desert. Still, it was the pilot and co-pilot who were calling the shots on the search.

For the moment, however, there were no shots to call.

"If we don't get a match soon, we'll have the best seats in the house to witness whatever is going to happen," the co-pilot said mostly to himself.

No sooner were the words out of his mouth, when an audible alert began to beep. Both pilots immediately switched their views from the flat screen mounted on the wall to the virtual-heads up displays directly in front of them.

The V-HUDs showed the same images projected on the flat screen, but the area covered was reduced. They also displayed an array of digital data fields showing, among other things, the speed, direction, position, and altitude of Transformer. Also displayed on the right side margin was a stationary red electronic box, called the Electronic Sighting Mechanism, or ESM.

Within three seconds of the audible alert, the ESM automatically tracked across the screen and framed one of the gray images, a 10-digit geographic coordinate immediately popping up on the screen to indicate the boat's precise location. A second set of digits underneath the geo-coords displayed the boat's bearing and speed. A quick check of the magnified IR images indicated there were six men onboard the boat.

Switching to his external comms, the pilot announced, "We have a match on the target profile. The ESM is engaged and locked on. Target is stationary in the river 800 meters west of the dam. Request permission to execute on target."

"Roger. You are green to execute. Repeat. You are green to execute," came the response from the other side of the country.

As the pilot maneuvered Transformer to assume an attack profile, Sheik Osman knelt down in the boat next to the device and positioned himself where, with the assistance of a small red-filtered flashlight, he had a clear view of the control panel. Steadying himself from the movement of the boat, he carefully punched in the detonation time. A flashing red prompt indicated that the time should be re-entered for validation. Osman punched in the time again, and a green light appeared.

Half a world away, the pilot established Transformer in the proper position and armed its single missile.

"Base, Base, this is Control One," squawked the radio speaker.

"Go Control One," the pilot replied.

"Abort. Repeat. Abort. You are no longer green. Repeat. You are no longer green. Mission is cancelled."

US mission aborted

—86—

It had been almost half an hour since Tarek had spoken with General Ali when his sat phone rang.

"Yes," Tarek answered.

"We have a problem," Ali said. "The Americans are calling off the strike."

"What!" Tarek said in disbelief. "Why?"

"Someone in the American government doesn't believe our information about the team, and the ambassador in New Delhi balked at the plan. He said it would violate Indian air space and create a diplomatic nightmare for the U.S. The Secretary of State is backing him up."

"Idiots! Do they know what the consequences of this could be?" Tarek asked.

"My agency contact is working the problem and is trying to have the decision reconsidered, but that could take hours," Ali replied.

"We don't have hours, General. The team is only a few minutes from the dam. They must be stopped now."

"I agree, but how?" Ali asked.

"Well, we have two pistols. We'll have to work with that."

HV/30, who had been listening to Tarek's side of the conversation, reached into his back pack. "We also have this," he said as he pulled out the pilfered hand grenade.

Tarek's eyes lit up. Smiling at HV/30, Tarek said, "General, our arsenal has just been upgraded. My partner has brought along a grenade, and a white phosphorus one at that. This thing will literally set their world on fire."

"Then do it, Tarek. Take them out."

87

We will only get one shot at this, Tarek said to HV/30. "I want you to bring us up slowly behind the other boat. Once we are as close as we can safely be without being discovered, I will get in the water. At my signal, I want you to gun the engine and blast past them into the night as fast as you can make this boat go."

"Rashid, what about you? You will be like a duck in the water," HV/30 said.

"Maybe, but you will create a diversion. While their attention is directed toward you I will swim up behind the boat and drop in the grenade. Then I'll get as far away as I can before it detonates," Tarek said.

"But then what? How will I find you?"

"It should be easy to spot the remains of the boat, so just come back to the area and I will call for you. Do you understand?"

"Yes, Brother, I understand."

"Now make sure you and Omar stay as low in the boat as possible. They may open up on you."

"Alright. We'll keep down," HV/30 said. He leaned forward and quickly embraced Tarek. "Brother, we've come a long way together. Keep yourself safe. I want Soriya to one day know the man that took revenge for her honor's sake. If I cannot do this myself, than there is no one else I would rather have kill Sheik Osman than you."

Tarek smiled. "Then let's get on with it."

HV/30 kept the outboard motor running at just above idle speed and slowly moved in the direction of the LT boat, remaining directly behind it. Tarek slipped off his shoes and shirt and repositioned himself at the front of the boat. He placed the grenade in a netted pocket on his pack and put his arms through its shoulder straps, cinching them up tightly. The muffled sound of the LT team's diesel engine grew louder as HV/30 guided the boat forward.

After what seemed like an eternity, Tarek could make out the faint outline of the rear of the boat no more than 30 meters ahead. It was holding still in the river. Tarek signaled back to Mahmoud to stop their forward movement, then slipped over the side into the cool water. Looking back at HV/30 he gave him a quick wave and began to swim toward the LT boat.

HV/30 waited a few seconds to ensure Tarek was well clear. After telling Omar to lie down, he gunned the motor and sped past the LT boat about 30 meters off its port side. Within seconds, a burst of gunfire erupted. HV/30 felt a deep pain in his side.

Tarek reached the LT boat just as the shots were fired. His view of what was happening on the boat was blocked by its protective shelter, but he was able to see the muzzle blast of an AK light up the night.

Taking advantage of the distraction caused by HV/30's maneuver Tarek worked his way to the starboard side. He took off his backpack and removed the grenade from the pocket as he moved around the boat. With his left hand Tarek reached up to the top railing and grabbed hold. He found a foot hold built into the side of the boat and pulled himself up out of the water to a position where he could see the members of the team in ready positions, their backs to him as the men stared out into the darkness in the direction where HV/30 had headed.

Studying the interior of the boat, Tarek looked for the best placement for the grenade. For an instant, he saw the glow of a red-filtered flashlight and was able to make out the silhouette of a man kneeling beside a large canister-like object.

"Forget about that dam boat," the kneeling man said. "Pull up the drag anchor and let's get to the placement point."

Tarek knew once the boat started moving it would be impossible for him to hang on. He had to make his move. The two diesel fuel cans were close enough to him that he could touch them. He pulled himself up a little higher and reached over the side of the boat, yanked the pin and held the grenade spoon down as he gently placed the grenade between the two fuel cans. His hands were wet, however, and the spoon slippery. It sprang free of his grip and flew across the boat striking the canister and making a distinctive pinging sound.

Suddenly, there was a cry. "Hey!"

He had been spotted.

Tarek pushed himself off the side of the boat and dove under the water, using the boat as a counter force to push against. In a second, he could hear the muffled sound of guns blasting and the hiss of bullets passing through the water near him.

He swam to a point directly underneath the boat where he was relatively safe from the rifle fire, but he would not be protected from the blast once the grenade detonated. He had to get away from the boat—preferably behind it, where the team would have trouble spotting him. Tarek could not see the boat's propeller but he could hear it and feel its vibration in the water. Diving deeper, he swam under the propeller, feeling the force of the water it displaced pushing against his back.

Then came the explosion, a combination of sound and concussive force that pushed Tarek even deeper and knocked the breath out of him. Fighting the natural impulse to breathe in, he struggled to make his way up through the water, finally breaking its surface with a desperate gasp for air.

Everything around him was in flames and an acrid stench permeated the air. Burning debris from the boat littered the area and an oily veneer coated the water's surface. Tarek could see three bodies a few meters away, all of them on fire. He knew he had to get away from the flames, or he would soon become a floating human candle.

He took a deep breath and dove back into the water.

—88—

Engineer Kamal had just begun his opening remarks to the assembled guests and dignitaries when a bright flash illuminated the black night behind him. Within seconds the noise of a powerful explosion followed. So sudden and unexpected, the flash and the sound it produced caused everyone to flinch. Standing on the speaker's podium with his back to the river, Engineer Kamal instinctively collapsed into a low crouch as startled cries rang out from the audience.

Quickly regaining his composure, Kamal turned to see the flames flickering well out into the river. Turning back to the panicked audience, he tried to assure them there was no cause for concern.

"I apologize for the disturbance, ladies and gentlemen; it appears the military has been conducting some training exercises this evening. Normally, we are notified in advance, but sometimes the proper notifications are not made. I think it best that we continue with our program. It would be a shame to let this disrupt our ceremony any further."

Sahar had instinctively gripped her father's arm tightly when the explosion occurred, but with Kamal's explanation, she began to relax her grip. "Oh, Father, that scared me," she said.

Advani nodded. "It was a surprise indeed, but I agree with Engineer Kamal; let us try to enjoy this event that so many have worked so hard to organize. It is yet a very special night for me and for India."

HV/30 had no problem finding the debris from the boat, but by the time he and Omar had returned to the area of the explosion, the debris had spread out, swept along with the current toward the dam.

Feeling weak, HV/30 sat down in the bottom of the boat and rested himself against the side. "Mahmoud? What's wrong?" Omar asked.

HV/30 reached inside his shirt then pulled his hand back out. It was covered with blood. "I've been shot," he said.

Omar knelt down beside him to see a pool of blood collecting on the bottom of the boat next to HV/30. "Oh my God, we have to get help," he said.

"No! We have to find Rashid. If we don't, he won't survive the dam. Now start looking for him. I know he is out there somewhere."

"Rashid!" HV/30 began to call. "Rashid!"

Almost immediately came a voice barely audible over the noise of the boat's motor. "Over here. Over here."

"There he is," HV/30 said pointing off the port side. "Omar, get us over to him. I'll pull him in."

Omar expertly maneuvered the boat, keeping a close eye on the man in the water to ensure he did not run him over.

As they moved closer, HV/30 said, "He is floating on a little piece of the boat. Thank Allah he found that to hang on to."

"Rashid are you okay?" he asked as he painfully leaned out of the boat. All he heard in return was a low moan.

"Omar, quick, toss me the flashlight on top of the pack," HV/30 commanded.

Omar threw it to him, and HV/30 turned on the light and shone it on the man in the water.

"No!" HV/30 exclaimed. "It's Sheik Osman."

Omar turned off the motor and moved up beside HV/30 to lean over the edge of the boat.

"It is! It's him!"

For a moment both men looked in stunned silence at Sheik Osman, who appeared to be injured and barely hanging on to the piece of wood.

"Help me," Sheik Osman pleaded.

HV/30 pulled the revolver from his waist band while keeping the light on Sheik Osman's grimacing face.

"Sheik Osman, do you know who I am? It's Mahmoud."

"Mahmoud," Osman replied weakly. "Praise Allah you have come. Please help me get into the boat."

HV/30 lifted the revolver, extending it into the flashlight's beam so Osman could see it. "Do you remember Soriya?" HV/30 asked.

"Mahmoud, yes I remember her. She is your daughter. Now please, put the gun down and help me."

"Do you remember the day you raped her, you bastard?"

"No, no Mahmoud. I don't know what you are saying. Please! I am suffering. I need your help!"

"Have you heard the expression that revenge is a dish best served cold?" Mahmoud asked.

"What are you talking about?" Osman asked. He appeared to struggle more and more to hang onto the wooden debris.

"I am going to kill you, Sheik Osman. I have waited for this day a long time and Allah has rewarded me for my patience."

Sheik Osman managed to raise one of his hands. "Mahmoud, do not do this. You are a good Muslim, I am a Muslim. You must know that you cannot kill me without a fatwa."

HV/30 said nothing as he slowly cocked the hammer on the revolver.

"He is right," Omar interjected. "Allah must decide his fate, just as he decided mine." Omar edged himself closer to the side of the boat to ensure Sheik Osman could see him. "It is me, Sheik Osman. Omar. Remember? You had your men throw me into the river from my father's boat and Allah in his mercy decided my fate. I am here alive in the boat, and now it is you in the river. Will Allah be as merciful to you as he was to me?"

"I am a Muslim; why don't you help me? Allah will reward you."

"Can you swim?" Omar asked.

"No, I am injured. I think my legs are broken and something is wrong with my arm. My back is burned. I am very weak."

HV/30 looked at Omar and lowered the still cocked pistol. Leaning forward, he slowly reached out toward Sheik Osman. Raising his injured arm, Sheik Osman reached up to grab HV/30's outstretched hand.

In one swift movement HV/30 pulled away the debris that Sheik Osman had been clinging to.

"There will be no virgins for you in paradise, Sheik Osman. The demons of hell are all that await you."

Osman began to flounder in the water as much as his broken body would allow. Within seconds he disappeared below the surface. His head popped up briefly as he gasped for air, then disappeared beneath the water once again, never to resurface.

"It's done," said HV/30. "My daughter's honor is avenged."

"Praise Allah, that monster is gone," Omar said.

"Yes, praise almighty Allah." HV/30 sat back down on the floor of the boat. "I feel so weak," he said. "Omar, I'm dying."

"No, no! You will be alright. There is a hospital at Crowe's Bazar. I will take you there."

HV/30 smiled. "No, it is too late for that but there is still time to find Rashid." HV/30 grabbed Omar's shirt sleeve. "Omar, you must find Rashid. Promise me you will find him."

Tears welled up in Omar's eyes. "Alright, I will find him. I promise. I will find him."

HV/30 nodded. "Thank you Omar. You are a good young man. May Allah watch over you."

Slowly, HV/30 loosened his grip on Omar's shirt and closed his eyes as his last breath passed from his body.

—90—

It was 8:15 on a Saturday morning when General Ali pulled into the Roosevelt Island parking lot off the George Washington Parkway. There were already several cars in the lot, and joggers and bicyclists were taking their morning exercise along the park's trails and bicycle paths.

Ali drove to the far end of the lot and parked close to a pedestrian bridge that crossed a branch of the Potomac River to the wooded island. As he got out of his car, he could see a man in the middle of the bridge, leaning against the railing. Even at a distance, Ali could see that the man was tall and strongly built, but it was his bald head and pastel shirt with matching tie, that confirmed it was Dan Barlow.

As Ali started toward him, Barlow turned his back and began to walk across the bridge toward the island. Once there, Barlow stopped on the dirt trail and waited for Ali to catch up, confident they would be out of sight, protected by the trees and the vegetation.

"Good morning, General. Let's walk. I have things to tell you," Barlow said.

The late spring morning was warm and humid and as they began to walk, Barlow slipped his suit jacket off and folded it over his right arm. Ali did likewise.

"Since I briefed you on the decision to call off the strike, some developments have occurred. Before Transformer left the area, an explosion was detected on the river. Transformer was given permission to check it out and it looks like the target boat was somehow destroyed.

"Thank God," Ali said. "Tarek succeeded."

Barlow nodded. "Yeah, I think your man came through, and we are all beholden to him for that."

"Were there any secondary explosions?" Ali asked.

"Oddly enough, no. It's amazing that whatever explosives they were carrying with them did not detonate."

Ali nodded his agreement.

Barlow and Ali still had no knowledge that the explosive the team had been carrying a low-yield atomic device which could only be detonated by an internal electronics system. Also unknown to them, the device was now lying in the mud at the bottom of the Ganges, its initiation sequence never fully activated. It no longer posed a threat to Farakka Barrage or anything else.

"Any evidence of survivors?" General Ali asked.

"It is difficult to say. We surveyed the area after the hit and there were bodies in the water, a couple of them on fire. But it is very unlikely, between the blast and the river currents that anyone would have survived."

"No sign of Tarek or his boat?" Ali asked.

"None." Barlow responded. "We were not able to look for very long before we were ordered to vacate Indian air space, so I would not give up hope at this point. As we agreed, General, in the event something like this would happen, we have contacted our Indian counterparts and told them that we've learned the ISI had just prevented an attack on Farakka Barrage and that an ISI officer is missing in action. They are looking for him. They know he prevented a major terrorist attack on their soil and if it wasn't for him, there would be a big hole in Farakka Barrage right now. They have promised that if they find him he will be treated well. Hopefully, word will come soon that they have located him."

"Let us pray that it is so," Ali said solemnly.

"General, you have done a great service for all the countries of South Asia by preventing yet another war between India and Pakistan. The last thing the U.S. wants to see is a war between your country and India. After all, there are enough wars going on right now, thank you."

"Let me tell you, if I had not felt I could trust you, we wouldn't be standing here talking about this."

"I appreciate that, General. You're a good man and it means a lot to hear you say you trust me." Barlow paused for a moment and continued. "Thanks to you, General, and your man Durrani, a war has been averted, but it would seem only temporarily. After all, the key players that you've told me you suspect are behind this are still in place."

Ali nodded. "Yes, I know. Ambassador Salim and General Huq and their cohorts are still there. Prime Minister Bahir is in no position to challenge them. He has no power base to speak of, particularly within the military, and that is what is needed to confront these men and contain the extremist movement that is tearing my country apart. Believe me, I have thought long and hard about trying to take some action myself, but I am isolated and, frankly, I am not certain which of my colleagues I can trust."

"General Ali, there are many Pakistani officers, some within ISI and some in the regular military, who feel the way you do. There are civilian leaders as well. We are in contact with them, and we want to facilitate your meeting with them. The truth is, General, we can't stop what is happening, but you and men like you can, and this is your opportunity."

Ali stopped in the middle of the sandy trail for a moment, and then pointed to a nearby bench. "Let's sit and talk, Mr. Barlow."

An hour later, a deal had been struck, and General Ali for the first time in months felt there was hope for his country.

—91—

It was early evening, nearly two months since the commemoration ceremony at Farakka Barrage. Sahar and Engineer Advani sat silently together on their favorite bench in Lodi Park, the occasional chirping of a small bird the only sound to be heard.

"Sahar, you haven't spoken about Tarek since the ceremony. I think it's time that we talk about what has happened. It's not good to hold your feelings inside yourself." Advani said, breaking the long silence that had fallen between them.

"I know you are right, Father, and I've wanted to, but it just hurts so much. I keep waiting for the hurt to go away," Sahar responded softly.

Advani was encouraged. This was the most Sahar had said on the subject since the Intelligence Bureau inspector informed them that Tarek was a Pakistani intelligence officer.

"I guess I never understood what deceit was or how hard it could be to experience," Sahar said.

"I know this has been hard for you Sahar, as it has been for me as well. To be deceived is indeed a painful thing."

Sahar sat motionless, staring vacantly into the deepening dusk. "I actually thought I loved him. How could my heart have been so wrong?"

"Maybe your heart was not wrong," said Advani, gently brushing a tear from Sahar's cheek.

"How can you say that?" Sahar replied with an uncharacteristic edge in her voice. "Tarek was a complete fraud. He lied to both of us about everything."

Advani nodded. "Certainly he lied to us about his purpose in coming to India, but was he a complete fraud? I don't think so, and I don't really think you do either."

Sahar shifted her position on the bench so she could more directly face Advani.

"Father, why are you saying this? You heard what the Intelligence Bureau said about Tarek. He came to meet you so he could steal the plans to Farakka Barrage, and then they were given to terrorists."

"Part of that is true, but even the Intelligence Bureau said Tarek had no knowledge that the plans were to be used in an attack and, most importantly, that as soon as he learned that an attack was being planned, he acted to stop it at great risk to himself."

"Well, that may be what Tarek told them, but it could be a lie as well," Sahar said.

Advani shook his head. "Tarek did not tell the IB anything. From the moment they found him on the riverbank until he was put on the plane to Dubai, he never said anything to them."

"Then how do they know any of this?" Sahar asked.

"Habibi told them."

"So they went to Dhaka and talked to Habibi?"

"They didn't have to," Advani said. "Habibi had already told the IB about Tarek before he went to Dhaka."

"Habibi was a spy for the Intelligence Bureau?" Sahar asked, a look of incredulity on her face.

"Not exactly," Advani said. "When Habibi was in New Delhi, he began to worry that he and Tarek would not be able to stop the terrorists alone. At one point, he tried to convince Tarek that they should approach the authorities and tell them a plot was afoot, but Tarek argued that without details about the plot it would be pointless, and the authorities would almost certainly jail both of them. When he couldn't change Tarek's mind, the morning we were preparing to fly to Calcutta, he secretly went to the IB himself. From that point on, they were aware that there was a plot of some kind, and they began to monitor Tarek."

"Father, how do you know this?"

"Habibi told me."

"You are in touch with Habibi? Sahar asked.

Advani nodded. "Yes, I've spoken with him on the phone a couple of times in the last two weeks."

"Why did you call him? Don't you want to be done with all of this? "

"I didn't call him. He called me." Advani said.

"Why? What does he want?"

"He wants us to know the truth about Tarek, that Tarek meant us no harm, and that his only goal was to stop an attack that might start a war, and . . ."

"And what?"

"And to tell you that Tarek is truly in love with you. He has been from the moment he met you."

Sahar did not respond for a few moments. "Where is he?"

"Tarek?"

Sahar nodded.

"He's in Abu Dhabi. He can't return to Pakistan, as it seems his office has fallen into unfriendly hands, and he would almost certainly be jailed. His life, as he knew it, is over."

"Am I supposed to feel sorry for him? Or somehow accept him back? No, this is not possible."

Advani reached out to take Sahar's hand. "Sahar, I would never want to cause you any pain, but I saw how happy you were with Tarek, and I believe the Tarek you cared so much about is a good man, despite his deception. I saw it for myself. Your heart wasn't wrong."

Another tear slipped down Sahar's cheek. "But he betrayed me."

"No, he didn't, Sahar. A lie and a betrayal are not the same thing."

"Oh really, father? Tell me, what is the difference?"

Hearing a soft flutter of wings, Advani looked up to see a pair of green parrots as they settled on the branches above where he and Sahar sat. They were the first parrots that he had seen in many weeks.

Sahar repeated her question. "So Father, what is the difference?"

Advani turned his gaze from the parrots to Sahar and smiled. "A lie can be forgiven."

About the Author: Duane Evans is a former CIA officer with field tours on four continents to include serving as Chief of Station, CIA's most senior field position. He is the recipient of the Intelligence Star for valor. Prior to joining the Agency, he was a U.S. Army Special Forces officer. *North From Calcutta* is his first novel.